THEY W[...] BEST AND THE BRIGHTEST....

Lt. Jack McCrary—scion of a proud naval dynasty—a man who would not break under pressure, but whose blind quest for vengeance portends untold destruction.

Betsy Kirkland—McCrary's fiancée—the beautiful daughter of a powerful congressman: fierce ambition would drive her to betray the very men struggling to save the man she loved.

Lt. Commander Ben Mount—the Jewish boy from Brooklyn who overcame anti-Semitism at Annapolis only to see his career ruthlessly threatened by a single fatal error.

Helen McCrary—Jack's sister—young, lovely, impelled by insatiable hungers to lead a dangerous double life—college girl by day, seductress of sex-starved submariners by night.

SUDDENLY THEIR LOVES, THEIR CAREERS, THEIR HOPES, WERE SINKING WITH THE *SEBAGO*...

FORTY FATHOMS DOWN

FORTY FATHOMS DOWN

J. Farragut Jones

A DELL/BRYANS BOOK

Published by
Dell Publishing Co., Inc.
1 Dag Hammarskjold Plaza
New York, New York 10017

Dell ® TM 681510, Dell Publishing Co., Inc.

ISBN: 0-440-12655-X

Printed in the United States of America

First printing—July 1981

FORTY FATHOMS DOWN

ONE

The long black submarine backed out of its pen into Connecticut's Thames River. Lieutenant Jack McCrary, the executive officer, stood on the bridge, binoculars hanging from his neck. In the dawn light he could see small waves breaking over the stern of the submarine as it moved into the main channel of the river. Standing beside him was Lieutenant Commander Gene Dunlop, skipper of the submarine. It was April 17, 1939, and the submarine was called the *Sebago*.

Jack McCrary glanced behind him and saw the dock crew coiling lines as they watched the submarine move away from them. Turning forward again, he saw the stern of the *Sebago* enter the swiftly moving waters of the main channel. He smelled pungent salt air, and seagulls shrieked as they flew in circles above the submarine.

"All stop!" Lieutenant Commander Dunlop called down to his helmsman in the control room.

"All stop!" replied the helmsman, Boatswain's Mate First Class Jethro Keller.

At the propulsion control station in the after compartment of the submarine, the order came through on the intercom. Machinist's Mate First Class Anthony Brouvelli pulled the levers that disengaged the four big diesel engines. The submarine slowed down, and everyone in its crew could feel it.

"Right full rudder!" shouted Lieutenant Commander Dunlop on the bridge.

"Right full rudder!" replied Boatswain's Mate Keller.

"All ahead one third!"

"All ahead one third."

The *Sebago* straightened out in the channel, and a bow wave formed as it gained way toward the sea. It was long and thin, lethal-looking as a stiletto, and was the only vessel moving on the Thames that morning except for a few small fishing boats. Jack raised his binoculars to his eyes and looked at the horizon ahead. He didn't expect to see anything of great significance, but he'd been serving on submarines for six years now, since he graduated from the Naval Academy at Annapolis, and he'd been trained to be on the lookout for trouble whenever he was on the bridge.

He wore a tan duty uniform with a brown leather jacket and his visored cap. Of average height, he was broadshouldered and had blond hair, blue eyes, and a ruddy complexion from spending so much time on the bridge of submarines. He was twenty-eight years old and was engaged to be married in September.

"Looks like it's going to be a nice morning," said Lieutenant Commander Dunlop, standing next to him.

"Yes, sir."

"Take the bridge, will you? I'm going to have a look below."

"Yes, sir."

Jack watched Lieutenant Commander Dunlop climb down the ladder into the submarine. Dunlop was one of the old salts of the submarine service, a potbellied man of forty-one who'd come up through the ranks. He was the senior submarine commander on the base, so when the *Sebago* was delivered, it had been turned over to him.

Jack McCrary rested his elbows on the bridge rail and looked at the sleek, deadly form of the *Sebago*'s bows. It was the first of a new series of submarines with higher-capacity battery cells and a new configuration of fuel and ballast tanks to make it pitch less in heavy seas. Otherwise it was basically similar to submarines of the previous *Salmon* class, with two main propulsion engines, two main generator engines, two auxiliary generator engines, four torpedo tubes aft, and four torpedo tubes in the bow.

The *Sebago* sliced resolutely through the choppy waters of the Thames. Jack McCrary scanned the horizon through his binoculars and wondered if the *Sebago* ever would go to war. Hitler had just gobbled up Czechoslovakia, and nobody believed his voracious appetite was sated. In the East, Japanese soldiers fought in China and Manchuria while their warlords made bellicose statements about the United States and Great Britain. The stormclouds of war were forming, and Jack wondered if the leaders of the world could make them go away.

"Permission to come to the bridge, sir," said Ensign Roy Delbert through the voice tubes from the control room.

"Permission granted."

Lean and gawky Ensign Delbert climbed to the bridge, a big smile on his freckled face. He was fresh out of submarine school, and this was his first submarine assignment. Raising his binoculars, he looked ahead to the mouth of the Thames.

"Lovely day," he said.

"Yes," McCrary agreed, scanning ahead through his binoculars.

"Where do you think the old man will take her down?"

"South of Block Island, I think. We need enough

water to check out our maximum operating depth."

"I can't wait," said Ensign Delbert eagerly.

Jack McCrary wanted to say "Neither can I," but it wouldn't be appropriate for an officer of his rank to show such emotion. He was executive officer of the submarine and was supposed to be calm and dignified. He had to inspire confidence in his junior officers and men. But Jack McCrary's mouth was dry with anticipation, and he felt excited by the prospect of going down with the *Sebago* for the first time.

The *Sebago*'s hull had been test-submerged in dock a few times and had been undergoing sea trials in the Atlantic Ocean for two weeks now. The only problems so far had been a failed electrical circuit between the conning tower and the bow torpedo tubes, and a sticky main induction valve in the conning tower. The electrical circuit had been repaired, but they couldn't discover what had been wrong with the main induction valve, so they stripped it down and put it together again, and it had been working perfectly ever since. Today the *Sebago* would stay down for an hour, running on batteries while all systems were checked. If everything went well, they'd come out again tomorrow, dive again, and fire torpedoes for the first time. The tests would continue for another three weeks, and then the *Sebago* would take its place in the Atlantic Submarine Fleet.

Lieutenant Commander Dunlop came up the ladder. "Anything going on up here?" he asked.

"No, sir," replied Jack McCrary.

Dunlop raised his binoculars and looked forward. "We'll be in the sound soon. I'll take the bridge now, Jack. I'd like you to go below and check the boat from bow to stern to make sure everything's all right."

"Yes, sir."

Jack saluted, then climbed down the ladder into the control room. He saw Lieutenant Junior Grade Robert Stearns at the navigation table, drawing lines on the plastic sheet that covered the chart of the area. The interior of the submarine smelled like metal and oil, the way a revolver smells when you hold its chamber close to your nose.

Jack stepped away from the ladder and looked around the control room. Chief Boatswain's Mate Jethro Keller stood at the helm, watching the dials and needles that kept him on course. At the forward hydroplane control was Boatswain's Mate Second Class Alfred Araujo, a Portuguese-American from New Bedford, Massachusetts, the old whaling city. Boatswain's Mate Third Class Mark Donahue from San Francisco manned the ballast controls. Jack glanced at the Christmas tree, the array of lights that glowed red when the various valves of the submarine were open and they were running on the surface, and green when the valves were closed and they were submerged.

The submarine trembled from the action of the diesel engines, and their rumble could be heard from the aft engine compartments. Jack looked at the innumerable levers, switches, dials, and wheels, his practiced eyes telling him all was in order. He decided to go forward first on his inspection tour of the submarine.

"Come left to one-six-five!" came Lieutenant Commander Dunlop's voice from the bridge as Southwest Ledge lighthouse bore off the port beam.

"Come left to one-six-five," repeated Keller at the helm.

Jack stepped through the oblong hatch forward of the control room and entered the officers' quarters. To his right, in a tiny room not much larger than the closets in many American homes, sat Yeoman Third Class Joseph Reilly, tapping away at his typewriter. Jack passed the compartments where he and the other officers slept, passed the officers' wardroom, and entered the forward torpedo room through another hatch. The *Sebago* had five waterproof hatches, and each could be closed if a section of the submarine had been damaged and was taking water.

In the forward torpedo room the crew commanded by Torpedoman First Class Hank Burns sat among the deadly twenty-foot-long fish that carried 666 pounds of torpex in their warheads and could sink any ship in the world if they hit in the right place. Sandwiched among the torpedoes were fourteen bunks and fourteen lockers for the crew members who lived in the room, the largest on the submarine. In the front of the room, surrounded by pipes, cables, control boxes, and dials, were the four torpedo tubes that comprised the main attack system of the submarine.

Jack looked around and asked the men some questions about their duties. He checked a few valves to make sure they were open, and a few others to make sure they were closed. He made certain that the proper switch connections were made between the torpedo tubes and the torpedo data computer (TDC) in the conning tower. Satisfied all was in order, he told the men to carry on, then moved aft through the room, angling through the hatch to the officers' wardroom again, continuing the inspection tour that ultimately would bring him to the aft torpedo room. He made his way through the officers' quarters and the control room, glanced into the radio room aft of the control room, and entered the crew's mess. On the forward bulkhead hung a framed picture of a Sebago, an Atlantic salmon covered with brown spots. He ground his teeth in annoyance as he entered the hatch that would take him to the first engine room.

Jack didn't like to go back to the engine rooms of the submarine, although he had to often. Through a strange quirk of fate—or maybe it wasn't so strange—his younger brother Ed McCrary, the black sheep of the family, was a seaman second class on the *Sebago*.

Jack stepped into the forward engine room and saw

his brother, in dark blue dungarees and a light blue chambray shirt, tightening a bolt on the side of a diesel engine, being watched and directed by Machinist's Mate First Class Albert Gomez of Los Angeles. Ed was shorter than Jack and much thinner, with the sharp features of their father rather than the softer ones of their mother, which Jack had inherited. Ed had been expelled from the Naval Academy because he'd been caught cheating on an exam.

Gomez, Ed, and the two other sailors in the compartment looked at Jack, who checked the big diesel engines and the various lines and tubes leading to them.

"Everything under control?" he asked Gomez.

"Yes, sir."

"Carry on," Jack said.

He glanced at his brother and felt a twinge in his heart, because Ed had been his baby brother and he'd loved him once, before he disgraced the family in the cheating scandal. The McCrary family had naval traditions that went back to the Civil War, and Ed had sullied those fine traditions because of his weakness and selfishness. Jack could never forgive him for it. He went through the hatch to the aft engine room, wishing that Ed had not been assigned to the *Sebago*, but Jack suspected that their father, a commodore in the Navy, had arranged for both of them to be on the same submarine, perhaps hoping that Jack would look out for his younger brother and keep him out of trouble.

Jack had no intention of looking out for Ed. If Ed ever screwed up in any way, Jack would throw the book at him. He rode Ed harder than any other sailor on the submarine, and was scrupulous about not showing him the slightest bit of warmth. Ed had made his bed—now let him lie in it.

Entering the aft engine room, Jack saw Machinist's Mate First Class Anthony Brouvelli standing before the long levers of the propulsion control station. His chambray shirt was unbuttoned halfway down, and a gold crucifix on a gold chain could be seen against his smudged white T-shirt.

Jack looked at the dials and gauges above the control station. He checked the positions of the levers on the console. "Everything okay, Brouvelli?" he asked.

Brouvelli was tall and lean, with an olive complexion. "So far—so good, sir," he replied.

"Good," said Jack, heading back to the last hatch, the one that led to the aft torpedo room. He glanced at his watch; it was 0730. He figured that in about three hours and a half the *Sebago* would be off Block Island, and then Lieutenant Commander Dunlop would give the orders to take her down. Bending toward the hatch, he hoped that the time would pass quickly.

TWO

In a little hotel off Scollay Square in Boston, Boatswain's Mate First Class Tommy Hodges lay on his back with his head propped up on the pillow and looked down at the pretty young blond girl who was making love to him. He was supposed to report to the Boston Navy Yard at 0630, which was only a half hour away, and it didn't look as though he was going to make it.

The girl's head bobbed up and down as she held his cojones daintily with her long elegant fingers. Meeting her had been an incredible stroke of luck. He'd just arrived in Boston at the bus station on Tremont Street, on his way to the first whorehouse he could find, when she'd come up to him out of the crowd and asked for a light for her cigarette. He'd given it to her and had the presence of mind to invite her for a drink. She'd accepted, to his great surprise, because she'd seemed to be sort of a classy dame, and several drinks later they'd wound up in this hotel room.

She licked at him with fiery intensity, and he sighed, reaching for his package of Lucky Strikes on the night table. He lit it with his old Zippo, swiveling his hips a little, and wondered if he had any more juice in him, because she'd been loving him wildly for most of the night. She'd told him her name was Helen but wouldn't divulge her last name. She was tall and athletic-looking, pretty strong for a woman, and he wondered who she was and where she came from. He figured that she couldn't be much more than twenty years old. He was thirty-five and had been in the Navy ever since he was seventeen.

She put the tip of his manhood into her mouth again, sucking vigorously, and he realized this would be it—he couldn't hold back any longer. Holding the cigarette away from his face, he looked at her through his narrowed eyes, wondering how such a nice girl could be such a wanton creature. He'd known women twice her age who couldn't excite a man half as well as she did, and then he felt that maddening itch in the root of himself, and his muscles tightened up. She looked at him through her big blue eyes and smiled as she moved her head up and down more quickly. Hodges gritted his teeth and squinched his eyes shut as the sweet ecstasy exploded outward.

"That was nice," she said, a little out of breath.

"Sure was," Hodges agreed, taking a puff from his cigarette.

She kissed his throat. "You've got a lot of nerve—smoking a cigarette while I was blowing you."

"I've noticed that cigarettes taste better that way," he replied.

"Mind if I have one of yours?"

"Help yourself, kid."

She rolled over and took one of his cigarettes, lighting it up with his Zippo. Engraved on the stainless steel was the outline of a submarine and the lettering SS CUTTLEFISH.

"You're on the *Cuttlefish*?" she asked, lying on her back beside him.

"I was," he replied.

"When?"

"Until about two years ago."

"What submarine are you on now?"

"I'm not on any submarine now."

"You're not in the Submarine Service anymore?" she asked, raising her head from the pillow. "Then why do you still wear your dolphins?"

"I'm still in the Submarine Service," he explained, "but I'm on special duty right now."

"What kind of special duty?"

"Oh, you wouldn't understand."

"Try me," she said. "I know a little about submarines."

He looked at her incredulously and turned down the corners of his mouth. "What do you know about submarines?"

"I know that the *Cuttlefish* and her sister ship the *Cachalot* were designed along the lines of the U-boats the Germans used during the war, and that they have two engines instead of the four that most American submarines have now."

Hodges blinked. "How did you know that?"

She smiled triumphantly and blew smoke into the air. "I know a few things about submarines."

"You've got a boyfriend on one of them?"

"Both of my brothers are in the submarine forces," said Helen, whose last name was McCrary.

"What boats?"

"None of your business."

"Why won't you tell me?"

"Because I don't want you to know."

"Why not?"

"My business."

"You won't even tell me your last name."

"You don't have to know that," she said.

"What if I want to call you sometime?"

"I'll call you. Just give me the number of your orderly room before you leave. What kind of special duty did you say you were on?"

"I didn't say. I'm working on a special ship rescue project."

"I think I heard something about that. Isn't Lieutenant Commander Mount in charge of it?"

"Yeah, the Jew."

Helen frowned. "Don't call him that."

"Why not? He's a Jew, ain't he?"

"Yes, but you shouldn't call him that."

"You know him?"

"I've heard of him," Helen said.

Hodges chuckled. "What a strange duck he is. Designs all sorts of stuff for submarines but's afraid to go down on one himself. They say that he faints dead away. Can't take the close quarters and all. He's a smart son of a bitch, though, like most Jews."

"I wish you wouldn't talk like that," Helen said.

"Why not? You like Jews?"

"Oh, shit," she said wearily. She rose from the pillow and sat on the edge of the bed, holding her cigarette to the side. "I think it's time for me to go."

"What's the hurry?" Hodges asked, placing his palm on her shoulder.

She shrugged it off and stood up, stretching and walking to the chair where she'd laid her underclothes the night before.

"Did I say something wrong?" he asked, watching her step into her pink underpants.

"Don't worry about it, Tommy," she said. "You can't help being what you are."

Hodges didn't know exactly what she meant but figured she was insulting him or looking down on him in some way. "What in the fuck is that supposed to mean?"

"Whatever you want it to mean."

"Hey," he said menacingly, getting up from the bed. "Don't start getting sassy with me."

She looked at him and told herself again that she ought not to fool around with ordinary sailors in the

"Silent Service." You never could tell when they might get violent. But there was something about the big tough bastards that excited her, and she couldn't help herself.

"I'm just being straightforward with you, Tommy," she said. "You wouldn't want me to lie, would you?"

Her retort confused him. "I don't know," he replied, shrugging his massive shoulders. "I don't like being sassed by a woman."

"I didn't mean anything by it, Tommy. Relax."

"I'm relaxed," he said, puffing his cigarette. He didn't know what to do, so he sat on the edge of the bed. "Where are you going?"

"I've got an appointment." She stood before the mirror and put on her wool skirt.

He admired her large round breasts in the mirror. Last night he'd had his full share of pleasure with them "What kind of appointment?" he asked.

"My dentist," she lied, not wanting to tell him she was a senior at Radcliffe.

"Got problems with your teeth?"

"Yes. Hook up my bra for me, will you?"

"Sure."

He got up and walked behind her, holding the delicate scraps of pink cloth in his stubby fingers and snapping them together. Reaching around her, he cupped her breasts in the palms of his hands.

"Why don't you stick around for a while?" he asked.

"Because I've got to go, and so do you." She lowered her hands, turned around, and smiled. "You mean you haven't had enough?"

He grinned, looking at her pert nose and pretty lips. "I could never get enough of you, kid."

She laughed. "I'll bet you say that to all the girls, Tommy."

He winked. "As a matter of fact I do."

She stepped away from him and lifted her blue cashmere sweater from the back of the chair, then glanced at her watch. It was a few minutes before eight o'clock, and her first class was at eleven. She was certain that she could make it back in time.

Putting on the sweater, she walked to the bathroom and closed the door. Hodges could hear her tinkling into the bowl, and he grinned as he put on his skivvy shorts. She was a great piece of ass, whoever she was. He hoped he'd be able to get together with her again some day, but right now he had to figure out what he'd tell the marines on guard at the gate of the Boston Navy Yard, because he'd overstayed his pass and technically was AWOL.

"Well, I'll think of something," he muttered as he reached for his blue bell-bottom trousers.

"Did you say something?" Helen called from inside the bathroom.

"Yeah, I said come on out here and let's play around some more," Hodges replied exuberantly, although he knew he didn't have much juice left.

"Oh, Tommy," she said reproachfully. He heard her turn on a water faucet. "You submariners are all so sex-crazy."

"I wouldn't talk if I was you," he replied, as he got on his knees and looked under the bed for his socks.

As she left, she found herself, unaccountably, crying —floods of tears. She was crying as she hadn't cried since she was eleven years old.

THREE

In a parking lot beside a public beach in New London Harbor, a lone 1935 La Salle sedan was parked. In the front seat sat a Japanese man wearing a dark brown suit and matching homburg. He was rather stout, moon-faced, and had steel-rimmed spectacles over his eyes. Hanging from his neck was a pair of binoculars, and beside him on the seat was a Leica with a 300 mm telephoto lens. His car was parked so that he faced the harbor, and he smoked a cigarette as he stared expressionlessly ahead. His view was restricted by a big wooden warehouse on his left and some sort of manufacturing building on his right, but he'd have ample time to observe any craft that sailed past that morning.

He looked at his watch; it was a few minutes after eight. Stubbing out his cigarette in the ashtray, he picked up his camera and checked it over once again. Upon arriving in the parking lot, he'd loaded it with a fresh roll of film. That had been at daybreak, and he'd been here ever since, sitting patiently, occasionally reading articles in the *New York Times* that he'd brought with him.

He blew a speck of dust from the lens. Then he saw

it in the corner of his eye—the sleek bow of a submarine. Raising his binoculars, he watched as the vessel sailed into view. The number 192 was on the conning tower and he knew it was the *Sebago*, the new American submarine. It looked almost exactly like the boats of the previous *Salmon* class, except that maybe it was a little longer, and its conning tower was somewhat lower. But it was hard to say for sure at this distance without a *Salmon* boat nearby to compare it with.

The Japanese man opened the door of his car. He got out, taking his Leica with him. Standing beside the car, he took off his glasses and dropped them into the inside pocket of his suit, then raised the Leica to his eye and focused on the conning tower of the *Sebago*. He already had the lens opening and shutter speed set, so all he had to do was shift to the viewfinder window and press the button. He wound the film quickly, raised the Leica to his eye again, and snapped another picture, thinking that his angle and the light showed the silhouette of the *Sebago* perfectly. He couldn't ask for better conditions. He managed to take three more pictures before the *Sebago* became obscured by the warehouse on his left. He watched as the bow disappeared behind the warehouse; then he returned to his car and put the Leica back into its brown leather case. Removing the binoculars from his neck, he placed them in their case, then put both camera and binoculars into his black pigskin briefcase.

He smiled as he lit another cigarette. Taking a puff, he turned the key in the ignition and pressed the button on the dashboard. The V-8 engine rumbled to life, and he shifted into first, letting up the clutch and driving in a wide circle to the entrance of the parking lot, where he turned left onto the road and drove away.

FOUR

"McCrary, you can take a coffee break if you want," said Gomez.

"Okay," said Ed McCrary, checking his watch to make sure of the time.

"Be back in ten minutes."

"Right."

Ed wiped his hands on a rag and stuffed it into the back pocket of his dungarees. He knew the other men in the engine compartment were watching him as he moved forward to the hatch. They always were watching him silently because the word was out on him: He'd been bilged from Annapolis and was the younger brother of the boat's executive officer. They weren't unfriendly toward him, but they weren't friendly either. He hadn't been accepted as a member of the crew. He was an outsider again.

He went through the hatch and entered the crew's quarters, where some of the men were lying on their bunks. He'd been an outsider all his life, never able to mesh well with other people. He tried—Lord knows he tried—but he never got anywhere. He didn't know that others mistook his natural shyness for arrogance, and that made them contemptuous of his awkward manners. His efforts to be liked and respected usually ended in humiliation. He just couldn't seem to get along easily with people.

He squeezed past the bunks in the crew's quarters and went through the hatch to the crew's mess compartment. The cook, a grizzled old sea dog, was in his little space, watching his mixing machine make dough for the biscuits he intended to serve with lunch. He looked at Ed as he appeared in the doorway.

"Can I get a cup of java, cookie?" Ed asked, trying to be friendly.

The cook grunted and drew a cup of the black steaming liquid. "Milk?"

"Yes, please."

The cook poured in some milk. Ed took the cup and sat at one of the tables, his back to the starboard bulkhead. Winowski, from the aft engine gang, was at the next table, reading a Superman comic book with his coffee. Winowski glanced up from his comic book.

"Hi, Winowski," Ed said.

Winowski grumbled something and looked down at his comic book again. What in the hell do these guys have against me? Ed wondered unhappily. Are they afraid I'll tell my brother if I see them doing something wrong?

Ed spooned some sugar into his coffee, then took a sip. It was hot, and he didn't like Navy coffee very much anyway, but he liked to sit and relax for a few moments. He tapped his fingers on the top of the table and tried to convince himself that he should be happy as an ordinary seaman on the *Sebago* because he was about as low as a fellow could get in the Navy, and if he screwed up he couldn't drop any lower than he was already.

If only his brother was on a different submarine. He was convinced that he would've got along a lot better on the *Sebago* if Jack wasn't the exec. It was hard for him to bear the cold disapproving looks that Jack always gave him. Jack hated him—that was clear. Ed couldn't blame Jack for feeling that way, for he'd brought dishonor to the family name.

If only he hadn't cheated on the physics examination. It was terrible that one little mistake could ruin a person's life. He'd wanted to do well on the exam so he could impress his schoolmates and make his parents happy, so he'd written some of the important formulas in tiny print on a small square of paper and hidden it up his sleeve. Naturally the proctor caught him looking at it. He'd been confined to quarters, and two weeks later they threw him out of Annapolis. The next day he enlisted in the Navy. He hadn't gone home and hadn't seen his mother and father since he left Annapolis. His kid sister Helen had come to see him a few times when he was a seaman recruit at Newport, Rhode Island, and then, when he was assigned to the *Sebago,* he was horrified to see his brother Jack standing on the deck.

What a moment that had been. Shakily, he crossed the catwalk and boarded the *Sebago,* walking up to his brother and saluting as he stated his name and rank and reported for duty. Jack looked at him as though he was a piece of shit and told him coldly to report to Yeoman Reilly for his assignment. Ed saluted and went below.

That had been two weeks ago. He'd pulled every shit detail on the boat ever since, but he was determined to stay together and do his duty somehow. He'd show them all that while a McCrary could make a mistake, a McCrary was tough and could be expected to weather any storm.

His coffee was cooler now; he took a sip. It sure wasn't like the coffee Mom used to make, but nothing was like the things that came out of Mom's kitchen. He took another sip and looked at his watch; he had five minutes left. It would be better to report back for duty a minute or two early, so no one would think he was trying to get away with anything. But of course if he got back too early, they'd think he was trying to brown-nose Gomez. He was damned if he did and damned if he didn't. What a mess.

The tan cap of an officer appeared in the aft hatch, and Ed stiffened behind his cup of coffee. It was Jack, returning from his inspection tour of the boat's forward compartments. Still bent in the hatch, Jack saw Ed and froze for a moment, then looked away and stepped through into the crew's mess compartment. He walked past Ed as though he wasn't there, and went through the hatch to the control room. Ed watched him go, his eyes getting salty. Jack had been his big brother once. He'd taught him how to play tennis and how to swim, but that had been in a world that was long gone.

Ed looked at his watch; he had four minutes left. He gulped down his coffee, dropped the cup into the tin basket next to the galley sink, and went aft to the engine room.

FIVE

Frowning, hating his brother so much that he felt knots in his stomach, Jack climbed the ladder to the conning tower. "Permission to come to the bridge, sir!" he shouted up.

"Permission granted!" replied Lieutenant Commander Dunlop.

Jack climbed the ladder to the bridge. Dunlop was there with Ensign Delbert and Lieutenant Nielsen, the latter an observer from the Royal Swedish Navy. Raising his binoculars, Jack saw that the *Sebago* was coming to the mouth of the river.

"Everything is secure below, sir," Jack said to Dunlop.

Dunlop grunted as he peered ahead through his own binoculars. "Well, we'll be clear of the river soon," he said. He lowered his binoculars and turned to Nielsen. "What do you think of her so far?"

"Well, it's much larger than our submarines," Nielsen replied in his Swedish accent. "It's hard to say whether that's an advantage or not."

"It all depends on what the particular submarine is being used for," Dunlop explained. "This submarine is large because it's designed to make long-distance patrols. Its cruising range is eleven thousand miles, so it needs space for additional fuel and provisions, plus more reasonable accommodations for its crew."

Nielsen smiled. "Then this submarine is not intended purely for the defense of the United States mainland, I do not suppose."

Dunlop smiled back. "You can suppose what you like, Lieutenant Nielsen, but as a naval officer I'm sure you know that the best form of defense is quite often offense."

Nielsen nodded. "I know, but the latest German undersea boats are only two-thirds this size, with approximately the same cruising range."

"I don't think they'll prove to be very reliable," Dunlop said, "and the living conditions below must be rather tight."

"I don't know—I've never been on one, sir," Nielsen lied.

"No? That's surprising, since Sweden is so close to Germany."

"There are all sorts of political problems between my country and Germany."

"Ah, yes—that Hitler."

Ensign Delbert's high-pitched voice cut through the conversation. "We're abeam of New London light, sir."

"I've noticed, Ensign Delbert," Dunlop replied. He looked ahead at the slanting rays of sunshine that came through the thick puffy clouds. "Looks like we might have some bad weather."

"We won't feel it when we're submerged, sir," Delbert said.

"But we won't be submerged that long," Dunlop replied. "Left full rudder!" he shouted down the conning tower.

"Left full rudder!" replied Boatswain's Mate First Class Keller.

The *Sebago* swung around the mouth of the New

London Harbor. It passed Southwest Ledge, cruised through the marker buoys, and headed east toward The Race off Fishers Island. A few trawlers were in the sound, and Fishers Island, a haven for millionaires, could be seen clearly off the port bow. Jack looked at Fishers Island through his binoculars. His future father-in-law, Congressman Adam Kirkland of the state of New York, had a mansion on the sheltered side of the island, and Jack scanned its northwest hills to see if he could spot it.

"Looking for enemy artillery emplacements?" Lieutenant Commander Dunlop asked good-naturedly.

"No, sir. I was looking for a home that my fiancée's father maintains there."

"Oh, yes, Congressman Kirkland. I hadn't realized that he had a home there, but I suppose he has homes in many places, a man with his wealth and connections."

Jack smiled. "As a matter of fact, he does."

"I'll have to be careful what I say around you from now on, since soon you'll have influence in the halls of Congress."

"I don't think the influence will amount to very much," Jack said. Congressman Kirkland wasn't happy about his daughter marrying a lieutenant in the Navy. He'd wanted her to marry a Wall Street lawyer or an industrialist, maybe even a crowned head of Europe. Jack was aware that Congressman Kirkland didn't like him very much, but he'd probably change his mind when he became a grandfather.

Jack wondered what Betsy Kirkland saw in him, because he wasn't rich and he wasn't that good-looking. He only had his lieutenant's bars and a family that had distinguished itself in the Navy. She'd told him once that she felt more comfortable with him than with any other man she'd ever gone out with, so maybe he was like an old shoe or a nice soft pillow to her.

"Come right to one-two-oh!" shouted Lieutenant Commander Dunlop.

"Right to one-two-oh!" replied Keller in the control room.

The submarine angled east and headed toward Block Island Sound. It wouldn't be long before the old man took her down for the first time. Jack would be able to tell his grandchildren someday that he was on the *Sebago* when it made its first test dive. It was the sort of thing that might give him satisfaction in his old age.

"Lieutenant Stearns, come to the bridge and bring your hand-bearing compass with you!" shouted Lieutenant Commander Dunlop.

"Yes, sir!" replied Lieutenant Stearns.

Moments later Stearns ascended the ladder, carrying his compass.

"Take a fix," Dunlop told him. "I want to know how far we have to go before we reach our point of dive."

"Yes, sir."

Lieutenant Stearns held the hand-bearing compass to his eyes and sighted down it at the lighthouse on the tip of Fishers Island. He'd sight on two more prominent landmarks, then go below with the bearings and draw lines on his chart. The *Sebago*'s position would be where the lines intersected.

Jack watched Stearns write down the bearing for the lighthouse and then aim at a water tower on the mainland.

Well it won't be long now, Jack thought.

SIX

The old synagogue was small, located on a side street in the Sheepshead Bay area of Brooklyn. Lieutenant Commander Benjamin Mount, in civilian slacks and sport jacket, opened the front door for his grandfather, Chaim Mount, who was seventy-six years old, a puny, wrinkled old man with a long white beard, wearing a black suit and a yarmulke.

Chaim Mount entered the synagogue, and Ben followed him, feeling queasy and uncomfortable. Ben wasn't religious—in fact was antireligious—but his grandfather had begged him to come along to morning prayers, and Ben couldn't refuse.

The interior of the synagogue was dark and gloomy. The only light came from a small stained-glass window behind the ark and a few low-wattage chandeliers. Some old men were standing in the pews, rocking back and forth in the rapture of their prayers. Ben cringed at the sight of them. He hated superstition and ritual but loved his old grandfather, so here he was in *shul* for the first time in years.

His grandfather entered an empty pew. Ben followed him and stood silently while his grandfather recited a brief prayer. Ben had no idea of what he was supposed to do in a synagogue. He'd known everything once, when he was studying for his bar mitzvah, but he'd forgotten it all—probably on purpose, as he remembered many things he'd learned in regular school during those days.

His grandfather opened the little blue velvet bag that contained his prayer articles. Ben did likewise, opening the red velvet bag that his grandfather had given him for his bar mitzvah when he was twelve. On top was his yarmulke, which he put on the back of his head. He had straight black hair, a Semitic nose, and a wiry build. He'd graduated first in his class at Annapolis and had been on the track team.

His grandfather turned to him. "Do you remember how to put on tefillin?" he whispered.

"No," Ben replied.

"Do what I do and say what I say."

"Okay."

His grandfather sniffed as he pulled his hand tefillin out of the bag. "Take out this one."

Ben fished around in his bag until he found his hand tefillin, which he took out and held up. "This one?"

"Yes, that one. We're not supposed to talk while putting on tefillin, but I guess we have to so I can show you." He spoke in the gutteral accents of the Polish *shtetl* where he'd been born and raised. "You put the box part right here like this." He placed the little leather box on his bicep. "See?"

Ben placed his own tefillin in exactly the same place. "Like this?"

"You're doing fine, *boychick*. Now take the straps like this and wind them around your arm like so." He wound the straps around his arm once. "See?"

"I see."

"Okay, wind the straps on the rest of the way and repeat after me: *Baruch ata adonai elohainu . . .*"

"*Baruch ata adonai elohainu . . .*"

His grandfather intoned the Hebrew words of the

prayer, and Ben dutifully repeated them as he wound on the tefillin. His grandfather was smiling, happy to be transmitting this special knowledge to his grandson, and Ben was glad that he could give his grandfather this moment, because the old man would be dead in a few years, and Ben didn't suppose that a man his grandfather's age had many sources of pleasure.

Next they put on the head tefillin and recited the appropriate prayer in the same manner. Ben knew that Jews had been performing this ritual for thousands of years, just because it had been written someplace that God told a Jew that they were supposed to bind His name between their eyes and and on their right arms. No Jew ever questioned it. The Jew who wrote it down might have been an epileptic or a madman, yet for thousands of years religious Jews had been doing this. *Why?* Ben wondered. *What do they get out of it?*

With their tefillin in place, they picked up prayer books and turned to the Eighteen Benedictions. The text was given in Hebrew, English, and a transliteration so that an ignorant Jew like Ben could speak the Hebrew words. His grandfather began to recite the first of the Benedictions, rocking back and forth. Ben spoke the ancient syllables with him but refused to move his body in that foolish manner. Ben was a modern man, a scientist and engineer, and there was only so much that he could do to please his grandfather.

They droned out the prayer together. It was a long one, and Jews were supposed to recite it three times every day. Ben didn't bother reading the English translation of the prayer, because he didn't care what it meant. He thought religion was for weaklings who needed something to believe in, or for ignorant superstitious people like his grandfather who didn't know any better. How much cleaner and more beautiful were the laws of science, which were precise and described the world as it really was.

Ben always had loved science. It had been his favorite school subject when he was a little boy, and quite early he had decided to become a scientist. He had gone to the Bronx High School of Science and had graduated in only three years. Growing up in the Sheepshead Bay area, he became interested in boats when he was a little boy. As he grew older, he became friendly with a classmate named Emilio Santucelli, whose father operated a fishing boat. Emilio invited Ben out on it several times, and on one of their trips to the Ambrose grounds Ben decided he'd like to become an engineering officer in the Navy. His school marks were outstanding and he was able to get a recommendation from his congressman. He became a plebe at Annapolis when he was eighteen years old.

On his first day at Annapolis he ran into the anti-Semitism that would follow him throughout his Navy career. Living in New York City and surrounded by a large Jewish population, he hadn't thought much about his Jewishness, but he was forced to think about it at Annapolis when the upperclassmen called him Jewboy Mount. At first it had flabbergasted him. People like his grandfather were Jews, but Ben had considered himself an American. He'd been born in America, and so had his parents. He thought the Jewish religion was a lot of baloney. But the upperclassmen and many of his own classmates descriminated against him because he was a Jew, giving him the dirtiest details to do, riding him unmercifully, trying to force him to drop out of Annapolis. But he was tough and strong, and things got easier once his plebe year was finished.

Quite often he wondered what *Jewish* really meant. He knew it didn't refer specifically to a religion, because he wasn't religious at all. It wasn't a nationality, because he had been born in Brooklyn New York. It wasn't a language, because he couldn't speak Hebrew or Yiddish. It wasn't something he carried in his blood, because doctors had never identified Jewish blood corpuscles as being any different from Christian blood corpuscles. When they called him a Jewboy, what in the hell had they been talking about?

Was it his nose that bothered them so much? Did he really act so much differently from the way they acted? He never figured out what it was, and he still didn't know, but he'd decided in his first year at Annapolis that his only hope was to fight back, and the only way to fight back was to be a better midshipman and a better student than any of them. They thought they could break him, but he took all they could dish out and graduated first in his class. He'd shown them. Many of them didn't like him, but he'd made them respect him. He'd beat them at their own game, and he still was doing it. Some people thought he might even become an admiral someday. Wouldn't that be something—a Jewish admiral. Stars on his shoulderboards.

Lieutenant Ben Mount smiled bitterly as he continued reciting the Eighteen Benedictions with his old grandfather. He thought of how easy and pleasant his military career would have been if only he'd been born into some other religion. How terrible to have to drag this Jewish baggage through life. It would be different if he believed in it, but he didn't believe in it at all.

He only believed in his brain and his will. He was certain that whatever the hardships and tribulations he would encounter in his life, his brilliant mind and iron will would carry him through.

Sometimes he secretly wished that a great obstacle would be thrust in his path, so he could demonstrate in spectacular fashion that he was the stuff admirals were made of.

SEVEN

The *Sebago* glided over the choppy waters of Block Island Sound. Jack McCrary had command of the bridge, and with him were Lieutenant Nielsen, Ensign Delbert, and Seaman First Class Darrell Goines. The brisk wind sent sheets of salt water flying toward the bridge, and a thick oily mass of clouds covered all but a few blue spots in the sky.

"Weather's getting worse," Goines commented, looking up at the sky.

"We should be back in port by three or so," Jack answered, his binoculars trained on the segment of the horizon where Block Island would appear before long.

Delbert looked at McCrary. "Think the old man might want to get in some submerged torpedo practice this afternoon?"

"I don't know."

In the control room Lieutenant Commander Dunlop was going over the chart with Lieutenant Stearns. Boatswain's Mate First Class Keller at the helm and Boatswain's Mate Second Class Araujo on the hydroplane controls watched the two officers make lines on the plastic and mumble coordinates to each other.

Stearns made an X in the Atlantic, south of Block Island, and looked up at Dunlop.

Dunlop was checking his watch. "We should be at our dive position in twenty minutes or so." He looked at Stearns. "Have the coordinates radioed to New London, then come up on the bridge for a final fix."

"Yes, sir."

Dunlop went up the ladder to the bridge. Halfway through the conning tower he felt out of breath and stopped for a moment. There was a dull ache underneath his left arm; he'd had it since he boarded the *Sebago* that morning. He hadn't been feeling well for a few weeks but had postponed seeing a doctor because he was anxious to take command of the *Sebago* and get underway. It couldn't be anything serious, he was certain. He'd probably twisted his arm in some way, and he was out of breath because he smoked too much. He'd have to cut down, maybe starting tomorrow morning.

A puff of salt air came down the conning tower, refreshing him. *I'm not as young as I used to be,* he thought, as he resumed climbing the ladder to the bridge.

In the control room Lieutenant Stearns wrote the dive position on a pad of paper and tore off the slip. He carried it back to the radio room, where Radioman Second Class Arthur Mason sat with his headphones on, listening to messages going in and coming out of the New London submarine base.

Stearns handed Mason the message. "Send this to New London right away."

"Yes, sir."

Stearns returned to the control room, and Mason looked at the message on the slip of paper. It was neat and clear—no problem. He tapped the key, and the dots and dashes flew into the atmosphere.

In the communications center at the New London submarine base, the message was picked up by Radioman Third Class Ralph Kerry, who was hung over and exhausted after a weekend of saloons and whorehouses in New York City. He took down the message but confused a dash for a dot and two dots for a dash. When he finished taking down the message, he signed his name to the bottom of the form and tossed it in his OUT basket.

The coordinates he'd written down were not the coordinates Radioman Mason had transmitted.

They were approximately ten miles away from the spot where the *Sebago* would make her first dive.

EIGHT

The offices of the *New York Standard* were in a grimy red-brick building a half block east of Herald Square in midtown Manhattan. Betsy Kirkland sat at her desk in the city room and looked at the copy on the sheet of yellow paper in her typewriter:

WILLIAM DILLWORTH 3RD
IS FIANCÉ OF MARY E. JOHNSON

> *Mr. and Mrs. Floyd Johnson of Old Saybrook, Conn., have announced the engagement of their daughter, Mary E. Johnson, to William Dillworth Palmer 3rd, son of Mr. and Mrs. Palmer 2nd of New York City and Palm Beach. A September 30 wedding at St. Bartholomew's Church in New York City is planned.*
>
> *Miss Johnson is an alumna of Skidmore College, where she was elected to Phi Beta Kappa. She is presently a student of Fine Arts at Columbia University. Her father is president of . . .*

I can't take much more of this, Betsy thought, staring dully at the words she'd written. She felt desperate, like jumping up from her chair and running out of the city room, out of the *Standard* building, and into the streets of New York, never to return again.

She looked around the big city room at the other reporters pounding their typewriters. The walls had been painted tan once but now were dark brown and looked like dirt. Paper overflowed from wastebaskets, and reporters chatted over telephones. Copyboys rushed around carrying pieces of paper.

Betsy knew that some of those reporters were working on important and interesting stories that dealt with politics, the international situation, and the coal strikes in Harlan County, Kentucky, but she was stuck on the society pages because that was the kind of job that women reporters usually got. In fact, were it not for her father, who was a congressman, she would have started out as a copygirl, even though she was a graduate summa cum laude from Vassar.

She closed her eyes and worked her jaw muscles, trying to hold down the anger and frustration. She simply couldn't bear to write another of those damned wedding announcements. That's all they ever let her write, along with birth announcements, charity parties, and who was seen wearing what at some stupid restaurant. She'd got a job at the *Standard* because she wanted to cover news stories, not inanities. She wasn't doing it for the money. Her family had plenty. She'd become a reporter because she'd thought it would be interesting work, but it was turning out to be the most boring activity she'd ever done in her life.

I've been here four months, and I can't take this anymore, she told herself. *I'm going into the office of the city editor right now and tell him that if he doesn't give me more interesting work, I'm going to quit. If he doesn't like it he can go fly a kite.*

She stood up and smoothed the front of her tartan plaid skirt. Squaring her shoulders, she marched among the desks and wastebaskets toward the closed door that was stenciled CITY EDITOR. She was tall and slender, with shoulder-length straight auburn hair combed into bangs on her forehead. Her nose was curved, and her lips were thin and pretty. Her high heels whacked against the linoleum on the floor, but no one looked at her; the city room was bedlam and there always were people running around.

She approached the door marked CITY EDITOR and knocked on it.

"Who is it?" asked Jimmy O'Rourke, who sat inside.

"Betsy Kirkland!"

"Come on in."

Betsy opened the door and looked at O'Rourke going over a sheet of copy on his desk. He wore wire-rimmed spectacles low on his pug nose and had a florid complexion; his stomach was as big as a barrel of pickles.

"What's on your mind?" he asked, not looking up.

She crossed her arms and looked at him as an obstacle that she somehow had to get through. Her mouth became a grim line. "I want a transfer," she said.

He took a cigar stub from his ashtray and chewed on it, still looking down at the sheet of copy he was editing. "Why?" he grumbled.

"Because I don't like the society desk."

"Why not?"

"It bores me silly."

"It doesn't bore Barbara silly, and she's been on the society desk for fifteen years."

"I'm not Barbara."

O'Rourke looked up at her. "No, you're not. Where do you want to transfer to?"

"Anywhere."

"You can't be more specific?"

"How about city hall?"

"They don't like lady reporters in city hall."

"Crime?"

"They don't like lady reporters in police stations."

Betsy wrinkled her brow. "I'd even work on sports, Mister O'Rourke, although I'm not that interested in sports."

He grunted and returned to the sheet of copy. "That's okay—I've got plenty of guys who are."

"Can't you send me upstairs to the national desk?"

"You don't have enough experience." He looked at her and smiled sarcastically. "Traditionally, reporters start in the city room."

"I can't stand society stuff anymore," she said evenly. "It's stupid."

He shrugged and looked back to his sheet of copy.

Betsy blinked and realized that the discussion had reached a crucial point. He had not honored her request for a transfer. She could either return to her desk and finish writing that idiotic wedding announcement, or she could quit. O'Rourke's behavior indicated he didn't care which way she went. Her father needed the *New York Standard* much more than the *New York Standard* needed him. She didn't know what to do.

"Anything else?" O'Rourke grumbled, chewing his cigar and not looking at her.

His tone of voice settled it.

"I quit," she said.

She turned around and walked out of his office, feeling a hundred pounds lighter. Floating across the city room, she thought how marvelous it was that only two words had emancipated her from the horrible drudgery of the society desk. No more weddings and afternoon teas. No more getting up at five-thirty in the morning so she could be to work at seven.

At her desk she opened the drawer and removed her few personal articles. *Well,* she thought, *I'm getting married in a few months, and I'll try to get a new job in the city near wherever Jack is stationed.*

She thought of Jack in his blue uniform. So dashing he was, so handsome, so reliable. He would be her refuge from dating and fooling around, which she didn't like very much, and her refuge from her overbearing father.

And the *New York Standard* could find some other sucker to write about weddings.

NINE

Lieutenant Stearns came to the bridge and stood behind Lieutenant Commander Dunlop, who was staring ahead through his binoculars.

"Sir?" said Stearns.

"What is it?" Dunlop asked, still looking through his binoculars.

"We have approximately one mile to go on the surface before we reach our point of dive."

Dunlop lowered his binoculars and turned to Jack. "Prepare the boat to submerge."

"Yes, sir." Jack leaned toward the hatch. "Prepare to submerge!"

"Prepare to submerge!" replied Chief Boatswain's Mate Keller in the control room.

Jack climbed down the ladder to the control room as all hands moved to their diving stations. At the propulsion control station, Machinist's Mate First Class Anthony Brouvelli stood before the console, ready to shift the drive from diesel to electric. In both torpedo rooms the men huddled around the tubes, although they knew this was a practice dive and no torpedoes would be fired. The cook in the galley continued baking bread; the dive wouldn't affect his duties at all. Boatswain Araujo was ready at his hydroplane control, and Boatswain Donahue had his hands on the ballast levers, waiting for the command to flood the tanks.

"All sections report!" Jack said into the control room intercom.

He listened as the sections reported one by one from the bow of the submarine to the stern. In the engine room, Ed McCrary leaned against a bulkhead and listened to Gomez report that his compartment was secure. Ed felt tense, because he still hadn't overcome the mild claustrophobia he always felt when a sub was about to dive. The thought that something could go wrong always entered his mind, a pipe bursting or a bulkhead caving in under water pressure. American submarines had been lost before on dives like this, but very seldom, and he knew that the odds were against something happening now. The *Sebago* after all was the pride of the United States submarine forces. It was unthinkable that an accident could happen.

Jack McCrary listened to his headphones as the reports came in. When Torpedoman Second Class Roberts told him that all was secure in the aft torpedo room, Jack faced Araujo and said, "Rig out the bow planes."

Araujo pressed a button and the hydroplanes, like the wings of an aircraft, flopped down on the outside bow of the submarine. They would be used to maneuver the boat up or down while it was underwater.

Jack looked at the Christmas tree. Each red light indicated that a valve was open, and each green one meant that a valve was closed and watertight. Only eight lights shone red among all the green. One was for the valve through which the radio antennae sprouted, one was for the conning tower hatch, four were for the exhaust valves on the four diesel engines, and the last two were for the main induction valves high in the conning tower. They were the largest valves on the boat and their job was to deliver air to the diesel engines.

The boat was ready to go. "The boat is rigged for diving, sir," Jack spoke into his intercom microphone.

On the bridge, Lieutenant Commander Dunlop looked at the ugly clouds above the submarine. "Lieutenant Stearns!" he shouted.

"Yes, sir."

"Let me know when we're over the dive position!"

"Yes, sir!"

Stearns stood beside Jack at the chart table and looked at the second hand of his stop watch. He'd figured out their speed against the current and had been watching the time since his last fix. When the second hand reached a certain point on the dial, they would be directly over the dive position designated by Lieutenant Commander Dunlop.

From the bow to the stern of the submarine, all hands were tense. It wasn't every day that you took a brand new submarine down for the first time, and although most of them were experienced submariners, and all had intensive training, there always was the shadow of doubt that something could go wrong. But this doubt was matched with the certainty that all systems had been checked and rechecked, they all knew their jobs thoroughly, and the likelihood of problems was nil.

"Thirty seconds to dive position!" Lieutenant Stearns shouted.

"Clear the bridge!" Lieutenant Commander Dunlop replied.

Ensign Delbert was the first one down the ladder, his hands sliding along the rails and his toes clacking past the rungs. Lieutenant Nielsen was next. Dunlop, alone on the bridge, looked around calmly. This was routine to him; he'd taken down new submarines before and had been on duty for almost twenty years.

"All ahead emergency!" he yelled, so that he could get all the push the diesels could deliver, which would force the *Sebago* down faster.

In the propulsion control room, Brouvelli pushed all the levers forward. The *Sebago* thundered through the waves and strained toward its top speed on the surface, twenty knots. Lieutenant Commander Dunlop felt exhilarated by the surge of speed and power.

"Stand by to dive!" he yelled.

"Stand by to dive!" repeated Keller in the control room.

Dunlop took one last look around and off his starboard bow saw an old trawler on its way north. He threw the trawler a playful salute and moved toward the conning tower hatch.

"Hard dive!" he called down.

"Hard dive!" echoed Keller.

Dunlop climbed down the ladder as the submarine's snout dipped into the dark waters of Block Island Sound. In the conning tower Lieutenant Nielsen was waiting to help dog the big hatch shut. The klaxon horn was honking the diving alarm. Nielsen stood to the side so that Dunlop could descend the ladder first to the control room. As soon as Dunlop's foot touched the deck of the control room, he turned to Stearns.

"Time?" Dunlop asked.

"Eight seconds," Stearns replied.

Dunlop grunted. He wanted to be under and at periscope depth in less than sixty seconds.

In the radio room, Mason tapped out the exact time in a message to the New London submarine base. In a few moments his radio antennae would retract and he'd be out of radio contact with the rest of the world. It was 1106 hours.

At his hydroplane control, Araujo had both the bow planes positioned at hard dive, pushing the *Sebago* into a sharp downward angle. The big bow buoyancy tank forward between the torpedo tubes already was filled with sea water and was dragging the *Sebago* down. The main ballast tanks on both sides of the hull also were filling with water and adding to the downward momentum. A submerging submarine was like a sinking ship taking on water, except that a special part of it was kept completely airtight. When it was time for the submarine to surface, compressed air blew the water out of the tanks and the vessel rose as a person would if he had a rubber tire filled with air around his stomach.

The *Sebago* was going down quickly. Stearns stood beside his chart table and watched the seconds tick away. The diesel engines kicked off and the submarine became weirdly silent. Jack McCrary was watching the Christmas tree and he'd seen the lights go green one by one as the valves and hatches were closed by the sailors in the control room. Now only two red lights were on: the ones for the main induction valves, which were the highest on the submarine and therefore the last ones to be closed.

Machinist's Mate Second Class Mark Donahue from Phoenix, had charge of those two valves, and the time had come to pull the levers that controlled them. He grasped them tightly and moved them backwards, while looking at the Christmas tree. The last two lights flicked to green, and the *Sebago* was watertight.

Jack looked at the all-green Christmas tree and believed that everything was secure. The dive was going so smoothly that one might think this crew had been taking the *Sebago* down for ten years. Lieutenant Nielson stood near the periscope and admired the efficiency of the *Sebago*'s crew. It was a standard that the Royal Swedish Navy would do well to emulate. He glanced at the *Sebago*'s Christmas tree and saw that it was all green.

Machinist's Mate Donahue drew air into the submarine from one of the high-pressure cylinders in the ballast tanks and watched the needle on the dial that indicated the degree of air pressure inside the hull. The needle moved an inch and a half, which meant that the interior of the boat was airtight.

"Pressure in the boat, sir!" Donahue called out.

"Hard Dive!" replied Jack.

Keller pressed the button that set the big klaxon horn off the second and last time. The submarine, now on full battery power, sank deeper into Block Island Sound. The sound of waves could be heard crashing against the conning tower.

"Open vents on main ballast tanks three and four!" Jack said.

Keller repeated the order, and Donahue pulled the levers. Araujo held the hydroplane at hard dive. Lieutenant Commander Dunlop, standing beside the ladder that led to the conning tower, looked at the Christmas tree and saw that all the lights shone green. Lieutenant Stearns looked at the ticking hand on his stopwatch. Jack stood beside Keller and waited for the silence that would tell them they were completely submerged. Outside, the waves of Block Island Sound rushed and bubbled against the sinking conning tower and then swallowed it up.

Beautiful, thought Lieutenant Commander Dunlop with a little smile. He moved toward the diving control station where Jack was standing and looked at the depth gauge indicator. It registered thirty-one feet; the boat would be considered fully submerged when it reached fifty.

"Time?" asked Dunlop.

"Thirty-five seconds, sir."

It's going very well, Dunlop thought with satisfaction.

"Reduce dive angle to thirty degrees!" Jack ordered; it was time to start leveling the boat out.

"Reduce dive angle to thirty degrees!" replied Keller.

Araujo turned his big hydroplane wheel, and the angle of the downward slide diminished. Keller instinctively glanced at the Christmas tree, and it still was all green. Jack and Dunlop watched the depth gauge indicator, and the needle crept around the dial to fifty feet. Stearns stared at the dial of his stopwatch. The only sound on the submarine was the faint whirring of the electric motors. Lieutenant Nielsen stood beside the conning tower ladder and admired the smooth businesslike efficiency of the *Sebago*'s crew.

The needle on the depth gauge touched fifty feet.

"Mark!" said Dunlop and Jack McCrary in unison.

Stearns read off the time on his stopwatch. "Fifty-six seconds," he said.

Dunlop grinned and nodded his head. "Excellent!" Jack turned to Keller. "Level the boat."

"Level the boat," repeated Keller.

Araujo turned the big steel wheel and watched the bubble in the angle indicator. When it settled in the middle of its horizontal tube, between the two red lines, the submarine would be completely level.

Dunlop moved toward the number one periscope to take a look above. He tipped his hat back, gripped the handles, and brought his right eye to the rubber-cupped eyepiece. Jack turned to the needle on the depth gauge indicator. The needle was creeping toward fifty-four feet when he suddenly felt a strange fluttering sensation in his ears. *What the hell's that?* he thought. He'd never experienced anything like it on any of his previous dives.

In the engine room Gomez had put Ed McCrary and Seaman First Class Patterson to work checking the diesels to make certain they'd be ready when the *Sebago* surfaced. Ed, rag in hand, was testing a tolerance in the fuel injection system on the starboard engine when suddenly he froze with horror at the sound of gushing water behind him. He spun around, and his eyes bugged out at a huge torrent of water blasting out of the main induction vent on the ceiling.

"Stop it!" he screamed, charging toward the vent, raising his hands to stanch the flow, but the violent pressure pushed his hands away, cascaded onto his head, and knocked him backwards.

Gomez ran to the intercom. "We're flooding! Take her up!" he screamed into it.

At the helm in the control room, Keller couldn't believe what he'd just heard over his earphones. His face drained of blood. "Sir," he said as steadily as he could to Lieutenant Commander Dunlop, "the engine room reports that it's flooding!"

"What?" said Dunlop, spinning away from the periscope. He looked at Keller. "What did you say?"

Keller looked into his eyes. "The engine room reports that it's flooding, sir!"

Everyone turned to the Christmas tree. All the lights still were green. If the engine room was flooding, how could all the lights be green? Dunlop decided this was no time to think—it was time to act.

"Blow all main ballast!" he shouted.

"Blow all main ballast!" Keller repeated.

Dunlop looked at Araujo. "Hard rise!"

"Hard rise!" repeated Keller.

At the ballast controls, Donahue's hands trembled as he pulled the levers that closed all air escape vents in the ballast tanks. Then he pounced on the lever that blew three thousand pounds per square inch of air pressure into the ballast tanks. Araujo spun the hydroplane wheel to the hard-rise position. Jack McCrary, electrified by the events of the last few seconds, looked helplessly at the Christmas tree, where all the lights shone green. He charged to the ballast control console, pushed Donahue out of the way, and began checking the levers himself, pulling or pushing each one to make certain it was all the way into its proper position. He quickly saw that they all were. Spinning around, he looked at the Christmas tree again. It still was all green.

Lieutenant Commander Dunlop dashed to the control room intercom. "Engine room report!" he yelled.

There was no answer, and everyone in the control room looked at each other, the full horror of the situation dawning on them.

"Engine room report!" Dunlop shouted louder.

There was still no answer, and Dunlop was faced with the toughest decision he'd had to make since the World War, but he made it quickly. "Secure all hatches!" he bellowed into the microphone.

The *Sebago* shuddered in the cold depths of Block Island Sound. Tons of water roared into the two engine rooms, making the stern of the boat dip lower than the bow. In the galley, the cook, Lawrence Gibbs of Topeka, Kansas, was removing a loaf of bread from the oven when he heard the captain's order to secure all hatches. As a trained veteran submariner, Gibbs reacted without thinking about it. He kicked closed the oven door with his knee, threw the loaf of bread on the counter, and dashed into the main corridor of the submarine, where his feet splashed into water that was ankle deep. He looked aft and his jaw dropped open at the sight of water pouring in his direction. Turning forward, his skin crawled with terror —the hatch to the control room was being closed.

"Wait for me!" he screamed, lunging toward the door, but it slammed shut in his face. He looked down, his hair standing on end, and saw the mechanism move toward its secure position. Lips quivering, he heard crashing sounds and shouting behind him. He turned and saw something like a waterfall, with bodies struggling through it. *Oh, my God,* he thought, turning toward the door again. He saw two eyes looking at him through the little glass window. "Open up!" Gibbs begged, although he knew that the person on the other side would not open up—once hatches were closed in an emergency they remained closed until the emergency was over.

The two eyes on the other side of the door moved away, and Gibbs could see frantic activity in the control room. "Open up!" he yelled as the fear and terror took hold of him. "Open the fucking hatch!"

Then something covered the little window, and Gibbs could see forward no more. He looked down at the water creeping up to his knees. His hands clawed at the thick steel hatch and he began to sob. Behind him he could hear men screaming.

TEN

Jack McCrary taped a piece of paper over the window to the hatch, his mouth dry and his pulse pounding. He'd been the one to close the hatch in Gibbs's face, and he'd looked into Gibbs's panic-stricken eyes afterwards, knowing that he'd doomed Gibbs to the possibility of death by drowning. But when the captain gave orders to close the hatches, you closed the hatches. There were no two ways about it, and there could be no exceptions. Sometimes you had to condemn part of the boat to save the rest of it, and every man in the submarine force knew it.

But he'd never forget those eyes. His jaw set, determined to follow orders and do his duty, he moved swiftly aft to the control room.

"All sections report!" said Lieutenant Commander Dunlop into the intercom.

He waited a few seconds, then heard: "Forward torpedo room secure!" in the unmistakable southern drawl of Torpedoman Hank Burns.

"Officers' quarters secure!" said Yeoman Reilly.

Then there was silence. Dunlop waited several moments, beads of perspiration on his brow, then said, "After compartments—can you hear me?"

He listened, but no voice came over the intercom. He looked at the depth gauge—the *Sebago* had sunk to eighty feet. Air could be heard hissing into the ballast tanks, and he hoped it would be enough to stop the downward momentum. Otherwise the *Sebago* would go right to the bottom of Block Island Sound.

A muscle in Dunlop's jaw twitched. Jack looked at his captain, wondering what he'd do next and whether it would be enough to save the *Sebago*. He looked at the depth gauge—the needle was moving steadily. The rear compartment must be loaded with water. He thought of the men in the engine compartments and aft torpedo room, and then it struck him with full force for the first time: His brother was back there.

"Oh, my God," Jack mumbled as he had a vision of Ed drowning in the engine compartment. He felt dizzy and hung onto a pipe for support.

"Hey!" somebody shouted.

Jack looked up and saw a jet of water shoot across the room from an overhead pipe above the ballast control console. Donahue reached up and turned the little wheel that controlled that pipe. In the radio shack Mason turned toward the sound; a stream of water hit him on the shoulder with the force of a punch from a man's fist. He sprang out of his chair and turned the knob that controlled that pipe.

A moment later two pipes burst on the overhead of the control room, and Araujo closed the valve that controlled one of the pipes while Ensign Delbert jumped onto the chart table and got the other.

Lieutenant Commander Dunlop stood with his back against the conning tower ladder and looked around at the interlaced network of pipes on the ceiling of the control room. He realized that water from the engine rooms was leaking into the ventilating system, but that was all right, they could turn everything off from the control room.

He turned to Jack. "Depth?"

"Ninety-five feet, sir," Jack replied, still shaken by the thought of Ed. Maybe he could be saved somehow, maybe he could find some space where there was air, but Jack knew it was unlikely. His soul shriveled as he wished he'd been kinder and more forgiving to his brother, but who could have guessed that something like this would happen?

"Are you all right, Jack?" Dunlop asked.

Jack snapped to attention. "Yes, sir."

"Are we still sinking?"

Jack looked at the needle—it was moving inexorably to the higher numbers. "Yes, sir."

Dunlop felt an ache in his left arm and decided he'd better ignore it because he didn't want his crew to know anything was wrong with him. Maybe he'd pulled a muscle when he was coming down the ladder. He looked around at his men, grim and steadfast at their posts. Even Ensign Delbert was under control, poised to follow any orders given him. Dunlop realized that the water in the stern was too heavy for the air in the ballast tanks and they would continue descending to the ocean floor.

He looked at Sterns at the navigation table. "How much water do we have?"

Stearns bent over the chart. "One hundred and thirty feet, sir."

Dunlop wanted to light a cigarette, but he knew they had to conserve oxygen. He kept his face immobile, knowing everybody was looking to him for leadership, and wondered what would happen when greater depths put increased pressure on the hull. Would something else blow? How long would it be before New London realized the *Sebago* was in trouble? They were supposed to stay down for an hour; he glanced at his watch. They'd only been under for five minutes. It would be a long time before New London became suspicious. Maybe too long. Dunlop wracked his brain for something that he could do to reverse the situation, but he knew there was nothing. Nothing at all. All he could do was hope that nothing else happened.

"Captain Dunlop!" said Yeoman Reilly's voice on the squawk box.

Dunlop stepped toward the intercom. "What is it, Reilly?"

"Sir, there's chlorine gas in the forward battery compartment!"

Dunlop pinched his lips together. Salt water must have worked itself into the bilges and was seeping into the forward batteries, where the chemical reaction would produce chlorine gas.

He looked at Jack. "Come with me."

"Yes, sir."

Dunlop walked to the forward control room hatch and stood to the side as Jack turned the wheel that opened the hatch. When he pulled the hatch open, Yeoman Reilly was standing there, his eyes tearing. Dunlop smelled the chlorine gas immediately, but it wasn't too strong yet. He turned to Reilly.

"Tell Keller to bring some tools up here."

"Yes, sir."

Reilly ran back to the control room, and Dunlop advanced into the officers' wardroom, which was atop the battery network. He felt a tightness in his chest and absentmindedly rubbed it with his fingers. The voltmeters showed a huge discharge taking place, which meant there was a short circuit down there somewhere. He heard footsteps and saw Keller moving forward, carrying the control room toolbox.

"You wanted some tools, sir?" Keller asked, holding up the toolbox.

"Yes," Dunlop said, and then all of a sudden he felt dizzy. Keller floated before his eyes, and the light grew dim. But a second later Dunlop's head cleared and he could see well again. He thought that maybe the chlorine gas had got to him. "Let's take up these floor plates and look at those batteries," he said.

Jack and Keller got down with the screwdrivers and began unscrewing a floor plate. Jack still was shaken by the knowledge that his brother was probably dead in the aft engine compartment and that things didn't look good for the rest of them. Something else might bust, and he could be drowned within the next few minutes himself. He'd always thought of himself as a lucky person, but now he realized that his luck might be running out.

He removed the screws holding down the floor plate, then wedged the blade of the screwdriver into the crack and pried the floor plate up. A nasty burning smell rose to his nostrils, and as he pulled the floor plate away he saw an ominous blue flickering in the darkness of the bilge.

"There's a short down here," he said.

"Let me see," replied Dunlop.

Dunlop bent over to get a closer look, and as he did so he felt a violent pain in his chest. He gasped, his eyes bulging, his legs wobbling, and dropped to his knees.

Jack and Keller looked at Dunlop in alarm.

"Are you all right, sir?" Jack asked.

Dunlop clutched his chest with his hands because it felt as though a monster was ripping it apart. He blinked and tried to breathe, but every movement of his lungs made sharp stabs of pain. His left arm was numb, and he realized he should have seen a doctor while he had the chance. Jack and Keller watched in horror as their captain pitched forward onto his face.

"Pharmacist's Mate!" Jack shouted back to the control room.

"Coming, sir!"

Jack looked at Dunlop writhing on the floor of the officers' wardroom. He wanted to do something but didn't know what. He could carry him back to his bunk, which was only ten feet away, but he'd learned in a first aid class that you shouldn't move anyone who was wounded or suddenly stricken ill until a doctor said it was okay. But there was no doctor aboard the *Sebago*—there was only Pharmacist's Mate Second Class Vincent La Gloria.

La Gloria ran forward with his little black bag and saw Jack and Keller kneeling over the captain, who had become still.

"What happened?" La Gloria asked as he grabbed for the captain's pulse.

"I don't know," Jack replied. "He keeled over all of a sudden."

La Gloria's skilled fingers prodded into the flesh and tendons of Lieutenant Commander Dunlop's wrist, but he couldn't feel anything.

"No pulse," La Gloria said in disbelief.

"No pulse?" Jack asked, unwilling to believe his ears.

La Gloria felt for a few more moments. "Nothing." He rolled Dunlop onto his back and placed an ear against Dunlop's chest.

Jack bit his lower lip as he heard crackling sounds coming from the bilges. The smell of chlorine gas was getting stronger. Everything was going wrong. It was a nightmare.

La Gloria raised himself from Dunlop's chest and looked into Jack's eyes. "He's dead, sir."

"Are you sure of that?" Jack asked, clutching after the straw.

"He's got no pulse and no heartbeat, sir. That means he's dead."

Jack looked down at Dunlop, and a shiver went up his spine. Keller and La Gloria were looking at him; he was now the commanding officer of the *Sebago*.

And the *Sebago* was sinking.

Jack looked at Keller, and their eyes met. Keller was

an old submariner, but he was looking to Jack for direction and confidence. Jack realized that every man on the submarine was now dependent on him. He had become top man, and from now on his word was law.

"You two help me lay him in his bunk," Jack said softly.

He grabbed Dunlop's still-warm wrists as La Gloria and Keller each took hold of a leg.

Then all the lights in the submarine went out.

ELEVEN

In the darkness Jack McCrary permitted himself to be afraid. None of his training had prepared him for this degree of sudden unexpected catastrophe. The corpses of his brother and numerous other men were in the after compartments of the submarine, and now death had come forward. The *Sebago* was sinking and out of contact with New London. Suddenly the responsibility for the submarine had been thrust onto him. He made fists in the darkness and clenched his jaw. He was going to do his best even though the people on shore might never know one way or the other.

"Break out the emergency lamps!" he shouted.

In the control room Lieutenant Stearns groped through the darkness and found the lamps. He passed them around, they were flicked on, and the forward compartments of the *Sebago* were bathed in a ghostly yellow light. Turning, Stearns looked at Lieutenant Nielsen standing beside the conning tower ladder.

"Well," Stearns said with a forced grin, "at least we have lights."

"The situation isn't hopeless by any means," Nielsen replied, realizing that Stearns was trying to lift the morale of the crew.

Araujo shrugged in front of his hydroplane wheel. "They'll get us out of here sooner or later," he said in a relaxed way.

The tension diminished a bit in the control room. In the officers' wardroom, Jack, Keller, and La Gloria carried the body of their captain to his berth and laid him down. The captain's eyes were open and staring wide; Jack leaned over and closed them with his fingers. "May your soul rest in peace," he muttered.

La Gloria crossed himself and said in unison with Keller, "May your soul rest in peace."

Jack looked at the body for a few seconds, he would have liked to say a more elaborate prayer, but there wasn't time. He turned to Keller. "Take up those floor plates out there while I talk with the crew."

"The chlorine gas is getting awfully thick in here."

"If it gets too much for you, put on a Momsen lung. I'll send someone back to help you."

"Yes, sir."

Jack looked at La Gloria. "Come with me."

"Yes, sir."

Jack tramped aft through the officers' wardroom and stepped through the hatch to the control room. La Gloria followed him, and Jack closed the hatch to keep the chlorine gas from seeping into the control room. Then Jack walked to the intercom, glancing at the depth gauge on the way. The *Sebago* had sunk to 155 feet and was still dropping. Jack grabbed the intercom microphone and pushed his cap back.

"Now hear this!" he said.

Everyone in the control room riveted their eyes upon him. In the forward torpedo room, Hank Burns and his men looked at the squawk box.

Jack decided not to mince words. "This is Lieutenant McCrary speaking," he said. "Lieutenant Commander Dunlop has just been stricken by what appears to be a heart attack, and I have taken command of this submarine." He looked at Stearns. "Lieutenant Stearns will be my executive officer. We're in a difficult situation down here and I'm not going to tell you that it's better than it is, but at the same time it's not as bad as some of you might think. We radioed our coordinates to New London as soon as we submerged, so they know where we are. When the time comes for us to surface and they don't hear from us, you can be sure they'll send someone to look for us. We only have about forty-five minutes to go until that happens, so just sit tight, follow orders, and remember your training. You'll be notified of any changes in the situation as they occur. That is all." Jack hung up the microphone and looked at the faces staring solemnly at him. "Any questions?" he asked.

Nobody said anything.

"Good. We're having a little problem with chlorine gas and a short circuit in the forward battery compartment. That means we've got to keep that forward hatch closed at all times." He looked at Donahue. "Since your station is closest to the hatch, it'll be your responsibility from now on to make sure that it's closed and to open it whenever somebody taps on it from the other side. Is that clear?"

"Yes, sir."

Jack turned to Stearns. "I'm going forward to work on the battery. You take over here in the control room until I get back. When she gets close to the bottom, give a warning, because we don't know how level it'll be down there. There might be some tossing and turning when we hit, and we want to be ready. Understand?"

"I understand, sir."

Jack looked around the control room and his eyes fell on Winowski and Electrician's Mate Third Class Homer Gilson. "You two come with me."

"Yes, sir."

"The rest of you carry on here."

"Yes, sir," they all said.

Jack led Winowski and Gilson to the hatch and opened it up. They stepped through and coughed at the odor of chlorine gas. Donahue dogged the hatch shut behind them. They passed through the narrow corridor, and Winowski and Gilson glanced into the captain's wardroom, seeing him pale and stiff on his blanket. They gulped and followed Jack to the wardroom, where Keller was prying up floor plates.

"How's it going, Chief?" Jack asked.

Keller looked up. "Can I speak to you alone for a moment, sir?"

"Sure."

Keller stood up and looked at Gilson and Winowski. "You two get to work pickin' up that floor plate down there."

"I got it, Chief," Winowski said, dropping to his knees and picking up a screwdriver.

Gilson kneeled beside the toolbox and took out a screwdriver, then inserted its blade in the slot of a screw and started turning. Jack led Keller into the tiny wardroom he shared with Lieutenant Stearns. A photo of Betsy Kirkland in her tennis whites was hanging on the bulkhead.

"What's the problem?" Jack asked Keller.

Keller put the tips of his fingers into his dungaree pockets. His sleeves were rolled up; the tattoo of an anchor showed on his left forearm and a hula girl on his right. "We've got to get somebody down in them bilges to cut the main battery cables, sir. The gas fumes are building up, and those sparks are liable to ignite them. The whole boat might blow."

Jack looked him in the eye. "Can you do it?"

Keller took his hands out of his pockets and tapped his big barrel chest. "There's not a hell of a lot of room down there, and I'm too big."

"Then I'll go," Jack said, turning and moving toward the corridor.

Keller grabbed his shoulder. "I don't think that's a good idea, sir, if you don't mind me sayin' so."

Jack looked back at him. "Why not?"

Keller wrinkled his brow. "You're the captain of this boat now, sir. You can't afford to take the chance; it'd be hard on the men if we lost two captains in a row so fast. Lieutenant Stearns is a good officer, sir, but he doesn't have the submarine experience you have. With all due respect, sir, I think you'd better get somebody else."

"Who?"

Keller looked away. "That's your decision, sir."

Jack wiped the perspiration off his forehead with the back of his hand. "You said it'd be best to send someone small down there?"

"Yes, sir. There's ain't much room."

Jack thought for a few moments. "I'll get Ensign Delbert. He's skinny as a rail."

"He's awfully young, sir. You think he can handle it?"

"He's an officer in the United States Navy, Keller. He can handle anything."

"Yes, sir."

Jack stepped across the corridor and entered the wardroom. He picked up the intercom microphone from the shelf behind the table. "This is the captain speaking. Will Lieutenant Stearns please respond."

Jack waited a few seconds, then heard: "Lieutenant Stearns speaking, sir."

"Stearns, send Ensign Delbert forward right away, then get back on the mike."

"Yes, sir."

Through the squawk box Jack heard Stearns tell Delbert to report to the forward battery. "He's on his way, sir," Stearns said.

"What's our depth?" Jack asked.

"One hundred ninety-five feet, sir."

"When do you estimate we'll hit bottom?"

"I'd say about another fifteen minutes, sir, unless something happens to change the buoyancy of the boat."

"How're the men?"

"Fine, sir."

"Carry on."

"Yes, sir."

The control room hatch opened, and Ensign Delbert came through, anxiety and concern on his face. "You wanted to see me, sir?"

"Come with me, Delbert."

"Yes, sir."

Jack and Keller led Delbert to where Winowski and Gilson were taking up the floor plates. The air was getting thicker with yellowish chlorine gas, and Jack noticed that the temperature was lower; evidently the heating system was out with the lights.

"You two get out of the way," Jack told Winowski and Gilson.

Winowski and Gilson stood and stepped back from the opening they'd made in the deck. Jack motioned for Delbert to get down and have a look. With Keller, they got on their knees and peered into the hole. They saw jagged blue-green bolts of electricity shooting back and forth from the terminals of the batteries. Keller aimed a flashlight down—the walls of the batteries were sagging and bubbling. Curls of smoke trailed up from the terminals. The smell of chlorine gas was intense.

"I've got a tough job for you, Delbert," Jack said. "I want you to go down there and cut the main cables."

Delbert's face went stony. "The main cables, sir?"

"That's right—the big ones that go aft to the generators. You know which ones I'm talking about, don't you?"

"Yes, sir."

"Do you think you can do it?"

"I'll try, sir."

"Good man." Jack looked at Keller. "Get him the wire cutter."

Keller dipped his hand into the toolbox and clanked around, finally bringing up the big wire cutter. The handles were sheathed with rubber to prevent the user from receiving an electric shock. Keller handed the wire cutter to Delbert.

"You'll have to be careful down there," Keller said. "There are a lot of bare wires and Buss bars."

Delbert nodded and worked the wire cutter in his hands. The blades made a metallic shearing sound. He took off his tan cap and handed it to Keller. "I guess I might as well get going," he said in his high-pitched adolescent voice.

"Maybe you'd better take a Momsen lung down there," Jack said.

"Good idea," replied Keller.

Keller got up and went to the officers' wardroom and took a Momsen lung off its peg. He carried it back and handed it to Delbert, who pulled it over his head and tied the strings around his waist. It fit something like a life preserver, and had been designed to help sailors escape from doomed submarines. It had a mouthpiece, a nose clip, and oxygen cells inside a rubber casing. The oxygen cells could be opened by an outside control, and a sailor could breathe the oxygen as he ascended from his submarine.

Delbert would use the Momsen lung as a gas mask if the chlorine fumes got too strong for him in the bilge of the submarine. He made sure the Momsen lung was secure, worked the wire cutter again, and said, "Well, here goes."

"Good luck, Delbert," Jack said.

"Take it slow," Keller added.

"You just keep shining that flashlight down here for me, Keller."

"Will do."

Delbert dropped his feet through the hole in the deck and touched them down on the narrow catwalk that ran through the network of buzzing melting batteries. Jamming the wire cutter into his belt, he eased his torso through the hole and carefully lowered himself until he was on his hands and knees on the catwalk. Blue-green zigzags of electricity floated eerily in the air around him, and the odor of chlorine gas and burnt rubber was strong.

"Are you all right down there, Delbert?" Jack asked.

"Yes, sir."

"Then get moving. You don't have much time."

"Yes, sir."

Delbert gingerly moved forward on the catwalk, and Jack looked at his wristwatch. He figured it would be approximately eight minutes before the *Sebago* hit bottom; if Delbert didn't have the cables cut by then, the impact of landing could pitch him onto the battery cells and electrocute him. Jack looked at Keller, and their eyes met. Then they peered down into the hole and watched Delbert's progress.

Delbert crawled forward on the catwalk, seeing water glisten in the bilges beneath him. He only had about eight feet to go, and up ahead he could see the main battery cables, thick as his forefinger and sheathed in rubber that was sizzling and melting. Just a few more feet, he told himself. I'm almost there.

Suddenly a squirt of water hit him in the face. He looked to his side and saw a thin pipe that had just burst. A valve was a few feet aft of it, and Delbert lunged for it, forgetting for an instant where he was. By the time he remembered, his knees and feet were already slipping off the catwalk. He yelped as he clawed to grip something so he could catch his balance, but there was nothing there. His arms fell on the tops of the batteries. There was a short sudden explosion followed by a big puff of white smoke.

"Delbert!" Jack shouted.

Delbert lay motionless, half on the catwalk and half on the batteries. The back of his head and his arms were smoking, and Jack could smell charred flesh.

"Oh, my God," Jack whispered.

"We're gonna have to send somebody else down there fast," Keller said, holding the flashlight on Delbert's corpse and trying to keep himself from retching.

"We don't have time," Jack said, moving his feet into the hole. "I'm going. Hold the flashlight steady for me."

Keller blinked. "I think you should send somebody else, sir. I could get Araujo up here in a minute. He's real skinny and he can climb like a monkey."

"I said hold the flashlight steady."

"Yes, sir."

Jack dropped through the hole and onto the catwalk. He eased forward onto his hands and knees and crept quickly toward Delbert's body. As he drew closer he caught a strong whiff of seared flesh, and it made him gag. He swallowed hard and kept moving, blue-green lights arcing around him. He saw the jet of water shooting over Delbert's body and hissing against the hot batteries on the other side of the catwalk. Touching Delbert's leg, he could feel no electricity, only warm flesh through the cotton twill trousers. He held onto Delbert's belt with one hand and leaned over the batteries to the valve that would cut off the connection to the pipe that was leaking. Turning off the valve, he wondered how many other pipes would burst under the fierce pressures they were being subjected to; not many, because most of the flow of water had been cut off farther back by the men in the control room.

The jet of water shortened as Jack wound the valve down. It dripped and then stopped altogether. Blowing air out the corner of his mouth, Jack pulled himself back to the catwalk and yanked the wire cutter out of Delbert's belt, inserting it into his own and wondering exactly how many men were still alive out of the fifty-six officers and enlisted men who had sailed from New London only three hours ago.

Jack crawled over Delbert's body and made his way down the catwalk to the end of the battery network. The chlorine gas burned his nostrils. He realized he should have paused to take the Momsen lung along with him, but he hadn't thought of it. He'd been too anxious to get down in the bilge and cut the cables. I've got to calm down, he told himself. I've got to think things through more carefully. Everybody's depending on me, and if I make one mistake all of us can be killed.

"Are you all right, sir?" Keller called from above.

"Just keep that light steady."

"Yes, sir."

Jack reached the end of the catwalk. Looking to his left, he saw the two big cables from the port bank of batteries; to his right were the cables from the starboard bank.

"Hold the light on the port cables!" he hollered to Keller.

"Yes, sir!"

The ray of light darted to the left and came to rest on the cables. Jack steadied himself on his knees and reached the wire cutter toward the nearest cable. He caught it in the steel jaws of the wire cutter and pressed the handles together with both his hands. His fingers and wrist muscles strained, and the wire cutter went *snap* as it bit through. Simultaneously the buzzing and electrical arcing stopped on the port bank of batteries, Jack used the tip of the wire cutter blades as pliers to pull the exposed cable ends away from each other so they wouldn't touch again by mistake, then reached farther and snapped the next cable, separating those ends also.

The chlorine gas made him cough, and he felt a burning sensation in the back of his throat. Chlorine gas could eat holes in your lungs, and we wished he'd brought the Momsen lung with him.

"You got them, sir?" asked Keller.

"I got the port ones. Now shine the light on the starboard cables."

"Yes, sir!"

Jack looked at his watch. It would only be four minutes until the *Sebago* hit bottom, and maybe less if Stearns had miscalculated or the bottom was closer than indicated by the chart. Gritting his teeth, perspiration dripping from his brow despite the lowering temperature inside the submarine, he caught the closest cable in the blades of the wire cutter, squeezed with all his might, and broke through. Quickly separating the cables, he reached over to cut the one that was left.

It became silent in the bilge. There were no more flashes from the battery terminals. Now to get the hell out of there. He jammed the wire cutter into his belt and turned around carefully because the tops of the batteries were hot and he didn't want to burn himself.

"You get 'em, sir?" Keller asked.

"I got 'em."

Jack looked at his watch; only three and a half minutes left. He crawled back on the catwalk and touched Delbert's hot body. Maybe he shouldn't have sent the kid into the bilge, but it was too late to worry about that now. He climbed over Delbert and made his way to the opening in the floor. Reaching up, he gripped the floor plates and pulled himself up. Keller grabbed an arm and helped him.

Jack handed the wire cutter to Keller, who put it and the screwdrivers into the toolbox.

"We'll leave the floor plates off," Jack said. "We might have to come down here again."

"Yes, sir."

"Let's get out of here."

Jack stood up and walked aft to the hatch that led to the control room. Just then the *Sebago* struck bottom. It's water-loaded tail hit a rocky shoal twenty feet high, bounced, and caused the bow to dive downward into the mud. The crew members were jolted forward suddenly, and they went sprawling, grabbing for pipes and knobs, anything to prevent them from crashing into metal and harming themselves.

In the forward torpedo room the shock of the blow caused one of the torpedoes to burst loose from its chain. It rolled and clanked toward the men, who struggled to regain their balance and get out of its way.

The torpedo was twenty feet long and weighed a ton and a half. The 666-pound torpex warhead wasn't armed, so there was no danger of its exploding, but Seaman First Class Donald Olds of Saginaw, Michigan, couldn't get out of the way in time, and it rolled over him, crushing his bones like toothpicks; his body managed to slow it down sufficiently for his mates to leap over it or take shelter in the little spaces around the torpedo tubes.

The runaway torpedo rolled aft diagonally over the backs of four torpedoes secured amidships in the compartment. It dropped off the ends of the torpedoes into the pit in front of the tubes, landing with a crash. There were only a few feet of room down there, so it couldn't roll very much anymore.

"Lash the fucking thing down!" screamed torpedoman Burns.

The men grabbed rope and chains—anything they could lay their hands on—and jumped on top of the torpedo, tying hitches on its nose and tail, lashing it to cleats, pipes, and the fittings on the torpedo tubes.

"Good work," Burns said.

Now they had time to look at the battered body of Seaman Olds. Bones protruded through his skin, and blood oozed onto the torpedoes he was lying upon. His head had been flattened to a third of its normal diameter. The men were aghast at the spectacle of death that had occurred so suddenly in their midst, and they could feel the bow of the *Sebago* still sinking.

"Hang on!" yelled Burns.

They groped for anything that might hold them secure, and the nose of the *Sebago* fell into the mud and stones of Block Island Sound. Its steel hull plates strained with the force of the landing, for the boat was suspended only by the rock under its tail and the mud under its nose. It trembled and yawed, then an ugly scraping was heard from the tail as the boat rolled sideways off the rock.

In the officers' wardroom, Jack hugged the legs of the mess table as Keller held onto a conduit pipe that ran up the wall. Araujo grasped the hydroplane wheel in the control room, and Lieutenant Stearns held his hands tightly on the chart table. The tail of the *Sebago* scraped clear of the rock and bounced down its side. Lieutenant Nielsen was holding the ladder that led to the conning tower, and a sudden motion caused his head to slam against the ladder, making him see stars. In the radio shack, Radioman Mason held onto his chair. At the ballast control console, Boatswain's Mate Donahue clutched the levers for support.

A trail of air bubbles arose from the stern of the *Sebago* as it rolled down the side of the boulder. It crunched and grated and then fell free. Every man still alive held onto something for dear life. The submarine's port ballast tank landed in the mud and cracked open, releasing a stream of diesel oil. The boat rocked backward and forward as it settled into the mud, then was still.

The *Sebago* had come to the end of its trial dive.

TWELVE

The sky was cloudy and ominous-looking as Boatswain's Mate First Class Tommy Hodges approached
the main gate at the Boston Navy Yard. It was 0830,
and he was ninety minutes overdue. A cigarette dan-
gling from the corner of his mouth, his hands in his
peacoat jacket and its big collar turned up, he moved
his long legs along casually so as not to attract undue
attention as he prepared to bluff or bullshit his way
past the two guards standing at the gate.

Hodges knew that once he got past those guards
he'd have it made. His commanding officer, Lieutenant Commander Benjamin Mount, was in New York
on a week's furlough, and Hodges was certain he could
handle Ensign Tolliver, who was a scientist like
Mount and didn't care much about Navy rules and
regulations.

Hodges walked confidently toward the guards and
set a course for himself that would bring him between
them and through the gate. Glancing at them, he
could see that they were scrutinizing him warily, so
he took his cigarette out of his mouth and waved it at
them.

"Hiya, boys," he said cheerily, approaching them swiftly and intending to pass them by as though they both were green lights.

"Wait a minute there, sailor," one of them said.

"Can't stop—I'm in a hurry," Tommy said cheerfully as he came abreast of them and didn't slow down.

"I said wait a minute there, sailor!"

"I'm in an awful hurry there, Corporal," Hodges said over his shoulder, still stepping out smartly.

"Halt!"

Hodges stopped cold in his tracks. The bluff hadn't worked. Now the bullshit would begin.

The two guards approached him. One was a corporal and the other a pfc. Through the window of the guardhouse near the gate Hodges could see another marine, probably a sergeant. Hodges had talked himself out of tougher situations, and he was certain he could talk himself out of this one.

"What's the problem?" Hodges asked in a friendly way.

"Let's see your pass," the corporal ordered. He was tall and wore a green uniform.

"My pass?" Hodges asked. "Whataya wanna see my pass for? You think I'm AWOL or something?"

"I said let's see your pass!" The corporal didn't crack a smile, and Hodge wondered where the Marine Corps found its zombies.

"Um, I got it right here someplace," Hodges said, fumbling in the pockets of his peacoat.

"And take that fucking cigarette out of your mouth!"

Hodges became angry at the sound of the corporal's voice, because a boatswain's mate first class ranks higher than a corporal. "Hey—who do you think you're talking to, young corporal!"

The corporal turned toward the guardhouse. "Sergeant!"

A marine with the build of a gorilla came out of the guardhouse, and the stripes on his arms indicated he was a gunnery sergeant.

"Hiya, gunny," Hodges said, turning on the charm again.

"What's the problem here?" the sergeant asked, looking Hodges up and down suspiciously.

"This guy's giving me some lip," the corporal said.

"Oh, yeah?" the sergeant replied, narrowing his eyes at Hodges. "What's your name, sailor?"

"Boatswain's Mate First Class Thomas Hodges."

"Lemme see your pass, Hodges!"

Hodges smiled and held out his arms. "Aw come on, Gunny—lemme go through, will you?"

"I said let's see your pass, sailor!"

"Aw shit, gunny." Hodges reached into his blouse pocket and took the yellow card from behind his green and red package of Lucky Strikes. "Here you go." He held it up for a second, then put it back in his pocket. "Okay?"

The sergeant frowned and held out his hand. "Give it here."

Groaning, Hodges took out the pass again and handed it to the sergeant, who looked at it and then his watch.

"You're a little AWOL, aren't you, sailor?" the sergeant asked.

"Am I?" Hodges asked, wide-eyed.

"You know fuckin' well you are!"

"You mean it don't say oh nine hundred hours?"

"Uh, uh. It says oh seven hundred hours." The sergeant pointed to the time on the pass card. "See?"

"Well whaddaya know about that!" Hodges said. "Gee, I thought it was for oh nine hundred hours."

"Sure you did," the sergeant said sarcastically. "Anyway, you're an hour and a half AWOL and I guess I'm gonna have to throw you in the brig until your C.O. comes and gets you out."

"But my C.O.'s on furlough."

"Tough shit. Let's go to my shack over there, and I'll call for a guard escort."

"But, Sarge," Hodges pleaded.

"No buts. Let's go."

"You can call my C.O.'s exec. His name's Ensign Tolliver."

"They can call him from the brig." The sergeant frowned. "Are you coming or am I gonna have to drag you?"

"I'm coming," Hodges said ruefully, following the three marines to the sentry box. He reflected that whenever he got in trouble, it usually had something to do with a woman. "You know, this is a very bad thing you're doing, Sarge. I'm working on a special ship rescue project here and it'll set the whole project behind if I'm in the brig."

"You shoulda thought of that before you went AWOL."

"I'm not AWOL—I'm right here on the fucking base!" Hodges said, waving his arms in the air.

The sergeant opened the door of the sentry box and picked up the telephone. He spoke a number, then mumbled a message. Hodges clicked his teeth together and tried to think of something to do, but his mind wouldn't come up with anything. The sergeant hung up the phone.

"Some people will be here directly to take you to the brig," he said to Hodges, stepping out of the sentry box. "And don't try to run away or anything like that, because I won't fire any warning shots, I won't fire over your head or anything like that, I'll just fire at the center of your back and bring you down." The sergeant tapped the holster of his service .45 for emphasis.

"Aw, Sarge," Hodges said.

"Don't aw Sarge me."

"But I'm working on a really special and important project. This'll fuck everything up."

"Tough shit," the sergeant said drily.

"You ever heard of Lieutenant Benjamin Mount?"

"You mean the Jew?"

"Yeah, the smart one—the genius. I'm working under him on a special project to rescue sailors from sunken ships, and you know it's important if he's in charge of it."

The sergeant looked Hodges in the eye. "Fuck him and fuck you."

"Aw, Sarge, you're making a lot of trouble for a lot of people for nothing."

"I'm not the one who went AWOL—you are."

"But I'm here—I'm not AWOL!"

A Jeep drove up to the gate from the outside and the corporal held up his hand to stop it. The driver put on his brakes and the corporal and pfc went to check his papers.

Hodges looked at the sergeant. "Are you sure we can't work something out, gunny?"

The sergeant turned down the corners of his mouth. "Shut up, you dumb swab jockey, before I write you up for insubordination. And put out that cigarette, got me?"

Hodges took the cigarette out of his mouth and sighed. "I got you."

He stubbed the cigarette out on the sole of his shoe, tore open the cigarette paper, and scattered the shreds of tobacco to the wind. Then he balled up the paper and threw it over his shoulder. A drop of rain fell on his white cap, and he wondered what Lieutenant Mount would say when he found out he was in the brig. He'd probably get annoyed, because he was a fussy son of a bitch and it'd probably screw up some plan he had.

Well, that's the way it goes I guess, Hodges thought as he waited to go to the brig.

THIRTEEN

The *Sebago* lay on its bottom in the muck twenty-eight miles south of Block Island. A trail of bubbles floated to the surface from a stern torpedo tube. A school of haddock swam past, paying no attention to it whatever. The port ballast tank was still leaking diesel oil.

Inside, Keller knocked a monkey wrench against the forward hatch of the control room. Boatswain's Mate Donahue looked through the window and then turned the wheel that opened the door. He pulled it open, and Keller entered the control room, followed by Jack McCrary. The first thing Jack saw was Lieutenant Nielsen lying with his eyes open at the bottom of the conning tower ladder, and Pharmacist's Mate La Gloria tying a bandage around his head.

"What happened to you?" Jack asked.

"I hit my head against the ladder," Nielsen replied weakly.

Jack looked at Stearns. "Any other injuries?"

"No, sir."

Jack glanced at the depth gauge. It read 234 feet.

"How long has it been since we first dived?" Jack asked.

Stearns looked at his watch. "Exactly forty-eight minutes, sir."

"That means we've only got twelve minutes until the people at New London start wondering what happened to us. I think we can hold on until then."

Jack looked at the faces of his men. In the glow of the dim yellow emergency lamps they looked anxious and tired. The strain was taking its toll of their energies, but they still looked fit for duty.

"Any word aft?" Jack asked Stearns.

Stearns looked down. "No, sir."

Jack was about to chew the inside of his lower lip, a nervous habit he had, but he thought better of it. The crew shouldn't see that he was indecisive and troubled. They should think he was confident and taking everything in stride. That's what leadership was all about.

"Sir," said Stearns in a voice that was almost a whisper, "where's Ensign Delbert?"

"He's dead."

Stearns's facial features collapsed. The men and officers looked at each other fearfully, then turned to Jack again. Jack realized he had to give them an explanation.

"He died in the performance of his duty," Jack said. "The forward batteries had shorted out and there was a danger that the sparks might ignite the fumes down there. He went into the bilges to cut the cables, but he tripped on the catwalk and got himself electrocuted. It was a very brave thing that he did, because by cutting the cables he probably saved our lives. His behavior should set an example for all of us." Jack noticed Keller looking at him weirdly. "Well," Jack continued, "I think the worst is over. We're settled on the bottom and I don't think there'll be any more nasty surprises. Our heating system has conked out, but we have plenty of blankets in the officers' wardroom. We also have enough canned food for a few weeks. We have oxygen bottles and carbon dioxide absorbent. I recall seeing some fishing boats when I was on the bridge, and they probably saw us go down." He looked at Keller. "Send up a smoke rocket."

"Yes, sir."

The rockets were in a canister above the helm. Keller pried off the lid, removed a rocket, and loaded it into its cylindrical ejector. "I'm ready to fire, sir," he said.

"Fire," Jack told him.

Keller pulled the thin stainless steel chain at the bottom of the ejector, and an abrupt *puff* was heard in the control room as the rocket shot up its tube and cleared the deck of the submarine. It roared up through the water, broke through the surface, climbed eighty feet in the air, and exploded, making a big red cloud.

There were two fishing boats on the surface and the fishermen saw the cloud, but submarines were always fooling around in the area so they paid it no mind. They simply watched the cloud rise into the sky and dissipate in the wind as they motored up the sound toward Cape Cod Bay.

Inside the control room Jack walked to the intercom microphone and said, "This is the captain speaking. Will Torpedoman Burns respond?"

He listened for a few moments, then heard Burns's agitated voice. "Torpedoman Burns speaking, sir."

"How's everything in your compartment, Burns?"

"We've had an accident, sir. A torpedo broke loose while we were rolling and pitching, and it landed on Seaman Olds. It killed him, sir."

"What about the torpedo?"

"We've managed to lash it down, sir."

Jack thought for a few moments. "There are two things I want you to do, Burns. The first is to release the marker buoy. The second is to remove Seaman Olds to the officers' wardroom and lay him on my bunk. There's chlorine gas in the wardroom, so you'll have to wear your Momsen lungs. Any questions?"

"Somebody'll have to open the hatch for us, sir."

"Machinist's Mate Donahue is on the way. Anything else?"

"No, sir."

"Carry on."

"Yes, sir."

Jack turned around and looked at Donahue. "Put on the Momsen lung and go forward to open the torpedo compartment hatch for Torpedoman Burns."

"Yes, sir."

Donahue took down a Momsen lung and put it on, placing the rubber mouthpiece between his teeth. Keller opened the hatch for him, and Donahue made his way into the smoky atmosphere of the officers' wardroom. Then Keller dogged shut the hatch.

In the forward torpedo room, Hank Burns flipped the latch that released the marker buoy. The device was attached to the deck of the submarine, and once released, would rise to the surface. It was painted bright yellow and had a telephone inside that was connected via cable to a telephone in the submarine control room. On the top of the buoy was stenciled SUBMARINE SUNK HERE. TELEPHONE INSIDE.

Marker buoys had been standard equipment on all U.S. submarines for the past two years. This was the first time one was used by a submarine in distress.

Donahue, a black-haired Irishman, opened the hatch to the forward torpedo room. Burns was standing there, a solemn look on his face. Burns motioned with his hand, and a crew of his torpedomen wearing Momsen lungs lifted the body of Seaman Olds, which they'd ensconced in the rubberized mattress cover they'd taken from his bunk. They carried the body into the officers' wardroom and laid it carefully on Lieutenant McCrary's bunk. Then they returned to the forward torpedo room, and Donahue stood by the hatch, ready to close it.

"Tell the captain that we've released the marker buoy," Burns said.

Donahue nodded, then closed the hatch. As he was about to dog it shut, he had an idea. Opening the hatch again, he called out to Burns, who was on his way to his bunk. Burns turned around.

"I was thinkin'," Donahue said, "that maybe I don't have to dog the hatch shut, because the reason the captain wants it closed is so that you won't get any chlorine gas in here."

Burns nodded. "Okay, shut it but don't dog it, and tell the captain what you done."

"Right."

Donahue closed the hatch and moved back toward the control room. As he approached the control room hatch, he saw two eyes looking out at him. The hatch was opened by Keller, and Donahue entered the control room. He saw Lieutenant Jack McCrary standing beside Lieutenant Stearns, both of them studying the chart.

"Sir," said Donahue, "the marker buoy is released, and Seaman Olds has been moved to your bunk."

Jack nodded. "Good."

"Torpedoman Burns and I decided that I needn't dog the forward hatch, because it's closed only to keep gas out of the forward torpedo compartment."

"That's acceptable," Jack replied. "All you men in the control room put on Momsen lungs and go forward to the officers' wardroom. Get all the blankets and food and bring them back here. Chief Boatswain's Mate Keller will be in charge."

The men reached for Momsen lungs and prepared to carry out this order. Jack turned to Stearns. "I think it's time you put together a roster of the men and officers who are still fit for duty."

"Yes, sir."

Stearns got on the intercom and called the forward torpedo room to find out who was fit for duty there, and Jack stepped toward Lieutenant Nielson, whose head had been bandaged by Pharmacist's Mate La Gloria, and who was standing beside the conning tower ladder again, calmly appraising the events going on around him.

"How do you feel?" Jack asked.

"I'm all right," Nielsen replied, although he was paler than usual. "What do you think has gone wrong with this submarine?"

Jack scratched his nose. "I don't know for sure, but offhand I'd say it was the main induction valves, because the flooding happened so quickly. It's either that or a rupture in the hull, which I think would be extremely unlikely."

"Didn't this boat have a problem with the main induction valve before?"

"Yes, but we thought it was repaired."

Nielsen tried to smile. "Well, quite often there are problems with new submarines."

"Yes," Jack replied. "Well, make yourself as comfortable as you can. I'm sure help will be on the way shortly."

"I hope so," Nielsen said.

Jack moved back to the chart table, where Stearns was working on his roster. Jack looked at the Christmas tree; all the lights were still green. He shook his head and ground his teeth together, feeling useless and impotent. He also felt angry, because if the main induction system had indeed failed, he knew whose fault it was. The main induction system and many other pieces of equipment on the boat had been designed by Benjamin Mount, the boy wonder of the U.S. Navy.

Jack and Ben had been in the same graduating class at Annapolis, and Jack hadn't liked Ben very much.

He'd considered him pushy and obnoxious, a typical Jew. Mount had acted as though he was too good for the rest of them because his marks were always highest. It galled Jack to think that such a person probably would become an admiral someday, able to lord it over officers who were better men than he. He already was a lieutenant commander, one rank ahead of Jack.

Jack hadn't liked Ben Mount before and now blamed him for the catastrophe that had befallen the *Sebago.* Ben Mount had designed the faulty main induction system. He wasn't as smart as he thought he was, the Jew bastard. And Ben Mount had killed Ed McCrary just as sure as if he'd pointed a gun at him and pulled the trigger. Jack felt a surge of emotion in his breast as he thought of Ed drowning in the forward engine room. It was guilt mixed with rage, and he swore that if he ever got out of the *Sebago* alive he wouldn't rest until he brought Ben Mount to a court-martial and had him thrown out of the Navy.

"I've got the roster together, sir," said Lieutenant Stearns.

Jack joined Stearns at the chart table and looked down at the roster he'd devised. Out of the six officers who'd sailed from New London that morning, three were still alive. Lieutenant Jordan, the engineering officer, had been somewhere aft when the engine rooms were flooded, and Ensign Delbert had died in the forward battery compartment.

Of the enlisted men, Jack counted twenty-three still alive out of the fifty who had sailed from New London. At the bottom of the roster Stearns listed the names of the men and officers presumed dead. Jack looked at the names, and the familiar faces floated before his eyes. When he came to the name of his brother he cleared his throat and looked away.

Enlisted men were carrying blankets and crates of food into the control room, and Jack looked at them, thinking about the men in the after compartments of the submarine and wondering if any might still be alive. It hadn't occurred to him before, but there could be an air pocket somewhere back there, and some of the men, perhaps even his brother, might be huddled in it, shivering in the cold water and waiting to be rescued.

He reached for the intercom microphone and held it near his mouth. "Hello, after engine room—can you hear me?" he said. "This is Lieutenant McCrary speaking—is anybody there?"

He waited a few seconds, but there was no answer. The men who'd been carrying supplies into the control room stopped to look at him, and he felt foolish. If any of the men in the after compartments could have communicated with the control room, they certainly would have done so by now.

"Get moving!" Jack said to the men who were looking at him. "Let's go!"

"You heard the captain," Keller growled. "Get your fucking asses in gear."

Jack looked at Stearns. "How long have we been down?"

Stearns looked at his stopwatch. "Seventy-two minutes."

"It won't be long now," Jack said. "We'll just take it easy and wait for them."

"Yes, sir."

Jack felt exhausted. He'd like to curl up someplace, go to sleep, and forget everything that had happened. It was getting cold inside the submarine; he zipped his leather jacket all the way up to his neck and put his hands in his pockets. He thought that the most serious problem facing him and the others trapped on the *Sebago* was the diminishing quantity of fresh air. After the men had loaded in all the supplies from the officers' wardroom, he'd order them to get down on the floor and exert as little effort as possible, so they'd use less oxygen. When things got bad he'd spread the carbon dioxide absorbent around the control room and the forward torpedo compartment. He'd bleed the emergency oxygen tanks to keep them alive. It probably wouldn't be necessary, though. Help would be on the way pretty soon. At New London, they probably were sending out a search party right now.

"All right," Jack said to the men after all the supplies were in the control room. "Let's cover up with blankets and get down on the floor. Try to diminish your breathing as much as you can. Rescue ships are probably on their way to us right now. Take it easy and everything will be all right."

In the dim light of the control room the men spread blankets on the floor and lay down. Jack sat with Lieutenant Nielsen and Lieutenant Stearns between the chart table and the conning tower ladder.

"This would all be bearable if I could smoke a cigarette," Nielsen said good-naturedly in his Swedish accent.

"You'll have one soon enough," Jack replied.

Across the room, Radioman Mason said to Yeoman Reilly, "Didn't the *S-51* sink somewhere around here about ten years ago?" He was referring to a submarine that had been rammed by a passenger ship while it had been running on the surface at night.

Jack shot to his feet and looked at Mason. "There'll be no more of that!" he shouted.

Mason looked sheepish. "Yes, sir."

"We haven't been rammed by any passenger ship and we're going to be rescued soon—is that clear?"

They all nodded and mumbled "Yes, sir."

Jack sat down on the floor, a muscle twitching in his jaw.

"Maybe you should lie down for a while, sir," Stearns said. "I'll wake you up if anything happens."

"If you're tired, then you lie down for a while, Bob. I'm not tired yet."

"Neither am I, sir."

Jack looked at Nielsen and forced a smile. "Well, I guess you'll have an interesting little adventure to talk about when you return to the Swedish Navy, Peter."

"I hope so," Nielsen replied drily.

"Keller!" Jack called.

"I'm here, sir," said a voice from the other side of the chart table.

"Where?"

"At the ballast station, sir."

Jack looked around the chart table and saw Keller lying sideways on the floor, using his hands for a pillow. "I think it's time to send up another flare, Keller."

"Yes, sir."

Keller got up and slammed another rocket into the ejector. He pulled the chain and the rocket went off, hissing through the water. It exploded through the surface and climbed high into the sky, bursting and becoming a red cloud.

But no one was there to see it.

FOURTEEN

At the New London submarine base, Rear Admiral Paul Mackie stood at the window of his office, sipping a cup of coffee and watching the *Porgie* back out of its pen into the Thames River. His office was on a high floor of the administration building, affording him a clear view of the pens and the Thames estuary in the distance. His son-in-law, Lieutenant Commander Ernest Ellington, was the commanding officer on the *Porgie*, which had recently completed its sea trials with flying colors and was now leaving for a thirty-day shakedown cruise to Panama. Admiral Mackie smiled as he sipped his coffee. He was glad that Ellington was going away for awhile, because Ellington and Admiral Mackie's daughter had been squabbling lately and Ellington's absence might calm things down between them.

There was a knock on the door.

"Come in," Admiral Mackie said, turning around.

Yeoman First Class Howard Richardson entered the office, a sheaf of papers in his hands. "The morning reports and messages, sir," Richardson said, dropping them into the admiral's IN basket.

"Thank you, Richardson."

"You're welcome, sir."

Richardson turned and left the office, closing the door behind him. Admiral Mackie sat in his chair and took the papers out of the IN basket, laying them in the middle of the desk and glancing through them.

Admiral Mackie had white hair, a white mustache, and pinkish skin. A graduate of Annapolis, class of '13, he had served aboard the *Skipjack* in the waters southwest of Ireland during the Great War. The *Skipjack* didn't sink any enemy ships, and neither did any of the other twelve American submarines assigned to duty in the Atlantic during the war, but the officers on duty learned of the superiority of British and German submarines and returned to the States with proposals for building a new, more effective fleet of American submarines. Mackie had been one of the leaders in this rebuilding effort and had stepped on many toes in Washington as a result. That's why he was only a rear admiral, unlike many of his classmates who wore more than one star on their shoulder boards.

Mackie sipped his coffee and looked through the morning reports and radio dispatches. He paused when he came to the radio message from the *Sebago* stating that it was submerging at 1106 hours. Mackie looked at his watch; it was 1228 hours. He continued to make his way leisurely through the reports and dispatches. When he came to the last one he realized there was no message from the *Sebago* stating that it had surfaced after it's one-hour test dive.

Admiral Mackie wondered whether to call his communications officer to check. This wasn't the first time a submarine was tardy in reporting its surface after a test submergence, and ordinarily it was nothing to be concerned about. But Lieutenant Commander Dunlop was an unusually scrupulous and thorough officer; one would not expect him to be lax about something like this.

Admiral Mackie decided to check. He picked up the

telephone and asked his clerk to buzz the communications officer, Lieutenant Randall Simpson.

"Simpson," Admiral Mackie said, "have we heard from the *Sebago* yet?"

"You didn't get the message indicating that she had dived, sir?"

"I'm referring to the message that indicated she surfaced after the dive."

"Oh, no, sir. That message hasn't come in yet."

"She was supposed to surface at one two oh six. Try to contact her, will you?"

"Yes, sir."

In the communications section, Lieutenant Simpson arose from behind his desk and walked to the radio room, wishing he'd thought of trying to contact the *Sebago* himself after it didn't call in at 1206. That would have impressed the admiral with his efficiency. Screwed up again.

He entered the radio room. Radioman Ralph Kerry was still on duty, sipping black coffee in an effort to wake up.

"Has anything come in from the *Sebago*?" Simpson asked, looking through the messages in Kerry's OUT basket.

"Not since they dived, sir."

"See if you can contact them."

"Yes, sir."

Lieutenant Simpson leaned against the bench where the radio was and placed his hands in his pockets as Kerry tapped out the message on his key: NEW LONDON CALLING SEBAGO—NEW LONDON CALLING SEBAGO—OVER. Kerry listened to the airwaves for several seconds, heard nothing, and tapped out the message again. He listened for a full half-minute this time, then looked up at Lieutenant Simpson.

"They don't answer, sir," Kerry said.

"Try them again."

"I already tried twice."

"Try one more time."

"Yes, sir."

Kerry tapped out the message, wishing Lieutenant Simpson would go back to his office and leave him alone. He listened to the crackling of the atmosphere; once more there was no reply from the *Sebago*.

"They're not answering, sir," Kerry said.

Lieutenant Simpson looked at his watch. "Try again every ten minutes."

Kerry sniffed. "They all stay down a little extra, sir. I'm sure they'll call in any minute now."

"I said try again every ten minutes."

"Yes, sir."

Lieutenant Simpson walked away, and Kerry cursed him under his breath. He felt lousy and didn't feel like remembering to call the *Sebago* every ten minutes. Those officers were all such a pain in the ass, always making extra work. Sometimes Kerry wished he'd never joined the Navy in the first place, although he'd been out of work, had no prospects, had no money, and it had been in the depths of the Depression.

In the outside corridor, Lieutenant Simpson stepped into his office and asked the clerk to connect him with Admiral Mackie's office.

"Sir," Lieutenant Simpson reported, "the *Sebago* hasn't called in since her first message. We tried to raise her twice but couldn't."

"Keep trying, Simpson."

"Yes, sir."

Admiral Mackie hung up the phone and felt annoyed. The submarine commanders were becoming too lax about radioing in their positions. If Dunlop was doing it too, it must mean that the situation really was getting out of hand. Admiral Mackie began drafting a directive reminding all submarine commanders to radio in their positions at the appropriate times and warning that anyone who forgot would be relieved of command.

That ought to straighten the situation out, he told himself as he sipped his coffee. Then he wrote 1106 on his memo pad. He decided that if he didn't hear from the *Sebago* by 1306 hours he'd send a ship to look for her.

I'm sure there's nothing wrong, Admiral Mackie said to reassure himself. Dunlop's probably staying down a little longer just to make sure everything's working okay on his boat.

FIFTEEN

Lieutenant Peter Nielsen sat cross-legged next to the conning tower ladder, a blanket draped over his head and shoulders, his eyes half closed, his face immobile. He held the blanket closed in front of him, to retain his body heat, for the temperature was dropping rapidly on the submarine. He figured that the water temperature outside was around thirty-five degrees and was transmitting its clammy coldness to the steel of the boat. If they weren't rescued soon, it would become extremely uncomfortable in the control room.

He knew that the U.S. Navy was reasonably efficient and that an effort would probably be made soon to get them out. But if that effort failed, he thought of how odd it would be that he, an officer in the Swedish Navy, with a Swedish father and German mother, would die in an American submarine off the coast of New England.

The Americans didn't know he was half German, of course. There had been no point in telling them that— or of his sympathies for the National Socialist government in Berlin. American public opinion had been riled up against Germany by the Jewish newspaper czars, and the U.S. Navy wouldn't have let him aboard their submarines if they had known the truth about him. But they didn't know. They'd let him aboard their latest, most advanced submarine, the *Sebago*, which he believed to be inferior to the latest U-boats, but it was possible that he'd never be able to relay the information to his friends in the Reich, because the *Sebago* might become his tomb.

Nielsen had always thought that he might meet death someday in a submarine. Many submarines had been sunk in war, and many also sank in peacetime during tests just like the one the *Sebago* was on. He'd known all the risks and was fatalistic enough to believe that something could happen to him, but he was fascinated by submarines and couldn't stay away from them. He thought submarines were the most interesting devices man had ever created, that they were far more remarkable technically than airplanes; he truly loved them, wanted to contribute to their perfection, and hoped to command one himself someday.

But now he thought it very likely that he would die in one. It was strange, the twists and turns a human life could take.

"Hey!" shouted Araujo, sitting a few feet away.

Nielsen looked in disbelief as a stream of oil squirted from the bulkhead and hit Araujo in the face. Araujo leaped to his feet, wiping away the oil with the back of his hand and worrying that he'd go blind, as Jack McCrary, Lieutenant Stearns, and Chief Boatswain's Mate Keller charged across the control room to the point from which the oil was shooting. As they fumbled to find the hole, the oil turned to salt water.

"The outside water pressure is backing up everything in these pipes!" Jack said as he located the source of the leak in the maze of pipes above the hydroplane wheels.

Keller followed the pipe with his eyes and saw a

main valve on the ceiling. He turned it shut, but it already was closed down. "There's something wrong with the valve!" he said.

The break in the pipe widened, and water poured into the control room, soaking Jack and Stearns.

"Check all secondary valves!" Jack shouted.

Before he could get the words out of his mouth, everyone in the control room was up and jumping around, frantically turning down the secondary valves. Slowly the flow of water diminished, then it stopped altogether.

"We got it, sir," Keller said.

Jack looked at the oil and water streaking its way aft over the control room floor, making a huge oleaginous puddle underneath the aft hatch. He wanted to order the men to get rags and sop it up, but he had to keep physical activity to a minimum—and they needed all the cloth they had for warmth.

"Forward torpedo room calling the captain!" said Torpedoman Burns over the intercom.

Jack walked to the intercom. "This is the captain speaking."

"Sir, we've got a leak in here!"

Jack's shoulders tensed. "How bad?"

"Not too bad, I don't think."

"Where is it?"

"I don't know. Somewhere down in the bilge."

"I'll be right there."

"Yes, sir."

Jack blew air out of the corner of his mouth. He decided to take Keller with him again, because Keller was the most knowledgeable man he had on the boat. "Keller, put on a Momsen lung and come with me."

"Yes, sir."

Jack looked at Stearns. "I'm going forward to check on the leak. Take command of the control room, and you might as well send up another smoke rocket."

"Yes, sir."

Jack walked closer to him and mumbled, "You're doing a fine job, Stearns. Keep it up."

"Thank you, sir."

Jack put on a Momsen lung, tied it around his waist, and sucked the tube, drawing oxygen into his lungs. He led Keller back to the forward hatch, and Donahue opened it up for them. They entered the officer's wardroom, now thick with chlorine gas, and stepped over the opening in the floor where Ensign Delbert's body lay on the batteries. When they reached the hatch to the forward torpedo room it was opened by one of the men there and they climbed inside.

Burns had winched some torpedoes aside and was unscrewing floor plates with the assistance of his crew. Jack and Keller walked to where they were and looked down into the bilge.

Sure enough, there was oil and water down there. The main ballast tank must have ruptured when it hit bottom. It was possible that the bow buoyancy tank was also damaged, and taking water.

"I thought I'd go down and have a look," Burns said.

"I don't think you're gonna find it," Keller said.

"It won't hurt to take a look."

Jack got on his knees and peered into the bilge. One of the sailors gave him a flashlight and he searched back and forth. There was only an inch or two of water and oil down there, not a serious leak.

"It's only a small leak," Jack said to Burns, getting up. "I don't think you'll be able to find it. I recommend that you just keep an eye on it."

"I'd like to go down and see just in case, sir."

"Go ahead if you want to, but if you don't find anything, don't worry about it. The leak won't be a problem for quite a while, and we'll probably be rescued by then."

"Okay, sir."

Jack looked at Keller. "Let's go."

They put the tubes of their Momsen lungs into

their mouths and walked back to the hatch. A sailor opened it for them and they entered the eerie yellow fog of the officer's wardroom.

I wonder what'll go wrong next, Jack wondered as he walked to the control room.

SIXTEEN

Admiral Mackie sat at his desk, studying a report about engine breakdowns on submarines. The report indicated that the Winton engines manufactured by General Motors were far more reliable than the H.O.R. engines made at the Navy Yard in Portsmouth, New Hampshire. He wondered how this could be, since both engines were essentially the same design. What the hell were they doing wrong up there in Portsmouth?

Something prompted him to look at his watch. It was 1315 hours. He was supposed to do something important that morning, but he'd become so engrossed in the report on engine breakdowns that he'd forgotten. A glance at his memo pad reminded him. The *Sebago!* He wondered if it had been heard from yet.

He picked up his phone and called Lieutenant Simpson, but he wasn't at his desk. Admiral Mackie told the telephone operator to connect him directly with the radio room.

"Lieutenant Simpson speaking, sir."

"Oh, so you're in the radio room, Simpson. I wondered where you were, because you weren't at your desk. Tell me—have we heard from the *Sebago* yet?"

"No, sir."

"You haven'tl"

"No, sir."

Admiral Mackie thought for a few moments. "Stay in the radio room, Lieutenant. I'll have further instructions for you in a few moments."

"Yes, sir."

Admiral Mackie broke the connection with his finger, then told his clerk to locate the operations officer and put him on the phone. Seconds later, Captain Allen Robertson came on the phone.

"I want you to report to my office immediately with the disposition of every ship and boat in the installation."

"Yes, sir."

Admiral Mackie drummed his fingers on his desk, then stood up and walked to the window. He looked out toward the Thames estuary; the *Sebago* was out there someplace, probably in trouble. The wind was blowing up a nasty chop in the river; if the *Sebago* was in trouble it wouldn't be easy to help her in weather like this.

There was a knock on the door.

"Come in."

Captain Robertson, a burly man with a black mustache, entered the office carrying a leatherbound looseleaf notebook. "I have the information you asked for, sir."

Admiral Mackie took the notebook and opened it on his desk. "I think we've got a problem, Captain. The *Sebago* went on her first test dive over two hours ago and hasn't been heard from since."

Captain Robertson furrowed his brow. "Have you tried to contact her, sir?"

"Every ten minutes, and we've received no answer whatever."

"Oh-oh," said Robertson.

"I think we'd better send somebody out to look for her. Who do you suggest?" Admiral Mackie looked down the listing of ships. "Where's the *Falcon*?" He was referring to the rescue ship normally docked at New London.

"In the Boston Navy Yard, sir. It's being fitted with new rescue equipment."

"Just when we need it, it isn't here," Mackie said. "I guess we'll have to send out a submarine."

"It'd take a while to get one underway, sir."

"How long?"

"A couple of hours at least."

Admiral Mackie frowned. "That's too long."

"We could reroute the *Porgie,* sir. She only cleared port about an hour ago."

Admiral Mackie thought for a few seconds. "Good idea." He picked up his phone and asked the clerk to connect him with the radio room.

"Lieutenant Simpson speaking, sir."

"This is Admiral Mackie. Contact the *Porgie* and tell her to change course and commence a search at the coordinates where the *Sebago* made her test dive."

"Yes, sir."

"Call me back to confirm that you've transmitted the message."

"Yes, sir."

Admiral Mackie hung up the phone and looked at Captain Robertson. "You may return to your office, Captain, but don't go where you can't be reached if I need you. Don't say anything about this, because it may not be anything serious. The *Sebago* might only be having radio problems. She might show up here in the river at any moment now."

"Yes, sir."

"If she does, let me know."

"Yes, sir."

"That is all."

Captain Robertson turned and left the office. Admiral Mackie walked to the window and looked out into the Thames. Clasping his hands behind his back, he strained to see if a submarine was entering the estuary, but except for a few fishing boats there was nothing there.

SEVENTEEN

Lieutenant Commander Ernest Ellington stood on the bridge of the *Porgie* and watched the eastern end of Long Island pass his starboard bow. On the bridge with him was his executive officer, Lieutenant McNally, and his navigation officer, Lieutenant Middleton.

Lieutenant Commander Ellington wore an oilskin raincoat and a wide-brimmed fisherman's cap, because the wind and waves were sending a cold saltwater spray up to the bridge. He had to keep cleaning the lenses of his binoculars with a rag so that he could see around him.

"I wonder how far we'll have to go to get out of this weather," said McNally, dissatisfaction and discomfort in his voice.

"It's liable to follow us all the way to Panama," Ellington replied.

Ellington was thirty years old, had brown hair, and had been a star quarterback on the football team at Annapolis. He had been looking forward to this shake-down cruise for a long time, because the arguments he was having with his wife were disturbing him considerably. She was a typical Navy brat, spoiled and obnoxious, and he'd married her because she was the daughter of an admiral. She also had been quite beautiful. He hadn't realized that she would make him so unhappy. He didn't dare divorce her, because her father was an admiral. He wouldn't be unfaithful to her because that would be dishonorable. All he could do was hope for long patrols away from home. He'd heard that the *Porgie* might be assigned to the South Pacific Fleet after its shakedown cruise, and Ellington hoped it was so. Patti probably wouldn't want to accompany him, because she wouldn't leave her mother for anything.

Ensign Hoskins climbed the ladder to the bridge. "Sir, a radio message has just come in from New London!"

"Stay down in the conning tower and read it to me."

Ensign Hoskins descended back to the conning tower. "It says: 'Proceed at once to forty degrees, forty-one north, by seventy-one, thirty west, and commence search operations for the *Sebago*, which dived at one one oh six hours and hasn't been heard from since.'"

Ellington didn't think he'd heard right. "I'll be right there." He turned to Lieutenant McNally. "Watch the bridge, will you, Johnny?"

"Did he say the *Sebago* is missing?"

"That's what I'm going to check."

Ellington climbed down the ladder and joined Hoskins in the conning tower. Dripping salt water onto the floor, he took the message from Hoskins and read it. "My God," he said. "It's really missing."

"Sounds like it, sir."

"Tell the navigation officer to turn this boat around and set a course for the coordinates indicated in this message."

"Yes, sir."

Hoskins descended the ladder to the control room, while Ellington returned to the bridge.

"Looks like the *Sebago* is missing," Ellington said gravely to McNally.

McNally stared at him. "It is!"

"Yes, and we've got to go looking for her."

At the helm, feisty old Chief Boatswain's Mate Abner Nowicki spun the wheel, and the bow of the *Porgie* turned to starboard. Ellington held onto the bridge rail as sheets of spray blew over the *Porgie's* deck. He knew Dunlop and Jack McCrary and the other three officers on the *Sebago,* and Chief Boatswain's Mate Keller had served under him when he was executive officer of the old *Bonita.*

Ellington's first evaluation was like Admiral Mackie's—that the radio gear on the *Sebago* had been damaged somehow. He hoped this was so as the *Porgie* turned around and barreled toward the coordinates given in the message, coordinates that were ten miles from the true dive position.

EIGHTEEN

Wrapped in a blanket, Lieutenant Robert Stearns sat on the floor of the *Sebago*'s control room, his head leaning against a leg of the chart table. The air was heavy and stank of oil and urine, because everyone was using the same bucket to relieve themselves in and dumping it into the bilge.

Stearns was a quiet, efficient officer, twenty-five years old and unmarried. At Annapolis he'd been known as a dreary drudge who studied all the time and never participated in parties or athletics. It was felt that his oddball personality would be unsuitable for submarines, but he was given the chance anyway. His commanding officers soon discovered that he was a perfectionist who followed orders to the letter. Crews respected him because he was fair and always knew what he was doing. He became an outstanding officer, and all who knew him thought he'd go far in the Navy.

But now, as he sat with his eyes closed, he thought that his naval career was coming to an end. While the *Sebago* had been sinking, he'd thought there was a chance that they'd pull out of it. But now, after being on the bottom for almost two hours, he believed that he and the others were doomed.

They couldn't use Momsen lungs and try to escape the submarine because they were down too far. No one ever had made an ascent with a Momsen lung from this depth. All American submarines were fitted with special hatches over the forward and after torpedo rooms. These hatches had fittings on them that were supposed to attach to a special rescue chamber, sort of a diving bell, which the Navy was in the process of developing, but as far as Stearns knew, the rescue chamber was not yet operational.

He had resigned himself to dying and thought it strange that he felt no panic or fear. At one point there'd be no more air and he'd just keel over. Or the *Sebago* would spring a leak that they couldn't fix and they'd drown. He and the others had done all they could do, and they didn't have much to hope for.

People often told Stearns that he reminded them of the actor John Wayne, because he had the same kind of ruggedly masculine face and talked with a slow western drawl. Stearns was from Texas, and his family was in the oil business. When he'd been a boy in Galveston, he'd seen the big ships come into port and had fallen in love with them. How strange that those ships would lead to this submarine.

"Stearns," said the low voice of Jack McCrary.

Stearns opened his eyes. "Yes, sir?"

McCrary was on his knees beside him, still wearing his brown leather jacket, his hat on the back of his head. "I've just had an idea, and I thought I'd check it out with you. The leak in the forward torpedo room made me realize that some of the secondary ballast tanks in the belly of this boat are still filled with water. Maybe the after trim tank is still filled with water too. Maybe if we blew them all, the displacement of water by air would bring us to the surface."

"I thought we blew all the tanks already," Stearns said.

"I thought so too, but evidently we didn't, because

there's water leaking into the forward torpedo room from the forward ballast tank."

"I suspect that the tank is leaking from the outside, sir. That's why it's filled with water."

Jack nodded. "Maybe, but I think it's worth a chance anyway. Let's go—if we pull all the levers together it might do something."

Stearns got up and followed McCrary across the control room to the ballast station.

"You pull those two," Jack said, "and I'll pull these two here."

Stearns placed his hands on the levers. "I just thought of something, sir. We're liable to blow ourselves onto our side, or maybe open another crack in the hull."

"Just from blowing the secondary tanks? I don't think so. Anyway, we can't be in much worse shape than we are now."

"Oh, I'm not so sure of that, sir."

"We've got to do something, Stearns," Jack said testily. "We can't just sit here."

Stearns thought he should keep his mouth shut and follow orders, but yet he didn't agree with McCrary at all. In his opinion, McCrary was much too impulsive, sometimes doing things just for the sake of doing them.

"I'm sorry, but I disagree, sir," Stearns said softly so that the others wouldn't hear him. "I think it might be better just to sit here."

McCrary moved his face closer to Stearns's and hissed, "If we just sit here we're liable to just die here! I think it's much better to try and do something!"

"But sir, we're liable to do something that will make our predicament worse and ruin any hope we have of being rescued."

"I think you're wrong, Stearns," McCrary whispered harshly. "I think you're being much too cautious as usual. I'm going to start counting, and when I say *three,* pull those goddamned levers."

"Yes, sir."

"Get ready now," McCrary said, gripping the blue steel levers.

"I'm ready, sir," Stearns replied, grabbing one with each of his fists.

"One—two—*three!*"

Stearns and McCrary pulled the levers at the same time. They expected to hear the *whoosh* of compressed air moving through tubes, but they heard nothing.

"I think the boat just moved!" McCrary said excitedly.

"I didn't feel anything, sir."

McCrary raced across the control room to the depth and trim indicators, and his heart sank when he saw that they'd registered no change. "Aw, shit," he said, his shoulders drooping.

Stearns joined him. "It was a good try, sir."

"You were right, Stearns. It didn't work."

"I wish that this time I had been wrong, sir."

"We might as well send up another smoke rocket," McCrary said disgustedly.

"Would you like me to take care of it, sir?"

"If you would."

"Yes, sir."

Jack sat heavily on the floor and looked at his watch. They'd been down for two and a half hours and they'd only heard the screws of little fishing boats passing overhead. What the hell was the matter with those people in New London. Didn't they know the *Sebago* was down yet?

At the rocket launcher Lieutenant Stearns pulled the chain. The rocket sped up from its tube, cut through the surface of the water, and exploded in the sky.

Not far away, the trawler *Mary B. Hathaway* was chugging north through Block Island Sound.

"Wow—looka there!" said Peter Medeiros, a new employee on the trawler. He'd recently moved to New London from Provincetown, Massachusetts. "What the fuck's that?"

"Must be one of them submarines screwin' around," replied Captain Hathaway, his gnarled hands gripping the wheel.

Medeiros looked at the expanding red cloud. "That's real pretty, ain't it?"

"You'll get used to stuff like that around here. Like I said, them submarines are always screwin' around."

"I wonder what it's supposed to mean?"

"Who the hell knows?" Hathaway grumbled, struggling to steer back to port. The sea was getting rough, and there was no point in staying out on it.

"I wonder what it's like to be on a submarine," Medeiros mused, still looking at the cloud.

"There's only one way to find out—join up," Hathaway said.

"Naw—to hell with that!"

Hathaway grunted as he steered his trawler over the surging waves.

NINETEEN

The *Porgie* thundered north through heavy seas. Lieutenant Commander Ellington stood in his slicker on the bridge, scanning the murky horizon through his binoculars. Waves washed over the deck and foam flew through the air as the submarine bucked up and down and crashed against the waves.

"What speed are we making?" Ellington shouted down the conning tower.

"Seventeen knots, sir!" replied Lieutenant Middleton.

"All ahead full!" yelled Ellington.

"All ahead full!" repeated Boatswain's Mate Nowicki.

In the propulsion control room the levers were pulled back all the way. The twin propellors bit into the water with extra force, and the *Porgie* leaped forward. Up on the bridge, Ellington felt exhilarated by the burst of speed. This was supposed to be the *Porgie*'s shakedown voyage, and he fully intended to shake her down.

"Any word from New London yet?" Ellington yelled down the conning tower hatch.

"No, sir!" replied Middleton.

"See if you can raise the *Sebago!*"

"Yes, sir!"

Middleton spoke to the radioman over the inter-com and told him to try and contact the *Sebago*. The radioman wrote the message on a pad and then tapped it out on his key. There was no answer. He tried again. Still no answer.

"I don't get a response, sir," he said to Middleton over the intercom.

Middleton called up to Ellington. "The *Sebago* doesn't answer, sir!"

"Keep trying!" Ellington yelled back.

"Yes, sir!"

"How far are we from the *Sebago*'s point of sub-mergence?"

"I'll check!"

Ellington swept the horizon with his binoculars but couldn't see much because the lenses were covered with salt spray. He wiped them with a rag and looked again, seeing angry clouds and boiling seas. *This is a hell of a day to get in trouble out here,* he thought.

"We're about eight and a half miles away on the surface, sir!" Middleton called up from the control room.

Ellington narrowed his eyes to slits and looked ahead. They'd arrive in Block Island Sound soon if the *Porgie* didn't develop mechanical problems in the heavy seas. If the *Porgie* were down, he tried to imag-ine what he'd do. He'd try to get her afloat again, and if he couldn't he'd release the marker buoy and shoot up smoke rockets at regular intervals. He nudged McNally.

"Watch for smoke rockets and a marker buoy!" he yelled over the roar of crashing waves.

"Yes, sir!"

Ellington wiped off his binoculars again and scanned the raging waters ahead. He wished he'd see a submarine zipping along out there, headed back to New London, but there was only the angry, relentless sea.

"Can we get any more speed out of this boat?" he hollered down the conning tower hatch.

"We're going full speed ahead, sir!" replied Boatswain's Mate Nowicki.

In the radio room, the radioman heard the *Porgie*'s call letters in his earphones. He tapped his key and replied that he had received the call. A brief message ensued, coming from New London. They wanted to know the *Porgie*'s position, rate of speed, and when it expected to be over the *Sebago*'s dive position.

The radioman gave the information to Lieutenant Middleton, who relayed it to Ellington on the bridge. Ellington told Middleton to produce the information and send it back to New London. Middleton went to work on his chart table, tabulated the information, and gave it to the radioman to transmit to New London.

New London confirmed that it had received the transmission and directed the *Porgie* to proceed with its mission.

TWENTY

"Torpedoman Burns calling the captain," said the voice on the loudspeaker.

Jack got up and walked to the intercom. "This is the captain speaking."

"I thought I'd report that we've been unable to find that leak, sir."

"I didn't think you would, Burns. It's an awfully small leak."

"We've been crawling around in the bilge ever since you were here, sir. I suspect there's more than one leak down there."

"How much water have you got in the bilge?" Jack asked.

"About six inches."

"That's not much."

"Not yet, anyway."

"When it comes close to the floor plates, you'd better move your men up here."

"Yes, sir, but I don't imagine that'll be for another few hours and I figure we'll be out of here by then."

"I'm sure you're right," Jack said, pleased by the optimism of the torpedoman. "We're taking a break for lunch here. I suggest you do the same up there."

"Yes, sir."

Jack took a few steps and sat down between Lieutenant Stearns and Lieutenant Nielsen. He'd removed cans of food from the control room emergency locker and passed them to the men, now the can opener was making its way around. Jack figured some food would give them some energy and maybe raise their morale. He had selected a can of spaghetti and meatballs and a can of pineapple chunks for himself. Lieutenant Nielsen accepted the can opener from Keller and opened a can of beans and a can of fruit salad. Then he handed the can opener to Jack.

Nielsen spooned some beans into his mouth and made a face.

"What's wrong?" Stearns asked.

The Swede began chewing. "It's not very good cold."

"Well, this isn't the Astor Hotel."

"Surely not."

"When we get out of here," Jack said, "I'll take you both to dinner at the officers' club. No, on second thought, I'll take the entire crew to the best restaurant in New London."

Nielsen raised his eyebrows. "I wasn't aware that New London had a best restaurant."

Stearns smiled. "Every town has to have a best restaurant."

"I doubt if New London has," Nielsen joked.

"But it must," Stearns replied. "Even if New London only had one restaurant, it would have to be the best restaurant in town."

"I think that what I'm trying to say is that New London doesn't have a good restaurant."

"That's another matter entirely."

Jack raised a forkful of spaghetti to his mouth and thought how strange it was that two grown intelligent men like Nielsen and Stearns coud have such an utterly ridiculous discussion in view of the desperate circumstances they were in. Probably they were trying to distract themselves. They wanted to pretend that everything was normal so they could relax and enjoy their cold canned food. Jack put a meatball into his mouth and began chewing. He didn't know how Nielsen and Stearns could be so lighthearted when twenty-six men and one officer were floating around drowned to death in the after compartments. It seemed sacrilegious somehow. Jack flashed on his brother Ed, the salt water and oil making the flesh on Ed's corpse pucker like a meatball. Suddenly Jack felt nauseated. He pulled the handkerchief out of his back pocket and spat the half-chewed meatball into it.

"Are you all right, sir?" Stearns asked, noticing his distress.

Jack nodded as he reached for his cup of water. He rinsed out his mouth and drank some water. There was a sickening ache in his stomach. He was aware that Nielsen and Stearns were looking at him.

"I guess I'm not very hungry," Jack said.

"Maybe you should eat some fruit, anyway," Stearns recommended.

"Maybe later."

"You might want to lie down for a while and take a nap. You've been under a lot of stress, sir."

"I'm not tired, Stearns. When I am I'll lie down, all right?"

"Yes, sir."

Jack felt himself becoming angry. *I wonder if I'm cracking up?* he thought. Somehow he had to put himself under control. Everybody on the boat was relying on him. If he cracked up and they were saved somehow, the admirals would never let him on a submarine again.

"Maybe I'll lie down for a while," he said to Stearns.

"I think that's a very good idea, sir."

"Wake me up if anything happens."

"Yes, sir."

TWENTY-ONE

The *Porgie* bucked and slammed its way into Block Island Sound. Lieutenant Commander Ellington looked up at the clouds and hoped it wouldn't rain. The wind and water lashed the bridge, and Ellington's eyes burned with salt as they looked for the *Sebago*. "Lieutenant Middleton!" he cried.

"Yes, sir!" replied Middleton in the control room.

"Come up here and take a fix!"

"Yes, sir!"

Middleton hastily put on his oilskins and hat and climbed the ladder, his hand-bearing compass hanging around his neck. A gob of salt water hit him in the face as soon as he arrived on the bridge.

"Whew—pretty nasty up here," he said, wiping his nose with the back of his hand.

"Never mind and take that fix."

"Yes, sir."

Middleton took fixes on a buoy, a smokestack, and a lighthouse. He scrambled back down the ladder to the control room so he could draw his lines quickly and see where they were.

"Call me when you've got it!" Ellington yelled.

"Yes, sir!"

On the plastic that covered the chart Middleton drew his three lines carefully. They intersected at a point near the southern entrance to Block Island Sound, and he drew a line from that point to the last position radioed in by the *Sebago*. Using his parallel rulers, he determined the bearing of that position from the reported position of Dunlop's boat.

"I've got the fix, sir!" Middleton called up the conning tower ladder.

He reached for his dividers and figured the distance between the *Porgie* and the *Sebago*'s last position. He heard Ellington descend the ladder, dripping salt water from his oilskins. Ellington took off his hat and wiped his face with a towel that Nowicki handed him. Then he advanced to the chart table, face red and eyes bloodshot from his hours on the bridge.

"Here *we* are," Middleton said, pointing, "and here *they* are."

Ellington studied the chart. He gave Nowicki a new bearing to steer, a bearing that would bring them closer to the last reported position of the *Sebago*. Middleton's tabulations indicated that they were less than six miles away.

"Middleton," he said, "give me a hoot when we're about five minutes from the last reported position."

"Yes, sir."

Ellington put on his hat again and snapped up his oilskin coat. He climbed the ladder and returned to the bridge.

"See anything?" Ellington asked McNally.

"No, sir."

Ellington looked around and saw nothing but sea and clouds. Even the seagulls were hiding. He thought about Lieutenant McCrary, whom he'd seen last Saturday night at a dance at the officers' club. McCrary had been with a beautiful young woman from New York whom he'd introduced as his fiancée. Later Ellington had learned that she was the daughter of Congressman Adam Kirkland of New York, chairman of the Naval Preparedness Committee. He wondered if McCrary would have better luck with the daughter of a congressman than Ellington himself was having with the daughter of an admiral. Sometimes Ellington admired Nowicki, who wasn't married and spent his shore time in whorehouses. Nowicki got what he needed, paid for it, and left, without having any headaches. But a naval officer couldn't spend his spare time in whorehouses. The admirals wouldn't like that. They'd shitcan you right out of the Navy.

Ellington realized he was daydreaming. It was a hazard that threatened all sailors who pulled watch duty, and had to be combated vigorously. Ellington shook his head to clear it out. A flying hail of surf helped. He wiped off his binoculars and raised them to his eyes, scanning the horizon from left to right. He lowered them and wiped them off. There wasn't a damned thing out there except ugly weather.

Ellington continued searching the horizon, and McNally beside him did the same. Gradually they advanced more deeply into Block Island Sound, and finally they heard Middleton's voice from the control room.

"Five minutes to the *Sebago*'s position, sir!"

"All engines ahead one third!" Ellington shouted back.

"All engines ahead one third!" repeated Nowicki.

In the propulsion control room, levers were pushed and knobs were turned on dials. The *Porgie* began to slow down. Ellington turned around on the bridge and examined all the water between him and the horizon. There was nothing out there, not even the suggestion of a submarine's hull.

"Take the bridge, McNally," Ellington said. "I'm going below to call New London. Keep your eyes peeled. The *Sebago* is supposed to be around here someplace."

"Yes, sir."

Ellington descended the ladder into the control room of the *Porgie*. He took off his hat, wiped his face with a towel, and trudged toward the radio room.

"I want you to send a message to New London," he told the radioman. *"Have arrived at Sebago diving position but do not observe marker buoy anywhere. Got it?"*

"Yes, sir."

The radioman hit his keys and the dots and dashes flew toward New London. Ellington looked down and saw that his oilskins were dripping onto the floor and making a puddle. His knees buckled slightly every time the *Porgie* fell off a wave. The radioman finished transmitting the message. Thirty seconds later New London told him to stand by.

He turned to Ellington. "They want us to stand by, sir."

"We're standing."

Ellington opened his oilskin jacket, took a pack of Chesterfields from the pocket of his brown leather jacket underneath, and lit a cigarette with his Zippo. His wet lips soaked the end of the cigarette. Inhaling, he leaned against the bulkhead, realizing how tired he was. He hadn't slept much last night because he was anxious to get underway on his shakedown cruise; on top of that he'd had a big fight with Patti. In addition, it was tiring to conduct a search in weather like this.

He heard dots and dashes coming from the radio and recognized the call signal for the *Porgie*. His radioman took down the message quickly and handed the sheet of paper to Ellington. It said: COMMENCE SEARCH OPERATIONS FOR SEBAGO. REPORT PROGRESS EVERY FIFTEEN MINUTES.

Puffing his cigarette, Ellington walked to the chart table and worked out a course so that the *Porgie* could explore the area systematically in ever widening circles, using the lost boat's last reported diving position as the center of the search. He told Middleton the bearings and turning points and ordered him to transmit them to Nowicki at the appropriate times.

"I also want three more men up on the bridge," Ellington added. "The more men we have up there the better."

"I'll send them right up, sir."

Ellington buttoned his oilskin coat, put on his hat, and with his cigarette hanging out the corner of his mouth, climbed the ladder to the bridge once again.

TWENTY-TWO

In the headquarters building at New London, Admiral Mackie sat behind his desk and looked at the message from the *Porgie* that Lieutenant Simpson had brought him. Captain Robertson sat in a chair in front of Admiral Mackie's desk. Simpson stood to the side, having just telephoned the radio room and ordered Kerry to transmit the message to the *Porgie* that ordered it to commence search operations.

Admiral Mackie frowned as he looked up at Captain Robertson. "Well, I guess we might as well face it: The *Sebago* is down."

Robertson leaned forward in his chair. "We don't know that for sure, sir."

"It's a damned reasonable assumption, Robertson." Admiral Mackie looked at his watch; it was nearly 1230 hours. "We haven't heard from them in over four hours. I think we'd better proceed as if they're down, but I don't want to notify the press yet. I want you to call the Boston Navy Yard and get the *Falcon* underway. It'll take a while for it to clear port, so get on it right now."

Robertson reached for the phone on Admiral Mackie's desk. "May I use your phone, sir?"

"No, use the one in your own office. I have to make some calls here myself. I also want you to get two more subs underway and send them out there to sweep the area."

"Yes, sir."

Captain Robertson arose and left the office. Admiral Mackie looked at Lieutenant Simpson.

"Return to your desk and report to me immediately whenever a message comes in from the *Porgie*."

Simpson walked swiftly from the office, leaving Admiral Mackie alone. Admiral Mackie looked at the message again and shook his head. If the *Sebago* truly was down, this could be a catastrophe for the Submarine Service. Submarines weren't too popular among many high-ranking admirals, and this incident could provide the ideal excuse for them to diminish the role of submarines even further. Also, it was the first in an entirely new generation of fleet submarines. If it was defective, it would mean that years of research and design had been wasted. Heads would roll, and one of them most likely would be the one belonging to the commandant of the submarine base at New London, himself.

Admiral Mackie knew that the time had come for him to notify Vice Admiral Charles Hill, the commander of the Atlantic Fleet, in Washington. Hill, nicknamed "Hardtop" for his fondness for aircraft carriers, was an outspoken critic of submarines. He believed that the World War had proved that submarines could easily be destroyed by concentrated depth charge attacks, and that submarines had become obsolete in modern navies. He had been opposed to the development of the *Sebago* but had been overruled by Admiral Cyrus Kane, the commander of the Navy, who didn't want to delete submarines from the Navy's table of organization without more evidence that they were useless.

If the boat was down, that certainly would be more

evidence, but anyway, the call to Vice Admiral Hill couldn't be postponed anymore. Admiral Mackie picked up his telephone and told his clerk to put him through to Vice Admiral Hill in Washington, and that the call was an emergency.

Admiral Mackie waited awhile, hearing clicks and buzzes from the earpiece of his telephone. Admiral Hill's clerk came on and said that the admiral was busy and had asked not to be disturbed.

Admiral Mackie cut in and identified himself. "This is an emergency, and I must speak to Admiral Hill at once!" he said to the clerk.

"Yes, sir."

There was another click and then the deep booming voice of Admiral Hill came on the wire. "What's the problem, Paul?"

"I'm afraid I have bad news, sir. It appears as though the *Sebago* is down."

The wire was silent for a few moments, then: "What happened?"

"It made its first test dive at one one oh six this morning and hasn't been heard from since."

"I see." Another pause. "What have you done?"

"I've sent out another submarine, the *Porgie,* to look for her, and I've alerted the *Falcon* in the Boston Navy Yard to stand by."

"But you don't know for sure yet that she's down."

"That's correct, sir, but I'm afraid the conclusion is inescapable at this point."

"You're probably right, Paul. Stay on top of the situation and let me know right away when you have more information."

"Yes, sir."

There was silence on the phone again. Admiral Mackie wondered whether he was supposed to hang up.

"I don't suppose you've notified the press yet," Admiral Hill said.

"No, sir."

"Good. We'll handle that from here when the time comes. One more thing: I want you to contact Boston and tell them to get the *Falcon* underway as soon as possible. If the *Sebago* is down, we should have the *Falcon* on the scene, don't you think?"

"Yes, sir."

"Carry on, Paul."

"Yes, sir."

"And whatever you do, don't breathe a word of this to the press."

"Yes, sir."

Admiral Mackie cut off the connection, then told his clerk to connect him with Rear Admiral Bernard Walmsley, the commandant of the Boston Navy Yard. Admiral Walmsley's clerk said that Admiral Walmsley was down in the yard someplace and that it would take a while to reach him. Admiral Mackie waited patiently, hoping the *Sebago* would turn up safe and sound with a reasonable explanation for what had happened, until Admiral Walmsley came on the phone. He and Admiral Mackie were old friends; they held the same rank and had known each other since they were midshipmen at Annapolis.

"What is it, Paul?" Walmsley asked.

"I just spoke with Admiral Hill about the *Sebago* situation. He told me to tell you to get the *Falcon* underway and send her to this command immediately."

"I'm afraid it won't be immediately, Paul. The *Falcon*'s engines are being overhauled and they're all in pieces, half in the hull and half in the workshops."

Admiral Mackie shook his head. "This is a hell of a time for the *Falcon* to be having her engines overhauled."

"It's a hell of a time for the *Sebago* to go down."

"I'd appreciate it if you'd let me know when the *Falcon* is ready to go."

"Will do."

"I assume you're notifying the members of the special sea rescue team you've got there."

"We're already trying to round them up. Their wonder boy C.O. is home on leave."

"You mean Mount?"

"Yes, Mount."

"Well, we all have our oddballs to contend with."

"Don't we though."

"That's all for now, Bernie. Be sure to call me when the *Falcon* is headed this way."

"Will do."

"And by the way, don't let anything leak to the press yet."

"Right."

Admiral Mackie hung up his phone and thought for a few moments. Then he called his clerk and told him to put in a call to Commodore Ray McCrary at the Bureau of Personnel in Washington.

TWENTY-THREE

Lieutenant Commander Benjamin Mount sat in the audience of the RKO Palace in Brooklyn and watched Al Jolson singing "Toot Toot Tootsie" on the silver screen. The movie was *Rose of Washington Square* and it also starred Tyrone Power and Alice Faye.

Jolson's face was painted black and he waved his hands in the air as he goggled his eyes and sang. Ben couldn't help chuckling, although he ordinarily didn't like movies. He'd come to this one to escape from his family. He dreaded these furloughs to Brooklyn and would much rather have remained at his job at the Boston Navy Yard, but he had so many furlough days accumulated that he'd lose some if he didn't go away for a while, and the people at the Bureau of Personnel would think it strange if he didn't use his furlough days.

Every furlough seemed worse than the last. He would like to use the time to travel and see something new, but that would make his parents unhappy; he always went home, where they fussed over him and embarrassed him and drove him nuts.

The normal conversational tone at home was a high-pitched scream; even when his parents weren't arguing they screamed at each other. His grandfather usually sat in a corner ignoring everybody and studying the Torah. It was a madhouse. His parents dragged him around, showing him off to neighbors, business associates, the local barber, everybody, and by the time Ben returned to his base he really needed a vacation. He felt guilty that he couldn't stand his family, but he couldn't stand them anyway.

On the occassions when he'd been invited to the homes of his Christian friends he'd been amazed at how tranquil everything had been. At meals they said, "Please pass the mashed potatoes," or "Please pass the butter," instead of banging on the table and grabbing. His parents acted as though they hadn't eaten for days, although they were well-to-do business people and overfed.

Ben understood why Christians hated Jews, because sometimes he hated Jews himself. From listening to his father he'd learned that in business dealings many Jews believed in behaving honorably with each other but that it was always open season on the *goyim*. He also knew that many Jews considered themselves far superior in every way to the *goyim*. Therefore it wasn't surprising to Ben that in countries like Germany there were movements to persecute the Jews. The terrible part of it was that Jews like him were persecuted for the behavior of other Jews. *The sins of the fathers shall be visited upon the sons*. He faced many more obstacles than the average naval officer because he was Jewish, and it hurt all the more because he didn't like being Jewish.

At least he was able to get out of his parents' house once in a while and go to a movie. He smiled and tapped his foot as Al Jolson jumped around and sang. The movie was about show business and he thought it awfully corny, but the music was nice. It pepped you up and made you want to dance—not that Ben knew how to dance.

He heard a commotion behind him but didn't turn around because he was transfixed by Al Jolson. Then he heard his mother's voice, and his blood ran cold.

"I know he's in here somewhere!" she said. "He told me he was coming here and he wouldn't lie to his mother!"

Horrified, Ben turned around and saw his mother coming down the aisle with a marine S.P. and an usher with a flashlight. *What the hell's going on here?* he wondered as he stood up.

"There he is!" his mother yelled, pointing at him.

The usher aimed his flashlight at Ben's face, and Ben raised his arms to shield his eyes.

"Are you Lieutenant Commander Benjamin Mount, sir?" the marine asked, walking toward Ben.

"Yes, I am."

"We've been looking for you, sir. There's an emergency at the Boston Navy Yard and you have to report back to duty."

Ben walked up the aisle with the marine, the usher, and his mother.

"I told them you'd be here, Benny," his mother said proudly.

"What's the emergency?" Ben asked the marine.

"I don't know for sure, sir. The lieutenant will tell you."

They entered the huge lobby of the Palace. Standing beside a purple stuffed sofa was a marine lieutenant and two pfc's.

"Here he is, sir," said the marine who'd brought Ben up the aisle.

Ben's mother tried to hold Ben's hand, but Ben pulled it away. She was a stout woman with peroxide blond hair, wearing glasses and too much rouge on her cheeks.

"Lieutenant Commander Mount?" the lieutenant said.

"Yes."

"You're to report to the Boston Navy Yard without delay. We have a seaplane waiting for you at the Brooklyn Navy Yard to transport you there."

"What happened?" Ben asked.

"I'm not supposed to say, sir."

"I see." Ben turned to his mother. "Well, it looks like I've got to go back to the base, Mom."

She stood on her tiptoes and kissed him, begging him to be careful, to wear enough clothes, to get enough to eat, and so forth, and he felt as touched by her concern as he was embarrassed by it. He removed her hands from his neck, smiled and waved, and walked off with the marines.

"Say good-bye to Pop for me!" he called back over his shoulder.

"Take care of yourself, Benny!" she replied. "Don't take no chances!"

Ben cringed as he followed the marines out of the lobby to the sidewalk on DeKalb Avenue, where three police cars were parked around the Navy car at the curb. A crowd of people were on the sidewalk gawking, with cops holding them back. The lieutenant held open the rear door of the Navy car for Ben, then followed him in.

The caravan pulled away from the curb and drove off down DeKalb Avenue, gathering speed and heading for the Brooklyn Navy Yard, the sirens on the police cars wailing and attracting the attention of passersby.

The marine lieutenant leaned toward Ben and said, "I guess I can tell you what the emergency is now, sir, but you're not supposed to say anything to any civilians, especially newspaper reporters."

"I won't say anything to anyone," Ben replied. "What is it?"

"A submarine is in trouble in the Atlantic Ocean, sir. The *Sebago*."

Ben closed his eyes, a chill going up his spine. He'd designed many of the systems on that boat two years earlier, when he was in Washington with the Bureau of Ships and Construction.

"Do you know what happened?" Ben asked the marine.

"No, sir. I don't believe the *Sebago* has been heard from since this morning, sir. They don't know for sure that it's down, but they believe it is."

"I see," said Ben.

His hand trembling slightly, he took out a package of Camels and lit one. He was wearing tan corduroy slacks and a brown tweed sport jacket. Puffing the cigarette, he looked out the window as the main shopping district of Brooklyn went past in a blur.

He knew that if the *Sebago* was down because of some mistake he'd made, he might as well kiss his Navy career good-bye.

And if lives were lost, he'd never be able to escape the ruthless persecution of his conscience.

TWENTY-FOUR

Commodore Ray McCrary sat at his desk in the Bureau of Personnel in Washington, examining officer efficiency reports. He was a short, compactly built man of fifty-eight, with gray hair and a bald spot at the back of his head. He intended to retire in a few years; presently he had thirty-two consecutive years of service in the Navy. They'd make him a rear admiral when he retired, which would give him a nice pension. During the World War he'd served on the destroyer *Concord,* which saw little action. Ray McCrary thought that if the *Concord* had been involved in a few major battle engagements, and if he'd handled himself well (as he was sure he would have), he'd be an admiral already, but those were the breaks of the game.

The phone on his desk rang.

He picked up the receiver and said, "Hello?"

"Commodore McCrary?" said the voice on the other end, which sounded as though it was coming long distance.

"Yes."

"This is Admiral Mackie at New London."

"Hello, Admiral—what can I do for you?"

"I'm afraid I have bad news, Ray. The *Sebago* is probably down."

Ray McCrary felt his mind breaking apart. "Down where?" he asked.

"We don't know exactly, but she test-dived for the first time at one one oh six and hasn't been heard from since."

Ray McCrary looked at his watch; it was almost one o'clock in the afternoon. "Well," he said, trying to keep his voice from faltering, "I'm sure you're doing everything possible."

"Yes, we have search boats out, and the *Falcon* is on its way from the Boston Navy Yard. I'll notify you personally as soon as anything develops."

"That would be very kind of you."

"Admiral Hill has ordered that no statements should be made to the press yet."

"Of course not."

"I'm very sorry about this, Ray," Admiral Mackie said consolingly. "I know both of your boys and I like them very much. I think that Jack is one of the best young officers in the submarine forces."

"It's good of you to say that," Ray McCrary said softly.

"Don't lose hope—the *Sebago* probably will turn up safe and sound."

"Yes."

They exchanged a few more words, then hung up. Ray McCrary stared at the photographs of his sons on his desk. It was impossible for him to accept the idea that two such vigorous young men could be lying at the bottom of the sea. He closed his eyes and sighed, wondering what to do with himself. He couldn't concentrate on officers' efficiency reports now. Maybe he should see the commanding officer about catching a hop to New London and be on the spot when the news came in.

No, that wasn't a good idea, he decided. They didn't

know for sure yet that the *Sebago* was down. It might have gone off on a little trip someplace, and its radio might be broken. Such things had happened before. It wasn't impossible by any means.

He decided to sit tight and await further developments. No sense in calling Martha yet. She was sickly, and this would land her right in the hospital. He didn't want to go through that until it was official that the boat was down.

Ray McCrary stood up and went to his window. In the distance he could see the Washington Monument and the Mall. It was a cloudy overcast day; in visibility like this it'd be difficult to spot a little boat like the *Sebago*.

Clasping his hands behind his back, he began to pace back and forth in front of his desk. First Ed's expulsion from Annapolis, now this. His wife was neurotic and saw a psychiatrist once a week. His career had been bedeviled by bad breaks, missed opportunities, and overlooked achievements. An awful lot had gone wrong. He prayed that he wouldn't lose both his sons, too.

TWENTY-FIVE

Boatswain's Mate First Class Thomas Hodges sat on the cot in his cell in the brig of the Boston Navy Yard. He was in his peacoat and wore his white hat cockily on the back of his head while staring at the floor wishing he had a cigarette.

He'd been in the brig since the marines had picked him up that morning. They took away all his personal belongings including his watch and cigarettes, and nobody had said a word to him since. He didn't know what time it was but was sure it must be time for lunch. He hadn't eaten breakfast and was ravenously hungry. Doors were slamming in the building all around him, but he was the only prisoner in this section of cells. They hadn't even given him anybody to talk with. He wondered how long they were going to keep him like this.

He heard a door open nearby, then footsteps in the corridor outside his cell. Jumping up, he ran to the bars and held onto them, squeezing his head through an opening so he could see who was coming. In the shadows of the corridor a marine corporal appeared.

"Hey, Corporal—you got a cigarette for an old sailor?"

The corporal shot him a quick malevolent glance and kept walking.

"Hey, Corporal—can't you even fuckin' say anything?"

The corporal stopped, turned slowly, and advanced toward Hodges's cell. "Who do you think you're talking to—swab-jockey!" he demanded. He had wide shoulders, a crewcut on his round, tough-looking skull, and a pug nose.

"I'm talking to you," Hodges replied, as the corporal drew his face to within a few inches of the bars.

The corporal pointed his finger at Hodges. "You'd better watch your fucking step while you're in here, sailor, or I'll whip your ass."

Hodges looked at him and got mad. "I'd like to see you try it, you fucking ape!"

The corporal's ears became red and he took a step backwards. "I guess you must be one of them wise guys, huh swabbie?"

"Fuck you," Hodges replied.

"You're the one who's gonna get fucked, swabbie. I'm gonna see the sergeant of the guard right now and tell him we've got a wise swabbie back here. I think he might want to throw you into the grease pit for the rest of the day."

Hodges looked the corporal in the eye. "Suck my dick," he said, and then spat a lunger at the corporal's nose.

The corporal stepped back, gagging and wiping his nose with his sleeve. "Now you've really done it!" he hissed. "I guess we're gonna have to teach you a lesson."

"Just don't try it alone," Hodges said.

"I'll be back," the corporal said, moving down the corridor.

"Just don't come back alone if you know what's good for you," Hodges said.

The door at the end of the corridor opened and closed, and Hodges sat heavily on his bunk. *I guess I've really done it this time,* he thought. *About ten marines are gonna come back here and bounce me off the walls.*

Hodges had heard stories about marines kicking the shit out of sailors in brigs. He'd even heard about sailors who'd been beaten to death. Marines who pulled guard duty in brigs were the cruelest, most insane sadists in the corps, and it was common knowledge in the Navy that any sailor was in trouble if he ever got in their clutches.

"Fucking seagoing bellhops," Hodges muttered, trying to pull some courage together. He was determined to go down fighting. Those bastards weren't going to push him around. They could kill him if they wanted, but he wasn't going to beg or play any other silly games for them. He'd been in a few brawls, and he knew how to handle himself. If they came for him, he was sure he'd be able to fuck up a couple of them anyway.

He stood up and took off his white hat, dropping it onto the cot. He took off his peacoat and dropped it beside the hat. Stretching, he danced around on his toes and punched the air a few times. He saw himself lying on the floor of the cell being stomped by a squad of marine guards, and punched harder. No one else was in this cell area, so there'd be no witnesses. They'd do whatever they wanted, and afterwards they'd say he tried to escape.

The door at the end of the corridor opened, and Hodges clicked his teeth. *Here they come,* he thought. He put his back against the wall of the cell and waited for them to come. He'd kick the closest one in the balls and go for the next one's eyes. After that it would be down and dirty to the bitter end.

A group of marines appeared in front of the bars.

The lighting was dim and Hodges couldn't make them out very well, but he was ready for the worst.

"Boatswain's Mate First Class Thomas Hodges?" one of them asked.

"That's me."

"I've got an authorization here for your release. Grab your hat and coat and let's go."

Hodges moved closer to the bars and saw that the marine who'd spoken was a lieutenant. He hadn't known that lieutenants went in for kicking ass, but evidently they did.

Hodges picked up his coat and hat. They were going to take him someplace else to beat the shit out of him. He'd play along with them as long as they wanted and when they tried to grab him he'd show them what a sailor was made of.

The corporal who'd taunted him opened the door of the cell and didn't look very happy. *I wonder what's wrong with him?* Hodges thought. Hodges stepped warily out of the cell and saw that three pfc's were with the corporal and the lieutenant.

"Move it out, sailor," the lieutenant said.

Hodges walked down the corridor, the marines behind him. They came to an iron gate, and a marine on the other side opened it up. There was a stairway ahead and Hodges thought the marines would take him below to a dungeon someplace, but they bypassed the stairs and came to another iron gate, which also was opened for them.

They traversed a series of corridors, and Hodges's anxiety mounted with every step. Finally they turned a corner and came to a large orderly room with four desks. Lieutenant Commander Benjamin Mount was looking out a window, his hands in the pockets of his civilian slacks. Ben turned around as Hodges and the marines came into the room.

"So here you are," Ben said, obviously pleased to see Hodges.

"I thought you were on leave, sir," Hodges replied, astonished to see Ben in the brig's orderly room.

"Something came up, and I've had to come back. Let's go."

"Let's go?" Hodges asked.

"Yes. Come on."

Hodges looked around at the marine guards. "But . . ."

"I've taken care of everything. Let's go."

Hodges decided to get moving and ask questions later. "Yes, sir."

Ben waved at a marine sergeant sitting at one of the desks. "Thanks for your help."

"My pleasure, *sir.*"

Ben walked out of the orderly room, and Hodges followed him. They crossed a graveled yard and came to the front gate of the brig. The gate was opened and they went outside into the Boston Navy Yard.

Hodges inhaled the salty air and smell of oil. He could hear engines chugging and people banging on steel with hammers. Ben walked toward the section of the yard where the buildings of the Ship Rescue Project were located. They passed huge buildings and little shops where ships and naval equipment were constructed and repaired.

"Why were you AWOL?" Ben asked, his voice curious and not angry.

"I really wasn't AWOL, sir," Hodges replied. "I just happened to return to the Yard around two hours late."

"An old sailor like you should have known better."

"Sometimes you get tied up, sir, and you can't get away."

"Was it a girl?"

Hodges grinned. "Yes, sir."

"I thought so." Ben was always amazed at the ease with which other men found women; it always was so difficult for him. "You'd better be careful about that from now on, Hodges, because I might not always be around to get you out of the brig."

"How come you're back from leave so soon, sir?"

"The *Sebago* is down, or at least they think it's down," Ben replied. "It hasn't been heard from since it went on its first test dive this morning at one one oh six hours. We may have to go and get her."

Hodges stopped abruptly, then continued walking again. He was surprised by the news. The submarine force wasn't very big, and anyone in it knew most of the other people. Hodges had served with Jethro Keller on the *Narwhal* and with Anthony Brouvelli on the *Cuttlefish,* which had been skippered by Lieutenant Commander Gene Dunlop for a while. He also knew Hank Burns from the *Narwhal.*

"Maybe its radio conked out," Hodges said.

"Even if it did, it should have returned to port by now. The engines are being put back into the *Falcon* right now, and when it's ready, we're going up to New London. Presumably they'll know where the boat is by then."

"Didn't it radio in its coordinates before it dived?"

"Yes, but no trace of it has been found in that area."

"Maybe somebody took down the wrong coordinates. Most radiomen got their heads up their asses most of the time anyway."

They came to a tall wooden building painted battleship gray. Stenciled on the door was SHIP RESCUE PROJECT. Ben opened the door and they went inside to a large loft area with machinery and workbenches along the walls. In the middle of the room was a diving bell about twelve feet high. Workmen were crawling around it, welding its seams and installing fittings. Inside, two men were welding equipment to its bulkheads. The welders' torches were sending showers of sparks into the air.

"Looks like our first test is going to be the real

FORTY FATHOMS DOWN . 143

thing," Ben said to Hodges. "You'd better get your duty uniform on and some chow because we might be leaving pretty soon."

"How soon, sir?"

"Within two hours. Don't stray anywhere that I can't reach you."

"Yes, sir. And thanks for getting me out of the brig."

"If the *Sebago* wasn't in trouble, I wouldn't have got you out, but you're welcome anyway."

Hodges smiled uneasily and walked away. The only reason Mount got him out of the brig was because he needed him, but at least he'd got him out. The Jew didn't do anything unless there was a good practical reason. He was as unemotional as a piece of wood.

Hodges made his way to a small washroom in the building, where there were lockers. He opened the door of his and changed into his work uniform, wondering if the boat really was down.

In the workshop Ben walked toward the rescue chamber that he'd designed. His hands in his pockets, he examined the work that was being done. The Navy had rescue chambers of other designs, but there'd been bugs in them and Ben had been given the assignment to develop a new one. A prototype had been tested in water tanks and air pressure chambers, and Ben was still adding refinements. Now the design process was coming to an abrupt end. The Mount Rescue Chamber had become operational.

Ben touched his hand to the smooth steel skin of the chamber. There were so many imponderables, so much that could go wrong. He knew that his career was riding on the success of the rescue chamber. If the *Sebago* was down because of the failure of a system he'd designed, and if his rescue chamber was fouled up too, he'd be dismissed from the Navy and he'd be lucky if he could get a job as an auto mechanic.

One of the workmen, his face smudged with grease, stepped out of the rescue chamber. "She's just about ready to go," he said with a proud grin.

"Good work," Ben replied.

TWENTY-SIX

Betsy Kirkland sat on the sofa in her living room on East 72nd Street. She was eating a cheese sandwich and wondering whether or not to call her father and tell him she'd just quit her job. She'd kicked her shoes off and her legs were curled up underneath her as she stared off into space, feeling depressed.

The thing that really got her was that nobody at the *Standard* had tried to stop her. While she was emptying her desk, she'd thought that O'Rourke would have made at least a token effort to persuade her to stay, but he hadn't and neither had anyone else. A few people she worked with wished her good luck perfunctorily and then returned to their desks as though they'd already forgotten her.

She wondered what she would have done if she was an ordinary working girl without a rich father. Girls like that couldn't quit their jobs if they didn't like them, she imagined. They had to stay and suffer. She was glad her father was rich. She would have gone insane if she had to keep writing wedding stories for the rest of her life.

Her telephone rang, and her first thought was that maybe it was Jimmy O'Rourke calling to ask her to return. If so, she decided to be a little stand-offish at first, then try to convince him to send her to the city hall beat.

She picked up the telephone. "Hello?"

"Betsy?"

"Yes?"

"This is Commodore McCrary speaking."

"Oh, hello, Commodore. I didn't recognize your voice at first." Betsy was surprised to hear from him, because he'd never called her before. "To what do I owe the pleasure of this call?"

"Betsy, dear, I'm afraid I have some bad news."

A chill passed over her, and she placed her cheese sandwich on its plate. "What's wrong?"

"I think you'd better get a good grip on yourself."

"I have a good grip on myself." She realized it must have something to do with Jack. "What is it?"

"I've just received word that the *Sebago* is in trouble," Ray McCrary said.

"In trouble?" Betsy asked, feeling a rise of hysteria. "You mean it's sunk!"

"All we know so far is that it's missing," Ray McCrary told her. He explained the circumstances as Admiral Mackie had explained them to him. "We don't know for sure what's happened, but I thought perhaps I ought to call you, since you and Jack are engaged to be married."

Betsy was shaken by the news. She wanted to do something, but didn't know what. "Are you going to New London?" she asked.

"Yes, I'll be leaving in about an hour."

"I think maybe I'd better go there too."

"What about your job? I called your office and was told that you'd gone home."

"I quit today."

"You quit today?"

"Yes."

"I thought that's what you said. If you go to New

London, ask for Admiral Mackie. He's the commandant and he's a friend of mine. He'll take care of you. How will you get there?"

"I think I'll take the train. It's a two-hour ride I believe."

"Then I'll be there before you. I'll tell Admiral Mackie to be on the alert for your arrival. I wouldn't worry excessively about this yet if I were you, because we don't know for sure that the *Sebago* is down."

Betsy's insides were quaking. "It doesn't sound very good to me."

"No, it doesn't," Ray McCrary agreed.

They agreed to meet in New London and hung up. Betsy sat with her hand on the phone for a few minutes, dazed by what Jack's father had told her. She couldn't believe that Jack might be dead on a sunken submarine. He always was so vigorous and enthusiastic, it was unthinkable that such a person could no longer be alive.

Feeling nervous and unstuck, she got up and paced back and forth in front of her sofa a few times. She looked out her living room window at the traffic on the street below, then went to her bedroom to pack a few things. Opening a drawer, she looked at the photograph of Jack on her dresser. He was wearing summer whites and was tanned and handsome. He was a wonderful guy and she loved him very much, although it wasn't a mad passionate romantic kind of love. She just enjoyed being with him; he made her feel better. She'd thought it would be nice to settle down with him. His presence made everything around him appear wholesome and pleasant. He didn't have much money, but she had enough for both of them. They'd have a happy life together.

Or so she'd thought before her future father-in-law had called. Her hands trembling, trying to keep from crying, she removed a few articles of underclothing from a drawer and laid them on the bed. Going to a closet, she took down one of her suitcases and opened it.

She normally wasn't religious, but as she packed clothing into the suitcase she prayed to God that the *Sebago* would be found and that Jack would be all right.

TWENTY-SEVEN

In the *Sebago*, the air was heavy and foul. Jethro
Keller sat underneath the depth gauge, looking
through slitted eyes at the others in the control room.
The lights were dimmer because the batteries in the
emergency lamps were running down. Keller's eyes
fell on Lieutenant McCrary, lying on the floor next
to Lieutenants Nielsen and Stearns, who were sitting
with their eyes closed.

We're like a bunch of corpses already, Keller
thought morosely, snuggling more tightly into the
blanket that he'd wrapped himself in. It had become
quite cold and damp inside the control room, and
occasionally he could hear chattering teeth. *It looks
like I'm gonna die down here,* he told himself. *It
looks like it's all over for old Keller.*

Like all submariners, Keller never believed that
something like this could happen to him. At various
times in his Navy career he'd wondered what it
would be like to die on a submarine, and he'd figured
it wouldn't be so bad: a depth charge would hit and
everybody would be drowned inside two minutes.
Fast and clean. Not a bad way to go at all.

It never had occurred to him that he would perish

slowly by suffocation aboard a submarine. Although such things happened, he knew they happened very seldom. The odds were against anything like that happening to him, and as an old crapshooter, he understood the odds.

Now he realized that the unlikely had happened. Not only that, but evidently the people in New London didn't even know where the *Sebago* was. He looked at his watch; it was two o'clock in the afternoon. It seemed to him that a ship of some kind should have passed overhead by now. He wondered what had gone wrong. Could the radioman have sent the wrong coordinates?

What a fucking mess, he thought. In a corner, somebody coughed. They had enough oxygen for another twenty-four hours, and after that it'd be curtains. Keller wondered if they'd die quietly, or if some of the younger ones would panic and turn the submarine into a loony bin. Keller wouldn't mind dying quietly, but he hoped he wouldn't have to die in a madhouse.

Taking a sip of water, he thought of his wife, Dolores. She lived in San Francisco and he hadn't seen her for five years. They didn't get along, so by mutual unspoken agreement he had stopped going to San Francisco to see her. They wrote once in a while. His allotment checks still went to her every month because he didn't have the heart to divorce her. He never thought about her very much, because he never had trouble meeting women in the ports he visited or the towns outside the bases where he was stationed. Strange that he was thinking about her now.

Keller ran his hand over the stubble on his cheeks. He always looked like he needed a shave, even after he just had a shave. He had wavy black hair and was built like a bear. Thirty-five years old, he'd joined the Navy when he was seventeen. He'd wanted to see the world, and he'd seen most of it. But the way things looked, he probably wouldn't see any more of it.

On the deck of the control room Lieutenant Mc-Crary twitched suddenly on the floor. "I think I heard something," he said, pressing his ear against the cold metal of the deck.

Stearns looked around thoughtfully. "I don't hear anything," he said.

Keeler got down on the deck and pressed his ear to the steel. His eyes widened as he heard the faint but unmistakable throbbing of submarine diesels. "I hear it too," he said. "It's a sub."

Everybody in the control room got down and listened. Some shouted that they could hear it too.

"Sssshhhh," said Jack, listening to the faint sounds. "I think it's getting closer." He looked at Keller. "I think you'd better send up a smoke rocket fast."

"Yes, sir!" Keller replied, jumping to his feet

TWENTY-EIGHT

The *Porgie* ploughed through the crested waves of Block Island Sound. Lieutenant Commander Ernest Ellington was on the bridge with Lieutenant McNally, Lieutenant Middleton, and Electrician's Mate Third Class Martin Gatewood. The *Porgie* had been patrolling the northern end of Block Island Sound for an hour, moving in ever-widening circles, and nothing had been seen.

Commander Ellington was becoming discouraged. He figured that he was nearly eight miles from the point where the *Sebago* had dived, and they should have seen some trace of her. New London hadn't reported that the boat had returned, so it *had* to be out here someplace. But where?

"Sir, I think I see something!" said Electrician's Mate Gatewood, standing with his binoculars on the starboard side of the bridge.

"Where?" asked Ellington, turning toward starboard.

"Over there, sir," Gatewood replied, pointing. "It looks like a smoke rocket."

Ellington, McNally, and Middleton looked in the

direction of Gatewood's finger and saw the gray haze of the afternoon. Then Ellington raised his binoculars and looked. Sure enough, there was a red smudge on the horizon. "I'll bet that's it!" he cried.

"It's a smoke rocket all right," McNally agreed, as he focused his binoculars.

Ellington leaned toward the conning tower hatch. "Hard right rudder!"

"Hard right rudder!" replied Nowicki in the control room.

The *Porgie*'s bow slammed sideways in the water as it turned in the direction of the red smudge.

"Middleton, get me a bearing on it!" ordered Ellington.

"Yes, sir!" Middleton wiped water from his hand-bearing compass and took aim.

"All ahead full!" Ellington yelled when the bow was pointed in the direction of the red smudge.

"All ahead full!" repeated Nowicki.

The *Porgie* surged forward toward the red smudge. Ellington looked at it through his binoculars. Yes, that surely was a smoke rocket, and it could only have come from the *Sebago*.

"I have the bearing, sir," Middleton said.

"Take it below and figure out the location of the rocket. Then tell Nostrand to send this message to New London: 'Have sighted smoke rocket at' whatever the coordinates are. 'Standing by.' Got it?"

"Yes, sir."

Middleton descended the ladder to the control room, and Ellington slapped Gatewood on the shoulder. "Good work," he said. "If it hadn't been for you, we might have missed it, because we were headed in the wrong direction."

Gatewood smiled and looked uneasy. It wasn't every day that he received compliments from the skipper.

McNally raised his binoculars and aimed at the

point on the horizon where he'd seen the smoke. It appeared to be only a few miles away, and the *Porgie* ripped through the waves toward it.

"I hope it's the *Sebago*!" McNally shouted above the roar of waves and the *Porgie*'s engines.

"It's got be!" Ellington replied.

In the control room, Middleton excitedly drew lines on the plastic overlay. When he had determined the location of the smoke rocket, he went to the radio room and told Nostrand to send it and the skipper's message to New London.

"There's another one!" shouted Gatewood on the bridge.

Ellington didn't have to raise his binoculars this time. The smoke rocket was close enough to be seen with the naked eye.

"Steer right four degrees!" he yelled down the conning tower hatch.

"Right four degrees!" repeated Nowicki.

The *Porgie* knifed full ahead toward the red cloud in the sky. Ellington held onto the bridge rail with both hands, flexing his knees whenever the submarine hit a wave. He was eager to get where that smoke rocket was, so he could see what was there. He hoped that the *Sebago* would be rolling peacefully on the surface, engines and radio out of operation. Then the rescue would be easy. But if she was down, the men and officers on board her might have had it.

Middleton came up to the bridge, a message in hand. "Just received from New London in response to our message, sir."

Ellington held the transcript low so the spray wouldn't get to it. CONDUCT THOROUGH SEARCH IN AREA OF SMOKE ROCKET. BE ON LOOKOUT FOR MARKER BUOY. SEND CONFIRMED COORDINATES TO THIS STATION.

Middleton raised his binoculars towards the red cloud on the horizon. "I don't see anything on the water," he said, the thrill of the chase upon him.

"We're not close enough yet. Wait a few more minutes."

The *Porgie* continued to pound its way northeast through Block Island Sound. Another red rocket shot into the air, and this time they were so close they could see the point where it burst out of the water. Ellington shouted a new bearing down into the control room so that the *Porgie* would pass closer to the spot from which the rocket had come. Then a third rocket exploded out of the water only fifty yards off the bows.

"All ahead one third!" Ellington ordered.

"All ahead one third!" The boat slowed down.

Ellington scanned the water through his binoculars, and as the *Porgie* lost forward way, he spotted a yellow marker buoy tossing on the waves.

"There it is—I see it!" Ellington yelled.

"I see it too!" Middleton said.

"Everybody keep his eyes on it," Ellington ordered. "Don't look at anything else but it."

"Yes, sir!"

Ellington gave orders that eased the *Porgie* closer to the yellow marker buoy. He told McNally to muster a deck detail and pick it up. McNally gathered his men and led them down the outside ladder of the conning tower. They started up the torpedo winch as Ellington inched the *Porgie* ever closer to the marker buoy. The hook on the end of a cable was lowered by the winch, and the men guided it to the buoy. The hook fastened onto the buoy and the winch raised it into the air. McNally removed the telephone and excitedly carried it to Ellington on the bridge.

Ellington pressed the telephone against his face. "Hello, *Sebago*—this is *Porgie*. What is your problem?"

The strained voice of Jack McCrary vibrated in the receiver. "The after compartments flooded immediately upon diving. We believe that the main induction valves failed to close. Twenty-six men and one officer were trapped in the after compartments. We also have a slow leak in the forward torpedo room. We're running out of air and it's very cold down here. That's the general picture."

"Okay, Jack," Ellington said, throwing military protocol to the winds. "We've got you now and we'll hang onto you. Help is on the way. Just sit tight and . . ."

A huge wave lifted the *Porgie* high in the air, stretching the buoy cable to its utmost. The cable snapped, twisting in the air like an angry snake. The connection went dead in Ellington's ear.

"Clutches out!" Ellington yelled.

"Clutches out!"

"Drop anchor!"

"Drop anchor!"

Ellington looked at the buoy cable disappearing into the sea. He turned to Middleton. "Send a message to New London," he said wearily. "Tell them what happened to the marker buoy. Give them the coordinates. Report that McCrary told me that twenty-six men and one officer had been trapped in the flooded after compartments."

Middleton wrote the information on his notepad, feeling sick at heart. When he finished writing down the information, he took it below to give to the radioman.

Ellington looked at McNally, who was pale as a sheet. Ellington slapped him lightly on the shoulder.

"Why don't you go below and get a cup of coffee."

"All right, sir."

McNally went down the conning tower ladder, and Ellington looked at the water on the starboard side of the submarine. He realized that now it might be impossible to find the *Sebago* in these seas.

Ellington frowned as he took out a cigarette. He hid his Zippo beneath the front of his raincoat and lit the cigarette, knowing that if he were aboard the *Sebago* right now he'd be frustrated as hell.

He couldn't help wondering which officers and crew members were alive down there and which were dead. He also wondered how they could be found now that the cable had been broken.

the overhead he could hear the waves slapping the side of the conning tower. Above that he knew a storm was gathering. The violent wind would turn the ocean into a fury. He was trapped, along with his crew, deep inside the Sebago.

TWENTY-NINE

Jack McCrary's heart nearly stopped beating when the connection was broken. He'd felt a rush of joy when he first heard Ernie Ellington's voice, and then suddenly it was all over. Something terrible had happened. He stared at the dial of the depth gauge in front of him, speechless. After the *Sebago* had been found, it had been lost again. Just like that.

"What's wrong, sir?" asked Stearns, who was crowding around McCrary with Lieutenant Nielsen and all the men in the control room.

Jack slowly lowered the phone from his ear. "The connection has been broken," he said in a hollow voice.

"Broken?"

"Yes."

Jack wanted to heave the telephone through the bulkhead, but he calmly hung it on its hook next to the depth gauge. He was still skipper and still had to set an example, although he'd much rather scream at the top of his lungs.

"It was the *Porgie*," he said. "They'll stay above us until help comes."

He looked up at the overhead and could hear the

rumble of the *Porgie*'s engines idling 240 feet above. He had no idea of how the *Sebago* could be located now that the cable was broken. The situation had looked bad before but now it was much worse. He wondered why the cable had broken.

"All right, everybody," he said, making his voice stronger. "Let's just sit tight and wait for them to come down and get us."

They all sat down and wrapped themselves in their blankets. In the dimness Jack reached into his back pocket and took out his wallet. Opening it, he looked at the picture of Betsy Kirkland. For the first time he felt certain that he'd never see her again. He believed that he and the others were doomed now, but he couldn't show it. He'd have to maintain discipline until the bitter end. They'll die like Navy men, not like dogs.

"Who's the girl?" Keller asked, looking over his shoulder.

"My fiancée," Jack replied, wondering why he'd never introduced her to his chief boatswain's mate. Who was more important to him than his chief?

Keller squinted his eyes at the photograph. "She's a real knockout. Isn't she the girl in the picture in your stateroom?"

"Yes, the same."

"I thought so. Well, I guess you'll be seeing her real soon, sir, because the *Porgie* is right up there and help is on the way."

Jack smiled, realizing that Keller was trying to raise the spirits of the crew. "You're right, Chief. I can hardly wait."

But in his heart Jack was sure that he'd never see Betsy again.

THIRTY

There was a knock on Admiral Mackie's door.

"Come in."

Lieutenant Simpson rushed into the office, a communications sheet in his hand. "Sir, we've just received a message from the *Porgie*! They've found the *Sebago*!"

Admiral Mackie stood up. "Where is it?"

"I think you'd better read the message, sir."

Admiral Mackie accepted the message and read it. Slowly he sat down. "Return to the communications section, Lieutenant, and notify me of any additional messages from the *Porgie*."

"Yes, sir!"

Simpson left the office, and Admiral Mackie stared at the message. So the *Sebago* really was down. Twenty-six men and one officer dead. And worst of all, the messenger buoy cable broken. Admiral Mackie reached for the button on his phone, but before he could press it his telephone rang. He picked up the receiver. "Yes?"

"Sir," said his clerk, Yeoman Richardson, "a woman is here to see you. She said that Commodore McCrary told her to come to your office. Her name's Betsy Kirkland and she's the fiancée of Lieutenant Jack Mc-Crary."

"Send her in and connect me immediately with Captain Robertson."

"Yes, sir!"

Admiral Mackie stood behind his desk, the phone pressed to his ear, as the door opened and a young brunette entered. She wore a brown wool suit, carried a shoulder bag, and Admiral Mackie thought her quite pretty. She held out her hand as she approached the desk, and Admiral Mackie gave it the little shake that men do when they shake hands with women.

"I'll be with you in just a second, Miss Kirkland," he said. "Have a seat."

She smiled and sat on one of the chairs. Captain Robertson's voice came through Admiral Mackie's telephone. "Yes, sir?"

"Report to my office immediately."

"Yes, sir!"

Admiral Mackie hung up his telephone and sat in his chair. He tapped his fingers on the desk and looked at Betsy Kirkland. "I imagine that Commodore Mc-Crary has informed you of the accident concerning the *Sebago.*"

"Yes," she replied. "And he told me to meet him in your office."

"I see. Well, he's not here yet, but I expect him shortly." Admiral Mackie softened his voice. "I'm afraid I have bad news."

Betsy leaned forward in her chair and said almost hysterically, "What is it?"

"The *Sebago* has been found. She's sunk somehow—we don't know how for sure—and twenty-seven of her crew are presumed to be dead. However, your fiancé still is alive, I'm happy to say."

Betsy didn't know whether to smile or cry. Admiral Mackie didn't know what to say to her. Usually when people in his command had died or were in danger, he'd merely sent letters to their next of kin. This was the first time he'd told somebody face to face.

The door of the office opened and Captain Robertson entered. "Yes, sir?"

Admiral Mackie handed him the message Simpson had given him. "Read this." Admiral Mackie turned to Betsy. "I'm sorry, Miss Kirkland, but I have important matters to attend to. You may stay in this office if you like, and wait for Commodore McCrary."

"Thank you very much, Admiral Mackie," she said.

Admiral Mackie introduced her to Captain Robertson. She and Robertson shook hands; it was clear that Robertson's mind wasn't on the introduction.

"I'm sorry to hear of what's happened to Jack," said Robertson.

"Thank you," she replied.

Robertson turned to Admiral Mackie. "Well, the situation could be worse," he said somberly. "What do you propose to do?"

"We'll have to drag for her," Admiral Mackie said. "Get the *Tioga* fired up. When it's ready to go, let me know. I'm going out there to direct the salvage operations, and you are too."

"Yes, sir."

Robertson turned and left the office. Admiral Mackie sat at his desk. He was about to say something to Betsy when his phone rang again. He picked it up.

"Sir," said Richardson, "Commander William Mulford of the British Navy is here to see you."

Admiral Mackie grimaced; he'd forgotten about Mulford. A few days ago he'd received a letter from Admiral Hill stating that Mulford, a staff officer in the British Navy, was to be given the red carpet treatment when he visited New London.

"Send him in."

"Yes, sir."

The door opened and Commander Mulford strode

in, tall and handsome in his uniform. He approached
the desk, his hat in his left hand, and saluted Admiral
Mackie.

"I'm Commander Mulford, sir," he said in his upper-
class British accent. "I believe Admiral Hill mentioned
me to you."

Admiral Mackie saluted back, then shook Mulford's
hand. "Yes, he has, but I'm afraid you've arrived at a
very bad time. We've just received word that one of
our submarines, the *Sebago,* is down."

"Oh, I'm so sorry to hear that."

"Please make yourself comfortable and bear with
me. I have a great many things to do. Unfortunately,
I can't turn you over to my operations officer, because
he's all tied up too. By the way, Commander Mulford,
this is Betsy Kirkland."

Mulford shook Betsy's hand and sat beside her. He
could see that she was distressed. Admiral Mackie
picked up his telephone and called Admiral Walmsley
at the Boston Navy Yard to find out how the work
was progressing on the *Falcon.*

Mulford leaned toward Betsy. "I take it that you
know someone on the *Sebago?*"

"Yes, my fiancé is the executive officer."

"I'm so sorry. However, I'm sure everything is being
done that can be done."

"I hope that will be enough," Betsy said.

Mulford wanted to remind her that all naval officers know that death might come to them whenever
they go to sea and that the women of naval officers
must be prepared for that eventuality, but decided
this was not the time to say those things. "All we can
do is pray that they'll be saved," he said.

"Yes, I suppose so. But I can't believe it. It's all so
sudden."

"When things like this happen, they always happen
suddenly."

She looked at his square solid-looking face, his

handlebar mustache and bushy eyebrows. "Are you a submarine officer, Commander Mulford?"

He smiled. "No, quite the contrary. My speciality is antisubmarine warfare."

The door to the office opened, and Commodore Mc-Crary walked in. He saw Betsy and walked toward her. She stood and they embraced.

"Are you all right, dear?" he asked, brushing her cheek with his lips.

"Yes," she replied. "You?"

"So far so good."

"How about Martha?"

"I haven't told her yet, nor Helen. I didn't want to say anything to either of them until we knew for sure what had happened."

Betsy took a step backwards. "Well, they know for sure now," she said. "The *Sebago* is down."

"Down where?"

"I don't know. You'll have to ask Admiral Mackie."

Ray McCrary looked at Admiral Mackie, who was engrossed with his telephone conversation. Then he noticed Commander Mulford, who stood up and held out his hand.

"Permit me to introduce myself," Mulford said. "I'm Commander William Mulford of the British Navy. I've just arrived, and it appears that it couldn't have been at a worse time."

"I'm Commodore Raymond McCrary."

They shook hands.

"I take it you're related to the Lieutenant McCrary on the *Sebago*."

Ray McCrary lowered his eyes. "He's my son."

"I'm so sorry to hear that, sir."

"Well, I suppose somebody's son had to be executive officer on the boat, and it happened to be mine. There are many other sons down there too."

Mulford felt ill at ease and moved from one foot to the other. "Yes, of course."

Admiral Mackie completed his conversation with Admiral Walmsley at the Boston Navy Yard and hung up his telephone. He got up and shook Ray McCrary's hand. "So good to see you again, Ray," he said. "I'm sorry it has to be under these circumstances."

"So am I," Ray McCrary replied. "Betsy here told me that the *Sebago* is definitely down."

"I'm afraid that's so."

"Does anyone know why?"

"Not yet. We understand that the after engine compartments flooded as soon as it dived. Your son indicated that the main induction valves malfunctioned, but we won't know for sure until she's raised."

"I take it you've located it?"

"Yes. The *Porgie* found its marker buoy, and the C.O., Commander Ellington, spoke briefly with your son, but then an accident took place and the cable of the buoy broke."

Ray McCrary closed his eyes. "My God."

"The *Porgie* is still at the site of the marker buoy. I'm leaving in a few minutes on the *Tioga* to look for it."

"Could I come too?"

"I don't think that'd be a good idea, Ray. The *Tioga*'s only a tug, and there won't be a hell of a lot of room. I think you'd be better off here. And now, if you'll excuse me, I have to make some more calls."

"I need to make some calls myself," Ray McCrary said. "Is there a phone I can use here?"

"My executive officer is in St. Louis on furlough. His office is next door. Make yourself at home in it."

"Thank you, sir."

Ray McCrary strode toward the door.

"Ray?" Admiral Mackie said.

Ray McCrary stopped and turned around.

"We'll get it up somehow," Admiral Mackie said.

"I know you'll do your best, Admiral."

Ray McCrary left the office, and Admiral Mackie

picked up the phone, asking the clerk to connect him with Admiral Hill in Washington. While the connection was being made, Admiral Mackie looked up at Mulford and Betsy. "Make yourself comfortable, you two. If you're hungry, there's a mess hall on the first floor of this building."

"I'll be all right here," said Betsy.

"Admiral, could I come out on the *Tioga?*" Mulford asked. "I have experience in detecting submarines, and perhaps I could be of assistance."

Admiral Mackie thought for a few moments. "Yes, maybe we can make use of you, Mulford."

Several seconds later Admiral "Hardtop" Hill came on the phone. Admiral Mackie told him that the *Porgie* had found the *Sebago's* marker buoy, and described the events that followed. He said that Admiral Walmsley in Boston had promised to get the *Falcon* underway to join the *Porgie* within ninety minutes. Lieutenant Commander Mount and his rescue crew were loading their gear aboard the *Falcon* already.

"Do you know what went wrong aboard the *Sebago?*" Hill asked.

"We think the main induction valves might have failed, sir."

"What the hell are main induction valves?"

"They bring air to the diesels for surface running and charging, sir. The *Sebago* reported trouble with her main induction valves in the past."

Admiral Hill was silent for a few seconds. Then he said angrily, "If the damned little pigboats sink during training exercises off Block Island, what the hell are they going to do in the middle of the Atlantic?"

"All boats and ships develop problems from time to time, sir," Admiral Mackie replied.

"But none so serious or as frequently as submarines," Admiral Hill shot back. "In my opinion, there have been too many damned submarine accidents in the United States Navy, and in view of their limited effectiveness anyway, I think it's time we took a closer look at our submarine program."

Admiral Mackie decided this wasn't the time to argue the merits of submarines with Admiral Hill. "Yes, sir," he said.

"How are you handling this?"

"I'm going out on the *Tioga* and drag for the *Sebago*."

"What the hell's the *Tioga?*"

"It's a tugboat, sir."

"When're you leaving?"

"Five or ten more minutes."

"Who are you going to leave in charge?"

"The only person I have available is my training officer, Commodore Briscoe."

"I take it that you haven't notified the press yet?"

"Not yet."

"You might as well do it now. Have your information officer send out a brief press announcement stating only the bare facts. He'll be swamped with reporters, and he'd better handle them well. You'll be held responsible if he doesn't."

"My public information officer knows how to handle the press."

At the sound of the word *press* Betsy Kirkland's ears perked up. Until now she'd been thinking only of Jack, but now she realized for the first time that she was sitting in the middle of the biggest news story since the *Titanic*. Her brain began to hum with possibilities. If she could do a little reporting, it might help prevent her from becoming too depressed over Jack. It also might help her land the kind of newspaper job she wanted.

Admiral Mackie finished his conversation with Admiral Hill and hung up his phone. He ran his finger over his white mustache, thinking that the disaster was going to make serious problems for the submarine service. He decided that before he left on the *Tioga* he'd better notify other submarine commanders to prepare for an onslaught of criticism from the anti-submarine people in and outside of the Navy.

"Admiral Mackie—may I ask you a few questions?" Betsy asked.

"Of course, my dear."

"Could you tell me exactly what time the *Sebago* went down?"

"Exactly what time?" He looked at the radio messages stacked on his desk. "Here—look at these. Everything I know is there, basically."

Admiral Mackie handed her the messages, not realizing that she was a reporter. She looked through them as Admiral Mackie lifted his phone again and called Commodore Briscoe. So absorbed was he with the *Sebago* situation, he didn't pay any attention to Betsy when she took out her notepad and began writing.

Sitting next to her, Commander Mulford stared out the window wondering what he could do to help locate the boat. He knew how to depth-charge an enemy submarine, but it had never occurred to him that someday he might have to locate a friendly one that had sunk.

THIRTY-ONE

Helen McCrary sat in her English lit class, listening to her professor, a wispy old woman, discuss Jane Austen and her great novel *Pride and Prejudice*.

"And so we see," the professor said, "that Jane Austen was perhaps the finest novelist of her day. She also was an accurate social reporter, for through her we perceive what it was like to be a young woman living in provincial England during the latter part of the eighteenth century. Moreover . . ."

Helen listened to her professor but really wasn't hearing what she said. This particular professor bored her to death, and Helen's mind drifted off into memories and fantasies. Helen didn't have a disciplined mind and couldn't make it do what it didn't want to do.

She found herself thinking of last night and the sailor she'd picked up in the bus station. She realized that she'd liked him better than most of the sailors that she picked up, perhaps because he was much older than she and more sure of himself than young sailors. He'd just calmly lain there and smoked a Lucky Strike while she sucked him; that had never happened to her before. Maybe she'd call him in a few days when she felt frisky. It'd be fun to see him again.

She looked around and wondered what her classmates would think if they knew about her private life. She imagined they'd be shocked. She had first let herself be seduced by a sailor when she was fifteen, and it had begun a whole new world for her. Since then she couldn't get enough sex. It took her mind off the boring life that she lived ordinarily. Sailors always carried rubbers in their wallets, so she didn't have to worry about getting pregnant. She only let them take their rubbers off when she sucked them, and a girl couldn't get pregnant that way.

Sometimes she wondered why she only was attracted to sailors. She'd taken a psychology course last term and figured it probably had something to do with her father and brothers. She'd decided not to worry about it. Her mother worried about everything, and all it ever got her were nervous breakdowns and weekly visits to her psychiatrist.

"Of course," the professor was saying, "Jane Austen was the daughter of a country vicar, so naturally she knew quite a bit about life in the English provinces. But who could have guessed that such a young woman, who led such a sheltered life, who had never traveled on the continent, could write such wonderful . . ."

Suddenly the door of the classroom opened. Miss Hawkes, the assistant dean, entered the room. "Excuse me," she said in the middle of Professor Stone's sentence.

Professor Stone stopped speaking, aghast at being interrupted.

"I'm sorry to disturb the class," Miss Hawkes said, "but I'm afraid I must ask Helen McCrary to come with me."

Helen blinked, not certain that she'd just heard her own name. "Me?" she asked dumbly.

"Yes."

Helen stood and picked up her notebook. She wore a checked skirt, white blouse, gray sweater draped over her shoulders, and bobby socks. She wondered what sort of emergency had taken place and decided something must have happened to her mother.

She followed Miss Hawkes out of the classroom and into the corridor.

"What's happened?" Helen asked.

"Your father is on the phone from Washington. He has something important to tell you."

Miss Hawkes led Helen down the corridor and two flights of stairs to the first floor of the building, where they exited, crossed the quad, and entered the administration building. In Miss Hawkes's small wood-paneled office on the first floor the phone was off its hook. She handed it to Helen, then left the office and closed the door.

Helen sat on a chair in front of the desk. "Hello, Daddy," she said.

"Helen?" asked her father.

"Yes."

"Something terrible has happened." Ray McCrary's voice was low and mechanical. "You'd better sit down if you're not already."

"I am, Dad," Helen said anxiously. "Is it Mom?"

"No. It's Jack and Ed. The *Sebago* has gone down, but Jack and Ed are all right." Ray McCrary didn't know that Ed was all right, but he assumed it. It would be unbearable for him to think that he was not.

An icy hand grabbed Helen's heart. "The *Sebago* has gone down?" she asked weakly.

"Yes. In Block Island Sound."

"You mean she's sunk?"

"Yes. I thought I'd better tell you before you read it in a newspaper."

"Are they going to be saved?"

"We hope so. Rescue ships are on the way right now. Another submarine is already there."

"Which one?"

"The *Porgie*."

Helen closed her eyes She'd once slept with Lieutenant McNally of the *Porgie*. She began to cry. "Oh Dad, if something happens to them I don't know what I'll do."

"We have to hope for the best, Helen."

"Have you told Mom?"

"Yes. I called her before I called you."

"How'd she take it?"

"She fainted. Wilma put her to bed." Wilma was their black maid. "Do you think you'd like to go to Washington and be with your mother?"

"Aren't you there?"

"No, I'm in New London. I caught a hop here earlier in the day. Betsy Kirkland is here too."

"I'd like to come to New London, Dad," Helen said. "I can take the train and be there in two hours."

"I'd rather you stayed with your mother. She needs somebody with her right now."

Helen panicked at the thought of being with her mother. "She's not alone—Wilma is with her. I'd rather be in New London with you. I want to be close to Jack and Ed."

Ray McCrary sighed. "If that's what you want, I suppose it's all right."

"I'll leave right now and see you in a little while."

"When you arrive at the gate, tell them who you are and say that you're supposed to go to Admiral Mackie's office. That's probably where I'll be."

"All right, Dad."

Helen hung up the phone and daubed at her eyes with a handkerchief. She felt disoriented. It seemed inconceivable that both her brothers could be trapped on a sunken submarine.

Holding the handkerchief in her hand, she rose from the chair and opened the office door. Miss

Hawkes was standing in the corridor, looking through a notebook. She glanced up at Helen.

"I hope everything's all right," she said, with a nervous smile.

"I have to go away for a few days," Helen replied, her voice sounding odd. "Something has happened to my brothers."

His face was ashen . . . The author rose to her chair
on . . . pale. She'd seen it at Home . . .
. . . hope Adventure . . . of . . . the . . . her . . . he . . . voice with . . .

I tried to look upon . . . my . . . through . . .
my voice . . . but . . . is . . . would . . . me . . . be . . . it . . .
. . . everybody . . .

THIRTY-TWO

Abe Rabinowitz sat in his office on the third floor of the *New York Standard* building near Herald Square. He was the national news editor for the paper, a stout man with thinning hair who had a button nose and wore eyeglasses. The phone on his desk jangled, and he ignored it as he edited a news story about the coal strikes in Harlan County, Kentucky. Finally, on the fifth ring, he lifted the receiver.

"Yeah?" he asked, cradling the phone with his shoulder as he continued editing the story.

"Abe Rabinowitz?" asked a female voice that sounded far away.

"That's me," he grumbled.

"This is Betsy Kirkland," said the voice. "Do you know who I am?"

"You work on the society desk, don't you?"

"I quit the society desk, and now I've got a red-hot story for you, Abe."

He wrinkled his nose. "Hold on . . . back up a little. Did you say you quit?"

"Yes. This morning," she said.

"Then what are you calling me for?"

"I've got a story for you."

"Listen, kid," Rabinowitz said roughly, "if you quit—down there, I sure can't use any of your stories up here."

"What if I was just about to give you a scoop on the hottest news story of the past twenty-seven years?"

"What the hell are you talking about?" Rabinowitz asked, his curiosity piqued.

"I'm telling you that I'm sitting right in the middle of the hottest news story of the past twenty-seven years, and I'm the only reporter in sight. I'll give you the story right now on the phone, and you'll beat every other newspaper and wire service in the world to the stands with it, but first you've got to promise me a job on the national desk of the *New York Standard*."

"You think the story's that good?" Rabinowitz asked.

"I know it is, and if you don't want it, I know the *Herald* will."

"What's the story?" Rabinowitz asked.

"Have I got your word?"

"I give you my word as a gentleman that if this story is as hot as you say it is, and if we stop the presses and put it on the front page, you'll be a staff reporter on the national desk from now on."

"And I want a byline."

"You got it, if the story's what you say it is. Now will you tell me?"

"Do you have your pencil and pad ready?"

"I sure have."

"Here's your headline," Betsy said. "Submarine sinks in Block Island Sound. Got that? Your subhead will be: Twenty-four men and five officers still alive."

Rabinowitz was sniffing like a rabbit. "How did you come by this information?"

"I'm sitting outside the commandant's office at the New London submarine base right now."

"What are you doing there?"

"My fiancé is the executive officer on the boat that went down."

"No other reporters are there yet?"

"No, but they're going to make the announcement at a news conference here in about an hour. If you stop asking questions, you'll be able to have the story on the streets by then."

"Is it still down?"

"Yes."

"How are they going to get the men out?"

"Let me tell you the story, and you'll find out how."

Rabinowitz's eyes glittered as he touched the tip of his pencil to his tongue. "I'm listening," he said.

THIRTY-THREE

Ben Mount stood on the aft end of the rescue ship *Falcon* and watched a derrick lower his rescue chamber onto the deck. He wore a tan duty uniform with regulation brown leather jacket, and beside him was Ensign Tolliver, Boatswain's Mate Tom Hodges, and four other enlisted members of Ben's rescue group.

Slowly the rescue chamber closed the distance between it and the deck. Across the harbor the skyline of Boston could be seen. The cloudy sky still threatened rain, and the wind was brisk. The force of the wind caused the rescue chamber to sway on its cable.

A dozen sailors from the *Falcon*'s crew stood on the stern, ready to guide the bell-shaped chamber down and tie it to the deck. They were commanded by one of the ship's officers and one of the boatswain's mates. Ben had wanted to guide the chamber down with the help of his crew, but the captain of the *Falcon* had told him icily that he'd handle all matters pertaining to the conduct of his ship's business and that Ben's only function would be to direct the operation of the rescue chamber when the ship was at the site.

Ben shuffled from side to side on the deck, clenching and unclenching his fists as the heavy steel unit came down. He was worried that the *Falcon*'s crew might damage it in some way. It had many delicate fittings and instruments, and glass windows all around it.

The rescue chamber touched down on the deck, and the deck crew lashed it to cleats. Ben stepped forward to inspect it and make sure no damage had been done. He touched it gently, as though it were a baby, looking at thru-hull fittings and the hatches. It was marvelous to design something on paper and then see it huge and palpable like this.

"How does it look to you, sir?" asked Hodges, who was checking it out with him.

"I think it's fine," Ben replied.

They heard footsteps behind them and turned around. The skipper of the *Falcon*, Captain Dennis Healey, approached with two of his younger officers. Healey had a black mustache and piercing green eyes.

"We've just received word," Healey said to Ben, "that the *Porgie* has found the *Sebago*."

Ben experienced a curious mixed emotion at hearing this. He was glad that the boat had been found but was afraid he'd no longer have a part to play in rescuing her. "Is she all right?" he asked.

"No," Healey replied. "She's stuck in two hundred and forty feet of water. Half her crew has been drowned in the after compartments. They believe her main induction valves failed."

In Ben's mind, the world went out of whack for a few seconds. He took a few deep breaths to come back. He'd designed the main induction valves for the *Sebago* and was chagrined to learn that they might have been the cause of the sinking. What he'd feared the most had happened.

"Does anybody know how they failed?" he asked, trying to keep his voice calm.

"No. The cable between the marker buoy and the *Sebago* snapped due to heavy seas before much information could be gotten."

"I see. When do you think we'll get underway?"

"About another half hour. By the way, Admiral Dexter is coming up from Washington to join us."

Ben nodded and kept his face expressionless as he heard this unwelcome news. Vice Admiral Rufus Dexter, the commander of the Atlantic Submarine Fleet, was reputed to be a very difficult character to deal with.

"Well," said Healey, "I've got a few things to do. I'll be on the bridge if you need me for anything."

"Thank you, sir."

Ben watched Healey walk away. Seagulls flew around the masts of the *Falcon*. Ben wondered if the *Sebago* had sunk because of a mistake he'd made in the design of the main induction valves. He wracked his brain to remember its details and specifications. He longed to return to his office and look at the original blueprints.

Hodges sidled up to him. He was wearing denims, a tan battle jacket, and a white cap low over his eyes. "Did I hear the skipper say that Admiral Dexter was coming aboard, sir?"

Ben looked at him. "Yes, and that means you'd better be on your toes."

"Aw, fuck," said Hodges.

"And you'd better not talk like that when the admiral is around."

"Yes, sir, but in my experience high-ranking brass mess things up more than they help them."

Ben looked at him sternly. "Admiral Dexter got where he is today because he knows what he's doing. I don't want you talking like that around me anymore, and certainly not around the younger men, who look to you for leadership. You're not supposed to undermine their faith in their officers—is that clear?"

"Yes, sir."

"Come with me. I want to inspect the inside of the bell to make sure nothing's been damaged in there."

"Yes, sir."

The wind plastered Ben's pants against his legs as he climbed the steel rungs welded to a side of the chamber. A few members of the *Falcon*'s crew watched as he undogged the hatch and lowered himself into the upper compartment. Hodges followed Ben inside and made sure he left the hatch open. He knew Ben would become claustrophobic if he didn't.

The upper compartment was like the inside of a tiny submarine—knobs, switches, levers, and dials everywhere. A hatch separated it from the lower compartment. In an emergency, the rescue chamber would be lowered into the water by a derrick on the fantail of the rescue ship. A crew of two would sit in the upper compartment, and the hatch to the lower compartment would be closed. It would be guided down by a cable previously affixed by a diver to the forward hatch of the submarine. The lower compartment would be open at the bottom, like an inverted teacup. When the chamber touched down on the submarine, one of the crew members would open the hatch to the lower compartment, get into it, and fasten the chamber to fittings on the forward hatch of the submarine. Excess water would be blown out of the lower chamber by air pressure, and then the submarine's hatch would be opened. The sailors in the submarine would transfer to the lower compartment of the rescue chamber. Next, they'd climb to the upper compartment, and the hatch separating both compartments would be closed. Then the chamber would be raised to the ship, the men unloaded, and another descent to the submarine begun.

Ben inspected the fittings and devices inside the rescue chamber, and Hodges followed him around, double-checking. Ben wanted to make certain that nothing would fail in the chamber. Perhaps some sailors had already died due to his negligence, and he didn't want more names added to the list.

Hodges had different reasons for making certain that the rescue chamber was in perfect working order. He'd been trained to ride in the upper compartment.

THIRTY-FOUR

A 1935 La Salle approached the front gate of the submarine base in New London. A marine guard came out of the sentry box and approached it as it came to a stop. As the driver rolled down his window, the marine saw that he was an Oriental wearing a brown suit and homburg, holding out a card.

"Hello," said the Oriental with a smile.

"What can I do for you, sir?" asked the marine.

The Oriental wiggled the card in his fingers. "I am reporter for the *Ogaki Sanjo*. I am here for the press conference. My name is Akiro Ito."

The marine took the card and looked at it. Other reporters had passed by his gate during the past half hour, but this was the first Jap. His press card appeared to be in order. The marine thought he'd better call the officer of the guard and report that a Jap reporter was on the base.

"Everything okay?" asked Ito in his Japanese accent.

"Yes, sir." The marine told him how to get to the administration building.

The marine opened the gate, and Ito drove his La

Salle onto the base. The marine returned to his sentry box and called the officer of the guard.

Ito drove slowly over the winding roads of the submarine base. There were beautifully landscaped lawns on both sides of the road, and he could see rows of neat yellow barracks buildings. Looking toward the waterfront, he saw large industrial buildings where he presumed submarine engines were overhauled and other equipment was serviced.

Ito thought it an incredible stroke of luck that he was permitted on America's foremost submarine base, and he imagined that something extraordinary must have happened. After taking photographs of the *Sebago* that morning, he'd returned to his hotel for lunch and a reading of the morning's newspapers. While sitting in the dining room of the hotel, he was paged to the front desk in the lobby, where he was told that his newspaper's New York office was calling him. He got on the phone and was told by his editor that an important press conference was being held at the New London submarine base at 3:30 in the afternoon.

Ito's face was expressionless, but he smiled inwardly at the thought that he, an undercover Japanese naval intelligence officer, had been admitted so easily into America's most important submarine base. *What fools these Americans are,* he thought. Although America was a large country with many resources, surely it was not clever enough to win a war against Japan. Everything he'd seen in America had convinced him of that. Americans were fat and lazy, they thought only of pleasure, they had no willpower and therefore lacked the ability to be good soldiers and sailors. Japan was becoming stronger every day while America was just sitting and eating. The world would be in for a big surprise if Japan and America ever went to war.

Ito made his way to the administration building. He hadn't paid much attention to the directions the marine had given him, because he'd flown over the submarine base numerous times in a private plane and taken aerial photographs. He probably knew where everything was beter than the marine. He also had photographed the naval installations in Maine, Rhode Island, Massachusetts, and Virginia. Through a network of spies he was kept apprised of developments in American warships. On one of his return trips to Japan he'd been awarded a special medal from Admiral Yamamoto.

He drove his La Salle into the parking lot across the street from the administration building. Taking his briefcase with him, but leaving his camera hidden under the seat, he got out of the car and walked toward the front steps of the building. He climbed the steps and entered the lobby, where a sailor was sitting at a desk.

"May I help you, sir?" the sailor asked, looking suspiciously at Ito.

"I am here for press conference," Ito replied, showing his card.

The sailor looked at the card, then told Ito how to get to the room where the press conference was being held. Following his directions, Ito walked down the corridor and opened a door on which was hanging a cardboard sign freshly stenciled PRESS CONFERENCE.

A dozen reporters were already in the room. Ito smiled and nodded to them as he carried his homburg and briefcase to a seat at the rear. Sitting with his homburg in his lap, he took a notebook out of his briefcase and placed it on the enlarged flat right arm of the chair. He lifted his fountain pen from his shirt pocket and waited calmly for the press conference to begin.

THIRTY-FIVE

In the control room of the *Sebago*, Boatswain's Mate
Second Class Alfred Araujo sat beneath his hydroplane wheel and tried to keep himself from becoming
hysterical. The air stank and he thought he was suffocating. His heartbeat had slowed down and was
irregular. He was monitoring it carefully, the palm
of his hand under his shirt and pressing against it.
The others were lying in the dimness like corpses.
Araujo felt dizzy and everything seemed weird. He
was considered a brave man and had been a Golden
Gloves champion before joining the Navy, but the
uncertainty of his present situation was pushing him
over the edge.

His eyes were smarting, and he rubbed them with
the tips of his fingers. Far above, he could hear the
submarine going round and round, back and forth.
It had been doing that for almost two hours now.
Occasionally Keller had shot up a smoke rocket.
Araujo wondered how much longer it would be before they were rescued.

He opened his eyes and looked at the ballast controls. There seemed to be a figure hovering there,
looking down at him. Araujo gasped as he recognized

Torpedoman First Class Frankie Duarte, a Portuguese-American like himself, also from New Bedford. Duarte had been stationed in the aft torpedo room when the engine compartments had flooded. What the hell was he doing here?

"How'd you get out here, Frankie?" Araujo asked.

Frankie didn't answer. He looked coldly at Araujo and pointed his finger at him. Araujo realized he was seeing Frankie Duarte's ghost. Araujo had once screwed Frankie's wife.

"Hey—I couldn't help it!" Araujo said, raising his voice and standing. "It was just one of them things, Frankie! You know how it is!"

"Get him," whispered Jack McCrary.

Jack, Lieutenant Stearns, and Keller jumped on Araujo and pinned him against the bulkhead.

"It's okay, Araujo," Jack said soothingly. "Everything's all right."

Araujo stared at the ghost of Frankie Duarte, his whole body trembling.

"What's wrong?" Jack asked.

"It's Frankie," Araujo mumbled.

"Frankie who?"

"Frankie Duarte from the aft torpedo room. He's right over there in front of the ballast controls."

Jack looked over there. "I don't see anything."

"Neither do I," added Stearns.

"Me neither," said Keller.

Donahue stood in front of the ballast controls. "There's nothin' over here, Al."

The specter began to fade. Araujo blinked his eyes and it was gone.

"Maybe I was seeing things," Araujo said, trying to smile. His nose had been broken in one of his amateur fights and his dark complexion was smooth as satin.

"Why don't you sit down?" Jack said.

"Yes, sir. Sorry."

"That's all right, Araujo."

Pharmacist's Mate Vincent La Gloria came forward with his little black bag. He took out a bottle, unscrewed the cap, and rolled out two yellow pills. "Take these," he said to Araujo. "They'll calm you down."

"Naw," said Araujo. "I'm all right now."

"Take them," ordered Jack.

"Yes, sir."

Araujo popped the pills, and La Gloria handed him a cup of water. As Araujo was drinking it, he heard a new sound above him. Everybody looked up.

"There's another ship up there," Stearns said.

Jack listened to the deep burble of new engines joining the high-pitched whine of the *Porgie*. "Sounds like a tug," he said.

"It's a tug all right," Keller agreed.

Jack turned to the others and smiled. "Cheer up, boys. They're gonna start getting us out of here now."

THIRTY-SIX

"Ship off the stern, sir," said Lieutenant McNally on the bridge of the *Porgie*.

Lieutenant Commander Ellington turned around and fixed his binoculars on the horizon off the stern. "I see her," he said. "Ask who she is."

McNally operated the blinker, and a few seconds later a light flashed on the horizon.

"The *Tioga*," Ellington said, reading the flashes. "Well, whaddaya know about that."

"Sir!" shouted Lieutenant Middleton in the control room. "You're wanted on the radio!"

"Coming right down!" Ellington nudged McNally. "Keep a sharp eye out."

"Yes, sir."

Ellington went down the ladder and walked across the control room to the radio shack. Radioman Nostrand handed him the mike. Ellington pressed the button on the side.

"Lieutenant Commander Ellington of the *Porgie* here, sir," he said.

"This is Admiral Mackie," said the voice on the loudspeaker. "I'm on the *Tioga* and we're coming with dragging gear. I understand you've got a buoy down to mark where the *Sebago* is."

"Yes, sir, but with the wind and tide we have to consider that it's moved somewhat."

"We'll drag the area until we find the *Sebago*. When we see your buoy, we'll flash you a signal. Then get out of our way. Any questions?"

"Should we stay out here, sir?"

"Did I tell you to go anywhere else?"

"No, sir."

"Any other questions?"

"No, sir."

"Over and out."

Handing the mike to Nostrand, Ellington lit a cigarette and climbed to the bridge.

"Anything going on?" he asked McNally.

"The *Tioga*'s coming."

They watched the *Tioga* chug closer and soon could see her crew running along the deck.

"All engines one third back!" Ellington yelled.

"All engines one third back!" replied Nowicki.

The *Porgie* backed up as the *Tioga* approached the buoy. The *Tioga* flashed a signal indicating that it had spotted the buoy. McNally flashed back that the *Porgie* had received the message.

"Hard right rudder!" yelled Ellington.

"Hard right rudder!"

The *Porgie*'s stern slapped against the waves as it turned and back away from the *Tioga*.

"All engines stop!"

"All engines stop!"

"Rudder amidships!"

"Rudder amidships!"

"All ahead one third."

"All ahead one third."

Waves crashed over the *Porgie*'s bow as it rumbled away from the *Tioga*. Ellington trained his binoculars on the *Tioga* and saw men on the stern operating the machine that lowered dragging gear into the water. The big hooks were attached to cable rolled around drums on the stern of the *Tioga*. A system of cranes and pulleys extended the chain five yards abaft the stern. A light on the mast of the *Tioga* began blinking.

"They want you on the radio again," McNally said to Ellington.

"Shit," mumbled Ellington as he went back down the ladder again. Dripping salt water onto the deck of the control room, he puffed his cigarette and made his way to the radio shack, where Nostrand held out the mike.

"Lieutenant Commander Ellington of the *Porgie* speaking, sir."

"Ellington, this is Admiral Mackie again," said the voice in the loudspeaker. "You have more buoys aboard, don't you?"

"Yes, sir."

"How many?"

"I don't know for sure, sir. I'd guess a dozen or so."

"Good. I want you to stake out an area for me one thousand yards square, and mark each corner with a buoy. The center of the square will be the position where we believe the *Sebago* went down. Is that clear?"

"Yes, sir."

"Any questions?"

"No, sir."

"Over and out."

Ellington handed the mike to Nostrand and trudged forward to the chart table, where he huddled with Middleton over the chart and tried to figure out where to plant the four buoys.

THIRTY-SEVEN

Ben Mount was in the rescue chamber when the whistle on the mast of the *Falcon* blew off, indicating that it was about to leave its berth. He could feel the *Falcon* tremble as it backed up, but his principal concentration was on the air motor, the innards of which he was examining with a flashlight and magnifying glass.

"How does it look, sir?" asked Ensign Tolliver, who, like Mount, was an engineering officer.

"I think it's okay," replied Ben, flicking the little wheels with the blade of a screwdriver.

In the lower compartment of the chamber Boatswain's Mate Hodges was checking the ballast tanks. He held a hose attached to a saltwater pressure outlet on the *Falcon,* and was pouring water into the ballast tanks to see if any dripped through cracks or faulty welds. So far the outsides of the tanks showed no sign of leakage.

"Lieutenant Commander Benjamin Mount to the bridge!" said a squawk box somewhere on deck. "Lieutenant Commander Benjamin Mount to the bridge!"

Ben looked up from the air motor. "I wonder what

the hell they want." He handed his magnifying glass and flashlight to Ensign Tolliver. "Continue looking over this motor, will you, Ritchie?"

"Yes, sir."

Ben picked up a rag and climbed out of the chamber. When his head cleared its top he saw the destroyer *Kendall,* which was berthed on the port side of the *Falcon,* moving forward—an optical illusion caused by the aft movement of the *Falcon.*

He climbed down the side of the rescue chamber and crossed the deck, wiping his hands on the rag. He looked up and saw figures behind the glass windows of the bridge. Seagulls flew around the masts of the *Falcon,* and the sky was thick with clouds. The air smelled like salt mixed with oil.

Ben entered a passageway in the superstructure of the ship and climbed the ladderwell that led to the bridge, wondering what was in store for him up there. He imagined they wanted to ask him about the readiness of the rescue chamber, or what support functions he'd require from the *Falcon* while the chamber was operational.

He arrived on the bridge deck and entered the *Falcon*'s control room through the hatch. The first person he saw was Vice Admiral Rufus Dexter, and Ben didn't know whether to report to him, Admiral Walmsley, or Captain Healey. He solved the problem by coming to attention and throwing a smart salute in the general direction of all of them.

"Lieutenant Commander Benjamin Mount reporting, sir," he said.

Admiral Dexter placed his arms behind his back and advanced slowly toward Ben. Dexter was big, built like a football fullback, with a meaty face, the snout of a bulldog, and big ears that stuck out. His white cap, covered with gold braid, was low over his eyes.

"So you're the wonder boy," Dexter said, looking Ben up and down.

Ben decided not to respond to the provocation and remained standing at attention.

Dexter scrutinized Ben, not bothering to conceal his disapproval. To Dexter, Ben represented all that was wrong with the Navy. Dexter's ancestors had come to America on the *Mayflower*, and he believed that he was a *real* American. He thought the Navy's officers should be drawn from the finest old families in the country, families like his, who had helped build America since its earliest days. Now the Navy was being dragged down by the sons of immigrants, by men who had no manners and no decent backgrounds, and by Jews like Mount.

Admiral Dexter looked Ben in the eyes. "Don't you consider yourself the wonder boy of the Navy?"

"No, sir," Ben replied.

"I should think not," Admiral Dexter said, "in view of the possibility that the *Sebago* probably is down because of you!"

"I've not yet been presented with any evidence, sir, that the boat is down because of me."

Admiral Dexter's eyes flashed with anger. "I've been told that the *Sebago* is down because of a failure in the main induction valves, and I understand you designed those valves and the systems that control them. Isn't that so, Mount?"

"Isn't what so, sir?" Ben asked.

Admiral Dexter's face became red. "I just asked you whether or not you designed the main induction valves on the *Sebago* and the systems that control them!"

"I did, sir."

"Then it appears that it's down because of you, or do you think we should blame somebody else?"

"I don't think we should blame anybody until all the facts are in, sir."

"If the main induction valves failed, and you designed them, what more facts do you think we need, Mount?"

Ben realized that Dexter's reason was being clouded by his animosity. "There could have been a flaw in the manufacturing process, sir, or there might have been something wrong with the metallurgy."

Admiral Dexter looked stonily at Ben. "I'm sure the inquiry will decide who or what is to blame."

"Yes, sir."

"There will be an inquiry, you know."

"Yes, sir."

"And if a naval officer is to blame, that naval officer will be court-martialed."

"Yes, sir."

Admiral Dexter glowered at Ben. "I hope your rescue chamber functions better than the *Sebago*."

Ben was aware that all eyes were on him. He had an urge to turn around and run out of the bridge. "The rescue chamber was constructed at the Boston Navy Yard by technicians working under my personal supervision, sir. It hasn't been tested extensively yet, but I think I can vouch for it."

Admiral Dexter smiled. "I imagine you would have vouched for the main induction valves you designed, too."

"No, sir, because they weren't constructed and installed under my personal supervision."

"You've got an answer for everything, haven't you, Mount?"

"Not everything sir—just the projects on which I've worked."

The muscles in Admiral Dexter's jaw quivered. He hated Ben more than ever now that Ben had stood up to him and had given reasonable answers to his questions.

"Return to your duty station, Mount, and bear in

mind that I'll be keeping my eyes on you throughout this operation."

"I'll do my best not to let you down, sir," Ben said.

He saluted smartly, did an about face, and marched out of the *Falcon*'s bridge.

Admiral Dexter watched him go, then turned and walked toward Rear Admiral Walmsley and the other officers who had been behind him.

"I don't like him," Dexter said, shaking his head.

Admiral Walmsley was frowning. He didn't approve of the way Dexter had spoken, and although he was junior in rank to Dexter, he thought he'd let him know.

"I've always found him to be a very capable young officer," Walmsley said.

Dexter raised his eyebrows. "Oh?"

"He's very intelligent and very organized."

"I imagine you're one of those who's responsible for the reputation he has as a wonder boy."

"As I said, he's very intelligent and capable," Walmsley insisted. "I think the Navy could use more officers like him."

"The inquiry will decide how intelligent and capable he is," Admiral Dexter replied.

THIRTY-EIGHT

Hank Burns lay shivering on his bunk in the forward torpedo room, listening to the sound of engines roving back and forth overhead. He'd figured it was a tugboat dragging the bottom for the *Sebago*. Burns didn't feel optimistic about the operation, because the irons could roll right over the hull and not grip onto anything. They might not even get close.

The air was disgusting and he felt nauseated. He thought Lieutenant McCrary should let them try to make it to the surface with their Momsen lungs. At least that would be a chance. He felt they had no chance if they remained on the boat. The oxygen couldn't last much longer, and they'd all die.

He heard a shuffling and rustling in the bunk beneath him. Torpedoman Guido Paroni crawled out and made his way across the torpedos to the head on the other side of the compartment. Burns saw Paroni open the door to the head, freeze, and yell "Hey!"

Burns leaped off his cot. "What is it?"

"The head's flooding!"

Burns climbed over the torpedoes and looked at the bowl. In the dim light he could see water and turds burbling out of it and pouring onto the floor. No one had noticed before because the air stank anyway, and the water had run underneath the torpedoes and dripped through cracks in the floor plates into the bilge.

The crew in the torpedo compartment huddled around and looked at the water pouring out. Burns tried to figure out what to do. He decided that a leak in the bilges had somehow worked its way into the sanitary tank.

He turned to Paroni. "Get a big piece of sheet metal."

"Right."

Paroni ran back to the torpedo workshop area and selected a piece of sheet aluminum a quarter of an inch thick and two feet square. He carried it to Burns, who kicked up the seat on the commode and placed the sheet metal on the opening.

"Stand on it," Burns said to Paroni.

"But I gotta take a piss."

"We'll get you a bucket."

Paroni stood on the sheet metal, and Burns crouched to see if it had stopped the leak. It was awfully dark down there."

"Get me a flashlight," he said.

One of the sailors ran off and came back with a flashlight, which he handed to Burns. Burns flicked it on and illuminated the commode. Water was leaking down the sides, but not as badly as before.

"Somebody get Paroni a bucket to piss in," Burns said as he walked to the intercom.

One of the sailors picked up a bucket from underneath a torpedo tube, and Paroni began unbuttoning his pants. Burns leaned toward the intercom.

"Forward torpedo compartment calling the captain," he said.

Burns waited several seconds and was beginning to wonder if something had happened to the people in the control room when Jack McCrary's low fatigued voice came through the squawk box.

"This is the captain speaking."

"This is Burns, sir. We've got another leak up here. This one's coming from the head."

"Do you mean the pipes in the head or the commode itself?"

"The commode, sir. Water and shit are just pouring out of it."

"I'll be right there."

Burns returned the mike to its hook and walked back to the commode. Paroni was pissing into a bucket that Tucker was holding for him.

"All right, you guys," Burns said, "let's move these torpedoes away from the head."

The sailors pitched in and began lifting away torpedoes. Burns's plan was to take up the floor plates in front of the head so that the water and shit could pour straight down into the bilge instead of running over the deck. The smell was horrible. *Jesus Christ, what a mess,* he thought. "Some of you guys get rags and clean this shit up!" he said.

The hatch was opened and Jack McCrary came through, followed by Keller. Burns thought McCrary looked a little green around the gills, as did Keller. He imagined that he probably looked the same way to them.

McCrary and Keller advanced to the head and took a look at Paroni standing on top of the sheet metal.

"If one man can hold it down," Jack said, "the leak can't be too bad."

"It could always get worse, sir," Burns said.

Keller nodded. "It could blow Paroni right into the air if it got worse all of a sudden."

McCrary looked at Burns. "You'll have to stop it up with a wood plug."

"That's what I was thinking, sir."

"Get a big piece and jam it right in there."

"Yes, sir."

"If it blows, evacuate the compartment immediately and bring your men aft to the control room."

"Yes, sir."

Jack and Keller put on their Momsen lungs and left the forward torpedo compartment. They made their way through the thick yellow gas in the officers' wardroom and passed the bunks where the bodies of Seaman Olds and Commander Dunlop had been laid. Jack thought that the leak situation in the forward torpedo compartment was deteriorating and that new problems could be expected as cracks widened and salt water worked itself into more places. The danger was that the escape hatch was in the forward torpedo room; if the room became flooded, they'd have to try to get out through the conning tower. But there were no fittings on conning towers for diving bells. That meant that if the forward torpedo compartment became flooded their chances for rescue would be greatly reduced. Jack told himself he'd have to make periodic checks of the forward torpedo compartment.

He stepped through the hatch into the control room; the men and officers huddling on the floor looked up at him. He knew they were cold and that the strain of the situation was wearing them down just as it was him. From above, he could hear the tugboat plying back and forth. He wondered if it ever would make contact with the *Sebago*.

"Send up another smoke rocket, will you, Keller?"

"Yes, sir."

THIRTY-NINE

In the bridge house of the *Tioga* Admiral Mackie saw the rocket explode red smoke into the sky.

"Damn," he said. "We've already dragged over there."

"Should I head that way again, sir?" asked Lieutenant Commander Nolan, the skipper of the *Tioga*.

"Yes, and try to cover the area as slowly as you can."

"Yes, sir."

Nolan gave the orders to his helmsman, and Admiral Mackie turned to look out the rear windows of the bridge house. He saw Captain Robertson on the stern, supervising the dragging gear. The seas were rough, but the *Tioga* had powerful diesels and ploughed steadily through them. Admiral Mackie looked at his watch; it was nearly four o'clock in the afternoon. He'd received word that the *Falcon* was on its way from the Boston Navy Yard, but the *Falcon* wouldn't have much to do if the *Tioga* couldn't locate the *Sebago*.

Admiral Mackie looked through the side window of the bridge deck and saw the *Porgie* out there, circling around awaiting further orders. The *Jeffer-*

son, a hospital ship from Newport, Rhode Island, was also on the way. The *Dale,* a destroyer returning from a patrol in the Atlantic, had radioed to say that it was proceeding to the scene also.

"Coffee, sir?" asked Nolan.

"Thank you," replied Admiral Mackie, accepting the white mug of coffee.

He took a sip and saw the helmsman turning the wheel, maneuvering the *Tioga* for another run through the area over which the smoke rocket had appeared.

The door to the bridge house opened and Commander Mulford stepped in, wearing a long black trench coat.

"I say there, sir," he said, advancing toward Admiral Mackie. "I was just down having a peek in the radio shack, and I saw that they have an oscillator on board. I think we might be able to send a message down to the *Sebago* with it. Shall I have a go?"

Admiral Mackie shrugged. "You might as well, but how will they respond?"

"They can bang on the hull."

"Could we hear that?"

"*We* can't, but I think some of our electronics might be able to pick it up."

"Go ahead and try, then."

"Yes, sir."

Admiral Mackie smiled as he watched Mulford leave the bridge. He liked Mulford; the British officer was bright, cheerful, and always looking for something to do. If he established contact of some kind with the *Sebago,* it wouldn't help the *Tioga* locate her, but it might give encouragement to the men trapped aboard.

The *Tioga* made a slow run through the area from which the smoke rocket had blasted, but its big hooks didn't catch anything. The helmsman swung the wheel around for another run, and Admiral Mackie began to think they'd never locate the downed boat. Even if the hooks actually touched it, they might not catch onto anything. They could drag right over it and not realize that anything was there.

If only that marker buoy hadn't broken, he thought as he gazed at the churning seas.

FORTY

Jack McCrary sat in the control room blowing on his hands. The submarine was clammy and ice cold, and his feet tingled with pain. Lieutenant Stearns bled oxygen flasks to improve the fetid air; when he finished, Chief Keller would spread more carbon dioxide absorbent around.

Jack had passed through surprise, confusion, fear, and resignation; now he was getting mad. His promising Navy career and indeed his very life might soon be over because of a faulty main induction system designed by an obnoxious Jew. He'd always known he might be killed but had not imagined it like this: drowning like a rat in only 240 feet of water. He felt like standing up and punching the bulkhead. If Ben Mount had been standing in front of him he would have torn him limb from limb.

Suddenly he heard a high-pitched *ping* against the hull. He straightened up and looked around as another *ping* hit. The pings began to come in dots and dashes.

"Mason—get this down!" Jack shouted.

"I am, sir," Mason stuttered, running out of the

radio shack, nearly tripping over the blanket that had been wrapped around him.

He listened to the dots and dashes and wrote down the message. Everyone in the control room looked at him, new hope in their eyes. Jack rose to his feet and approached Mason, standing next to him and reading the message as it was written down: HELLO SEBAGO—THIS IS TIOGA—CAN YOU READ ME? RESPOND BY BANGING ON HULL.

Jack dove on the toolbox and came out with a hammer. Stuffing the hammer into his belt, he climbed the ladder to the conning tower and began tearing cork off the conning tower walls.

"Mason—get up here!" he yelled as his fingers clawed away the cork.

"Yes, sir."

Mason climbed the ladder as McCrary began banging the hammer against the wall of the conning tower. He'd been communications officer on the *Porpoise* and remembered enough Morse code to pound out. YES—YES—YES—YES.

McCrary stood in the dim light, breathing heavily and hoping that the *Tioga* heard his message. He closed his eyes and said a little prayer. The pinging began again: WHAT IS YOUR SITUATION?

Jack looked at Mason and told him to translate what he was going to say into Morse code. Then he explained that the after compartments were flooded, that twenty-six men and one officer were presumed dead in them, there were leaks in the forward torpedo compartment, they were running low on air, and it was very cold. He also said he surmised that the main induction valves had failed upon diving. He reported that Gene Dunlop had died of a heart attack, and that he, Jack McCrary had taken command.

Mason made the dots and dashes on his pad and handed them to Jack.

"Read them to me," Jack told him. "I can't read and bang at the same time."

Mason read the signals one letter at a time, and Jack hammered them out on the hull. Gritting his teeth, he pounded until one arm got tired and then switched to his other arm. Despite the cold he felt perspiration forming in his armpits and on his shoulders. His lungs strained to draw oxygen out of the air as he slammed the hammer against the hull; he hoped they were reading him above in the *Tioga*.

He finished the message and leaned against the bulkhead, gulping for air. He pushed his hat back on his head and wondered why he felt so happy, since his ability to communicate with the *Tioga* was no insurance that the *Tioga* would be able to find the *Sebago*.

After several minutes, the pinging began again: CANNOT READ YOU CLEARLY. PLEASE SEND EVERY WORD THREE TIMES.

"Stearns—get up here!" Jack shouted. "You, too, Keller, and bring another man with you."

Stearns, Keller, and Donahue climbed the ladder that led to the conning tower.

"Are we communicating with them?" Stearns asked.

"Yes, but not very well," Jack replied. "We have to repeat every word three times, and my arm's getting tired." He handed him the hammer. "You try it for awhile, and when you can't do it anymore, let Keller have a try."

"Yes, sir."

Stearns took the hammer, and Mason read the signals. Stearns commenced hammering while Jack leaned against the periscope and watched. He'd prayed before that the *Tioga* would hear him, and it did, so this time he prayed that the *Tioga* would locate the *Sebago* somehow, even though the sea was huge and time was running out.

FORTY-ONE

President Franklin Delano Roosevelt sat with Harry L. Hopkins in the Oval Office of the White House. Roosevelt was asking Hopkins's opinion about a letter he wanted to send to Adolf Hitler and Benito Mussolini requesting assurances that they would not attack thirty-one specified countries in Europe and the Near East.

"I don't think the letter'll make a bit of difference about anything," Hopkins said. "If those two want to attack somebody, they'll do it no matter what assurance they've given."

"But still, I think we ought to go on record about this matter," the President said.

"You can make it a matter of record if you want to, but those two will just laugh at you and this country."

The phone on President Roosevelt's desk rang, and he lifted the receiver.

"Yes?" he said.

"Admiral Kane would like to see you, Mister President," said his secretary. "He says it's urgent."

"Send him in."

"Yes, sir."

President Roosevelt hung up his receiver. "It's Admiral Kane," he said to Hopkins. "He wants to see me about something urgent."

"Should I leave?"

"I don't think that'll be necessary."

The door to the Oval Office opened and Admiral Cyrus Kane, the chief of naval operations, entered. He marched to the desk and saluted the President, who smiled and waved.

"What can I do for you?" President Roosevelt said.

"Sir, something serious has happened and I thought I'd better brief you on it before someone from the press asks for your statement."

"I hope we're not at war with anyone," Roosevelt said jokingly. "If we were, I imagine I'd be the last one to know, wouldn't I?"

Admiral Kane took some correspondence out of a manila envelope, his hands trembling. He was getting on in years; he had sunken cheeks and deepset eyes. President Roosevelt had been planning to replace him but hadn't figured out who to replace him with.

"Why don't you have a seat, Cyrus?" President Roosevelt suggested.

"Yes, sir."

Admiral Kane sat on a green leather chair beside Harry Hopkins and managed to remove the papers from the envelope. He glanced them over quickly, then looked at President Roosevelt.

"Mister President," he said solemnly, "I'm afraid I have to tell you that our newest submarine, the *Sebago,* sank during sea trials this morning somewhere in Block Island Sound."

"The *Sebago*? Down?" Roosevelt had once been assistant secretary of the Navy and still kept himself up to date on naval matters. He'd known about the sea trials at New London. He looked at his watch; it was four o'clock in the afternoon. "It went down this morning, you say?"

"Yes, sir."

"What time?"

Admiral Kane shuffled through the papers on his lap. "One one oh six, sir."

"And I'm just finding out about it now?"

"We didn't want to notify you until we knew something definite, sir." Admiral Kane stared at the President's eyeglasses and hoped the President didn't guess that he was lying. He hadn't notified the President because he'd assumed that Admiral Hill had.

"Does the secretary of the Navy know?" the President asked.

"Yes, sir."

"When was he informed?"

"I don't know for sure."

"Have you spoken with him?"

"Yes."

"When?"

"Shortly before I came here."

"What did he have to say?"

Admiral Kane reddened. "He told me that I should brief you personally, since I knew more about the matter than he."

President Roosevelt looked at the papers on Admiral Kane's lap. "Do you have all the information there?"

"Yes, sir."

"May I look at it?"

"Yes, sir."

Admiral Kane handed over the papers, and President Roosevelt began to read them. "Come behind the desk here and take a look, will you, Harry?"

"Sure thing, Mister President."

Harry Hopkins arose from his chair and came behind the desk with the President, reading the information over his shoulder. When they had finished reading, Hopkins returned to his seat.

President Roosevelt looked at Admiral Kane. "We've got to get those men out of there," he said.

"We're doing our best, sir."

"You've got to do better than your best. It is absolutely necessary that we get those survivors out of there. The whole world will be watching. Losing the submarine is a serious blow to our prestige, but failing to rescue her survivors will be much worse."

Admiral Kane nodded. "I understand, sir."

President Roosevelt looked at the papers again. "Who's in charge of the rescue operations?"

"Admiral Dexter, the commander of the Atlantic Submarine Fleet."

"Tell him I expect him to get those survivors out. I don't care how he does it—he'd just better do it."

"Yes, sir."

That's all, Admiral Kane. Thank you for coming over here."

Admiral Kane stood and saluted. "Yes, sir." He did an about face and marched out of the office, closing the door behind him.

"Whew," President Roosevelt said. "We certainly don't need this right now."

"We sure don't," Harry Hopkins agreed. "The rest of the world doesn't respect us militarily as it is, and now our newest, most advanced submarine has sunk on her first test dive."

"With all hands on board," President Roosevelt added. "What a catastrophe. Perhaps I'd better get in touch with some of the families of the crew.

"That might be a good idea."

President Roosevelt shook his head in dismay. "I'll have to do something about Kane. He should have been retired long ago."

"Some of them don't like to let go," Harry Hopkins said.

"If they don't like to go, then I'll have to pry their

fingers loose. I think Dexter is a good man, though. He's as tough as they come.

"If anybody can get those survivors out, it's Dexter."

President Roosevelt took a cigarette from a gold case on his desk, inserted it into his holder, put it into his mouth, and lit it. Angling the cigarette and holder in his teeth, he looked through the papers Admiral Kane had brought.

"I think I'd better get a statement out on this right away, don't you, Harry?"

"I think that would be a good idea, Mister President."

"Help me with it, will you? You're good at this sort of thing."

"Very well, sir." Hopkins took his fountain pen from his shirt pocket. "Do you have a sheet of paper that I can use?"

FORTY-TWO

The *Sebago* wives were a strange-looking bunch, Betsy
Kirkland thought as she sat with them in the administration building. They'd been trickling in all afternoon, having been notified that the boat was down.
Commodore Briscoe, whom Admiral Mackie had
placed in charge of the base while he was away, had
come to the briefing room to assure them that everything possible was being done to rescue their husbands. Now they were sitting together, fretting and
awaiting further news.

Betsy noticed a distinct difference between the wives
of officers and the wives of the men. The officers'
wives were better dressed and more sophisticated,
but compared to the women of Betsy's acquaintance
they didn't appear sophisticated at all. She imagined
that all three of them, the wives of Gene Dunlop, Ensign Delbert, and Lieutenant Jordan, had graduated
from small teachers' colleges in the Midwest and led
relatively sheltered lives. She thought Delbert's wife
particularly unattractive, with her pockmarked face
and frizzy blond hair. Betsy had talked with her
earlier and found out that she and Delbert had been
married only eight months. Dunlop's wife was trying

to be strong and brave, but looked like she might break down at any moment. Betty Jordan was a quiet, petite woman who appeared to be saying prayers.

Most of the enlisted men's wives fit into the category that Betsy would call "poor but proud." They appeared ill at ease in the presence of the officers' wives, whom they obviously considered to be their betters, and were coping with their emotions less effectively. Some sobbed softly into handkerchiefs, others chain-smoked, and a few appeared to be bored. One of them, in a flaming red dress and high-heeled shoes, her hair done up like Rita Hayworth's, looked like she'd come straight from a night club in Brazil. Surprisingly, she'd had a Brooklyn accent when she'd introduced herself as Laurie Burns, wife of Torpedoman Hank Burns.

They were sitting in a room ordinarily used for briefings, their chairs backed against the four walls. Through the window Betsy could see the angry gray sky. Occasionally a whistle went off somewhere. Betsy had spoken with most of the wives and was preparing to leave the room to phone in another story to the *Standard* when the door opened and an ensign poked his head in.

"Miss Kirkland?" he asked, looking around.

Betsy raised her hand. "Here I am."

"Commodore Briscoe would like to speak with you, ma'am."

Betsy rose from her chair, smoothed the front of her skirt, and followed the ensign into the hall. She'd known that somebody would want to speak with her before long, because the *New York Standard* must have hit the streets already with its special edition and her byline.

The ensign opened the door to Admiral Mackie's office, and Betsy stepped inside. Commodore Briscoe sat behind Admiral Mackie's desk; he was a bald fussy-looking man who Betsy suspected still lived with his mother. A newspaper was lying on his desk; she could see that it was the *Standard.*

"Have a seat, Miss Kirkland," Briscoe said.

Betsy sat and crossed her legs.

Briscoe raised the copy of the *New York Standard.* "What's the meaning of this, Miss Kirkland?" he asked.

"What do you mean?" she asked back.

"Did you write this story?"

"I certainly did."

Briscoe narrowed his eyes at her. "Are you aware that you've misused confidential information?"

"I hadn't been aware that it was confidential information," she retorted. "Nobody indicated to me in any way that it was."

"You didn't indicate to anyone that you were a newspaper reporter either."

"Nobody asked me whether or not I was a newspaper reporter. I saw no reason to make the announcement to anybody. Everyone seemed very busy and intensely preoccupied with the sinking."

Briscoe smiled sardonically. "I think you're being difficult, Miss Kirkland."

"I think you're being unreasonable, Commodore Briscoe. No one placed any prohibitions on me here, and I've violated none that I know of."

Briscoe pointed his finger at her. "You've used your privileged position among us here to reveal information that could be damaging to the United States Navy."

"I only told the truth about the *Sebago,*" Betsy insisted, "and if that's damaging to the Navy, it's the Navy's fault, not mine."

"Miss Kirkland," Briscoe said sternly, "I'm afraid I must ask you not to contact your newspaper anymore while you're on this base."

"You have no right to ask me that!" Betsy declared.

"I have every right!" Briscoe replied. "This is a military installation and I am in command!"

"I'm a civilian and you have no right to command me to do anything!"

"While you're on this submarine base I have!"

Betsy leaned forward and smiled at Briscoe. "I think I'm going to call my father," she said. "I'm going to tell him that you're trying to prevent the truth about the *Sebago* from being told to the American people. Do you know who my father is, Commodore Briscoe? He's Congressman Adam Kirkland from the State of New York."

Briscoe went pale.

"And then do you know what I'm going to do, Commodore Briscoe? I'm going to call my editor and tell him the same thing. I think he might want to do a story about the cover-up here in New London."

"Now just a moment, Miss Kirkland . . ." Briscoe stuttered, holding up his hand and trying to smile. "We're not trying to prevent the truth about the *Sebago* from getting out."

"Then what are you trying to do?"

"We're trying to prevent rumors from spreading."

Betsy pointed to the copy of the *New York Standard* on Briscoe's desk. "Have I reported rumors or have I reported the facts?"

"Um . . ." Briscoe wrinkled his forehead in an effort to think.

"Commodore Briscoe, I don't think we have anything more to say to each other about this matter, do we?" Betsy asked.

"Ah . . . no."

"Then you won't mind if I leave your office?"

Briscoe pulled himself together. "You may leave if you like, but I hope you won't report the details of this conversation to anybody." He smiled ingratiatingly.

Betsy stood and adjusted her shoulder bag. "I won't say a word about it, provided no one interferes with my work. It's been lovely talking with you, Commodore Briscoe."

Briscoe stood as Betsy left. After she'd closed the door behind her, he sat and snarled at the walls of the office. No woman had ever talked to him like that in his life, and he felt like strangling somebody.

Betsy returned to the room where the wives were. She wanted to gather more information for the story she was doing on them. Opening the door to the room, she entered and walked toward Patricia Delbert.

"Betsy!"

Betsy turned around and saw Helen McCrary, her future sister-in-law. Helen was sitting on the other side of the room; she must have just arrived. They embraced and touched cheeks, although they didn't like each other very much. Helen thought Betsy was a snob, and Betsy considered Helen a typical Navy brat.

"Did you just get here?" Betsy asked, sitting beside Helen.

"No," Helen replied. "I arrived around half an hour ago. I've been with my father downstairs."

"How's he taking it?"

"All right, I suppose. It's hard to know what's really going on inside Father. He's in the radio room, monitoring incoming messages."

Betsy hadn't known that Commodore McCrary was in the radio room. She reminded herself to mention it in her next story. "Any news?"

"The *Tioga* is communicating with the *Sebago* through Morse code."

Betsy wrinkled her forehead. "I thought radio waves couldn't go under water."

"I don't think they can," Helen said. "Dad told me that the *Tioga* is using something called an oscillator, and the sailors on the *Sebago* are banging on the hull."

"The *Tioga* can hear them banging?"

"Evidently."

"What did the *Sebago* say?"

"Dad wouldn't tell me much. I guess he doesn't want me to worry."

Betsy looked over Helen's head and imagined the next headline on the *Standard:* SEBAGO SENDS FIRST MESSAGE.

She decided to go downstairs and talk to Commodore McCrary. Maybe she could wheedle some information out of him. She was certain that she was the only reporter who'd be permitted to go down to the radio room, and it'd be another scoop.

The young ensign poked his head into the room again. "Mrs. Dunlop, would you come with me, please."

Arlene Dunlop stood and left the room, carrying her pocketbook in both hands. She was wearing the housedress she'd had on when she'd received the news that her husband's boat was down. She was a stout woman. Trying not to appear troubled, she followed the ensign to the office of Commodore Briscoe.

"Have a seat, Mrs. Dunlop," Briscoe said kindly.

Arlene Dunlop sat down, a look of consternation on her face.

"I'm afraid I have something very terrible to tell you," Briscoe said.

Arlene Dunlop lowered her head and covered her face with her hands. "I know what it is already," she whispered, and began to sob.

FORTY-THREE

Admiral Isoroku Yamamato stood on the bridge of his flagship, the aircraft carrier *Soryu,* and observed the sea exercises his fleet was undergoing in the Sea of Japan. The purpose of the exercise was to land the crack 29th Division on the island of Hokkaido. The sky swarmed with bombers and fighter planes, and steaming toward Hokkaido with the *Soryu* was her sister ship, the aircraft carrier *Hiryu,* plus the heavy cruisers *Tone* and *Chikuma,* and four destroyers. Two troopships were in front of the aircraft carriers and behind the cruisers, while the destroyers protected the fleet's flanks.

Admiral Yamamoto watched the movement impassively through his binoculars. He was a husky man with a stern face, fifty-six years old. On either side were staff officers, also observing the exercise. For the past several months Admiral Yamamoto had been devising strategies for attacking strongly held islands, and this was the first time his strategies were being put to the test. The exercise was going well so far, but he knew that the success of the strategies in actual combat would depend on who controlled the air and how well the islands were defended.

A young lieutenant with a sheet of paper in his hand advanced toward Admiral Yamamoto. "A message has just come in for you from Tokyo, sir."

"Read it to me."

"It's rather long, sir."

Admiral Yamamoto took the message from the lieutenant and read it. He grunted, pursed his lips, and cocked his head to one side. Then he handed the paper to his senior staff officer, Admiral Ansei Ushiro.

"America's newest submarine has just sunk during its first test dive with all hands aboard," Admiral Yamamoto told his officers as he raised his binoculars to his eyes. He turned down the corners of his mouth. "The Americans have a tin Navy."

FORTY-FOUR

Jack McCrary clenched and unclenched his hands in the pockets of his leather jacket. The *Tioga* had been passing back and forth overhead for almost an hour and a half but had not made contact. Araujo had the hammer and was banging a new message to the *Tioga:* YOU ARE NORTHEAST OF US.

Stearns heard the *Tioga* change direction and head toward the *Sebago* again. "Tell them they're headed toward us again!" Stearns shouted up the ladder to the conning tower.

Radioman Mason, sheets of paper piled around his feet, translated the message into dots and dashes and gave them to Araujo, who commenced banging on the hull again. YOU ARE HEADED OUR WAY.

Jack became tense as the *Tioga* approached once more. He prayed that it would hook the *Sebago* this time. Everyone aboard the submarine looked up as the sound of the *Tioga*'s engines drew closer. It came directly overhead, and for an intense moment they thought it was slowing down, but instead it kept going.

"Shit!" Jack said.

Peter Nielsen stood on the other side of the conning

tower. "Evidently the water is distorting the direction-
al qualities of the sound. We think the *Tioga* is overhead, but it isn't."

"It's close, though," Keller said.

"But not close enough."

Stearns called from the control room.

"Tell him he's passed overhead again!"

Mason translated the message and Araujo pounded
it out. YOU JUST PASSED OVER US.

"Araujo," Jack said. "Go below and have La Gloria
relieve you."

"Yes, sir."

Araujo handed the hammer to Keller and began
climbing down the ladder. Jack listened to the sound
of the *Tioga*'s engines getting farther away. *I wonder
how much more of this we can take?* he asked himself.

Commander Mulford looked over the radioman's
shoulder as the message from the *Sebago* was translated: YOU JUST PASSED OVER US.

"Damn!" said Mulford. He grabbed the intercom
microphone and pressed the button. "Commander
Mulford calling Admiral Mackie," he said.

"This is Admiral Mackie," said the squawk box.

"They said we just passed over them again."

Admiral Mackie made an exasperated sound. "We'll
turn around and go back again."

"Yes, sir."

"Anything else?"

"That's all for now."

From the window of the radio shack Mulford could
see that the *Tioga* was turning around again. If the
Tioga were a British destroyer and the *Sebago* an
enemy submarine, he could have finished her off long
ago with depth charges, because you don't have to
hit right on target with depth charges, you just have
to come close.

The *Tioga* turned around and made another pass. On the bridge, Admiral Mackie frowned at the darkening sky. It would soon be nightfall, and if he didn't find the boat by then he'd have to work under searchlights. He raised his binoculars and looked at the *Porgie,* the hospital ship *Jefferson,* and the destroyer *Dale.* A short while ago he'd received a message from the *Falcon,* stating that it was on its way through the Cape Cod Canal; he expected it to arrive after dark.

Back in the radio room, Mulford told the radioman to send another message by oscillator: WE'RE COMING BY AGAIN.

The *Tioga* pushed through the high waves. On the bridge, Admiral Mackie wondered if they'd ever hook the elusive quarry. The irons might catch onto an old sunken wooden ship, maybe even a rock ledge. Admiral Mackie was becoming discouraged. He thought the unthinkable: that the boat might never be located, that the hammering would become softer and softer, and that finally it would stop forever.

In the radio room, Mulford stood beside the radioman and listened through a set of headphones. He heard the steady roar of the *Tioga*'s engines and the crashing of waves against the bow. Then he heard the clanging. The radioman wrote the message down and handed it to Mulford: YOU PASSED OVER US AGAIN.

Mulford radioed the message to Admiral Mackie, who told Captain Nolan to turn around and go back. The radioman transmitted the message that they were on their way again, but everyone on the *Tioga* had come to believe that their chances of hooking the *Sebago* in those heavy seas was extremely unlikely.

Captain Robertson on the stern of the *Tioga* watched the gear drag through the foaming wake. He wore a thick wool sweater underneath his brown leather jacket and still he shivered as he stood next to the winch. His black mustache was dripping brine, and drops of water hung on his earlobes like earrings.

Four sailors were with him, their knit caps over their ears and their faces red from the cold.

Suddenly the ratchet on the winch began to chatter. Robertson stared at it in disbelief. The winch was designed to operate like a fishing reel: When something was hooked it would play out cable.

"We've got something!" Robertson yelled to the bridge.

Admiral Mackie heard the ratchet before he heard Robertson's voice. "All engines stop!" he ordered.

"All engines stop!" repeated the helmsman.

"Drop anchor!"

"Drop anchor!"

On the bow of the *Tioga,* a seaman pulled a lever that loosed the huge anchor. It thundered off the hull and splashed into the water below, trailing huge links of chain.

Admiral Mackie turned to Lieutenant Commander Nolan. "Tell Robertson to make sure she has plenty of play. We don't want to lose contact the way the *Porgie* did."

"Yes, sir."

Nolan ran out of the cabin, and Admiral Mackie picked up the mike. "Admiral Mackie calling the radio room."

"This is the radio room," replied Commander Mulford.

"Send a message down to the *Sebago* that we believe we've hooked her."

"Yes, sir!"

Overjoyed, Mulford tapped the radioman on the shoulder and repeated the admiral's order.

"We have?" the radioman asked, his face lighting up.

"We think we have," Mulford replied. "Hurry and send the message."

"Yes, sir."

* * *

In the conning tower of the *Segago* Jack and the others heard the *Tioga*'s engines stop above them.

Keller smiled broadly, showing his gold incisor tooth. "Hey, sir—maybe they've hooked us."

Jack shook his head. "I haven't heard anything. If they hooked us I think we would have heard something." He looked at Lieutenant Nielsen. "Did you hear something?"

"No, sir."

A series of *pings* hit the hull, and Radioman Mason wrote down the message. Jack looked over his shoulder and couldn't believe his eyes: THINK WE'VE HOOKED YOU.

Jack looked at Nielsen. Keller let out a cheer and jumped into the air, nearly hitting his head on the top of the conning tower.

"Calm down," Jack told Keller. "They might have hooked something else, because we haven't heard anything down here." He turned to Mason. "Tell them that we have no indication that they've hooked us."

Mason translated the message into Morse code and told La Gloria how to bang it out.

In the radio room of the *Tioga* the radioman handed the message to Mulford: NO INDICATION THAT YOU'VE HOOKED US.

Mulford pinched his lips together. "I'm going to the bridge," he told the radioman. "Contact me there if anything happens."

"Yes, sir."

Message in hand, Mulford climbed the ladder to the bridge of the *Tioga*. Admiral Mackie was looking at the ocean through his binoculars. It was nearly six o'clock and dusk was falling.

"Admiral Mackie—take a look at this," Mulford said, holding out the message.

Admiral Mackie lowered his binoculars and looked

at it. He frowned. "I was afraid of this," he said. "We might have hooked something else."

"And we might have hooked it too. It's possible that they didn't feel it."

Admiral Mackie shrugged. "Those grappling irons are awfully big. They should have made a noise when they hit the hull, don't you think?"

"Not necessarily, sir. Don't forget that those hooks were just floating along slowly underwater. They could have latched onto something very gently."

"But we would have pulled them somewhat, because we were moving and they were still.

"Not if the ratchet gear on our winch was working properly."

Admiral Mackie thought for a few moments. "I forgot about the ratchet gear. It's supposed to play out cable if the irons grip something, isn't it?"

"Yes, sir."

Commander Nolan pointed out the bridge window. "Sir, there's a ship approaching."

Admiral Mackie raised his binoculars and took a look. He saw a big ship on the horizon.

"I'll bet it's the *Falcon*," Admiral Mackie said. "It should be due about now."

The squawk box on the wall started up. "Radio room calling Admiral Mackie."

Admiral Mackie picked up the intercom microphone. "This is Admiral Mackie."

"You're wanted on the radio, sir."

"I'll be right down."

Admiral Mackie hung up the mike and walked toward the rear of the bridge house. He descended the stairs and Mulford followed him to the radio room. The radioman got to his feet and held out the mike for Admiral Mackie, who took it and pressed the button.

"This is Admiral Mackie on the *Tioga*," he said.

"Hang on a moment, sir," said the voice on the

squawk box. "Admiral Dexter would like to speak with you."

Admiral Mackie listened to some static in the squawk box, and then Admiral Dexter's booming voice came through: "Have you found the *Sebago* yet, Mackie?"

"We've just hooked something and we believe that's it, sir."

"You don't know for sure?"

"No, sir."

"I understand that you've made contact of some kind."

"That's correct, sir. We're communicating with our oscillator, and they're banging on their hull."

"Did they confirm being hooked?"

"They said they had no indication that they'd been hooked."

"Then maybe you didn't hook them."

"That's true, sir." Admiral Mackie explained Mulford's theory of how a boat could be hooked without the crew's knowing it. "Since we seem to be over her. I think we should proceed on the assumption that we've hooked her."

There was silence for a few moments, then: "I'm not so sure about that. I'll think it over and make a decision before morning. I'm taking command of the rescue operations as of now, Mackie."

"Yes, sir."

"Make certain your anchor isn't dragging."

"Yes, sir."

"Over and out."

"Admiral Mackie handed the microphone to the radioman. "Well, the big cheese is here," he said.

"He's the commander of your Atlantic Submarine Fleet, isn't he, sir?" Mulford asked.

"That's him."

"I'd like to have a talk with him sometime."

"It may not prove to be such a pleasant experience,

but I'm sure it would be rewarding nonetheless." Admiral Mackie looked at the radioman. "Tell the people on the *Sebago* to get a good night's rest, and that we'll try to raise them in the morning."

"Yes, sir."

Admiral Mackie smiled at Mulford. "I guess we might as well have dinner."

"Sounds like a fine idea."

"We'll have to spend the night on this boat," Admiral Mackie said as he walked toward the door. "I imagine it'll be rather cramped."

"I'm sure it won't be as cramped as it is on the bottom," Mulford replied, following Admiral Mackie out of the radio room.

The sound waves of the *Tioga*'s oscillator zinged against the hull of the *Sebago*. Radioman Mason wrote down the message and handed it to Jack as the others in the conning tower huddled around him. GET REST. WILL TRY TO RAISE YOU IN THE MORNING.

Jack looked at Mason. "Tell them good night."

"Yes, sir."

Mason transformed the message into Morse code, and La Gloria banged it out. Jack descended the ladder to the control room and saw Stearns leaning against the chart table, his eyes bleary and face pallid.

Jack smiled at him. "You're doing a fine job, Stearns."

"Thank you, sir."

Jack looked around the control room. "All of you are doing a fine job."

The men looked sheepish and shy; Jack always thought it curious that grown, grizzled sailors always acted like little boys whenever they were praised. He wiped his mouth with the palm of his hand and tried to plan the night on the submarine as La Gloria hammered out the message on the inside of the conning tower. He decided it would probably be best if they just had dinner and went to bed. If the men were asleep they'd use less air, and they could huddle together for warmth. It would also keep their minds off their troubles. He'd assign a watch to bleed oxygen into the air periodically and spread carbon dioxide absorbent.

"Stearns," he said, "we're going to eat and then hit the sack. Break out the food while I go forward to check on the torpedo compartment."

"Yes, sir."

"Keller—come with me."

"Yes, sir."

Lieutenant Nielsen stepped out of the darkness. "Could I go with you too, sir?"

"Very well. Keller, you stay here."

"Yes, sir."

Jack and Nielsen put on Momsen lungs, then Donahue opened the hatch for them and they entered the dark and eerie officers' wardroom. The atmosphere was yellow-greenish. As they moved along the passageway, Nielsen glanced into the captain's stateroom and saw the corpse of Lieutenant Commander Dunlop. Nielsen swallowed hard. He'd asked to come with Jack because he'd been feeling light-headed and strange in the control room. He'd thought that he was on a ghost submarine and that he was one of the ghosts. Now, seeing the corpse of Gene Dunlop, a shiver crept up his back. *I'm not a ghost,* he told himself, *I'm still alive.* He began humming a song to cheer himself up, but stopped after a few bars when he realized he was humming *Die Fahne Hoch,* the marching song of Germany's National Socialist party. Nielson bit his lip to force himself back to the reality of his situation. If Lieutenant McCrary had recognized *Die Fahne Hoch* he would be suspicious. McCrary was no fool—Nielsen realized he had to be careful. An Aryan male should be able to stay in control of himself at all times; he'd have to strengthen his will and start behaving properly.

Jack opened the hatch to the forward torpedo compartment and stepped inside. He realized that the deck was wet. Burns jumped out of his bunk when he was aware that Jack was in the compartment. Jack bent over and touched his finger to the deck. The water came up to his first knuckle. Nielsen held his breath, expecting the worst; a strange odor of musk enveloped him.

"Still leaking, eh?" asked Jack.

"Slowly but surely, sir."

"How's the head?"

"We've got it plugged up pretty well, but it's still leaking too."

"Let me have a look."

Jack walked toward the head and shone his flashlight on it. Burns and his men had whittled down a huge chunk of wood and jammed it into the bowl. Jack shone the flashlight around the bowl and could see filthy water leaking down onto the floor plates.

"It's not that bad," Jack said.

"Not yet, anyway," Burns replied.

"You heard the pinging against the hull?"

"Yes, sir. We thought it was the rescue ship in contact with us."

"It was the tugboat *Tioga,*" Jack explained. Burns and the men crowded around him. "They say they've hooked us with their gear and they're going to bring us up in the morning."

"They say they hooked us, sir?" Burns asked, half-closing one eye.

"That's right, Burns."

"When did they do that, sir?"

"Within the past fifteen minutes."

"I thought I heard something topside a little while ago. Maybe that's what it was."

Jack stared at him. "You heard something top-side?"

"Yes, sir."

"What did it sound like?"

Burns shrugged. "I dunno. It was just a noise."

"Was it metallic?"

"Could have been. Maybe something fell off the *Tioga*, or maybe water pressure buckled something topside."

Nielsen cleared his throat. "We're vulnerable to water pressure in our hull, not topside. I don't think we're received any damage topside, do you, Lieutenant?"

"No," Jack said. "Maybe the sound Burns heard was the *Tioga* hooking us."

"It may very well have been," the Swedish officer said, his spirits improving.

"We'll have to report this to the *Tioga* when it contacts us in the morning." Jack looked at the sailors around him. "Well, keep your chins up, boys. Things are getting better all the time."

"Yes, sir," they all mumbled.

"Burns, let me know if anything happens up here."

"Yes, sir."

"I think you should have chow about now and then put the men to bed. Maintain a watch throughout the night, in case the leaks get worse."

"Yes, sir."

"Carry on."

"Right, sir."

Jack and Nielsen returned to the control room, where they found Stearns distributing cans of food for the dinner meal. Jack noticed La Gloria bending over Electrician's Mate Homer Gilson, who was lying on the floor.

"What's going on over here?" Jack asked.

"Gilson is coming down with something, sir," La

Gloria replied, rolling some pills onto the palm of his hand.

Jack knelt down and looked at Gilson, who was shivering uncontrollably.

"Has he got a temperature?" Jack asked.

"One hundred and one degrees, sir."

"That's not so bad," Jack said jauntily, as he stood erect again. "He'll be all right. I'll lend him my blanket and double up with Lieutenant Stearns. The men in the forward torpedo compartment reported that they heard the *Tioga* hook up with us, so I imagine we'll all be out of here in the morning."

The men looked at him with expressions that indicated they didn't know whether to believe him or not. Jack tried to appear cheerful and optimistic as he advanced to the chart table and picked up a can of pork and beans. He opened it with the can opener, took a fork, and leaned against the Christmas tree, wondering how the ships above intended to get them out.

FORTY-FIVE

Lieutenant Commander Ben Mount stood before the mirror in his *Falcon* stateroom, tying his necktie. It was time for chow in the officers' mess, and he knew that Admiral Dexter would be there to taunt him; he wanted his appearance to be faultless. There was nothing worse than being criticized for wearing a wrinkled shirt or for the way your tie was tied, and he knew that officers often harassed people they didn't like in that picayune manner. Ben had learned at Annapolis to be above reproach; that was the only way to stay out of trouble.

He put on his blue jacket. He looked shipshape; the only problem was that his nose was too big for the U.S. Navy. Grinning at himself, he left his stateroom and stepped into the narrow corridor.

Two young lieutenants were several paces ahead of him, and he followed them through corridors and up ladderwells to the officers' mess. Ben loved to walk through ships even though he'd been in the Navy for seven years. He loved the clean metallic fragrance, the logic of the way everything was arranged, even the exposed pipes and cables that ran along the bulkheads and overhead. A ship was a big complex machine with no frills, nothing false. The officers and men were straightforward and businesslike; if they didn't like you they didn't pretend that they did.

He entered the officers' mess, where many of the officers were already seated at a big U-shaped arrangement of tables. On the walls were color prints of Navy ships. There were some plaques the *Falcon* had won, and maroon drapes covered the portholes. Ben found an empty space and sat down. The ritual was to wait patiently until the captain arrived; then the meal would be served by black and Filipino attendants.

Ben liked Navy food. He preferred it to the heavy Eastern European fare his mother prepared, and even to the fancy food of expensive restaurants. Navy food was plain, clean, and nourishing—exactly what food was supposed to be. Ben liked everything to be rational and functional. He couldn't stand gaudiness and superficiality.

The mess filled with more officers, and a lieutenant sat beside him. No one could sit on the other side, because Ben had the last chair on the end of the table.

"Good evening, sir," the lieutenant said. "I don't believe I know you."

"I'm Lieutenant Commander Mount."

"Oh——Commander Mount. How do you do. I'm Lieutenant Randall."

Ben shook his hand. Ensign Tolliver arrived, spotted Ben, and sat on the chair opposite him. "It's raining, sir."

"We'll be all right if the wind doesn't kick up."

Ben introduced Tolliver to Randall, and it turned out that they'd both dated the same girl somewhere along the line. Ben listened curiously, because other men's escapades with women seemed so strange to him. He'd never been obsessed with women like most of the other men he knew—perhaps he didn't have the proper amount of hormones or something. Whatever the cause, he was glad of it, because women took up so much of a man's time and he needed all the time he could get for his work.

Yet there were hours in the middle of the night when he'd awaken with a dull sexual hunger, but he'd start thinking about hydraulic valves and water pumps and soon the sexual hunger would dissipate so that he could fall asleep again.

Admiral Dexter entered the mess followed by Admiral Walmsley and Captain Healey of the *Falcon*. Ben and the other officers shot to their feet. Admiral Kirkland and his party sat at the head table, and then Ben and the others sat down.

"Sorry to keep you waiting, gentlemen," Admiral Dexter said. He turned to Captain Healey. "'Do we have a chaplain aboard?"

"No, sir."

"Then would you say grace, please?"

"Yes, sir." Captain Healey bowed his head and folded his hands.

"Wait a minute!" Admiral Dexter said.

Captain Healey looked at Admiral Dexter, as did everyone else.

Admiral Dexter smiled maliciously. "I assume that Captain Healey is going to say a Christian form of grace, and it has just occurred to me that we have an officer of the HE-brew persuasion aboard. I thought perhaps, out of fairness to the officer of the HE-brew persuasion, that I ought to give him the opportunity to leave the mess until the prayer was over, because I wouldn't want to subject him to a form of religion in which he might not believe."

All eyes fell on Ben, and he felt warm underneath his collar. But this sort of thing was not new to him. "Were you referring to me by any chance, Admiral Dexter?" he asked innocently.

Admiral Dexter looked to his right and left. "Why, who else would I be referring to, Commander Mount?" he asked.

"I didn't know, sir. I thought perhaps there might be some other officer of the HE-brew persuasion aboard."

"No, Lieutenant Mount—you're the only officer of the HE-brew persuasion aboard."

"Well, Admiral," Ben said, "perhaps I should have advised you before this meal that I'm not a very religious person. One prayer is as good as another for me, and you therefore need not have delayed the meal on my account."

"You're not a very religious person?" Admiral Dexter asked, a playful note in his voice.

"No, sir."

"That's strange. I thought people of the HE-brew persuasion were very devout people."

"I don't suppose that people of the HE-brew persuasion are any more devout than any other people, sir."

"Is that so?" Admiral Dexter asked, and Ben could tell from the tone of his voice that he was about to throw in a harpoon.

"Yes, sir."

"Well, Commander Mount, perhaps you can tell me, then, if people of the HE-brew persuasion are no more devout than other people, why do they consider themselves the Chosen People?"

Ben had dealt with this particular provocation many times. "Well, Admiral Dexter, some people of the HE-brew persuasion—those who consider themselves religious—believe themselves to be the Chosen People because somewhere in the Bible they are referred to as the Chosen People by God. In other words, sir, people of the HE-brew persuasion aren't trying to assert that they're the Chosen People; they're only repeating what they believe God told them in biblical times."

"That's very interesting," Admiral Dexter said. "I didn't know that. But tell me something, Commander Mount. Do you think you're a chosen person?"

"Chosen for what, sir?"

"Do you think you're special in any way?"

"In what way, sir?"

"You're being awfully elusive today, Commander Mount."

"I don't mean to be, sir. I'm just trying to figure out what it is you want to know."

"Shucks, Commander Mount—you know what I'm trying to say. I guess the problem is that we gentiles sometimes have difficulty expressing ourselves as clearly as you people of the HE-brew persuasion. I guess what I want to know is: Do you think you're better than the gentiles here?"

Ben looked around at the faces of the officers staring at him. He wondered how many of them wanted to see him trip and fall. Then he looked at Admiral Dexter again. "Better in what way, sir?"

Admiral Dexter smiled. "Why, I do believe that you're toying with me, Commander Mount. I think you're trying to make me appear foolish with your clever tongue, but I don't suppose I should be surprised, because I've often heard that it's extremely difficult to get a straight answer out of a person of the HE-brew persuasion."

"Well, sir," Ben said, "if you will permit me to say so, I must confess I find it difficult to give a straight answer unless I've been asked a straight question. I'm afraid I don't know what you mean by *better*. Do you mean stronger, more intelligent, more worthy of existence, a better engineer, a better officer, a better citizen, or what?"

Admiral Dexter chuckled. "Oh, how crafty you

are, Commander Mount. You've got a real silver tongue, haven't you? Well, since you continue to dodge my question, I guess I'll go ahead and ask Captain Healey to say grace. Captain Healey?"

Captain Healey folded his hands together and bowed his head. The other officers followed his example, and he said, "Lord, we thank you for this bounty that we are about to receive. Amen."

Ben took the napkin from underneath his silverware and folded it on his lap. The door to the kitchen opened, and the stewards carried in tureens of soup.

Admiral Dexter looked at Ben. "That little prayer didn't offend you in any way, did it Commander Mount?"

"No, sir."

"That's good, because I wouldn't want any officers of the HE-brew persuasion to be forced to engage in religious practices in which they don't believe."

"That's thoughtful of you, sir."

A black steward placed a tureen of soup on Ben's table and ladled it out. Ben's stomach was tied in knots. His verbal bout with Admiral Dexter had caused him to lose his appetite, but he knew he had to eat—not only because he needed to maintain his outward composure but because he needed food as well as rest. Tomorrow would be an important day for him, perhaps the most important in his life.

FORTY-SIX

In a bistro not far from Fisherman's Wharf in San Francisco, Dolly Keller sat at the bar, drunk at five o'clock in the afternoon. She wore her brunette hair shoulder length, with a pompadour above her forehead. Her cheeks were heavily rouged and her mouth was thick with lipstick. She was thirty-two years old and wished she still was twenty-two.

Next to her sat a fisherman, his arm around her shoulders. He'd came to port that morning on a boat filled with tuna, had been paid, and shortly thereafter had met Dolly in a bar. They had drunk whiskey and wine in several bars in the area and now were slowing down.

"Hey baby, where d'ya live?" the fisherman slurred into her ear. His name was Tony. Dolly stared at her glass of muscatel. The lights behind the bar were making pretty colored reflections in the amber liquid. She'd heard Tony ask her a question but didn't quite catch what it was. All the damn fishermen asked her questions, but as long as they bought her wine and danced with her, she didn't care what they said.

"Didn't you hear me?" Tony asked, shaking her

shoulder. He needed a shave and still smelled like the hold of the scow he'd been on.

"Did I hear you what?"

"I asked where you live?"

"Whaddaya wanna know where I live for?" She looked at him and wrinkled her nose.

"So I can take you home."

"I don't wanna go home."

He winked at her and made a crooked smile. "Sure ya do."

"I do not."

"Then whaddaya wanna do?"

"Sit here and drink."

"But that's what we've been doing all day." He hugged her shoulder. "Let's go to your place and have some fun."

"What kind of fun?"

He winked. "You know what kind of fun."

A bit of drool spilling from the corner of her mouth, she summoned together all her strength and threw his arm off her shoulders. "How dare you make an indecent proposition like that to a woman like me!"

"Aw, shit, Dolly. Don't gimme that," he said, grabbing onto the bar so he wouldn't fall on his face. He bumped into the sailor sitting next to him, and the sailor turned around.

"Watch what you're doing, pal!" the sailor snarled.

"Sorry," said Tony, pushing on the bar to make himself erect again.

The sailor looked at Dolly. "Is this guy bothering you, lady?"

"Naw, he's okay."

The sailor looked into her eyes, and she looked into his. He likes me, she thought happily. She wondered whether to make a play for the sailor and dump Tony. She'd always liked sailors. In fact, she was married to a sailor. *I wonder where in hell he is,* she thought.

Tony looked at her, his eyes crossing as he tried to focus. "Don't you like me, Dolly?"

"Sure I like ya, Tony."

"Then let's go have some fun."

"I'm having fun right here."

"You know what kind of fun I mean." He winked lewdly.

"I'm afraid I don't know what you're talking about," she said icily, looking over his shoulder at the sailor, and smiling.

Tony grabbed her shoulder. "Hey—what the fuck you mean you don't know what I'm talking about? I been spendin' all my money on you all day long and you don't know what I'm talking about? Are you fuckin' kidding me?"

"Well!" she said indignantly. "Just because you bought me a few drinks—that doesn't mean we're married!"

Tony staggered to his feet. "A few drinks! Lady, you drink like you got a hollow leg!"

"I *beg* your pardon!" Dolly said, imitating Bette Davis in a movie she'd seen recently.

"You mean after I bought you all them drinks you ain't gonna give me none of what you're sittin' on!"

"What!" Dolly said. Mortified in front of her friends in the bar, she hauled off and tried to slug him, but her aim was off and she missed.

Tony, ducking out of the way, collapsed against the sailor again, and the sailor turned around. "Hey, buddy—will you cut the shit!"

The sailor looked at Dolly again, and she looked at him. He was young and scrubbed clean, not an old wharf rat like Tony. She smiled at the sailor, and he smiled back.

Tony turned to the sailor. "Sorry."

"Mister, I think it's time you went home," the sailor said menacingly.

Tony looked at the sailor in disbelief. "Oh, you do, do you?" he asked. "Who the fuck do you think you are? Just because you're wearin' a uniform, you think you can tell people to go home?" Tony took a few steps backward and put up his dukes. "I'd like to see you make me go home!"

The bouncer came behind Tony and lifted him into the air.

"Hey!" Tony screamed. "What the hell's goin' on here?"

"You're goin' right out that door, you fuckin' scumbag!" the bouncer said.

"What'd I do?"

"You're making' trouble."

"But I musta spent twenny dollars in this bar today."

"Tough shit!"

The people at the bar laughed and slapped each other on the shoulders as the bouncer gave Tony the heave-ho out the front door. The bouncer smacked his hands together a few times and disappeared.

The sailor moved to Tony's stool and took a pack of Lucky Strikes from the pocket of his blouse. "Cigarette?"

"Thanks," said Dolly, removing one from the pack. She looked at the other side of his blouse and didn't see any silver dolphins. At least he wasn't on submarines.

He lit her cigarette with a match, then lit one for himself. "What's your name?" he asked, blowing a cloud of smoke into the air.

"Dolly. What's yours?"

"Eddy."

"Eddy what?"

"Eddy Holmes. Can I buy you a drink?"

"If you wanna."

Eddy called the bartender, and Dolly looked discreetly up and down the bar to see if any of her friends had noticed the handsome young sailor who was making a play for her. He sure was cute. And he appeared to have money.

The bartender came over and poured Dolly another glass of muscatel.

"Thanks," she said to Ed, fluttering her false eyelashes.

"My pleasure."

The bartender drew a glass of beer for Ed and placed it in front of him.

Dolly and Ed sipped their beverages, looking at each other over the tops of the glasses. Dolly thought she was falling in love again, and Ed thought that if he was lucky the old bag might give him a blow-job before the night was over.

"Dolly!"

Dolly turned and saw her friend Alice walking quickly toward her, a newspaper in her hand. Alice's coat was buttoned up; she must have just come in.

"Come on over and have a drink," Dolly said, certain that Ed would pay.

"Have you seen the papers?" Alice asked, raising the one she was carrying.

"I don't read the papers," Dolly said drunkenly. "They're only full of lies. Right, Ed?" She elbowed Ed in the chest.

"Right."

"Look at this!" Alice said, unfolding the newspaper and holding it up.

Dolly squinted as she read the headline:

SURMARINE SINKS IN ATLANTIC
Local Man Aboard

"Lemme see that paper!" Dolly said.

Alice handed her the paper, and Dolly looked at

the photograph of a sailor inset into the corner of a photograph of the *Sebago* taken on the day it was commissioned.

The sailor was her husband, Jethro Keller. She dropped the newspaper and her face drained of color. "Oh, my God!"

"Now take it easy," Alice said, sidling up to her and holding her shoulders.

"Whatsa matter?" Ed asked.

"Her husband's on a submarine that just sank."

Ed picked up the paper and looked at the picture of the *Sebago*. He read the first few paragraphs of the story. Dolly grabbed her glass of wine and gulped half of it down. The bartender leaned over to read the paper that Ed held up for him, and the other people at the bar crowded around.

The bouncer materialized out of the smoke. "What's goin' on over here!"

The bartender pointed to Dolly. "Her husband's on a submarine that just sank!"

"The one on the East Coast?"

"Yeah."

"Hey, Dolly—I didn't know you were married!"

"Well, I am," Dolly told him polishing off her glass of wine. "Hey, Mickey," she said to the bartender, "gimme another one, willya?"

"Sure thing, Dolly."

"Hey, Dolly," said the bouncer, "if you're married, how come you don't wear no ring?"

Dolly didn't answer him, reaching for the newspaper instead. "Lemme see that."

Ed gave her the paper and she bent over to read it. The other bar patrons crowded around her to read it too. Dolly found out that twenty-seven men were dead on the submarine, and the newspaper said it hadn't been able to determine whether Chief Boatswain's Mate Jethro Keller of San Francisco was among the casualties. Dolly looked at the photograph of Jethro. She hadn't seen him for a long time, and he looked different. Lost some hair and gained some weight. But he still looked like the mean son-of-a-bitch he always was.

Dolly handed the newspaper to Alice. "Oh, shit," she said wearily. "I need a drink." She swung around on her seat and faced her glass of muscatel. Raising it to her lips, she gulped half of the wine down.

"Did you read the last part of the article?" Alice asked.

"The beginning was enough for me," Dolly replied, the bar spinning around her. "I think I better go home."

"It said that the Navy in flyin' family members of the crew to the place where the submarine sank. You oughtta call the Navy and tell them who you are, so they can send you."

Dolly shook her head. "Nah. I haven't seen Jethro for years. I don't think he'd wanna see me if he's alive, and if he's not alive, I don't wanna see him."

"But Dolly, he's your old man!" Alice insisted.

"I told you that I ain't seen him in years. We never got along."

"So what?" Alice said. "Take the trip anyways. It'd look funny if you didn't go. The Navy might stop your allotment."

Suddenly Dolly became sober. That check came in regularly every month, and she'd got used to it. It kept her going so that she didn't have to work if she didn't want to. It had never occurred to her that someday it might stop coming in. And if Jethro was dead, there might be some insurance money.

"You're right," she said. "I'm gonna call the Navy." She stood up and rearranged her hair, trying to think of how to call the Navy. "Does it give a number in the article, Alice?"

"No."

"Then who do I call?"

"We can call the newspaper, or maybe we can look in the phone book."

"Yeah, the newspaper," Dolly said. "I'll call the newspaper." She turned to Ed. "Got a nickel, honey?"

FORTY-SEVEN

In Block Island Sound five ships and one submarine lay at anchor, their mast lights flickering through the mist and rain. On the *Falcon,* Ben Mount made his way through the corridors to the office being used by Admiral Dexter. He'd just received word that the admiral wanted to see him immediately. Ben carried a briefcase full of plans and sketches that he'd been working on, knowing that Admiral Dexter would want to be briefed on his plan to bring up the crew of the *Sebago* in the morning.

Ben reached the office and knocked on the steel door.

"Come in."

Ben entered the office and saw Admiral Dexter seated behind the desk. Admiral Walmsley and Captain Healey were seated on either side of him. Ben advanced to the desk and saluted Admiral Dexter. "You wanted to see me, sir?"

Admiral Dexter's hat was off and the large bald area on the top of his head shone in the light of the overhead lamp. "Have a seat, Commander Mount."

"Yes, sir."

Ben sat on one of the chairs in front of the desk.

He looked at Dexter, Walmsley, and Healey; the latter two did not appear particularly hostile to him.

"We wanted to know exactly how you intend to employ your rescue chamber tomorrow," Admiral Dexter said.

"I thought you'd ask me that, sir," Ben replied, "so I brought some material along to show you how everything will work." He opened his briefcase and spread some of the drawings on the desk in front of the three officers. "The first step in the rescue operation will be to send a diver down and have him fasten a downhaul cable to the escape hatch above the forward torpedo compartment." Ben pointed to the drawings of the escape hatch and the specially designed fitting on the end of the cable. "Then the chamber will ride down the cable to the escape hatch. When it touches, the crew inside the chamber will clamp it to the matching fitting at the top of the sub's hatch. A crew member will tap a signal on the hatch to the men inside, and they'll open the hatch climbing out of the submarine into the chamber. We believe we can fit six or seven of them at a time. The chamber will be raised to the *Falcon,* the submarine crew will debark, and the chamber will go down again. It will continue making trips until all the crew members are out."

Admiral Dexter scrutinized the drawings. "You make it sound easy, Mount."

"It won't be that easy, sir."

"I know it won't be that easy," Dexter said gruffly. "Any number of things can go wrong. For one thing, this rescue chamber's never been used before. We don't even know if it works."

Admiral Walmsley cleared his throat. "It's worked on tests we've conducted at the yard, sir."

"But it hasn't been tested in deep water yet."

"That's true, sir."

"And the water out there's awfully rough." He

pointed his stubby forefinger to a drawing of the rescue chamber. "I wouldn't stake my life on this damn contraption."

Ben shrugged. "Well, sir, I don't see any alternative but to try to get them out with this rescue chamber."

Dexter looked askance at Ben. "You can't think of any alternatives, Mount?"

Ben sat on the chair and leaned forward. "No, sir."

"A smart feller like you can't think of anything else?"

"No, sir."

"It seems to me that there's something rather obvious that a smart feller like you should have thought of, Mount."

"What's that, sir?"

"We could send divers down to close off your faulty main induction valves, and then we could pump out the flooded compartments." Admiral Dexter looked at Admiral Walmsley for his comment.

"But sir," Admiral Walmsley said, "we don't know for sure that the main induction valves have broken down. If they're not, using the divers that way would waste precious time."

Admiral Dexter looked at Captain Healey. "What do you think, Dennis?"

"I think we should try the rescue chamber first, sir. We should get those men out of there before we start pumping out the submarine. Those men probably aren't in very good shape, and I think we should get them out as soon as possible."

Admiral Dexter turned to Ben. "I imagine you favor using the rescue chamber too."

"Yes, sir, I do—for the reasons Admiral Walmsley and Captain Healey mentioned, and one more. If you start pumping water out of the rear compartments, there's no telling how the submarine may react. It may wrench loose suddenly from the bottom, and if her hull's damaged, it could become worse. If the hydroplanes have been damaged, the submarine may broach. If the ballast and trim system are out of order, the submarine will be uncontrollable. There are too many variables involved if you pump out the rear compartments, sir. I think we ought to send down the rescue chamber first thing in the morning and get those men out of there as quickly as we can."

Admiral Dexter looked at the drawings and pondered what Ben had said. The bright light of the overhead lamp cast sharp shadows on his face and made him appear Oriental. "The rescue chamber is a variable too," he said. "We don't know if it will work."

"It'll work," Ben said.

"How can you be so sure?"

"I've checked it over thoroughly and I can't find anything that could go wrong with it."

Admiral Dexter gazed into Ben's eyes. "You probably would have said the same thing about the *Sebago* before its first dive."

"If I had checked it as thoroughly as I've checked the rescue chamber, and if I'd found nothing wrong, yes—I would have said that. But I didn't, and quite frankly I can't understand why you would say that."

"I'm trying to suggest, Commander Mount, that you could be completely sure of yourself and still be wrong."

"I understand that, sir," Ben said, "and I'm sure your remark could be applied to any of us here, you yourself included."

Admiral Dexter appeared irritated. "Yes, I suppose it could."

An uneasy silence fell over the office. Ben leaned back in his chair and waited to hear what Admiral Dexter would say next. Admiral Dexter and the other officers looked over Ben's drawings and specifications. After a while Admiral Dexter looked up at Ben.

"You may return to your cabin, Lieutenant Mount,"

Dexter said. "Rescue operations will begin at the crack of dawn. I expect you to be at your station and ready to go work at that time."

Ben arose from the chair and stood at attention in front of Admiral Dexter's desk. "Yes, sir," he replied, throwing a salute.

He returned his drawings to his briefcase, executed an about-face, and marched out of the office.

FORTY-EIGHT

The chapel was empty and dimly lit as Helen Mc-Crary entered at nine o'clock in the evening. It was a small wooden building, austere compared to other churches Helen had seen. Purple cloth covered the altar, and a plain cross was affixed to the wall behind it. A light on the ceiling was focused on the cross, and Helen couldn't take her eyes off it as she stepped sideways into a pew.

She took off her kerchief and unbuttoned her raincoat. Kneeling, she clasped her hands together and bowed her head to pray. She said the Lord's Prayer and then asked God to save the lives of her brothers. She whispered into her fingers that she loved her brothers very much; she pointed out that Jack and Ed were decent human beings and asked God to deliver them from the depths of the sea.

She prayed only a few minutes and realized she had nothing further to say. It wouldn't be proper if she got up and left after just having arrived, so she decided to stay on her knees a while longer to show her devotion to God.

She rested her forehead against her clasped hands and wondered what she was doing in the chapel in the first place. Except for obligatory weddings and funerals, she hadn't been to church in years. She was a young intellectual and didn't believe in God. How could anyone believe in God in 1939, when science had explained everything?

I really shouldn't be here, she thought, as her knees began to ache. I don't have much faith in this stuff. God really doesn't help people. Religion is just for ignorant, uneducated people.

And yet, while worrying about Jack and Ed, something had compelled her to come to this barren chapel and pray for them. She thought she was being ridiculous and a hypocrite, but she was here, and she had to admit that she felt a little better, that the chapel afforded her a small degree of consolation.

She remained on her knees, thinking about Jack and Ed. Jack was her favorite, so handsome and dashing, but she thought that perhaps she loved Ed more, because he was so pathetic, like a little puppy dog who was lame. *My poor brothers,* she thought. *Please help them, O Lord.*

She rested her forehead against her hands, and her breath sounded heavy in her ears. She thought that hundreds, maybe millions of people were praying to God for favors at that moment, and if there was a God, why would He listen to her, Helen McCrary, who disobeyed so many of His moral laws. She knew she was a sinner and an unrepentant one. She had no right to ask favors of God.

She thought about Jack and Ed and realized that she cared for them much more than the shipload of sailors who'd marched through her life. She gladly would have forgone the pleasure of sleeping with all those sailors if she could have her brothers back safe and sound.

"Lord," she whispered, "if you bring me back my brothers, I promise that I won't sleep with any more sailors and I'll go to church every Sunday. I really do promise this with all my heart and soul. Please give me back my brothers."

She stayed on her knees awhile longer, and finally the pain in her legs became severe. She said the Lord's Prayer again, then stood and buttoned her raincoat. Putting on her kerchief, she stepped out of the pew and left the church.

FORTY-NINE

Commander Dobbs, the public information officer for the New London submarine base, made offices and typewriters available to members of the press, and Betsy Kirkland sat in one of the offices, typing a story about the men aboard the *Falcon* who would direct the rescue operations in the morning.

She knew some of the officers personally, and therefore could provide more information on them than the reporters who had to rely on press handouts from Commander Dobbs. She'd never met Lieutenant Commander Mount, although she'd heard a lot about him. She knew that Mount wasn't well liked among officers in the Navy because he was considered an arrogant know-it-all. She was aware that much of the hostility toward Mount was the result of anti-Semitism, for she'd often heard anti-Semitic comments made about Mount when she'd been with Jack in the officers' club. She'd decided not to use the anti-Semitic angle in her story. No use looking for trouble. But she anticipated interviewing Mount and wondered if he really was as smart as everybody said. If he was nasty to her, she'd rip him apart in anything she wrote about him.

There was a knock on the door.

"Come in."

A young ensign poked his head into the office. "Miss Kirkland—there's a call for you from your father. You can take it in Commander Dobbs's office."

Betsy rose and followed the ensign to Commander Dobbs's office. It was vacant so she sat in Dobbs's chair behind the desk. The young ensign left and closed the door behind him.

Betsy picked up the phone. "Hello—Daddy?"

Her father's deep voice sounded far away. "Betsy?"

"It's me, Dad."

"Well I'll be darned," he said. "Somebody just handed me a copy of the *New York Standard* and your name is right on the front page. I had to look at it twice before I realized it was you. It *is* you, isn't it?"

"Of course it's me, Dad. Who else could it be?"

"Well I'll be darned. I'll bet the commander there would like to string you up by your heels."

"He's out on the *Tioga,* but the officer he left in charge tried to string me up. He didn't get very far, though."

"Why not?"

"I mentioned your name."

"Good grief."

"Well, you're my father, aren't you?"

"Well, yes, but . . ."

"And you want the American people to get the truth about the *Sebago,* don't you?"

"Of course."

"Then what's the problem?"

He sighed. "I don't suppose that's much of a problem, but the Navy is going to be awfully mad at you."

"What do I care? They'd better be careful that I don't get mad at them."

"My goodness," Adam Kirkland said. "My daughter has become a real reporter. I guess I'd better be careful of what I say to you from now on, because if I don't I'm liable to read all about it on the front page of the *New York Standard*."

"Don't worry about that, Daddy. All your secrets are safe with me."

"That's nice to know. Listen, dear, I and a few other congressmen are visiting there tomorrow. I look forward to seeing you."

Betsy found a piece of paper on Commander Dobbs's desk. "Let me write this down," she said. "Will it be an official visit?"

"Are you interviewing me?"

"Yes."

"Good grief."

"Is it an official visit?"

"Of course it is," Adam Kirkland said wearily.

"Has the press been notified yet?"

"No, but I have a funny feeling that they are now."

"You're right," Betsy admitted. "Who's coming along with you?"

Adam Kirkland told her the names, and Betsy wrote them down. "I understand that we'll all go out on the *Falcon* and watch the rescue operations," he said.

"Can I come with you?"

"You?"

"Yes, me."

"But you're a reporter! It wouldn't be fair if you were the only reporter permitted on the *Falcon!*"

"All's fair when it comes to getting a scoop," Betsy said. "C'mon Dad. After all, I'm your daughter."

"I know," he groaned.

"Can I?"

"Oh, all right."

She smiled happily. "Thanks, Dad. You're wonderful."

He was silent for a few seconds, then said, "You're in an awfully good mood."

She realized he was questioning her feelings in relation to the danger that Jack and the *Sebago* were in. "If I brood about Jack I'm afraid I'll wind up in the hospital, so I'm trying to keep myself occupied."

"Are the McCrarys there?" he asked.

"Jack's father and sister Helen are here."

"Don't they think it odd that you're so busy at a time like this?"

"They haven't said anything."

"They're probably thinking something, though. I'd be more mindful of their feelings if I were you."

She thought about that. "Maybe you're right," she admitted. "I'll be more careful when I'm around them." She asked her father when he would arrive tomorrow, and he told her the approximate time. They made arrangements to meet at the dock the next day, said good-bye to each other, and hung up their telephones.

Betsy walked to her office, thinking about Jack. She wondered if other people thought the way her father did: implying that she mustn't really care for Jack if she was calmly writing newspaper articles about the submarine disaster.

Do I really love him? she wondered. *Would I be able to do my work if I really loved him?*

She didn't know whether she really loved him or not, and she wasn't sure that she knew what love really was. She knew that she cared about him. She knew that she enjoyed being with him. But she also knew that she wasn't gaga over him the way many of her girl friends were over their men. Was it because she was too intelligent to go gaga over someone, or was she simply not in love?

She approached the office she'd been using, and saw that she'd left the door open. She entered the office and was surprised to see the reporter from the Japanese newspaper bending over her desk. He straightened up when he was aware that she'd returned, and he fumbled with his glasses.

"Ah, Miss Kirkland," he said. "I have been looking for you. I am Akiro Ito—reporter for the *Ogaki Sanjo* —we met earlier in the day. I would like to ask you something."

"What is it?" she asked, trying to be pleasant although she'd just caught him looking at her personal notes.

"I have been told that you are daughter of Congressman Kirkland, is that correct?"

"Yes, it is," she said.

"I wonder if you would permit me to interview you for article in my newspaper?"

Betsy smiled. "I don't think I could tell you very much. My father is the congressman, not me."

Ito pointed his finger in the air. "Ah, but you have so much important information in the stories that you have written for your newspaper. It seems to me as though you know quite very much."

"Everything I know I put into the stories. If you wanted to use one of them, I'm sure something could be worked out with my editor."

"Ah, I see," Ito said. "Well, I think I shall call my editor and ask him." He bowed. "Good evening, Miss Kirkland."

"Good evening."

The Japanese man bowed again and left her office. Betsy sat at her typewriter, trying to remember his name. She'd been introduced to him earlier in the day at one of the press conferences. She wondered if he'd been trying to steal information from her desk or if he genuinely wanted to interview her. It doesn't matter anyway, she thought, because I don't know anything special.

She looked at the paper in her typewriter and saw that she'd been writing about Lieutenant Commander Ben Mount. Picking up the sentence where she'd left off, she began hitting the typewriter keys, wondering if she'd get an opportunity to interview Mount tomorrow.

FIFTY

It was midnight. Jack McCrary lay underneath two blankets, huddled against Lieutenant Stearns, and Lieutenant Nielsen was sleeping underneath the same blankets on the other side of Stearns. They'd decided to pool their blankets and sleep together for maximum warmth.

Jack had awakened a few minutes before and was listening to the sound of breathing all around him. Some of the men were fast asleep and breathing deeply, while others, like him, were awake and wondering what the morning would bring.

Jack's leather jacket protected his torso from the cold of the deck, but his legs felt as though sheathed with ice. His head rested on his raincoat, and he rolled onto his back, looking past the chart table at the ballast and trim control console.

The air was foul, and something was dripping somewhere. When he'd awakened he hadn't known where he was, but it quickly came back to him: He was on the *Sebago* and it was down. His chest ached, and he thought he might be coming down with pneumonia. If they weren't rescued in the morning, they almost certainly would be dead by tomorrow night. The oxygen bottles were half empty and water was rising in the forward torpedo compartment. Tomorrow would be decisive.

Jack told himself that he never should have volunteered for submarines. Everyone knew they were more dangerous than surface vessels. Jack had thought he could get his own command faster, and he'd been right. He was skipper of a submarine, and he was only twenty-eight years old. But the people who said submarines were dangerous had been right too. If he hadn't volunteered for the submarine service he'd be safe right now. It had been a foolhardy thing to do, and he regretted it.

It was hard for him to imagine that on the day after tomorrow the world might be here but he wouldn't. Betsy and Helen and his father would be here, but he wouldn't. And neither would Ed. Poor Ed. May his soul rest in peace. If I ever get out of this, I'll be nicer to people, he thought. I won't be so foolhardy. I'll be especially respectful of Mom and Dad, because they don't have much longer to live. He also swore that if he got out alive he wouldn't rest until the person who'd caused the disaster was thrown out of the Navy.

If he and the others weren't rescued they'd get weaker and die. There might be a few minutes of suffocation and panic, but then it'd be all over. Maybe they could escape with the Momsen lungs, but it was a long shot. No one had ever used them to escape from a sunken submarine before. They were too many things that could go wrong.

Jack clenched his jaw and rolled toward Stearns again. *Why am I having these morbid thoughts?* he wondered. *Why am I losing faith? I imagine that they'll get us out of here tomorrow, and if they don't, well, all I can do is try to die bravely, like a McCrary.*

FIFTY-ONE

The alarm clock went off on the desk beside Ben Mount's bunk. He reached over and turned it off, then lit a cigarette from the pack lying next to the alarm clock. Taking a puff, he rolled out of bed and put his feet on the deck. He turned on the lamp and looked at the clock; it was four-thirty in the morning.

He stood and looked at the papers and drawings on his desk, puffing his cigarette. When it was half-way gone he stubbed it out in the ashtray, put on his robe, and went to take a shave and shower.

In the crew's quarters of the *Falcon* another man was also smoking a cigarette and thinking of the day ahead of him. He was Boatswain's Mate First Class Andrew P. Butsko. Captain Healey had told him yesterday that he'd been selected as the first driver to go down in the attempt to find the *Sebago*.

Butsko was a heavyset man with blond hair. His nose was crooked; it had been broken in a barroom brawl in San Diego. He had a reputation for being mean and troublesome, and his career was hanging in the balance because he'd been arrested a few weeks before by police in Providence, Rhode Island, for allegedly beating up his girl friend, a waitress in a saloon. His case would come to trial in around a month.

Despite that, he'd been selected to make the first descent. Captain Healey considered him the best diver in the Navy. He told him he'd be going very deep: to 240 feet. He added that if Butsko found the boat he'd be a hero, and no court ever would convict him of beating up a woman.

Butsko grunted as he puffed his cigarette. He was in a stateroom with three other divers, all asleep. From deep in the bowels of the ship he could hear motors humming. Soon it would be daybreak. Soon he would go down to the bottom of the sea and find—what?

It would be nice if he could find the *Sebago* and become a hero. What a laugh that'd be: a guy like him who liked to fight and mess up other guys' faces—a hero. His ex-girl friend in Providence would shit her pants when she found out about it.

Because the truth was that he *had* beat her up. To be more specific, he'd broken her jaw and knocked out three teeth. He'd found out that she'd been fucking the bartender she worked with, and he taught her a little lesson.

She thought he was going to go to jail for it, but oh, boy, was she going to be surprised if he found the *Sebago*.

Admiral Dexter felt a hand on his shoulder.

"Wake up, sir," said the steward. "It's five-thirty."

"I'm up," Dexter growled, rolling over.

"I've brought you some coffee, sir."

"Good."

The steward left the cabin and Admiral Dexter rolled over. The pot of coffee and cup were on the desk just as the steward had said. He sat up and poured himself a cup, taking a sip of the hot, pungent stuff, feeling it enliven him inside.

The big day had arrived at last. He'd had difficulty sleeping, and it had reminded him of when he had been a little boy tossing and turning throughout the night before Christmas because he was so anxious to open his presents.

But today there were no presents. Only a severe task ahead: one that could mean life or death for twenty-eight men on the bottom of the sea, life or death for the submarine service, and perhaps life or death for his career.

We've got to get them out of there, he thought as he raised the cup of coffee to his lips.

It was still dark when Ben Mount came onto the deck. He looked up at the sky and was pleased to see stars amid the patches of cloud. Perhaps the weather would be better today. He walked across the deck to the starboard rail and saw six-foot waves. The seas were rough but not as rough as yesterday.

He made his way aft to the rescue chamber. The deck rose and sank beneath his feet, and he bent his knees to compensate. Midway across the afterdeck he stopped and looked behind him to the superstructure of the ship, where he could see lookouts high in the turrets, scanning the horizon through binoculars.

Looking over the port rail, he could see the *Tioga, Jefferson,* and *Porgie* lying at anchor with all their night lights on. Lookouts were posted on them, too, for someone always is awake on a ship at sea. Soon their crews would be up and performing their duties in the rescue operations.

Ahead of him he could see the rescue chamber like an elongated ball on the after deck. He came closer to it, feeling almost as though it was human, perhaps even his child, for he'd worked on it so long, designing and building it from nothing.

"Is that you, Commander Mount?" asked a voice.

"Tolliver?"

"Yes, sir."

Ensign Tolliver stepped out of the shadows behind the rescue chamber. A short man, he had barely made the height requirement for admission to the Naval Academy. He often acted with exaggerated masculinity to compensate.

"I couldn't sleep," Tolliver said, "so I thought I'd come out and take a look."

"Everything all right?"

"Yes, sir."

"How do you feel?' Ben asked. Tolliver was to go down with Hodges.

"Okay, sir."

Ben placed his hand on Tolliver's shoulder. "I know you can do it, Ritchie. If you can't, no one else can either."

"I'll do my best, sir."

"If you do your best, I'm sure everything will be fine. Now let me take a look at this thing."

Ben moved toward the chamber and examined it to make sure nothing had happened during the night. The cables holding it fast were just as Ben had left them the previous evening. There was some brine on the metal, and the windows had fogged on the inside because all the hatches had been closed during the night. Ben figured the chamber would make its first descent around ten o'clock.

He looked at his watch. "They'll be serving chow in a few minutes," he said. "Let's get going to the mess."

"Yes, sir," replied Tolliver, following him.

In the crew's mess, Tommy Hodges sat at one of the long tables, eating scrambled eggs and bacon. He'd noticed everyone looking at him when he went through the chow line, and now they still were looking. He realized that the word must be out on him:

He was going down to the *Sebago* in the chamber. All the attention made him feel like a movie star.

"Pass the salt," he said to the sailor sitting next to him, a little guy with yeoman's insignia on his arm.

"Sure," the yeoman said, grabbing the salt and passing it to Hodges. "Hey, aren't you the guy who's going to ride that diving bell today?"

"Yeah," Hodges replied, sprinkling salt on his scrambled eggs.

"I heard this is the first time the thing has ever been used."

"Yeah."

"Good luck," the sailor said.

"Thanks," Hodges told him.

"Hey," said the sailor sitting opposite Hodges, "what's that Mount like?"

Hodges shrugged. "He's just another fuckin' officer."

"They say he's a genius."

"He's pretty smart, but like I said, he's just another fuckin' officer, which means that he's a pain in the ass like the rest of them."

The sailors around Hodges guffawed as they ate their breakfast. The best way to get along with other sailors was to put down officers.

"Isn't it strange bein' under a Jew officer?" asked a redheaded sailor on the other side of the table.

"No," Hodges said.

"Is he rich?"

"How the fuck should I know?" Hodges answered. "He never let me look at his bankbook."

"They say he's afraid to go down in the thing himself."

"He's got something called claustrophobia," Hodges explained. "He gets sick when he's in little places."

"There's always something wrong with Jews," somebody said. "They just can't take it."

The sailor sitting to the left of Hodges got up from the bench. "Good luck, feller," he said.

"Thanks."

The sailor walked away with his tray, and Hodges bit into a slice of toast. He wondered how much luck he'd need today, and if something went wrong, whether or not he'd be able to handle it.

Stearns was passing out the canned food for breakfast while Hodges bled oxygen into the control room. Near the radio shack Pharmacist's Mate La Gloria was urinating into the bucket. The stench in the room was almost unbearable. Jack picked up the microphone from the intercom.

"This is the captain speaking," he said. "Will the forward torpedo compartment please report."

There was silence for a few moments, then: Torpedoman Burns speaking, sir."

"How's everything up there?" Jack asked.

"No change."

"How's the leak?"

"We've got about six inches above the floor plates now."

"That means it came up about four inches during the night."

"Yes, sir."

"Seems as though it's getting worse."

"Seems that way."

"You have breakfast yet?"

"We're just getting started."

"How's your oxygen holding out?"

"We've got enough for about twelve more hours."

"We should be out of here long before that," Jack said. "Help should be on the way anytime now."

"Yes, sir."

Andrew P. Butsko crossed the afterdeck, his hands in the pockets of his bell-bottom dungarees and his white hat low over his eyes. Dawn was breaking, casting a ghostly glow on the ocean. He was headed toward the divers' station, which occupied a large deckhouse on the fantail of the *Falcon*. The station contained all the divers' equipment plus a decompression chamber in case a diver came up too fast and got the bends.

As Butsko neared the station, he looked at the huge rescue chamber hanging from chains on the afterdeck. He recognized Mount and some of his crew standing underneath it and talking. A group of sailors were at the port rail, watching the *Tioga* moving about.

Butsko entered the station. His three diving partners were there already. He guessed they were jealous of him. Each of them probably wanted to be the first one down, but he had been chosen.

Fuck you guys, he thought as he opened the door of his locker.

On the *Tioga*, Captain Robertson supervised the crew members who were fastening the dragging gear to a large wooden platform. The crew members stepped back when they were finished, and Robertson checked the fittings. The cable appeared secure. He signaled to Admiral Mackie, who signaled back to winch the platform overboard.

"Okay, boys," Robertson said, "let 'er go."

The winch strained the tackle taut and lifted the heavy platform over the starboard rail. The chief boatswain's mate among them started counting, and when he said *three* the tackle boom swung out and the platform slammed against the side of the *Tioga* on the way down. It crashed into the water, disappeared for a few moments, then rose to the surface again.

On the bridge, Admiral Mackie turned to the helmsman. "All ahead one third," he said.

* * *

As the *Tioga* moved away from the floating platform, the *Falcon* moved toward it. On the bridge of the *Falcon,* Admiral Dexter watched the platform bobbing on the waves. It was becoming brighter now; they might have a fairly decent day for the rescue operations. Congressman Kirkland glanced at his watch, it was seven o'clock in the morning.

Captain Healey maneuvered the *Falcon* close to the floating platform, then stopped his engines and threw down four anchors. His deck officers got the derrick working, and the big claw on a chain went over the side, grabbed onto the platform, and raised it into the air. It moved the platform over the *Falcon*'s fantail and then lowered it. When it hit the deck, a crew of sailors unfastened the cable and secured it to a big cleat near the divers' station.

Then Captain Healey went to get Andrew P. Butsko.

On the *Sebago,* Jack and his crew looked at the overhead as they heard ships maneuvering around above them. Something finally was happening. The *Tioga* was moving away and a larger ship, probably the *Falcon,* was moving into position. Rescue operations were getting underway. Jack heard the large ship stop its engines overhead, and then some clanking sounds came down.

"They're getting ready to do something," Keller said, a note of hope in his voice.

"They'll have us out of here soon," Stearns remarked.

I hope so, Lieutenant Nielsen thought, using all his self-control to appear calm.

Just then a *ping* hit the *Sebago*'s hull.

"Mason!" shouted Jack.

Mason, dozing in the radio shack, took out his notebook and pen. "I'm getting it down, sir."

The oscillator on the *Falcon* sent its message down

to the *Sebago,* and Mason deftly decoded it. He came out of the radio shack and handed the message to Jack: DIVER COMING DOWN.

"They're on their way," Jack said with a smile.

Andrew P. Butsko sat on the bench in the diving station. He wore his big bulky diver's suit, and his helmet was on a shelf in another part of the station. His eyes were closed, and his head rested against the cold steel bulkhead as he thought about the task ahead of him and the problems he might encounter at the depth to which he was going.

Under the extreme pressure of those depths, the human body sent an excess of nitrogen into the bloodstream. This alteration of blood chemistry caused different men to react in different ways. Some became giddy, others became morbid, and some forgot where they were or what they were doing there. Butsko had been at extreme depths before and experienced mostly the first symptom: He'd felt as though he was in the first stages of a drunk. If the same thing happened today, and it probably would, he would have to struggle to remain concentrated on his mission, otherwise he and the trapped sailors on the submarine would be doomed.

The door to the station opened and Captain Healey entered. "Are you ready, Butsko?"

"Yes, sir."

"Let's go."

Butsko rose and followed Captain Healey out of the divers' station. The other three divers followed, also in their deep-sea suits, and then a crew of sailors went inside to get the helmets and iron boots.

Butsko walked to the fantail of the *Falcon,* passing Ben Mount and the rescue chamber. Admiral Dexter was standing on the fantail, his forehead wrinkled as he watched Butsko approach. Butsko felt weird having so many eyes on him. He looked at his diving platform suspended by a chain from one of the derricks on the stern of the *Falcon*. The cable leading down to the *Sebago* had been threaded through a fairlead on the platform.

"How do you feel, Butsko?" Admiral Dexter asked.

"Fine, sir."

"Don't take any unnecessary chances down there."

"No, sir."

"Stay in constant contact with us through your radio."

"Yes, sir."

"Good luck."

"Thank you, sir."

Admiral Dexter shook his hand and looked him in the eye. Then he stepped away and Butsko sat on the bench next to the diving platform. He put his feet into the iron boots, and crew members fastened them to the pants of his diving suit. When they were finished, two other sailors set his helmet over his head and fastened it to the metal ring on the collar of the diving unit. The little glass port on the front of the helmet was open, and Butsko breathed the last fresh air he'd get for awhile.

Captain Healey kneeled in front of him. "Are you all right, Butsko?"

"I'm fine, sir."

"Do you have any questions?"

"No, sir."

Healey grinned and slapped Butsko on the arm. "Good luck, sailor."

"Thank you, sir."

Butsko got up and walked laboriously to the diving platform, standing in the middle of it and holding onto the cables that went up to the derrick. A sailor closed his face plate, and Butsko breathed the air pumped in through his helmet. It smelled rubbery, but that didn't bother him.

"Everything okay?" asked Captain Healey's voice through the earphones inside Butsko's helmet.

"Yes, sir."

"Hang on."

Butsko held the chains tightly, and the platform lifted into the air. He looked down at the crew raising their faces to him, and then was swung out over the water. Slowly the platform descended into the water, sliding down alongside the cable that led to the *Sebago*. The platform splashed down, and he was up to his knees in water. It rose to his chest, and then a wave crashed over his helmet and he was under the surface of the sea.

His exhalations burbled out through the valve of his helmet. He looked down at the rays of the sun as they slanted through the clear green water.

"Everything all right, Butsko?" asked the voice of Captain Healey.

"Everything's fine sir."

Andrew P. Butsko dropped deeper into Block Island Sound. He looked at the depth gauge strapped to his wrist, he was down to thirty feet already. The water was becoming dimmer, and soon he'd have to unhook his searchlight from his belt. He knew what he was looking for. Yesterday he'd been taken aboard the *Porgie* by Lieutenant Commander Mount, who had shown him the hatch above the forward torpedo compartment that he was supposed to look for on the *Sebago*. Mount had walked him back and forth on the deck of the *Porgie* a few times to familiarize him with its configuration, so he'd know where he was and what direction to move in when he landed on the *Sebago*—if he landed on it. There was no certainty that the cable was hooked onto the sunken submarine.

Butsko sank deeper into Block Island Sound. He took his searchlight off his belt and turned it on, sending a ray of light down toward the cloudy bottom. A school of small fish passed through the light. Butsko felt the pressure of the sea against his chest and legs.

"Butsko, how are you?" Healey asked.

"Okay so far," Butsko replied.

"How far down are you?"

Butsko looked at his depth gauge. "Ninety feet."

"Steady as she goes, Butsko."

"Yes, sir."

The water became darker as Butsko dropped lower. Everything was silent except for his exhalations through the valve of his helmet. He passed some clumps of floating seaweed and wondered if his folks in Pittsburgh had found out on the radio that he was the first diver going down to the stricken boat. He hoped it was at the bottom of the chain. It would be nice to help get those guys out of there. They must be in pretty bad shape by now. He wondered how he'd hold out if he'd been trapped on a sunken submarine for nearly twenty-four hours.

He looked at his depth gauge and saw that he was nearing two hundred feet. He flashed his searchlight in the direction of the chain below him. His flesh crawled when he perceived a long thin configuration way down there. It could be a rock formation or it could be the *Sebago.*

"I see something," he said.

"What is it?" asked Healey anxiously.

"I don't know yet, but it looks as though it might be the submarine."

"How deep are you?"

"Just about two hundred feet."

"If it's there, you should be seeing it soon."

Butsko strained his eyes to see the configuration more clearly. As he sank lower, the huge hulk of the submarine could be perceived. Butsko blinked his eyes; yes, the lines were clean, and the conning tower sprouted two periscopes. Bubbles rose from the forward part of the submarine.

"I see it!' Butsko said.

"Are you sure?" asked Healey through his headphones.

"Yes, sir. It's the sub—I can see it perfectly."

"Where will you come down?"

"On the foredeck, sir. The irons have hooked onto the railings near the deck gun."

"Perfect," said Healey. "Tell us when to stop."

"Yes, sir."

The platform began to drop at a slower rate. Butsko looked below and saw the railing of the submarine come closer. When it was five feet away, he said, "Stop!"

By the time the platform stopped, it was two feet above the guard rail. Butsko fastened to his belt the cable that he'd attach to the escape hatch over the forward torpedo compartment. Then he took a length of rope and tied it to the side of the platform. He jumped off the platform and dropped to the deck of the submarine. Stumbling, he lost his balance and fell to his knees, then gripped the guard rail and stood up again.

"I'm standing on the deck of the submarine," Butsko said.

"Wonderful!" Healey exclaimed.

"Lower the platform two feet."

"Right."

The platform was lowered. When it touched the deck, Butsko said, "Stop!"

The platform lay on the deck. Butsko turned around and saw that the escape hatch was about twenty feet away.

"I see the forward hatch," Butsko said.

"How do you feel?" Healey asked.

"Fine, sir."

"Good. Connect the cable to the hatch, and then we'll bring you right up."

"Yes, sir."

Butsko turned and walked in slow motion toward the escape hatch of the *Sebago*.

FIFTY-TWO

In the forward torpedo room Torpedoman Hank Burns heard the platform land on the deck. Electrified, Burns opened his mouth and looked up. He heard Butsko's heavy metal boots clomping closer.

"It's the fuckin' diver!" Burns said.

His crew cheered and clapped their hands. Burns reached for the intercom microphone. "Forward torpedo compartment calling the captain!" he shouted.

There was a pause, then Jack's voice came through the squawk box. "This is the captain."

"Sir, we can hear the diver working overhead!"

"We can hear him back here too, Burns."

Burns didn't know what else to say. "Well, I just thought I'd let you know," he muttered.

"Keep the men calm," Jack told him. "We'll all be out of here soon."

"Yes, sir."

Burns hung up the mike and turned to his men. "The skipper said stay calm. He said we'll be out of here soon."

The men lay back in their bunks and listened to the sound of footsteps above them.

* * *

Butsko made his way across the foredeck of the *Sebago,* flashing his searchlight ahead of him. Every step sent him into the air several inches, and he had to wait until gravity brought him down so that he could make his next step. Closer and closer he came to the escape hatch. It was weird to think that underneath his feet were twenty-eight trapped men.

Finally he reached the escape hatch and slowly kneeled in front of it. He could see the fitting where he was supposed to fasten the shackle of the downhaul cable that the rescue chamber would ride on. The fitting felt like marshmallow to his gloved fingers. He looked at it more closely, and it became a woman's breast. He giggled as he bent over to kiss it, but the plate glass window of his mask scraped against the fitting.

"What's going on here?" he asked himself. He looked around him, and wondered if he was dreaming all this. His head began to spin, and he heard the voices of women singing. He held onto the escape hatch and tried to clear his head.

"Are you all right, Butsko?" asked the anxious voice of Captain Healey.

"Ah, I don't know," Butsko replied, blinking his eyes and trying to focus them. He wanted to dance like Fred Astaire across the deck of the submarine. Maybe Ginger Rogers would come and dance with him.

"Butsko, what's going on down there?" demanded Captain Healey.

"Um . . ." Butsko wondered who was calling his name.

"Butsko, are you in trouble?"

"Ah . . ."

"Butsko!" Healey shouted. "Get ahold of yourself! You've got nitrogen sickness."

The words *nitrogen sickness* brought Butsko back to

reality. He remembered that when you had nitrogen sickness you had to take deep breaths to bring more oxygen into your body. He huffed and puffed, and slowly his mind cleared. Focusing on the hatch beneath him, trying not to listen to the singing girls, he unfastened the downhaul shackle from his belt and hooked it to the fitting on the middle of the escape hatch.

"I've done it, sir," he said, still feeling drunk.

"What have you done, Butsko?" Healey asked, an edge to his voice.

"I've hooked the shackle to the fitting on the escape hatch."

"Are you sure?"

Butsko pulled the shackle, and it was properly fixed. "Yes, sir."

"How are you feeling?"

"A little dizzy."

"Can you make it back to the platform, or should I send somebody down to help you?"

Butsko wanted to finish the job alone. "I can make it back, sir."

"Are you sure?"

"I'm pretty sure."

"We can very easily send somebody down."

"I can do it, sir," Butsko insisted.

"Call if you have any trouble."

"Yes, sir."

Butsko pulled the rope that led to the diving platform, and he floated over the deck. *I'm gonna make it,* he told himself. *They're gonna pin a medal on me when all this is over.* He landed on the platform and dragged himself to his feet. Gripping the cables that led up to the *Falcon,* he said, "Take me up, sir."

"Are you steady on the platform, Butsko?"

"Yes, sir."

"We're going to bring you up slowly so you don't get the bends."

"Yes, sir."

"Hang on tight."

"Right, sir."

Butsko gripped the chains as the platform began to rise. He resisted an impulse to wave good-bye to the submarine, and giggled instead.

Ben Mount looked through his binoculars at the destroyer turning broadside to the *Falcon*. It was only a hundred yards away, and he could see photographers lining the guard rail, taking pictures of the *Falcon*. Ben realized that the sinking of the *Sebago* was a major news event. A single-engine airplane flew past overhead, and Ben raised his binoculars to it. He could see a photographer leaning over the side, taking a picture of the *Falcon* below him.

Ben frowned as he lowered his binoculars. Twenty-eight men were trapped on a submarine, and it was turning into a circus. He realized that sooner or later reporters would ask him questions about the SS 192 and his rescue chamber. He didn't look forward to it at all.

A lieutenant approached Ben. "Sir," he said, "Captain Healey wants you to know that our diver has hooked onto the *Sebago*, and that you should prepare your rescue chamber for its first descent."

"When will they go down?" Ben asked.

"We have to bring the diver up slowly, so I'd guess around an hour."

Ben looked at his watch. "Thank you."

While Butsko was being raised slowly to the surface, a light cruiser came alongside the *Falcon* and tied up to it. A catwalk was set up between the vessels, and a group of distinguished visitors crossed from the cruiser to the *Falcon*. Among them were Vice Admiral "Hardtop" Hill and a group of congressmen from the Naval Preparedness Committee headed by Representative

Adam Kirkland of New York, its chairman. Following these personages were members of Hill's and Kirkland's staffs, and Betsy Kirkland, who was accompanying her father, representing the *New York Standard,* and anxious to see Jack if and when he was rescued.

Admiral Dexter came forward, all smiles, to greet his visitors on the foredeck. He saluted Admiral Hill, shook hands with the congressmen, and told them all was going well so far. He invited them to come to the bridge with him so they could watch the rescue operations.

Adam Kirkland walked beside Admiral Hill, happy to be on a ship again. He too was a graduate of Annapolis and had served four years in the Navy as an officer before leaving to help manage his family's business interests when his father died. He'd regretted having to leave the Navy, but he had only one other brother, who couldn't manage all the family affairs himself. He was an officer in the Reserve and still had the Navy in his blood.

Tall, with a mane of white hair, he walked with the others across the deck listening to Admiral Dexter tell them that a diver had made contact with the *Sebago* and that the rescue chamber would make its first descent soon.

Betsy walked beside her father, writing on her notepad. They entered the superstructure of the ship and climbed the ladderwell to the bridge.

Butsko heard a *swoosh* as he came up out of the water. Clearheaded now, he felt embarrassed by the way he'd behaved on the deck of the *Sebago.* The derrick raised him into the air and then swung him over the fantail of the *Falcon,* where he was lowered gently.

The platform touched down, and Captain Healey stepped forward to open the face plate and shake Butsko's hand. "Well done, Butsko," he said.

"Thank you, sir."

"You'd better get into the decompression chamber quickly."

"Yes, sir."

The *Falcon*'s doctor and a group of other officers and men accompanied Butsko to the decompression chamber in the divers' station, and Healey looked at the downhaul cable that Ben Mount's crew was fastening to the bottom of the rescue chamber. Healey walked to Mount and stood before him.

"It's your show now, Mount," Healey said.

"Yes, sir."

"Get them out as quickly as you can."

"Yes, sir. "

Healey walked back to the derrick, and Ben turned to Ensign Tolliver and Boatswain's Mate First Class Tommy Hodges. "Well," he said, "if you don't know what you've got to do by now, you'll never know." He extended his hand. "Good luck."

Tolliver and Hodges shook hands with him, then climbed the steel ladder and got into the rescue chamber. Ben saw them pull the hatch shut on top, and a few seconds later sailors from the *Falcon* untied the mooring cable from the nearby cleat. Then the derrick hoisted the chamber into the air and swung it over the sea.

Slowly the derrick lowered the rescue chamber to the water.

The oscillator signals hit the *Sebago*'s hull and Mason wrote down the message. When he had it all he handed it to Jack McCrary. RESCUE CHAMBER ON THE WAY DOWN. IT CAN CARRY SEVEN MEN EACH TRIP. EVACUATE YOUR INJURED FIRST.

Yeoman Reilly brought Jack a sheet of paper, and Jack huddled with Stearns, Nielsen, and Jethro Keller at the chart table to decide who should go up first.

Jack decided that he, as the captain, would have to go up in the last trip, and that Mason and La Gloria would have to stay until the last trip also.

"I think I should go up on your trip too, sir," Keller said.

"Why?"

"Because I'm the ranking enlisted man, sir."

Jack shrugged. "Okay."

Stearns said he'd go up whenever Jack designated him, but Nielsen decided he should go up on the last trip too, and told Jack.

Jack looked at him. "No, you're going up on the first trip, Nielsen."

"The *first* trip!" Nielsen spat out. "But it would not be proper for an officer to be among the first to leave! An officer should be among the last. Like you."

Jack shook his head. "I'm the captain of this boat —that's why I go last. And you're a guest here—that's why you go in the first batch. You're not even in this navy, Nielsen. Have you forgotten?"

Peter Nielsen became stern. "It would be a disgrace for me to be in the first group to leave. I beg you to let me go last."

Jack pointed at him. "I am the captain of this boat, and I'm making the decisions. You're going up in the first trip, and I don't want to hear anything more about it. You're wasting precious time."

"Yes, sir," Nielsen said, raising his chin in the air.

Jack conferred with Stearns and Keller and decided that Araujo and Goines from the control room would be among the first to go. Then he decided to go forward to the torpedo compartment to see if anyone was sick there. As he was giving orders to have Araujo and Goines helped forward, he decided that it might make sense to have the entire control room crew and officers move permanently to the forward torpedo compartment. He issued orders to effect this transfer and told Hodges to assign men to carry their food and water forward.

The control room crew and officers put on Momsen lungs and prepared to move forward to the torpedo room.

The rescue chamber hung over the sea. Tolliver and Hodges sat inside the tiny upper compartment, looking out the ports. The rescue chamber was suspended from the derrick by a cable and was also connected to the *Falcon* with an air intake hose, air exhaust hose, and a line that included a telephone cable and air power to operate the air motor.

"Are you two all right?" Ben's voice asked over the squawk box.

"Yes, sir," replied Tolliver.

"We're going to set you down, now. Hang on."

"Yes, sir."

Tolliver and Hodges waited tensely for a few moments, then felt themselves being lowered to the water. They splashed down, and the chamber rolled over onto its side, Tolliver and Hodges hanging onto grips welded to the inner walls.

"Still okay?" Ben asked.

"Yes, sir," Tolliver replied.

"Take her down, Ritchie."

"Yes, sir."

Tolliver pushed the lever, and the air motor started up, reeling in the downhaul cable Butsko had attached to the *Sebago*. Hodges operated the controls that blew the ballast and flooded the lower chamber. The rescue chamber slowly sank beneath the waves.

Inside, the air motor whirred loudly. Tolliver and Hodges looked around the tiny compartment for leaks and signs that something might be wrong. But they could find nothing. The chamber was working perfectly. Its motor reeled in the cable and pulled it ever closer to the *Sebago*. Hodges looked at the depth gauge on the bulkhead. Only 220 feet to go.

"How're you doing, Hodges?" Tolliver asked.

"Fine, sir. You?"

"So far so good."

Tolliver looked at the depth gauge as the rescue chamber dropped through the sea toward the boat on the ocean floor.

On the fantail of the *Falcon,* Ben watched the chamber sink out of sight. He looked at his watch. Ten fifteen. Turning around, he looked up at the bridge. A lot of brass and civilians up there. One of them was a female.

He looked again at the bubbles trailing to the surface from the descending chamber. He was standing beside the winch near the boatswain's mate operating the controls. The sun shone brightly and the wind was strong, making moderately high waves. The winch grumbled as it paid out cable for the rescue chamber. Captain Healey had returned to the bridge, leaving Ben in charge of the rescue operations.

"It's your show now," Healey had said. It was true. All the people out there were wondering whether the rescue chamber would work and if Ben Mount could save the submariners on the *Sebago*.

Ben pressed the button on the microphone. "How're you doing, Tolliver?"

"Fine, sir," said the voice on the squawk box.

"No problems?"

"No, sir."

"Can you see anything yet?"

"Only water, sir."

"How far down are you?"

"Fifty-five feet, sir."

"How's Hodges?"

"Fine, sir."

"Carry on."

* * *

Jack and the crew looked at the overhead and heard the rumble of ships' engines above them. They'd heard the diver working on the deck and they'd heard him leave. They knew the rescue chamber was on its way down, and they also knew that no one had ever been rescued from a downed submarine before. In the flickering dimness, with water rising to the tops of the torpedoes where they were standing, they hoped and prayed.

The ponderous bell sank deeper into the sea. Hodges looked at his watch. Ten fifteen. The depth gauge told him he was at one hundred feet. He was tense but not worried, and wished he could smoke a cigarette. He looked at Ensign Tolliver, whom he didn't like very much. Tolliver was smart, but he had a tendency to be chickenshit. Like too many ensigns, he thought that the only way to get respect was to be harsh and rule by fear.

Tolliver looked at his watch and the depth gauge. He was hatless and his straight black hair was parted on the side and combed neatly. Tolliver was almost an entire foot shorter than Hodges, and Hodges thought he looked like a little boy. A little boy playing naval officer.

Tolliver kept his hand pressed against the lever that operated the air motor. The motor whined as it pulled the chamber deeper. Hodges saw beads of sweat on Tolliver's forehead. He took off his own hat and ran the back of his hand across his forehead; it came back dry. Tolliver is nervous, Hodges thought. I hope the fucker doesn't crack up on me.

"How's everything going?" asked Ben Mount over the intercom.

"Everything's fine, sir," Tolliver said. "Everything is working perfectly."

"How far down are you?"

"One hundred and twenty-five feet."

"Carry on."

On the bridge of the *Falcon,* amid the crowd of high-ranking officers and people from Washington, Adam Kirkland turned to Admiral Dexter and asked, "Do we know yet why the *Sebago* went down, Admiral?"

"We don't know for sure," Dexter replied, "but we believe the main induction valves failed immediately upon their diving."

"Do you have any idea yet why they failed?"

"No, sir, but you can be sure that we'll hold an inquiry immediately after we've raised her." He pointed to Ben Mount on the afterdeck near the winch. "That officer down there might very well be responsible. He's the one who designed the induction valve system."

Congressman Kirkland raised his binoculars and looked down at the figure the admiral had pointed to. "What's his name?"

"Benjamin Mount."

"Oh, the boy wonder. I've heard of him."

"We'll find out how much of a boy wonder he is when this episode is over, Congressman."

"I'm sure you'll see to it that he gets a fair hearing."

"Yes, sir."

Standing on the other side of her father, Betsy also looked at Ben through her binoculars. "What's *he* doing down there?" Betsy asked.

"He designed the rescue chamber, and he's directing its operation."

Betsy sensed the seed of a good story. The officer who designed the system that failed on the *Sebago* had also designed the equipment being used to rescue her crew. *I'll have to interview him,* she thought.

Jack looked at the faces of his officers and men as they stood crowded together. Their eyes were downcast, and they were solemn as in church. Not one of them tried to catch his eye or do something that would make him notice them and maybe assign them to the first trip going up.

The light was dimmer than ever and the stench was horrendous. Jack felt anxious to get out of the damned deathtrap submarine. He felt sick and woozy, and imagined everybody else did too.

It occurred to him that he should make a full report to the officers above as soon as possible. Since he couldn't go up on the first trip, he'd have to send Stearns, because Stearns knew everything that had happened. So did Nielsen, who would be on the first trip, but it wouldn't be appropriate for a Swedish officer to make the report.

"Lieutenant Stearns?" he called out.

"Yes, sir," replied Stearns, standing near the torpedo tubes.

"I want you to go up in the first trip, so that you can make a full report to Admiral Mackie of what has happened."

"Very well, sir."

Lieutenant Nielsen was sitting on one of the bunks. "Does that mean I will go up in a subsequent trip, sir?"

"No. I told you that since you're not in this navy you'll have to go up first. Torpedoman Blanchard?"

"Yes, sir?"

"You'll have to go up on the second trip instead of the first."

"Yes, sir."

Next to the torpedo tubes, Lieutenant Stearns felt happy—and annoyed with himself for feeling happy. The strain and stench were getting him down, but he felt that he, an officer, should not go up in the first trip. But he knew Jack was right and that one of the boat's officers should make a full report as soon as possible.

He also knew that something might go wrong and that the rescue chamber might not work. No one had ever been rescued from a sunken submarine before, and perhaps no one would be rescued now, either.

Hodges and Tolliver sat inside the rescue chamber. The depth gauge needle was at 220 feet. Hodges felt relatively calm, but he could perceive that Tolliver was nervous and edgy. Tolliver's face was damp with perspiration, although it was cold inside the rescue chamber, and his eyes kept darting around like those of a trapped animal. He hoped that Tolliver wasn't going to go nuts but was sure he could handle it if Tolliver did. He'd just whack Tolliver over the head with his monkey wrench and continue with the mission on his own.

There was a grinding metallic *clunk* as the rescue chamber touched down on the deck of the *Sebago*. Tolliver and Hodges looked at each other. They looked at the depth gauge. It read 236 feet.

"We're here, sir," Hodges said with a smile.

The chamber rocked from side to side as it settled down, then it was still. Tolliver turned off the air motor and took the microphone. "We're on the deck of the *Sebago*, sir," he said.

On the *Falcon*, Ben felt a thrill pass through him. "Everything all right?"

"Yes, sir."

"Fill your main ballast tank and empty the lower compartment."

"Yes, sir."

Hodges and Tolliver manipulated the levers and knobs that controlled these functions. The additional weight of water in the ballast tanks, and the vacuum being created in the lower compartment, made the rubber gasket on the bottom of the rescue chamber adhere firmly to the escape hatch.

It won't be long now, Hodges thought as he watched the lower compartment's air pressure needle drop.

Jack jerked his head around when he heard the metallic thunk. "It's here," he said. "Let's get ready to go."

He threaded through the press of men in the compartment and stood under the escape hatch, looking up at it. *Please Lord, make everything go right,* he thought. "Bring Araujo and Goines over here," he said. "The rest of you going up in the first trip stand by."

Araujo and Goines were helped forward, and the other men rearranged themselves as they looked up and listened to the sounds of the rescue chamber above them.

"Seal completed," said Hodges to Tolliver.

"Open the hatch."

"Yes, sir."

Hodges got down and undogged the hatch that separated the upper compartment of the diving bell from the lower one. He wondered if water would gush up when he opened the hatch, but he pulled it open and nothing happened. Looking below, he could see a small puddle of water over the sub's hatch, but that was to be expected. He dropped into the lower compartment and slid four steel bolts into rings around the hatch, to make the chamber more secure to the submarine.

"We're opening the submarine hatch," Tolliver said over the intercom.

"Everything okay?" Ben asked.

"Everything seems fine so far, sir."

Ben chewed his lips as he waited for the next report. A crowd of officers and sailors clustered around him, listening to the squawk box that carried Tolliver's voice.

On the *Sebago*, Jack stared at the hatch as he listened to it being undogged. He was breathing through
clenched teeth, praying that the hatch would open and
he'd see the face of a human being inside the rescue
chamber.

The hatch opened a crack and he saw a ray of electric light. It opened all the way, and he saw the face
of Hodges smiling down at him.

"How's everything going, sir!" Hodges said cheerily.

"So far so good," Jack replied. The men around
him smiled happily and winked at each other.

"Lemme pass this air hose down to you so you can
ventilate out a little bit." Hodges passed the hose
down, and Jack heard the steady whoosh of air. "You
can start sending your men up now, sir," Hodges said.
"We can only fit seven each trip—I guess you know
that."

Jack and the men near him lifted Araujo up to the
chamber, and Hodges pulled him in.

In the upper compartment, Tolliver spoke into the
mike. "We're taking the first man aboard, sir," he reported.

"Good work," replied Ben over the squawk box.

Tolliver hung up the mike and went down to the
lower compartment to help Hodges pull the first group
aboard. He grabbed a sailor's arm and helped him up
while gazing down at the upturned faces below him.
It was dark and they all looked haggard, with bloodshot eyes and bleached skin.

"Move to the upper compartment," he told the
sailor he'd just pulled aboard. "Let's go. We don't
have all day."

"Anybody got a bottle of whiskey up there?" joked
one of the crew.

Hodges chuckled as he grabbed the next man. "No,
but I got a nice blonde for you. I'm gonna send her
right down."

"Wowee!" said the sailor.

Jack watched his men go up one by one. Finally it was Stearns's turn. Stearns looked at him and smiled. Jack held out his hand.

"Have a nice trip, Bob," Jack said.

"Thank you, sir."

The crew members lifted Stearns, and he was grabbed by Hodges and Tolliver, who pulled him into the chamber.

"Move to the upper compartment, sir," Tolliver told him.

Stearns climbed up with the other men, and Tolliver leaned toward the submarine. "That's all for now," he said. "We'll be back for the next trip in a little while."

"Bon voyage," Jack said.

"Hey, where's that blonde?" shouted a sailor.

Hodges removed the bolts and closed the hatch as Tolliver climbed into the upper compartment of the rescue chamber. Hodges dogged the wheel and Tolliver reached for the mike.

"We've taken seven men aboard," Tolliver reported, "and we're preparing to come up."

"Everything working okay?"

"Yes, sir."

"Take it slow and easy."

"Yes, sir."

Hodges climbed into the upper compartment and grinned at the group of sailors crowded into the small space. "Everybody okay?" he asked.

They nodded and smiled. Even Araujo managed a wink. Hodges closed the hatch separating the upper compartment from the lower and turned the wheel that made it fast.

"The hatch is secure sir," he said to Tolliver.

"Prepare to ascend."

"Yes, sir."

Stearns watched in amazement as Tolliver and

Hodges worked their little levers and wheels. Water was blown out of the ballast tank and the air pressure was raised in the lower chamber, breaking the seal between it and the *Sebago*. Tolliver pulled the lever on the air motor and the chamber began to rise. Stearns couldn't believe that he was on his way to the surface. He'd been on the stricken submarine for nearly twenty-seven hours and there had been times when he'd thought he'd never get out.

Now he was out, and all he could do was hope this strange little vessel would bring him all the way up.

"How's it going down there?" asked Ben over the squawk box.

"Fine so far, sir," Tolliver replied.

Stearns listened to Tolliver talk with the voice on the squawk box. He looked around at his men. Araujo's normally swarthy complexion was ashen, and Goines appeared to be sleeping. The others looked out the ports or at the top of the rescue chamber. The air was much better than in the control room of the *Sebago,* but he didn't know whether or not to trust the rescue chamber completely. He heard Tolliver end his conversation with the voice on the squawk box.

"Who was that?" Stearns asked him.

"Lieutenant Commander Benjamin Mount. He's in charge of the rescue operation."

Stearns frowned. He knew that Ben had designed the main induction valves on his boat and was worried that something might be wrong with the rescue chamber, too.

Betsy Kirkland looked at Ben Mount through her binoculars. It seemed odd for such a young man to be the center of a rescue effort that included several ships and thousands of men.

"Calling Admiral Dexter," said Ben's voice on the intercom.

"What is it, Mount?" Dexter asked.

"The chamber is on its way up with seven of the *Sebago*'s crew members aboard."

Dexter waited for a few moments. "Anything else?"

"No, sir. Everything's proceeding according to plan."

"Let me know immediately if anything goes wrong."

"Yes, sir."

Admiral Dexter turned to Congressman Kirkland. "Well, the first batch is coming up at last."

"I'd like to go down to the deck and see the men when they come out of the bell," Kirkland said.

"Fine."

Admiral Dexter led the group out of the bridge and down the ladderwell to the deck.

"Will Lieutenant McCrary be coming up in the first group?" Betsy asked Admiral Dexter.

"No," he replied with a smile. "He's the captain now, and he'll be the last one out of the submarine."

Betsy thought of Jack as she followed her father and Admiral Dexter down the ladderwell. The other congressmen and aides followed behind them. Betsy realized that Jack was a hero. He'd commanded the submarine through the worst crisis in the history of the submarine forces, and he'd be the last one to leave the boat. She had a little Argus camera in her pocketbook, and she was going to take a picture of him as soon as he stepped out of the rescue chamber. She also wanted to photograph Ben Mount, who in some ways could be considered more important than Jack in this news story.

The group reached the deck and followed Admiral Dexter back to the winches. The hospital ship *Jefferson* had tied up to the *Falcon* during the past hour, and a motor launch had transferred some members of the press to the *Falcon*; they formed a group of twenty men on the fantail near the winch, held back by a group of sailors and a railing. The *Tioga* had returned to New London.

Betsy and her group passed through an opening in the railing and approached Ben Mount beside the winch. Ben didn't notice them; he was talking on his microphone and looking over the fantail of the *Falcon*. Finally he heard them and turned around. Betsy smiled when she saw the look of surprise on his face. He snapped to attention and threw a smart salute to Admiral Dexter. Betsy removed her Argus from her shoulder bag.

Admiral Dexter made the introductions. "Lieutenant Commander Mount, this is Congressman Adam Kirkland."

"How do you do, sir," Ben said.

"How do you do."

Betsy focused on Ben Mount and snapped his picture as Admiral Dexter introduced him to the other congressmen and their aides. With his hawklike nose and voluptuous eyes, she thought he looked like a different breed of human being than the admirals and congressmen speaking with him.

"And this," said Admiral Kirkland, "is Betsy Kirkland, Congressman Kirkland's daughter."

Ben smiled as he held out his hand. Betsy noticed that he had straight white teeth. "How do you do," he said.

"Hello."

Their hands touched and she shook hands awkwardly.

"I'm a reporter for the *New York Standard*," she told him. "I'd like to interview you when you have time."

"I'll have to get permission for that," he replied.

"From whom?"

"Admiral Walmsley, I think."

Betsy turned to Admiral Walmsley. "Would you let

me interview Lieutenant Commander Mount when he has time?" she asked sweetly.

Admiral Walmsley looked at Admiral Dexter, who glanced at Congressman Kirkland. Admiral Dexter nodded to Admiral Walmsley.

"Of course you can," Admiral Walmsley said to Betsy, "when Lieutenant Commander Mount is free."

"*Commander Mount!*" said a voice in the squawk box.

Without a word or an apology, Ben dashed to the squawk box and picked up the microphone. "What is it?"

"I should have mentioned before, sir," Tolliver said, "that two of the *Sebago's* men are ill and that you should have medical personnel standing by."

"Will do," Ben said.

Betsy snapped another picture of Ben as he made arrangements for doctors and nurses to come over from the *Jefferson*. She looked behind her and could see the other photographers taking pictures too, but she knew hers would be best because she was closest.

Congressman Kirkland cleared his throat. "Mount appears to be a very able young officer," he said.

Admiral Dexter looked at Admiral Walmsley, then turned to Congressman Kirkland. "Yes," he admitted reluctantly, "he's very able."

"It'll be marvelous if his rescue chamber saves all those men down there."

"It certainly will," Dexter had to agree.

FIFTY-THREE

Hodges looked at the depth gauge. It read 20 feet. "We're almost up, sir," he said to Tolliver.

Tolliver spoke into the microphone. "We're at twenty feet, sir."

"See you in a few moments," Ben said over the squawk box.

Stearns looked at the depth gauge and watched the needle move toward the lower numbers. His veins and arteries were humming with excitement. How wonderful to know you're going to live!

The chamber whooshed out of the water and was raised into the air. Everyone aboard looked out the ports at the sea and sky and ships all around.

"We're out!" shouted one of the survivors.

"Stay calm," Tolliver said crossly.

Stearns closed his eyes and gave thanks for his rescue. For a long time he'd thought he might die in the submarine, but now he was going to be all right.

The chamber was raised clear of the railing and swung over the deck of the *Falcon*. The sailor on the controls eased back the derrick, and the rescue chamber slowly came down. Sailors and civilians applauded; flashbulbs exploded. Crew members from the *Falcon* stood by with Ben Mount as the rescue chamber came closer. They reached up and grabbed it, guiding it to its mooring.

The crew members tied it down, and Ben stood beside it as admirals and congressmen crowded around him. The wheel on the outer part of the hatch turned as it was being opened from the inside, and then it swung wide. Ben looked in and saw Tolliver, Hodges, and the men from the *Sebago*. Betsy snapped another picture with her Argus. Hodges jumped out of the chamber, and Tolliver followed him. They reached in and helped Araujo out. Araujo stumbled out and looked around him in a daze.

"How are you, sailor?" Admiral Dexter asked with a big smile.

"I'm okay, sir."

A doctor and a medical aide led Araujo away as Tolliver and Hodges helped Darrell Goines out. Admiral Dexter shook Goines's hand, and Goines dropped to his knees and kissed the hollystoned deck of the *Falcon*. Betsy snapped the picture. One by one the others climbed out and were received warmly by the officers and congressmen before passing on to the medical personnel from the *Jefferson*. Cameras flashed and reporters took notes.

Lieutenant Stearns was the last out, and he didn't need anyone to help him. He stood erect and proud; everyone could see that this was an officer who'd been through hell but still knew who he was and what he represented.

"Welcome back, Lieutenant," Admiral Dexter said warmly, pleased by the proud demeanor of the young officer.

"It's great to be back, sir," Stearns replied.

"This is Congressman Kirkland from Washington."

"How do you do, sir," Stearns said.

"It's good to see you, Lieutenant," Kirkland replied, shaking his hand.

"It's good to see you, too."

Betsy stepped toward Stearns, whom she knew fairly well. "How's Jack?" she asked.

"He's fine," Stearns said. "He's a credit to the Navy."

"So are you, young man," Admiral Dexter said, slapping him on the shoulder.

"I'm prepared to make my report whenever you want to hear it, sir," Stearns said.

"There's plenty of time for that," Dexter replied. "I think you should be checked out by the doctors first."

"Yes, sir."

Stearns stepped toward the *Jefferson* and saw Ben Mount, whom he'd been introduced to briefly once at a party in the New London officers' club.

Ben held out his hand. "Welcome back to the world, Stearns."

"It sure looks nice up here," Stearns said. "If it weren't for your little rescue chamber, I guess we wouldn't be here."

Ben smiled. "Well, I hope it's not my fault that you were down there. I look forward to reading your report."

"All I can do is explain the way it happened."

"I'm sure that will be very helpful."

Stearns decided that he shouldn't tell Mount about how mad Jack McCrary was at him; there was no sense getting mixed up in that mess. Stearns left Ben and headed for the *Jefferson,* and Betsy opened the back of her Argus, for she'd finished off her first roll shooting pictures of Stearns and Ben Mount shaking hands.

Mount walked to where Dexter was standing. "Sir, I think you all ought to stand back, because we're sending the chamber down again."

Dexter and the group with him backed up, and Tolliver and Hodges got into the rescue chamber again. Ben poked his head inside. "Are you both sure you can handle another trip?"

"Yes, sir," said Hodges and Tolliver in unison.

Ben thought Tolliver looked nervous. He could send someone else down with Hodges, but he didn't have anyone as well trained as Tolliver, and it would be damaging to Tolliver's career if he was relieved in front of all those admirals and congressmen.

"Carry on," Ben said.

Hodges pulled the hatch shut, and Ben stepped back. The derrick lifted the rescue chamber into the air and swung it over the water. Then the rescue chamber slowly began to descend for its second trip to the bottom.

The *Tioga* had returned to New London after transferring its cable to the *Falcon* that morning, and now Admiral Mackie sat alone in his office, awaiting further news on the rescue operations. Glancing through the stack of newspaper reports that his public information officer had brought him, he realized with great displeasure that Betsy Kirkland's stories had placed the Navy in a bad light. She had revealed that the *Sebago* had gone down around ten miles from its reported diving position, which made the Navy appear incompetent. She had also told of the confusion of the officers, the misery of the wives waiting anxiously for word of their husbands, and the Navy's reluctance to provide information to the press.

Admiral Mackie had not had any idea that Betsy was a reporter. He recalled how he'd shown her the messages and dispatches on his desk, and he knew that he could be called on the carpet for his indiscretions with her. He could be transferred to a desk job in Washington for this one.

There was a knock on the door of his office. "Come in."

Lieutenant Simpson came in with a piece of paper in his hand. "This just came in from the *Falcon*, sir."

Admiral Mackie took the message and read it. It stated that the first group from the *Sebago* had been brought aboard the *Falcon,* and that Lieutenant Stearns had provided a list of those presumed dead on the submarine. The first name on the list was Lieutenant Commander Gene Dunlop, but Mackie already knew that Gene had died. His eyes roved down the list, stopping at the names of men he knew personally. When he came to Seaman First Class Edward McCrary, he groaned. He'd thought the lad might have been killed, because his station was in the engine compartment that was flooded first.

Admiral Mackie looked up at Lieutenant Simpson. "Has Commodore McCrary seen this list yet?"

"No, sir."

"Get him for me, would you?"

"Yes, sir."

Lieutenant Simpson left the office, and Admiral Mackie lay the sheet of paper on his desk. He'd have to notify those people whose husbands or sons had died, and he didn't know exactly how to go about it. Ordinarily he'd have sent telegrams, but now they were sitting outside his office. He'd have to speak to them individually—or maybe together, he didn't know yet which. But at least he could talk straight to Ray McCrary. Ray was an old friend and an old Navy man. Ray would be able to take it.

Lieutenant Simpson opened the door of the office, and Commodore McCrary, accompanied by Helen, entered.

"Have a seat," Admiral Mackie said somberly.

Ray McCrary sensed that something was wrong, and sat down slowly, trying to maintain his equanimity. Helen believed that Admiral Mackie had called them in to inform them that Jack and Ed were all right. It was impossible for her to think that they were not.

"I'm afraid I have bad news for the both of you,"

Admiral Mackie said. "The indications are that Ed was one of the unlucky ones."

Ray McCrary closed his eyes, and Helen was stunned. She couldn't believe what she'd just heard. She looked around her and realized that she wasn't dreaming, and that it really had happened. She began to sob, groping around in her handbag for her handkerchief.

"I'm very sorry to have to tell you this," Admiral Mackie said softly. "I truly am."

Dolly Keller had arrived in New London in the middle of the night and had been assigned a room in the nurses' quarters. She'd been half drunk, but now was sober, bathed, and attired in a demure little outfit that her friend Alice had found for her before the flight from San Francisco. Alice had cautioned her not to wear much makeup and to behave herself so as not to jeopardize her allotment or any insurance monies that she might be entitled to in the event of Jethro's death.

Dolly sat by herself in a corner of the room wishing for a drink. She decided that the other women were a bunch of stiffs. Except for Mrs. Burns, who looked as though she knew her way around.

All the women looked up at Commodore Briscoe and Captain Robertson.

Commodore Briscoe cleared his throat. "Admiral Mackie would like to speak with the following people," he said. He called out Mrs. Delbert's name, and then fourteen others. The women realized that news had come in about the men on the *Sebago* and wondered whether Admiral Mackie was first going to talk with relatives of the survivors or with relatives of those who would not come back.

Patricia Delbert figured correctly that he was first going to break the news to the relatives of the deceased. Numbly, trying to preserve her composure, she joined the other women and followed Captain Robertson into the hall.

When they were gone, Commodore Briscoe closed the door. He placed his hands behind his back and squared his shoulders. "We've just received the names of the men who didn't make it," he said. "Wives and relatives of those men have just been called to Admiral Mackie's office. Those of you here can have the comfort of knowing that your men are safe and are being removed from the *Sebago* at this moment."

Commodore Briscoe turned and left the room. Laurie Burns burst into tears, and Dolly Keller realized that she must really love her guy. Some of the other women were happy, and others seemed confused or disbelieving.

Dolly sucked a tooth and thought about Jethro. She realized she was glad he still was alive. That son of a bitch is too mean to die, she thought, wondering how he'd act when he saw her waiting for him.

The rescue chamber splashed up from the water for the second time, and the derrick moved it over the deck. The crowd of officers and congressmen watched as it was lowered to the deck and tied down by the crew.

The door opened, and the first man out was Boatswain's Mate Third Class Mark Donahue, who appeared drunk as his hand was clasped by a congressman he'd never heard of before.

"Welcome back, sailor."

"Thank you, sir."

The others piled out to be greeted and fussed over by officers, congressmen, and doctors. In the mélange Ben Mount drew Hodges aside.

"How's everything going?" he asked.

"Okay," Hodges replied, grinning and feeling like a hero.

"I've noticed that Tolliver hasn't been looking too well. What do you think?"

Hodges tried to look wise as he always did when an officer asked his opinion about something. "Well, he's more screwy than he usually is, sir."

"You think he can handle what he's supposed to do?"

"I think so, sir."

"Would you feel more comfortable down there with someone else?"

Hodges shrugged. "There *is* no one else, sir."

"What if there were?"

"Yeah, I guess I'd feel better with somebody else, but I'm sure Ensign Tolliver's all right."

"Thanks, Hodges. Don't mention what I just said to Tolliver."

"No, sir."

Ben looked at Tolliver, sipping coffee and chatting with some officers from the *Falcon*. Hodges moved off to get some coffee from the jug the cooks had set up. Ben wondered what to do about Tolliver. He knew Tolliver was high-strung but had overlooked that defect because Tolliver was a good engineer. He hadn't forseen that Tolliver would have to take the chamber down on rescue operations; the *Sebago* had sunk before a special crew for the chamber could be trained. The chamber was still in a development stage as far as Ben was concerned. It hadn't been tested thoroughly. There still might be bugs in it.

Ben walked over to Tolliver. "Can I speak with you alone for a moment, Ritchie?"

"Yes, sir."

Ben and Tolliver walked toward the derrick, where no one was standing. Ben looked down at Tolliver and saw that Tolliver appeared tired.

"How're you feeling?" Ben asked.

Tolliver narrowed his eyes. "I'm all right, sir. Why do you keep asking?"

"Because I want to make sure that everything is all right."

"If anything was wrong sir, you can be sure I'd tell you."

"You seem tense."

Tolliver looked levelly at him. "There's a lot to be concerned about down there, sir," he said crisply. "How tense would *you* be if you'd gone down in the chamber twice?"

Ben didn't bat an eyelash, but he was stung by what Tolliver had said. He knew everyone thought he was defective and weak because of his notorious claustrophobia.

"Carry on," Ben said to Tolliver. "If you have any problems, be sure to let me know."

"Yes, sir."

Tolliver returned to the rescue chamber, and Ben looked at Lieutenant Nielsen, who was chatting confidently with the group of congressmen. Ben hoped Tolliver would be able to manage the four trips, because if he didn't there would be no one else with experience to send down with Hodges.

No one except himself.

Helen walked slowly to the docks of the Thames, thinking about her brother Ed and regretting the many arguments she'd had with him, the many insults she'd hurled at him over the years. He was two years younger than she, and she'd always considered him a spoiled brat. She thought her mother lavished too much attention on him and her youngest sister, sixteen-year-old Arabella.

Her father was calling her mother in Washington to tell her the bad news, and Helen had felt a need to take a walk and get some fresh air.

She looked at the sunny sky and the big puffy clouds. The smell of salt was strong in the air, and sea gulls flew in long swooping circles overhead. Be-

low her were the submarine pens and the docks where
large ships tied up. There also were buildings and
warehouses painted gray. Three sailors approached
her on the path and looked her over but didn't say
anything, because they too had been sobered by the
tragedy.

She came to the area where the submarine pens
were and paused to gaze at the one closest to her. It
was long and sleek; she'd always liked the way submarines looked. Some men were on deck, and she
thought of Ed working on the deck of the *Sebago*
only yesterday morning. Now he was dead, drowned
in one of the after engine compartments, probably
clawing wildly at the steel bulkheads as the water
covered his head.

Helen faltered. The image of Ed drowning was too
much for her. She looked around and saw a bench outside a Quonset hut. She walked quickly to the bench
and sat down, because she was afraid her legs would
give out beneath her.

She took a handkerchief out of her pocketbook, bent
over, and sobbed. She thought of all the times she'd
teased Ed and been mean to him. She'd cursed him
when she found out he'd been expelled from Annapolis, and now he was dead. Her poor little baby brother
was dead and she hadn't done very many nice things
for him when he was alive. She'd hated his pimples
and his awkward manner, and she'd resented him because he'd been her mother's favorite. She realized
now that he'd only been a little kid and couldn't
help being what he was. She could have been kinder
to him. He always tried to get her approval, and
she always pushed him away. No wonder mother loved
him so. If she hadn't, the kid would not have received any love at all.

Helen cried into her handkerchief. She wished she
could have done one kind thing for Ed before he
died. She could have seen him when she was in New

London visiting Jack, but she never even tried. Ed was an embarrassment to her, and now she realized that she had failed him and that there was nothing in the world she could do to make it up to him.

Helen let herself go as she cried. She'd opened the floodgates and couldn't close them. She saw her pettiness and vanity quite clearly. She realized she was not a nice person, that she'd given herself freely to people she hardly knew but had never given any of herself to her little brother, who'd needed her the most. She sobbed uncontrollably at the thought of little Ed ripping his fingers bloody against the steel walls of the submarine.

"I say there—are you all right, Miss?"

Helen looked up and saw a tall man wearing the long black trench coat and insignia of a British naval officer. She realized where she was and that she'd been making a spectacle of herself. "I'm all right," she said, dabbing tears from her cheeks.

"Are you sure?"

"Quite sure."

The officer looked at her and made a move to walk away, then stopped and looked at her again. Wrinkling his brow, he sat down next to her on the bench. "I imagine," he said softly, "that you've lost someone on the *Sebago*."

Helen turned to him, dabbing her eyes with her handkerchief. "Yes," she replied.

"I'm very sorry," he said.

"Thank you."

"I hope you won't mind if I sit with you a moment," he said, obviously ill at ease, "but I lost my father and my uncle at sea in the war, and I can understand what you're going through."

There was something mature and decent about him that she found soothing. "I don't mind if you sit with me," she told him.

He sighed as he sat down. "It's a terrible thing to lose somebody suddenly like this."

"Yes, but especially when you feel that you haven't been very kind to that person."

"Death always makes us take a closer look at ourselves and the way we treat other people."

"I only wish that I could have seen how mean I'd been to him while he was still alive."

The British officer put his hand on her shoulder. "Don't blame yourself unduly," he said consolingly. "It's not your fault that he died, and I'm sure you did your best while he was alive."

Helen shook her head. "No, I didn't do my best when he was alive. I could have done much better."

"They say that a schoolboy's hindsight is better than an admiral's foresight. You see things differently now, but back then you couldn't help being what you were. All you can do now is look ahead and make sure your relationships with other people are on a more even keel."

"If only we could go back," she whispered passionately.

"Yes, if only we could. But we can't, and I think that the sooner we realize that, the better. I'm sure this would be the way your husband would want it."

"My husband?" asked Helen, bewildered for a moment. "No, he wasn't my husband. He was my brother Edward, a foolish frightened little boy, and I wasn't a good sister to him. To tell you the truth, I'm not sure of what he'd want from me."

"I am. I'm sure he'd want you to carry on. If he was a real sailor, that's what he would have wanted. I'm a sailor myself, and I know what sailors are like."

"I guess I should know too," Helen said. "My family is a naval family and has been for years."

"Then you know what you must do."

"Yes," Helen said. "I know." She looked into the

British officer's eyes. "It's been helpful for me to talk with you," she said. "You came along in the nick of time. May I know your name?"

"Commander William Mulford, ma'am."

"I'm Helen McCrary."

Mulford became confused, because he knew that Jack McCrary, the executive officer of the *Sebago,* was still alive. "Did you say your brother's name was Edward?" he asked.

"Yes."

Mulford wrinkled his brow. "Is Jack McCrary your brother too?"

"Yes."

"You had *two* brothers aboard?"

"Yes."

"How extraordinary!"

Helen noticed the wedding ring on Mulford's finger and thought his wife a very lucky woman.

"You've given me consolation, Commander Mulford," she said, "and I'm very grateful. I hope that someday I can do something for you."

He smiled. "There's no telling what might happen. Who knows—perhaps someday you can do something for me."

They reached toward each other and shook hands as the sun shone down on them and sea gulls soared overhead.

FIFTY-FOUR

The rescue chamber touched down on the *Sebago* for the third time. Hodges entered the lower compartment and inserted his bolts into the fittings on the escape hatch. He opened the hatch and looked down at Jack McCrary.

"We're ready for the next load, sir," Hodges said.

Jack had seven men ready, and Yeoman Reilly was the first to go up. Torpedoman Cooper was second and Electrician's Mate Bean was third. Jack watched them go, revived by the fresh air pumped down from the rescue chamber. He looked at his watch; it was one thirty in the afternoon. The rescue operations were going smoothly, and he felt confident that he'd be on the surface soon. What a glorious moment that would be, standing in the fresh air, safe at last!

Electrician's Mate Wakefield was the last one to go up into the chamber. Hodges looked down to Jack. "We'll be back for you in a little while, sir."

"I'll look forward to seeing you, sailor."

Hodges closed the hatch, and it was dark again in the forward torpedo compartment. The water was nearly to the tops of the torpedoes piled on the floor, and Jack estimated that it would cover the torpedoes by the time the rescue chamber returned. He climbed over the torpedoes to one of the bunks and sat down. Keller was on the next bunk and Vincent La Gloria was lying with his bag of medicines on the bunk above.

Jack was so exhausted he couldn't think straight. He saw lights flashing in the darkness, and bells chimed in his ears. When he got topside he'd go to bed for awhile, and then he'd be all right. In a few days he'd be fit for duty again.

It seemed strangely desolate aboard the submarine with most of the men gone. He'd never been on a submerged submarine with so few people aboard. It was eerie to look around the torpedo compartment and see it so dark and empty. He was surprised to feel sad about leaving the boat. He'd been through such an ordeal with the boat that he felt especially close to it. It was like a big wounded creature. He chuckled; lack of sleep was making his mind strange.

"Did you say something, sir?" Keller asked.

"No."

"Thought you said something."

Jack got out of his bunk. "I'm going aft to the control room," he said."

"What for?"

"Just to make a last check."

"Want me to go with you?"

"Stay here."

Jack put on a Momsen lung and walked aft to the hatch. He opened it, stepped through to the officers' wardroom, and closed the hatch behind him. The officers' wardroom was filled with a greenish yellow mist from the chlorine gas. Jack continued aft, and paused to look in the stateroom he'd shared with Lieutenant Stearns. Seaman Olds was lying on his bunk, wrapped in a mattress cover. Jack looked at the photograph of Betsy Kirkland on the wall. *I'll be seeing you soon, my darling.*

Jack passed his quarters and looked in those occupied by the stiff corpse of Commander Gene Dunlop. *You poor son of a bitch, you should have taken a desk job long ago, but you love the sea too much.* Only yesterday morning Dunlop had been alive, commanding the *Sebago* and taking her out to sea. Now he was dead.

Jack opened the door to the control room and went inside. How strange to see it empty. He looked at the chart table, where he and Stearns had made so many frantic calculations. He glanced at the Christmas tree, the lights still glowing green, although dimly. *That fucking Ben Mount,* he thought. *I'm going to nail that son of a bitch Jew when I get out of here.*

Jack looked into the radio shack; Mason had left everything shipshape, as though for inspection. *If men are trained properly, they'll perform their duties properly regardless of the circumstances,* Jack thought. He decided to keep Mason in mind in case he ever got his own submarine command and needed a good radioman. There were others aboard this boat he'd like to have with him again too: Keller and Burns, and Lieutenant Stearns, who'd been like a rock throughout the entire disaster.

Jack looked around, and his eyes fell on the piece of paper he'd taped over the hatch that led to the galley. He wondered what he'd see if he peeled off that paper. He knew he shouldn't look—that it might be something terrible—but his curiosity overcame him and he reached out, tearing the paper away.

He looked through the rectangular piece of glass. A hairy arm dangled in the water before his horrified eyes.

Hodges looked at the depth gauge; it read 180 feet. He and Ensign Tolliver were crowded together with the seven crewmen. Hodges realized that with every trip the *Sebago* men looked worse and worse. Their eyes were haunted, and their complexions were turning green. It must be hell to be on a sunken submarine and not know whether you'd get out or not.

Suddenly a terrible grinding noise came from the air motor, and the ascent slowed down. The people in the chamber looked at each other in panic, and Tolliver began slamming the lever back and forth. "Let's go, you bastard!" he shouted.

He worked the lever, and the chamber wobbled. Then he reached for the monkey wrench, and before Hodges could stop him, he whacked it against the side of the air motor.

It stopped, and so did the rescue chamber. Tolliver raised the monkey wrench to hit it again, but Hodges grabbed his arm.

"I don't think you should do that, sir," Hodges said calmly, smiling as widely as he could.

Tolliver's face became contorted. "Take your hands off me this instant!"

Hodges kept smiling as he let Tolliver go. "If you hit it again, you're liable to make it worse. I think I can fix it, sir."

Tolliver looked around and saw that the men from the *Sebago* were alarmed. He realized he had to get a hold on himself.

"Okay—have a look at it, Hodges."

Hodges changed seats with Tolliver and began to fiddle with the air motor.

"What's going on down there?" asked Ben Mount over the intercom.

"The air motor's stalled," Tolliver reported.

"Stalled you say!"

"Yes, sir."

"How'd that happen?"

"I don't know how. It just stopped."

"If you can't get it going soon, let me know. I might have to send a diver down to help you get up here."

"Hodges is trying to fix it, sir."

Hodges moved the lever back and forth slowly, keeping his eyes shut and feeling for the niche that might get the motor working. He touched it on the third try and the motor started.

"Hodges fixed it, sir," Tolliver reported.

"Good work, Hodges."

The rescue chamber began rising slowly again, and Hodges sat at the controls smiling, trying to calm the fatigued survivors. If Tolliver had hit the air motor again with that wrench, he might have broken it for good, and then they'd all be stuck down there.

He decided he didn't want to go down with that damn Tolliver again.

Ben wondered what had gone wrong with the air motor. He was the person who had selected it. It was basically the motor used by the seabees to raise and lower loads on construction projects where there was no electricity; he'd modified it for use in the rescue chamber. He could take it apart and put it together blindfolded. He realized now that maybe the chamber needed a bigger motor. He'd thought he could save the Navy some money by modifying an existing one; maybe he should have designed exactly what was required and asked manufacturers to bid for the contract.

He'd thought the motor would be adequate, but it wasn't. Probably more extensive tests would have revealed that, but they hadn't had time for more tests. He knew that Tolliver and Hodges didn't understand the motor as well as he did and couldn't fix it as well as he.

He realized that he ought to go down with that air motor in the rescue chamber the next time, but he couldn't. With his claustrophobia he might become a blithering idiot. He told himself that his iron will should be able to overcome any claustrophobia that might afflict him, but his iron will hadn't saved him when he'd panicked on the old S-5 and had to be tied to his bunk. The stain of that incident had followed him throughout his naval career, leaving him vulnerable to all manner of insults.

He'd avoided going down on subs ever since but wondered if he morally could refrain from going down on the rescue chamber on the next trip. The air motor was malfunctioning, and he was the only one who could fix it quickly. Ben wondered if any of the doctors nearby might have a pill of some kind that might quiet him down and permit him to cope with the close quarters of the rescue chamber, but he couldn't ask them for a pill. There were too many admirals around. It would be embarrassing. Maybe he could give Tolliver and Hodges some basic instructions on how to fix the motor. He could get some spare nuts and bolts from the engineering officer of the *Falcon*. It probably wasn't necessary for him to go down.

Ben motioned with his hand for Captain Healey to come over.

"What is it, Mount?" Healey asked.

"I need some spare parts for the air motor in the chamber. Could you send one of your engineering officers over so that I can tell him what I need?"

"I'll get one for you right away."

Ben watched Captain Healey walk quickly toward the superstructure of the *Falcon* and was relieved. He'd figured out a solution to the problem. He would not have to go down in the rescue chamber.

In the chamber, the air motor continued to whine and grind intermittently. Hodges wondered if it would make it to the surface.

"Ain't nothin' to be worried about," he said. "It sounds like this all the time."

"It didn't sound like that when we first started coming up," said the perspiring Yeoman Reilly.

"It does it from time to time," Hodges said with a smile. "Like I said, it ain't nothin' to worry about."

The chamber splashed out of the water and was raised into the air by the derrick, which then lowered it once more to the deck.

"I told you I'd get you up all right," Hodges said.

The rescue chamber was tied to the deck, and Hodges opened the hatch. He jumped out and saw Ben standing nearby. The people on the deck made less of a fuss over the men coming up now; this was the third trip and the novelty was wearing off. Hodges walked up to Ben and said, "Sir, I don't want to go down there with Tolliver again."

Ben was holding a cheesecloth bag of nuts and bolts that the *Falcon*'s engineering officer had given him. "Why not?"

"He's cracking up, that's why not. When the air motor started giving trouble, the crazy bastard attacked it with a monkey wrench."

Ben made the decision instantly. "Tolliver's not going down again."

"Who is?"

Ben thought. He tried to think of a way out for himself, but there was none. No one else knew the machine as well as he. He'd have to pull himself together and go down in the damned thing.

"Me," Ben said.

Hodges blinked. "You!"

"Yes."

Ben turned away from Hodges and walked toward Tolliver, who was talking with some officer friends of his. Ben noticed, in the corner of his eye, the congressman's daughter—he forgot her name—taking a picture of him.

"Tolliver, I want to talk with you alone," Ben said.

"Yes, sir," Tolliver said, stepping away from his friends and walking toward the winch with Ben.

They stopped next to the winch. Ben looked over

Tolliver's shoulder at the *Sebago* men being led away by doctors and nurses. Soon it would be time to take the chamber down on the last trip.

"Tolliver," Ben said, "I'm going down with Hodges on this trip."

Tolliver flinched as though he'd been slapped in the face. "Why?"

"Because I am."

"But you can't . . ."

Ben interrupted him. "I'm in charge of this project, Ritchie. I'm the one who asks the questions and gives the orders, not you. You may go to your quarters if you like or you may remain on deck, but I'm going down on the last trip."

Tolliver looked angry. "Yes, sir."

Ben walked toward Captain Healey, who was standing with Admiral Dexter and Congressman Kirkland.

"Captain Healey—may I have a word with you alone, please?"

Admiral Dexter smiled. "Alone? You can't speak with him in front of us, Commander Mount?"

"I didn't want to disturb your conversation, sir."

"It's no disturbance at all, Commander Mount. What's on your mind?"

Ben looked at Captain Healey. "I'm going down in the rescue chamber on its last trip, sir, and I wondered if you'd man the intercom for me."

Healey and Dexter stared at Mount, because they knew of his claustrophobia.

Admiral Dexter was the first to speak. "*You're* going down in the rescue chamber, Mount?"

"Yes, sir."

"Why?"

"Because a slight problem has developed with the air motor, and I've decided that I should go down on the next trip since I know that air motor better than anyone else."

"I see."

Admiral Dexter pondered what Ben had said, then turned to Congressman Kirkland. "Would you excuse us, please?"

"Certainly," replied Congressman Kirkland.

Ben, Admiral Dexter, and Captain Healey walked toward the chamber.

"Listen, Mount," Dexter said, "you know you're not fit to go down in that rescue chamber."

"There's no one else who can work on the motor as well as I can, sir," Ben replied. "I have to go down, and I will."

Admiral Dexter snorted. "I'll be the judge of that, young man."

They stopped next to the rescue chamber. "Sir," Ben said, "if that air motor breaks down again, you may lose the people on it and the people in the submarine as well. I don't think you want that, do you?"

"Why can't Ensign Tolliver go down again?"

"Because he doesn't know that motor as well as I do. I can take it apart and put it together again with my eyes closed, and I'm the only one who can do that. That's why I'm going down on the next trip, if that's okay with you, sir."

Admiral Dexter narrowed his eyes. "But what about your claustrophobia?"

"I can handle it, sir."

"They say you've got it awfully bad."

"It's not that bad."

"I hear they had to lash you to your bunk once."

"That was a long time ago. I can handle it now."

"Are you sure?"

Ben wasn't sure, but he said, "Yes, sir."

"If you go to pieces down there, you might lose your life and the lives of some good men," Admiral Dexter said firmly.

"If I don't go down there, the lives of those men will stand a greater chance of being lost."

Admiral Dexter looked at Captain Healey and

wanted to ask his opinion, but he knew that the decision had to be his, and no one could help him with it. He looked at Ben again.

"Are you sure you know what you're doing, Mount?"

"Yes, sir."

"I want you to understand something, Mount, and I'm going to tell it to you in plain English so you'll have no doubts as to my meaning. If you fuck up down there, and if any lives are lost because of you, and if you somehow come back alive, you're going to wish you hadn't, because I'll have your ass. Is that clear?"

"Yes, sir."

Admiral Dexter held out his hand. "Good luck, Mount."

"Thank you, sir."

They shook hands tightly and looked into each other's eyes. Ben hoped that his fear of Dexter would be greater than his fear of small enclosed spaces. He turned and walked toward the rescue chamber.

"Hodges!" he called out.

"Yes, sir!" replied Hodges, who was talking to a Navy nurse.

"Let's go!"

"Yes, sir!"

Ben climbed inside the rescue chamber and sat beside the air motor. He took the set of wrenches and the nuts and bolts out of the bag and looked them over as Hodges came through the hatch.

"You're really going down in this thing, sir?" Hodges asked.

"That's right. If you don't want to come down with me, you'd better say so now."

Hodges settled onto the other seat. "I'll go down with you sir," he said jovially. "If you get out of line I'll just hit you over the head with a monkey wrench."

"I knew I could rely on you, Hodges. Dog the hatch, will you?"

"Yes, sir."

* * *

Betsy Kirkland watched the chamber rise in the air. A group of officers were conferring in earnest near her, and she saw that one of them was Lieutenant Bob Stearns.

"Bob?" she called out. "Could I speak with you a moment?"

"Sure."

Stearns detached himself from the group of officers and walked toward Betsy, who was standing by herself. Her father had gone to the bridge to speak with somebody ashore.

"What is it?" Stearns asked, as he approached Betsy.

"What's the big fuss about?" she asked.

"Oh, everybody's talking about Ben Mount. He's got claustrophobia, but he's going down in the chamber this trip. Everybody's wondering if he'll go berserk down there."

Betsy looked at the chamber high in the sky. "He's got claustrophobia?"

"He's got it so bad that they say he had to be tied to his bunk on his first dive."

"Then why's he going down?"

"Well, there's a problem with the air motor and he thinks he's the only one who can fix it."

"But what will happen if he gets an attack down there?"

Stearns shrugged. "That's what everybody's talking about. They're also wondering what'll happen when Mount and Jack come face to face down there, because Jack hates Mount."

Betsy wrinkled her nose. "Why does Jack hate him?"

"Well, a lot of people don't like Mount. They think he's a little overbearing. He's a Jew, you know."

"Yes, I know."

"Another thing is that Jack thinks that the *Sebago* sank because of Mount. Mount designed the main induction valves, which evidently didn't work properly."

"I see." Betsy said, biting her lower lip. She watched the bell descend toward the water.

Ben looked out the port of the rescue chamber at the blue sky. His mouth was dry and his breath came in short gasps. He'd be in the water soon, and that's when the trouble would begin. He'd think of the millions of tons of water around him, and how they could crush him to death.

"How's everything going in there?" asked Admiral Dexter on the intercom.

"All right, sir," Ben replied. He realized he sounded as though he was choking.

"How's the motor working?"

"So far so good."

On the deck of the *Falcon*, Admiral Dexter looked at the sky and thought about Ben Mount. He still didn't like Mount, and he still didn't like Jews, but he thought Mount was being very brave, and Dexter believed that the most important quality a man could have was courage. *Maybe he's not so bad after all,* Dexter thought. *Maybe I've been a little too hard on him.*

The chamber dropped into the water and was covered by the waves. Ben looked out the port and saw a dark green infinity. He broke out in a cold sweat, imagining the walls of the chamber closing in on him. He squinched his eyes and willed the walls to move back.

"Are you okay, sir?" Hodges asked.

"Yes," Ben replied in barely more than a whisper.

"You think maybe you might want to lie down, and I'll take over the motor?"

"I can handle it," Ben said.

I've got to handle it, he thought. He knew that Hodges was getting scared and realized he had to maintain an outward show of calm although he felt trapped and suffocating. He smiled at Hodges and tried to relax. Then the air motor screeched. He nearly jumped out of his skin.

"That's what it was doing before," Hodges said.

Ben took deep breaths to calm down. "Sounds like the armature's loose."

"Hope it don't get too loose."

"I can fix it if it does." Ben stretched to reassure himself he had plenty of room in the rescue chamber. "How far down are we?"

Hodges looked at the depth meter. "Around thirty feet."

Ben tried to convince himself that he was perfectly safe inside the rescue chamber. If anything terrible happened, a diver could cut them loose from the *Sebago* and the derrick could raise them up. There was nothing to worry about, so why was he so worried?

Hodges watched Mount sweat and ball up his fists. Mount glanced around nervously. He was scared shitless but was holding himself together somehow. Hodges thought it might be a good idea to distract him.

"Hey, sir—you got a girl friend?"

Ben was astounded by the incongruity of the question. "A girl friend?"

"Yeah, a *girl friend*. You know what a girl friend is, don't you, sir?"

Ben couldn't help smiling. "Yes, I know what a girl friend is. No, I don't have one."

"You shoulda seen the girl I picked up in the bus terminal in Boston the other day," Hodges said. "What a piece of ass. It was because of her that I got back to the yard late and you had to spring me out of the brig."

"I figured it had something to do with a woman," Ben told him.

"Oh, you shoulda seen her, sir. She woulda made

you forget all about your slide rule, and I know how much you like your slide rule because you're always playing with it." Hodges gesticulated as he described her. "She had long blond hair that looked like gold, sir, and I know she was a real blonde because she had blond hairs on her pussy. I got real close so's I could look and make sure. And she had tits like grapefruits—you know what I mean? They were round and firm and fully packed, just like my Lucky Strikes. And she had these long legs that she wrapped around my waist, and *whoo-wee,* sir, she was like a wild bronco when I was riding her. You shoulda seen her, sir. You woulda fallen in love with her, too."

"How old was she?" Ben asked, genuinely interested in what Hodges was saying. He'd always been curious about Hodges's personal life.

"About twenty-one."

"That young?"

"Yes, sir, and she was a real frisky little bitch, let me tell you. She sucked my joint for me, and I didn't even have to ask her."

Ben wondered why he never met girls like that. "What does she do for a living?"

"I didn't ask her, but she was real smart, sir. Just like you. You woulda liked her."

"I'm sure I would've, Ben replied. He was grateful to Hodges for distracting him. He glanced out the port. The water was darker. The fear crept up his spine again. "What did you talk about with her?"

"Oh, we didn't talk that much really, sir. All she wanted to do was fuck, and that was okay by me."

"How far down are we now?"

"Seventy-five feet."

The air motor screeched again, and Ben worked the lever back and forth until the noise stopped. "Tell me more about the girl," he said, hearing the anxiety in his voice. "What was her name?"

"She wouldn't tell me her last name, sir. I figure she was married."

"What was her first name?"

"Helen."

"Did she have 'the face that launched a thousand ships and wrecked the ancient towers of Ilium'?"

"Huh?"

"It's a line from a poem."

"This girl was prettier than any poem I ever saw. She had an ass that was so sweet and round—I'll tell you something, sir: this girl had it all. You know what I mean? *All*."

"Maybe you should marry her."

"Marry her? She wouldn't even give me her last name, I told you. She wouldn't give me her phone number either. Like I said, I think she's married to some jerk someplace and she likes a little strange cock once in a while. Know what I mean? But she said she'd call me and hey, sir—tell you what I'm gonna do—I'll give her your phone number when she calls and I'll line her up with you. You can fuck her too. Then maybe Tolliver can fuck her. We can all fuck her."

Ben chuckled. "Just because she goes to bed with you, that doesn't mean that she'd want to go to bed with Tolliver and me."

Hodges wagged his forefinger in the air. "You may not be right about that, sir. I've known girls who've screwed the entire crews of submarines. You believe that? You probably don't, but it's true. I've even heard of girls who've screwed the entire crews of destroyers, and that's a lotta guys, sir. So I think that maybe this Helen will screw you and Tolliver, because I think she's a little crazy and she just might be interested.

"I heard of a girl who slept with the entire Navy football team once," Ben offered.

Hodges waved his hand in the air. "A football team is only eleven guys. That ain't so much, sir."

Admiral Dexter's voice came over the squawk box. "Is everything all right down there?"

"Yes, sir," Ben replied.

"How far down are you?"

Ben bent toward the depth gauge and read the numbers. "One hundred and seventy feet, sir."

"How're you feeling, Mount?"

"Fine, sir."

"Carry on."

"Yes, sir."

Hodges waited a few moments, then leaned toward Ben and whispered, "Do you think he can hear what we're saying down here?"

"I don't think so, because you have to speak into the mike in order for him to hear."

"That's good, because if he could hear us he might want some of Helen too. I don't know if she'd go for an old geezer like him."

Ben never would have believed that he could laugh in a tiny diving bell 170 feet in the sea, but he laughed. Hodges's ridiculous conversation had changed the mood inside the chamber.

"Keep talking," Ben said.

"What do you want me to talk about, sir?"

"Tell me about your other girl friends."

"Why don't you tell me about yours?" Hodges asked with a wink.

"I don't have a girl friend."

"Aw, don't give me that, sir: a nice lookin' feller like you. I'll bet you've got a nice little Jewish girl back there in Brooklyn that you're hiding from everybody."

"I really don't have a girl friend," Ben said.

"Then you oughtta . . ."

Hodges was interrupted by a screech and a clunk issuing from the air motor. The rescue chamber jerked up and down a few times, and the sounds became more violent.

"Oh-oh," Ben said.

"It's the motor again," Hodges grumbled.

"Shit."

"Now stay calm, sir. It'll be okay."

The motor stopped. Ben worked the operating lever back and forth and the motor whined a few times, but the rescue chamber wouldn't move. He glanced at the depth gauge and saw that they were at 195 feet. Looking around him at the walls of the chamber, the old panic came over him and he broke out into a cold sweat. His mouth went dry, and he looked up at the top of the rescue chamber.

"You okay, sir?" Hodges asked.

"To tell you the truth, no," Ben said.

"Oh, fuck." Hodges wiped his face with his hand. "Here I am stuck in the water with a Jew officer who's gonna have a nervous breakdown."

Hodges's remark struck Ben as funny, and the atmosphere lightened a bit. Ben tried to pull himself together and focus on fixing the motor. He reached under the bench he was sitting on and pulled up the little cloth sack full of nuts, bolts, and tools.

"I think I can fix it," Ben said.

"Mind if I say a little Catholic prayer?"

"I'd rather you told me about your other girl friends," Ben said as he opened the sack.

"Well, there's Fifi . . ."

Ben interrupted him. "C'mon, you really don't know anybody named Fifi."

"Yes, I do," Hodges replied indignantly. "Fifi La Tour. She's a stripper at the Old Howard."

Admiral Dexter's voice came over the squawk box. "You've stopped moving. Is anything wrong?"

Ben got down on his knees in front of the air motor. "Tell him what's happened."

"Me?"

"No, the other guy in here."

"I don't want to talk to no admiral."

"Neither do I. Tell him what's going on down here, Hodges. That's an order."

"Yes, sir."

Hodges took the mike down from the wall. "Um, the air motor just conked out, sir," he said.

"Who is this speaking?" demanded Admiral Dexter.

"Boatswain's Mate First Class Thomas Hodges, sir."

"Where's Commander Mount?"

"He's taking the air motor apart, sir. He told me to talk to you and answer your questions, sir."

"Ask Mount—I mean Commander Mount—when he expects to have the motor fixed."

Ben spoke as he took the face plate off the motor. "Tell him I don't know."

"He says he don't know, sir."

"Can't he give me an estimate?"

"Can't you give him an estimate?"

"No."

"He says no, sir."

"How deep are you?" Admiral Dexter asked.

"One hundred and ninety-five feet, sir," Hodges replied.

"I want Commander Mount to notify me as soon as the motor is fixed."

"Yes, sir."

"Over and out."

Hodges hung up the mike. "How's it coming, sir?"

"The armature's loose, just as I thought."

"Think you can fix it?"

"Yes."

"Thank God!"

"Tell me all about Fifi La Tour," Ben said as he removed the first of the worn bearings that held the armature.

"Fifi La Tour?" Hodges said, aware that his stories were alleviating Mount's claustrophobia. "Well, Fifi

La Tour is around thirty-two years old, and like I said she's a stripper at the Old Howard. You ever been to the Old Howard, sir?"

"No."

"Do you know what the Old Howard is?"

"A burlesque house on Scollay Square."

"Right. Well Fifi La Tour is the headliner when she appears there. Do you know what the headliner is, sir?"

"She gets top billing."

"Right, sir. Well anyway, she's got this act where she's got a hand puppet that looks like a swan, and she peels off her clothes with the swan's beak. You get the picture, sir?"

"I got the picture."

"Well, one night I happened to be hanging around the stage door of the Old Howard, and . . ."

Ben listened to Hodges's story as he rebuilt the air motor with the parts Captain Harris had given him. He felt light-headed and zany, as though this was a dream. Hodges's conversation reminded him of James Joyce. It was like *Ulysses in Nighttown*. There they were nearly two hundred feet underwater, and the sea could crush him and drown him as though he was made of paper. But it hadn't yet, and the mission was half over. He hadn't cracked up. He was sure he could make it all the way as long as Hodges kept talking about his bizarre sex life.

Jack sat with Keller, Mason, Burns, and La Gloria. The water was three inches over the torpedoes now, and he looked at his watch. It was almost three o'clock in the afternoon. The rescue chamber seemed to be taking longer this time, but maybe that was just his imagination. He felt anxious now that he was so close to being saved. He couldn't wait to get out of the submarine and look at the sky again.

A heavy metal object grated against the escape hatch.

"It's back!" Torpedoman Burns said happily.

Keller got up from his bunk and stood beneath the hatch. He heard Hodges fasten the chamber and open the top part of the escape hatch. Keller unlatched the bottom half and pulled it down, dodging the few gallons of water that had become trapped there.

"Step lively, boys," Hodges said, reaching down for Burns. "Come on up here, you old son of a bitch."

"Hodges, I never thought I'd be so happy to see your ugly face!"

Mason went up next with his radio codebooks, and next was Vincent La Gloria with his medicine bag. Keller took one last look around him and jumped up into the hands waiting for him, and finally it was Jack's turn. He looked aft to the hatch that led to the officers' wardroom. "So long, skipper," he said in the direction of Commander Dunlop's corpse. Then he stepped on a can of oil and held up his hands. Keller and Hodges grabbed him and pulled him up to the rescue chamber.

Keller climbed to the upper compartment, and Jack followed him up. As Jack's head came level with the deck of the upper compartment, he looked around and saw Ben Mount sitting next to the air motor. Jack froze in his tracks. He'd been thinking about Ben Mount and how Mount had caused the *Sebago* to go down with all hands, killing thirty men including his brother Ed, and now Mount was before him, that dirty Jew bastard. Jack glowered at Ben as he climbed into the upper compartment.

"Hello, Jack," Ben said, for he remembered Jack from their student days at the Naval Academy.

Jack grunted, unable to conceal his anger as he climbed into the chamber, and sat between Keller and Burns. Ben wondered what was bothering Jack, but had no time to worry about it now. He handed a marker buoy to Hodges.

"Tie this to the hatch."

"Yes, sir."

Hodges closed the sub's hatch, fastened the marker buoy to it, and removed the downhaul cable. He climbed into the upper compartment of the chamber, dogging closed the hatch that separated the two compartments.

"We're ready to go, sir," Hodges said.

Ben took the mike down from the bulkhead. "Admiral Dexter?"

"This is Admiral Dexter speaking," said the voice on the squawk box.

"We're ready to come up, sir. Tell the man on the derrick to take it slow and steady."

"All right, Mount."

They all sat looking at each other for a few moments, and then the chamber began to rise. Ben looked at Jack, who was glowering at him.

Hodges cleared his throat. "Should I keep talking about pussy, sir?"

"No, that's all right," Ben said, feeling reasonably calm. Somehow Hodges's chatter and the circumstances of the rescue had shifted his mind out of its mode of fear. He didn't enjoy being on the rescue chamber, but it didn't scare him very much anymore.

"You talkin' about pussy again?" Keller asked Hodges. "Shit, last time I saw you, and it musta been two years ago, you were talkin' about pussy."

"Pussy's all he ever talks about," Burns said.

"That's cause he don't get any," Keller suggested.

"I get more than you," Hodges told him.

"Bullshit!"

"You ain't had pussy since pussy had you," Hodges said.

Admiral Dexter's voice came over the intercom. "How's everything going down there?"

"Fine, sir," Ben said.

"Would you put Lieutenant McCrary on, please?"

"Yes, sir."

Ben passed the mike to Jack.

"Lieutenant McCrary speaking, sir," Jack said into the mike.

"How are you, Lieutenant?" Admiral Dexter asked.

"A little tired but otherwise fine, sir."

"I've spoken with several of your men and officers, and they say you've done a fine job. You're a credit to the Navy, McCrary."

"Thank you, sir."

"I'll look forward to congratulating you in person when you get topside."

"Yes, sir."

"Carry on."

Jack handed the mike back to Ben Mount, who hung it up on its hook. Ben was perspiring, and Jack thought he looked extremely shifty-eyed. *There sits the man who killed my brother Ed and twenty-nine others.*

Ben noticed Jack staring at him. The atmosphere in the rescue chamber was becoming oppressive again. The walls closed in on him and he couldn't move his arms.

Hodges noticed Ben getting tense again. "Hey, Burns," he said, "I'll bet you can't wait to see your old lady!"

"Shut up about my old lady," Burns said.

"Oh boy, I wish I met her before you did. I woulda married her myself. What a woman. I believe you told me once that she even knows how to cook."

"She's a damn fine cook," Burns said. "We'll have to invite you over for chicken sometime. She can do anything to a chicken except make it come back to life again."

"Your wife looks better than any chicken I ever saw," Hodges replied. "What's her name again?"

"Laurie."

"Yeah—Laurie. What a sweet name. I met a girl named Laurie once in Norfolk. What a piece of ass she was. She worked in her father's store and I happened to walk in to buy a pack of cigarettes. Nearly wound up marrying the girl. Maybe I shoulda."

Ben leaned toward the depth gauge and read 150 feet. It wouldn't be long now. He thought he'd conquered his fear sufficiently to go down in another submarine someday. The claustrophobia still bothered him, but not as much as before. He thought he could keep it under control if he remembered to stay relaxed. If only he could take Hodges with him whenever he went down in a submarine.

The side of Ben's face felt warm, and he realized that Jack was still staring at him. He turned to Jack and saw that he was indeed staring at him. With his scraggly beard and hollow eyes, Jack looked like an angry terrier about to attack.

"Are you all right, Jack?" Ben asked.

Jack nodded. "Yeah, I'm all right."

"It must have been hell down there."

"It was. You know why we sank, don't you?" he asked accusingly.

"No, I don't."

"The main induction valves failed."

"That's what I heard, but we don't know that for sure yet, do we?"

"I think we do. We also know who designed that defective system."

Now Ben realized why Jack had been hostile to him. Jack thought he was responsible for the sinking of the *Sebago*. "I designed it," Ben said.

Jack pointed his trembling finger at Ben. "Those men down there died because of you."

It became silent in the chamber. The men looked at each other nervously. Hodges was glad that the derrick was pulling them up, because nothing that happened in the chamber could stop them or slow them down.

Ben wiped perspiration off his cheek and looked at Jack. "I think you're a little distraught, Lieutenant. You'd better calm down."

Jack ground his teeth together. "Ben Mount," Jack said in a deadly tone, "I'm not going to rest until you get what's coming to you for what you did to those men down there."

Ben tried to smile. "The inquiry will decide who or what was to blame."

Jack pointed at Ben again. "We all know who was to blame—it was you, you *Jew bastard!*"

Ben stiffened on the little bench he was sitting upon. "Lieutenant McCrary," he said, "you'd better put yourself under control *right now.*"

Jack narrowed his eyes, and his voice came in a rasping whisper. "I'm going to get you, Mount. I swear I'm going to get you."

"Lieutenant McCrary," Ben said, "I'm just going to warn you one more time. If you don't calm down, I'm going to put you on report, and *I* won't rest until you're punished for insubordination."

Jack's lips quivered. He wanted to jump on Mount and pound his face in. Keller put his hand on Jack's arm.

"Take it easy, sir," he said soothingly. "Everything's been going okay. Don't blow it now."

Jack took a deep breath. He didn't want to blow it now. He'd hold himself back, and at the inquiry he'd nail Ben Mount's dirty Jew ass to the wall.

"I'm okay," Jack said. He looked at Ben. "Sorry, sir."

Ben didn't reply. He knew Jack wasn't sorry. He knew Jack was out for his blood and wouldn't stop until he got it.

The chamber broke through the surface of the water and lifted into the sky.

"We're out!" shouted Keller, clapping his hands.

"Ho!" yelled Burns. "Out!"

The men in the rescue chamber cheered and re-joiced while Jack and Ben stared at each other and made plans.

The rescue chamber came down to the deck and the sailors tied it fast. Hodges opened the hatch and the fresh air blew in. Ben breathed deeply, pleased that he'd made it despite claustrophobia, a broken air motor, and the provocations of Jack McCrary. The stain on his honor was wiped out. "Let's go, gentle-men," he said. "Let's get out of here."

Torpedoman Burns was the first one out; he gave an Indian war whoop as his feet touched the deck. Admiral Dexter came over to speak with him, and Burns treated him like an old buddy although he'd never spoken to Dexter in his life before. Vincent La Gloria came out next and crossed himself in the name of the Father, the Son, and the Holy Spirit. Radioman Second Class Mason left the chamber and wondered if they might make him Radioman First Class Mason. Keller climbed out of the rescue cham-ber and Lieutenant Stearns was there, holding out his hand.

"Welcome back to the world," Stearns said, shaking Keller's hand.

Keller looked up at the sky. "I never thought we'd get out of there," he confessed.

Jack McCrary came out of the rescue chamber, and the officers on the deck applauded. He was trembling and felt as though his mind was becoming unraveled. With the responsibility for the men on the *Sebago* suddenly removed from his shoulders, he thought he might faint.

Betsy broke through the throng and ran to him. "Oh, Jack!" she cried, and hugged him.

"Hello, Betsy," he said, placing his hands on her waist.

"Are you all right, Jack?" she asked, noticing something was wrong.

"Yes, I'm fine," he said.

Jack heard a commotion behind him and turned around. He saw Ben Mount being slapped on the back and congratulated by some officers and men. Jack narrowed his eyes and clenched his teeth. "That son of a bitch!" he hissed.

"What's wrong, Jack?"

"Oh, never mind."

Admiral Dexter walked up to Jack, and Jack gently pushed Betsy away so he could shake hands with the commander of the Atlantic Submarine Fleet.

"Welcome back, Lieutenant," Admiral Dexter said.

"It's good to be back, sir."

Admiral Dexter grasped both Jack's shoulders. "You're a credit to the Navy, McCrary. It was a terrible accident, and you did a fine job."

Jack balled up his fists. "Sir, I wouldn't want to speak out of turn, but I feel that I would be disloyal to my commanding officer and the men who died aboard the *Sebago* if I didn't point out to you that accidents do not happen—they are caused. I hope the full weight of military justice will be brought to bear against the person or persons who caused this accident." Jack turned and looked significantly at Ben Mount.

Admiral Dexter followed his eyes and looked at Ben. "You may rest assured, Lieutenant McCrary, that a full and impartial inquiry will be made."

"That's all I ask for," Jack replied. "I hope you will permit me to speak with you about this when the commotion dies down."

"Of course, Lieutenant. After you finish with the doctors, we can talk in my cabin."

"Thank you, sir."

Twenty feet across the deck, Jethro Keller was drinking coffee and joking with Burns, Hodges, and other enlisted men. A lieutenant with a roster walked up to him. "Are you Chief Boatswain's Mate Jethro Keller?" the lieutenant asked.

"Yes, sir."

"I thought you might want to know, Keller, that your wife is waiting for you on the dock in New London."

Keller was puzzled. "My wife? I think you've made some kind of mistake, sir. My wife is in San Francisco."

"You're Chief Boatswain's Mate Jethro Keller, aren't you?"

"Yes, sir."

"And you're married to a woman named Dolores Keller?"

"Yes, sir."

"Well, she's waiting for you on the dock, Chief. The Navy's flown her here from San Francisco."

Keller gulped. "They have?"

"Yes, and I know you'll be as happy to see her as she will to see you."

"Yes, sir. Thank you, sir."

The lieutenant smiled and walked away. Keller looked toward New London, his jaw hanging open. Dolly here?

FIFTY-FIVE

The *Falcon* eased toward the pier. Dolly Keller watched it, wringing her hands. She was afraid of what Jethro would say when he saw her. He might not recognize her. Maybe he'd think she wasn't pretty anymore. Maybe she never had been pretty and that's why he'd lost interest.

The people crowded on the pier were happy and sad at the same time; although some of the *Sebago* men were coming back, many were not. There was no Navy band to greet the returning sailors, only their families and ambulances to take the sick ones to the hospital immediately.

None of the people waiting were more torn apart in their hearts than Commodore Ray McCrary and Helen. Jack was coming back, and Ed was not. They watched the *Falcon*'s crew throw out her lines.

Ray McCrary had talked to his wife an hour before. She was in the Bethesda Naval Hospital, having had another breakdown when she'd heard about Ed. She had been heavily sedated when Ray spoke with her. He'd tried to soothe her but she had just kept crying.

He felt weary and old as Helen stood beside him and held his arm. He felt as though he had no more fight in him. He'd been through so much; perhaps the time had come to retire. Thirty-two years of service was enough. He and his wife would live on his pension. He hadn't given her much of his time; maybe that was one reason she'd had so many emotional problems. She'd always been fragile, and he should have helped her more, but the Navy had demanded **so** much from him. Now it had even taken one of his sons.

Helen watched the gangplank come down, vowing that in the future she'd be a good sister to Jack, to make up for her neglect of poor Ed. As the British officer named Mulford had said, you can't bring back the dead, but you can be kind to the living. She would be a better person instead of the little slut she had become.

The first figures came down the gangplank, two medics carrying a man in a stretcher. The crowd surged closer. Behind the first stretcher came another, carried by two orderlies. Then came an officer in a tan hat and brown leather jacket.

"Jack!" Helen shouted, letting go her father's arm. "Jack!" She pushed through the crowd.

Jack came down the gangplank, looking into the crowd. He heard his name being called and saw Helen waving to him. Stepping off the gangplank, he held out his arms as she rushed toward him and clasped him to her.

"Oh, Jack," she said, tears streaming down her cheeks. "I'm so glad you're back."

Jack kissed her cheek. How good it was to see her again.

"Welcome home, son," Ray McCrary said, holding out his hand.

"It's good to see you, Dad," Jack replied, shaking his father's hand.

"Where's Betsy? I thought she was on the *Falcon.*"

"She'll be down in a little while."

"I'll bet you were glad to see her."

"I wasn't actually able to spend much time with her, because I had to be checked over by the doctors, and Admiral Dexter wanted to speak with me."

"There'll be time later," Ray said. "We'll have dinner together tonight."

"How's Mom?" Jack asked. He glanced at Helen, who was wiping away tears with a handkerchief.

"She isn't feeling well," Ray said.

"I didn't think she'd take it well."

Ray nodded sadly. "No, she didn't take it well."

Near them, *Sebago* crew members came down the gangplank and ran into the arms of their families. There was crying and laughter. Jethro Keller stepped to the top of the gangplank, squinting down into the crowd. He walked down the gangplank, his white cap low over his eyes. He was a little bowlegged, and his bell-bottom dungarees flopped around his shoes. Some people were embracing and talking excitedly with each other; others were looking expectantly up the gangplank. A busty woman with short brown hair moved toward him, her hands folded in front of her. *Holy shit,* he thought. *It's Dolly, all right.*

He walked toward her, wondering what to say. She looked shy and awfully old, but he could perceive the young girl she used to be. She stopped in front of him and shuffled nervously. "Hi, Jethro," she said. "Remember me?"

Emotion welled up in Keller's heart. "Sure I remember you, Dolly."

He held out his big arms and enclosed her in them. She felt safe and happy that he'd welcomed her so warmly. He kissed her forehead as though she was his little sister.

"They told me you'd be here," he said, "but I didn't believe it."

She shrugged. "Well, I'm here."

"It was awfully nice of you to come, Dolly."

"The Navy paid for everything."

"It was nice of you to come anyway."

She rested her cheek against his big chest. "I didn't think you'd remember me, Jethro."

"I couldn't forget you, Dolly."

"I thought maybe you had."

"Well," he said, "I know I haven't been a very good husband to you, but I do think of you once in a while."

"Well, I guess I haven't been much of a wife, either."

"No, as a matter of fact, you haven't."

"I don't want to get into an argument with you right now, Jethro," she said, "but if you hadn't left me alone so often, I wouldn't have done the things I did."

"I don't want to get into an argument either," he replied, "but a Navy wife is supposed to get used to being alone."

They separated and looked at each other. The years had not been kind to either of them. Yet there was still a strange, indefinable attraction.

Jethro winked at her. "Let's get a drink someplace, Dolly."

"Now you're talkin'," she said.

After the crew of the *Sebago* had debarked, the admirals and congressmen came down the gangplank. Betsy Kirkland walked beside her father, troubled by the few moments she'd spent with Jack. He'd seemed angry and distracted. Although he had tried to be polite to her, his mind was somewhere else. She supposed it was because of the tribulations he'd suffered, but it seemed that he should have been happier to see her.

She'd often wondered whether he really loved her. She was an heiress and the daughter of a congressman who might be helpful with his Navy career. She'd always been suspicious of her boyfriends, thinking they were interested in her because of her money. She often wished that she was just an ordinary girl, so that if a man said he loved her, she'd know that he meant it.

Now the old suspicion was returning, and she reproached herself. Jack had just been rescued from death and should be expected to act differently for a while. Yet she couldn't help remembering that she had always had doubts about him and that she was not passionately in love with him. This was a terrible time to have these doubts: on the day his life was saved. She also knew that she enjoyed his company and had lots of good times with him. She decided she was confused.

At the bottom of the gangplank she looked for the assistant photo editor from the *Standard* who was supposed to meet her and pick up her film. She saw people hugging and kissing and shaking hands. A young man in a wrinkled raincoat and battered fedora walked up to her.

"Are you Betsy Kirkland?"

"Yes, I am."

He took his identification card from his pocket. "I'm from the *Standard*. I'm supposed to pick up a package from you."

Betsy turned to her father. "Dad, why don't you go ahead. I'll catch up with you."

"I believe I'll go say something to the McCrarys," Congressman Kirkland said, looking distastefully at the man from the *Standard*. He didn't approve of his daughter's occupation.

Betsy opened her shoulder bag and handed the rolls of film to her colleague, who put them into the pocket of his raincoat. She gave him a sheet of paper that identified the people in the pictures.

"I hope you can get these to New York quickly," she said. "We want to beat the other newspapers to the stands."

"There's a plane waiting for me at New London Airport. I've got a car with a chauffeur in the parking lot right over there."

The man ran off, and Betsy looked around at the crowd of noisy people. Seeing her father shaking hands with Jack's father, she walked in that direction, threading her way through the sailors and civilians. Helen was the first to see her, and the women kissed each other on the cheek.

"I'm so sorry to hear about Ed," Betsy said to Helen. Then she shook hands with Ray McCrary and expressed her condolences to him. She hugged Jack and kissed his gaunt bearded cheek. "I'm so glad you're back," she said.

"I'm sorry I haven't had much time to speak with you," he replied, "but we'll all have dinner together tonight, all right?"

"Sure."

"I'm afraid I won't be able to join you," Congressman Kirkland said in his bass stentorian voice, "There's a key vote in the House tomorrow on farm appropriations, and I have to be there."

The McCrarys expressed their regrets, and Helen looked around at the crowd. Suddenly she felt as though a horse had kicked her. She found herself looking into the eyes of Tommy Hodges, who was only ten feet away. He appeared as shocked to see her as she was to see him. Frightened, she held Jack's arm.

"What's wrong?" he asked.

"Nothing. I'm just so happy to see you, Jack," she said, shuddering at the thought of what would happen if Hodges came over to talk with her.

I've really got to stop playing with sailors, she thought. *It's starting to get out of hand.*

Tommy Hodges had no intention of saying anything to Helen. He thought she was married to Jack McCrary and was afraid he'd wind up in the brig

again with marines bouncing him off the walls. He
walked quickly, heading for the petty officers' club.
He'd had a hard day and wanted to loosen up. There'd
probably be a party over there, and who had a better
right to join it than he did?

His hands in his pockets and his white hat on his
forehead, he made his way to the club. He thought
of Helen McCrary. A guy could never tell who he was
going to wind up in bed with. He was liable to pick
up some old babe in a park some day and find out that
she was the wife of an admiral.

The wife of an admiral. He wondered what kind of
fuck the wife of an admiral would be.

She'd probably be fairly old if she was an admiral's
wife, but if she was half as good as that lieutenant's
wife he wouldn't mind at all.

FIFTY-SIX

It was night on the Thames River. On the *Falcon*, Ben Mount knocked on the door of the office being used by Admiral Dexter.

"Come in."

Ben entered the office and saw Admiral Dexter sitting at the desk, his collar unbuttoned. The only illumination came from a lamp on the desk, and Admiral Dexter had a mug of coffee in his hand.

"Have a seat, Mount."

"Yes, sir."

Ben walked to the chair in front of the desk and sat down.

"Would you like a cup of coffee?"

"No thank you, sir."

"You may smoke if you like."

Ben took out one of his cigarettes and lit up. Admiral Dexter sipped his coffee and looked at Ben. "Well, it's been quite a day, hasn't it?"

"Yes, sir."

"You did a fine job, Mount. I want you to know that."

"Thank you sir."

Admiral Dexter leaned back in his chair. "I know

I've been a little hard on you, Mount, but as far as I'm concerned you've proven yourself to me today. Your rescue chamber worked, and you put your life on the line to save the men of the *Sebago*. That's the sort of thing that impresses me. I know I'm arrogant and overbearing at times, but the two things I admire most are competence and courage, and you demonstrated both those qualities in great abundance today."

"Thank you, sir."

Admiral Dexter rose behind his desk and held out his hand. Ben stood up and shook it. The admiral looked at Ben as though he was making a solemn vow of some kind. Then they both sat down.

"I'm afraid this thing isn't all over for you yet, Mount," Admiral Dexter said. "There's going to be an inquiry, and young Lieutenant McCrary has made some very serious allegations here in this office. I tried to reason with him, telling him that even if the *Sebago* had sunk because of an error that you had made, you still weren't entirely to blame, because you're part of a team in the Bureau of Ships and your designs are checked by other officers. In addition, the *Sebago* had undergone a number of tests already and its problems had presumably been solved. Dunlop himself had never given any indication that anything was wrong. I realize I've said some rather harsh things to you, Mount, but now, as far as I'm concerned, the sinking was a tragic and deplorable accident, and nothing more."

Ben puffed his cigarette. "The inquiry may indicate otherwise."

"It may indeed," Admiral Dexter said, "and if it does, you can be sure that Lieutenant McCrary will make the most of it. However, I've thought this matter over. If you *did* make a design error that caused the *Sebago* to go down, you're not the only officer in the Bureau of Ships. Somebody else should have caught it by now."

"Sir, you know as well as I do that if I made a design error, my career in the Navy will probably be over."

Admiral Dexter nodded. "You're probably right. They might not kick you out of the Navy, but you'd spend the rest of your career behind a desk in a remote corner of the world."

"I'd leave the Navy if that happened."

"So would I if it happened to me. But let me tell you something, Mount. There's more at stake here than your career or mine." Admiral Dexter leaned forward and hit his fist lightly on the desk. "The future of the submarine forces are at stake. Unless I miss my guess, old Hardtop Hill will be in charge of the inquiry, and you know how he feels about submarines."

"He doesn't think much of them," Ben said.

"No, he doesn't. He likes aircraft carriers. I happen to like carriers too. I like all ships. But I know that one submarine with fifty men aboard and a spread of three torpedoes can sink an aircraft carrier or any other ship afloat. This country is headed toward a war, Mount—you know it as well as I do. It will break out any day now. And when it does, we're going to need submarines, lots of them, to sink enemy warships and freighters. If our submarine forces are crippled as the result of this inquiry, this country could conceivably lose the war. You may think I'm blowing up this incident out of proportion, but I am not. Very serious consequences can befall this nation if the finger of blame points to the submarine forces."

"I agree with you, sir," Ben said. "I don't think you're blowing it out of proportion at all. In fact, I've been thinking along parallel lines myself."

"Good, I'm glad to hear that." Admiral Dexter took another sip of coffee. "I want to ask you a straight question, Mount, and I want you to give me a straight answer. Why do you think the *Sebago* went down?"

"I don't know, sir."

"Are you sure you don't know, Mount, or are you just being crafty?"

"I'm telling you the truth, sir. I don't know why she went down. I worked very carefully on the main induction valves and every other system that I designed for the boat. I don't believe I made any mistakes, and if I had, someone would have found them somewhere along the line, as you already pointed out. As soon as I have a chance, I'm going back to Washington to study my original blueprints. I can send you copies if you like."

"Please do, because I'll probably be on the inquiry panel myself. Unfortunately, one of our biggest obstacles will be McCrary. He's being very stubborn about this. I think he holds you responsible for the death of his brother."

"I imagine that's true," Ben said, "but I've known him since Annapolis, and he's never liked me." Ben managed a smile. "But then of course, neither have you."

Admiral Dexter coughed. His face became red and he wiped his mouth with the napkin that the steward had brought with the coffee cup. "That's all over now, Mount," he said. "We've got to stand shoulder to shoulder for the sake of the submarine forces. We'll begin work on raising the boat tomorrow, and I imagine the inquest panel will start taking testimony in a week or two. I expect you to be fully prepared to fight for the submarine forces with me."

"I'll do my best, sir. When the *Sebago* is towed in, I hope someone will advise me of precisely what malfunctions occurred."

"You'll be notified, Mount, and if you need anything else, don't hesitate to contact me. I'll expect you to keep yourself available to me in the same manner. Oh yes, there's one more thing: I don't want you to give any interviews to the press. If they ask to speak with you, tell them you can't say anything until after the inquiry, and then after the inquiry you should tell them that you have nothing to say about the matter that you hadn't told the panel. Understand?"

"But I already promised an interview to Betsy Kirkland—you know, the congressman's daughter."

"Cancel it," Admiral Dexter said. "She's the worst one of them all."

FIFTY-SEVEN

Jack and Betsy were seated alone in the dining room of the officers' club. Jack's father had just excused himself to call his wife at the Bethesda Hospital, and Helen had said that she wanted to spend some time alone in the chapel. The officers' club, set on a hill, afforded a view of the harbor, where the *Falcon* was tied to the dock. Jack placed his hand on Betsy's.

"I'm so glad that we finally have a chance to be alone," he said.

Her eyes roved over his face. He was shaven and had taken a nap, but his eyes were still melancholy and sunken deep into their sockets. "Yes," she said, smiling. "I was so worried about you."

"I thought of you a lot down there, Betsy. I realized how fortunate I am to be marrying you, and how much I would lose if I had . . ."

She placed her hand on his. "Well, you're safe now, darling."

His eyes became clouded. "Yes, but Ed isn't safe. He's still out there—still on the *Sebago*."

"Don't dwell on that, Jack. It was a terrible thing, and nothing can be done about it now."

"You're wrong," he said. "Something can be done about it."

"What?"

"The person who caused the *Sebago* to sink can be punished for it," Jack said vehemently.

"Who's that?"

"Ben Mount!" Jack spit the words out as though they were poison.

"Now, dear," she said, "you don't know yet that Commander Mount is to blame."

"Oh, yes, I do know. The main induction valves failed, and he designed them. Everybody thinks he's so smart, but thirty men died because of him and he's to be punished for it!"

Betsy removed her hands from Jack's and crossed her arms beneath her breasts. She thought his bitterness most disagreeable. "But Jack," she said, "the facts aren't in yet. You shouldn't condemn him so quickly. In this country a person is presumed innocent until proven guilty."

"I know he's guilty, and soon the whole Navy will know."

"How do you *know* he's guilty?"

"I know."

"Now really Jack," she said, sounding like a schoolteacher. "There's a big difference between knowledge and speculation."

Jack sat upright in his chair. "Why are you defending Mount?"

"I'm not defending him. I'm just saying that you're condemning him before he's been proven guilty."

"He'll be proven guilty, don't worry about it."

"I don't know how you can be so sure."

"The Jew will pay for this—don't think he won't."

She closed her eyes, very troubled now.

"What's wrong?" he asked.

"I don't like it when people say *Jew* that way."

"Well, he is a Jew, isn't he?"

"Yes, but you say it like an insult."

His face became contorted by anger. "Maybe I meant it that way. Why—do you like Jews?"

"I don't have any particular prejudices about them. Some are all right and some aren't. I spoke with Mount briefly and I thought he was a decent and quite intelligent man."

"Oh, you did, did you?"

"Yes."

"Doesn't it mean anything to you that he killed my brother?"

"Why do you keep insisting that he killed your brother. You talk as though he shot Ed with a gun."

"He might as well have shot him with a gun. The end result would have been the same!"

Betsy was annoyed by Jack's unreasonable and cruel remarks. She tried to hold her tongue, but the words gushed out. "Do you know what I think?" she asked. "I think you feel guilty about the way you always used to treat Ed, and now that he's dead, you're transferring the guilt to Ben Mount."

Jack looked as though he'd been slapped in the face. He took a cigarette from his pack and lit it with trembling hands.

Now that Betsy had said what had been on her mind, she regretted it. "I'm sorry, Jack," she said.

He puffed his cigarette. "If you meant what you said, you shouldn't be sorry," he said in a strangled voice.

"Well, I did mean what I said," she admitted. "I think you're making Ben Mount the scapegoat for things you and other members of your family might have done to Ed. I've never heard any of you except your mother say anything nice about him."

"Leave my family out of this," Jack said testily.

Betsy lifted her snifter of cognac to her lips. She couldn't stand it when people refused to discuss matters in a rational and objective way. She'd noticed this tendency in Jack before, but until now their arguments had been about relatively insignificant things.

Maybe I should try to be more understanding, she thought. *He's been through a terrible experience and maybe I'm judging him too harshly. He'll probably be all right in a few weeks when he calms down.*

"I think I'd better go to my hotel," Betsy said.

"I'll drive you there," Jack replied, flicking ashes into an ashtray.

"That's all right—I'll take a taxi. I think you should get some rest."

His eyes flashed with anger. "What's that supposed to mean?"

"What's what supposed to mean?"

"Are you trying to say that my opinions are worthless because I'm tired?" he asked. "Well, it's true that I'm tired, but I still believe that Ben Mount killed my brother and twenty-nine other good men, and I'll believe it in the morning too!"

"I don't feel like arguing with you, Jack," she said. "I just want to go to my hotel." She stood up.

He shot to his feet and pulled back her chair. They walked out of the dining room.

FIFTY-EIGHT

The next morning a group of naval officers from the Bureau of Ships arrived in New London and began making plans to raise the *Sebago* and tow her in. The planning stage lasted ten days, and then the actual work began. A team of divers went out and were lowered to the submarine, attaching hoses so that her 360 tons of diesel fuel could be pumped out. Then the water in the after compartments was pumped out. At the end of May ships sailed out with pontoons and derricks to bring her up. Divers and machinery were lowered to slip supporting cables under the hull, and the work proceeded into July. The ships anchored over the *Sebago* and stayed in position all that time, like a floating construction company.

The inquiring panel convened in Washington in early June and began hearing testimony. The panel was chaired by Admiral Cyrus Kane, and on it were Vice Admiral Charles "Hardtop" Hill, Vice Admiral Rufus Dexter, Rear Admiral Bernard Walmsley of the Boston Navy Yard, and Rear Admiral Tobias Cranshaw from the Bureau of Ships and Construction.

One by one the *Sebago* survivors appeared before

the panel and told of their experiences during the fateful test dive and the hours that followed. The admirals on the panel asked questions and made notes. The hearings were held in the Navy Building on Pennsylvania Avenue, and on hot days the sound of traffic could be heard through the open windows.

Betsy Kirkland covered every day's proceedings from the press gallery, writing her stories in the evenings and wiring them to New York so that the *Standard* could be on the streets with her information in the morning. News of the disaster had moved off the front page, but in journalistic circles it was believed that Betsy might win a Pulitzer prize for the work she'd done.

The crew and officers of the *Sebago* paraded through the hearing room, and even Lieutenant Peter Nielsen gave testimony before returning to Sweden. Finally it came time for Lieutenant McCrary to testify. Since he had been the commanding officer of the boat while it was down, the panel wanted to hear him last. Everyone in the submarine forces had heard of the vendetta between Jack and Ben Mount, and everyone was anxious to hear what Jack would tell the panel.

Jack McCrary arrived in Washington on a Tuesday evening; he was scheduled to testify the next morning. The first thing he did at the airport was call his father and mother; he said he'd seen them later in the evening. Then he called Betsy at the Washington bureau of the New York *Standard*.

"Hello, Betsy," he said. "I just arrived in Washington. Can I see you, or are you still working?"

"I'm still working, but I'll be finished in about an hour. Why don't we meet next door in the cocktail lounge of the Hamilton Hotel?"

"Great! I can't wait to see you!"

"I look forward to seeing you too," she replied.

Betsy hung up, her heart like a chunk of lead. She had seen Jack only a few times since their argument in the officers' club at New London, and their relationship had deteriorated badly. She had been forced to admit to herself that she truly did not love him. She had liked him once, and perhaps even had been infatuated with him for a while, but now the pressure of events had revealed to her a stubborn, vindictive side of him that she didn't like at all. When he had called her yesterday to tell her he was coming to Washington today, she had decided that she must break off their engagement. The longer she waited, the worse it would be.

She had his engagement ring on her finger and intended to give it to him that evening. It would be painful, but she felt that she had to do it. Her experience with Jack had taught her that you never really could know anyone until you saw how they behaved in difficult circumstances. She'd also learned that she'd been immature in her attitudes toward men and that the time had come for her to stop being a girl and start being a woman.

She finished her story and brought it to the night editor whose responsibility it was to wire it to New York. She combed her hair in the ladies' room and applied some makeup to her face. Then, lifting her shoulder bag into place, she left the offices of the *Standard* and went next door to the cocktail lounge in the Hamilton Hotel.

It was nine o'clock when she arrived, and most of the diners had left. She took a table in a dark corner where she could observe the door, and ordered a glass of dry Spanish sherry from the waiter. She looked around at couples having cocktails and dinner and wondered if she'd ever know the kind of happiness they seemed to be sharing.

Jack arrived in his white summer uniform. All female eyes turned to him; he looked tanned and splendid. He spotted her, walked to her, and kissed her cheek.

"I'm so happy to see you again," he said, sitting beside her and holding her hand.

"I'm happy to see you, Jack," she said with a half smile.

He saw immediately that something was wrong. "Are you all right?" he asked.

"Yes," she replied.

"What are you drinking?"

"Sherry."

"I think I'll have a scotch." He raised his hand, and the waiter came over. He gave his order to the waiter, who scurried off to the bar. Jack rubbed his hands. "Here we are together at last," he said.

"Yes," she agreed.

He smiled. "Well, you certainly don't seem happy to see me."

The time had come to end the charade. "Jack," she said, "I'm afraid that I have something very important to tell you."

He became serious. "What is it?"

She couldn't look into his eyes. She took a sip of sherry, then looked toward the bar. "Jack, dear, please try to understand what I'm going to tell you, and please don't be too hurt."

"You don't want to marry me," he said suddenly.

She looked down. "You know."

He nodded sadly. "Something's been wrong between us. Would you tell me what it is?"

"I'd rather not." She squeezed the ring off her finger and placed it in front of him. "I'm sorry, Jack," she said. "This is the most difficult thing I've ever done in my life."

He picked up the ring and looked at it in the light. The diamond wasn't very big, but it was the biggest he could afford. "Well," he mumbled, "I always figured you thought you were too good for me."

"It's not that at all, Jack," she replied. "I never have felt, and don't feel now, that I'm better than you. I've just come to realize that we're sort of incompatible."

He looked sharply at her. "This has something to do with the way I'm going after Ben Mount, doesn't it?"

"Yes," she admitted.

"You think that I should let him get away with all the murders he's committed?"

She shook her head. "Jack, I don't want to go all through this with you again. I can't stand it anymore."

He dropped the ring into his jacket pocket. The waiter approached the table and set down a glass of scotch and soda. Jack raised it to his lips and gulped half the liquid down. "Ah," he said, placing the glass on its doily. He looked at Betsy. "Well, I guess it's better to find out these things now than later."

"That's what I thought, Jack."

He tried to smile. "Somehow I always had the feeling you'd never stand by me if I needed you."

"I never could bring myself to stand by someone who I thought was doing something wrong."

"You think I'm wrong about Ben Mount?" he asked.

"You know I do."

"Well, I think you're wrong too."

"We see the world differently," she explained. "That's why we shouldn't get married."

"I guess you're right." He raised his glass and drank the rest of the scotch and soda. "Well," he said, trying to smile, "I guess we really don't have very much left to say to each other."

"No," she agreed, "I don't suppose we do, but I hope we'll be able to remain friends in some way."

"We'll see," he said briskly. He slapped the palm of his hand lightly on the table. "Well, I guess I might as well get going. No sense in prolonging the agony, I always say. I'll pay the waiter on my way out. I guess I'll be seeing you around, huh?"

"All right, Jack."

He looked at her and shrugged. "To think I'll never kiss that pretty face again. But that's the way it goes, I guess." He stood, threw her a little salute, picked up his hat, and went to pay the waiter. Then, without a backward glance, he marched out of the cocktail lounge.

Betsy raised her glass of sherry to her lips. She felt numb but relieved. It was all over. Finally. And as she placed her empty glass on the table, she wondered if she'd ever fall in love again.

Jack arrived for the first day of testimony in a starched white uniform, looking handsome and healthy. He was sworn in and sat in the chair before the panel. The admirals asked him questions, and he answered them crisply and respectfully.

Betsy sat in the press gallery, taking notes and waiting for Jack to drop his first bomb. They'd spoken briefly in the corridor before the session began, and he'd been cool to her, which she'd expected.

"Lieutenant McCrary," Admiral Kane was saying, "could you please tell us now exactly what first made you think something was amiss when the Sebago began her dive."

"I felt a change of air pressure in my ears, sir."

"What was so unusual about that?"

"I had never experienced that before, sir," Jack replied.

"Where were you at that moment, Lieutenant McCrary?"

"I was standing next to the chart table, sir."

"What was your reaction when you felt that change in air pressure?"

"I looked at the Christmas tree, sir."

"That's the display of lights indicating whether the various openings in the boat were opened or closed—is that correct Lieutenant?"

"Yes, sir."

"What did they indicate?"

"They indicated that all the openings were closed, but of course since the *Sebago* subsequently sank, the system must have malfunctioned due to inadequate or inappropriate design."

Admiral Dexter cleared his throat. "Please answer the question without adding any comments of your own, Lieutenant. This panel will decide what malfunctioned and why."

"I'm sorry, sir."

Admiral Kane resumed his line of questioning, and Betsy looked at Commodore Ray McCrary, sitting in the audience and listening to his son's testimony. She'd seen him at the opening of the session that morning, and he'd come over to say hello, but it was clear that a wall had risen between them now that she'd broken her engagement with Jack.

"What did you do when Boatswain's Mate Keller reported that the engine rooms were flooding, Lieutenant McCrary?" Admiral Kane asked.

"I looked at the Christmas tree, sir."

"What did you see?"

"All the lights were green, sir."

"What did you do then?"

"I didn't do anything, sir, because I was awaiting Commander Dunlop's response to the situation. However it occurred to me that if the engine rooms were flooding, it must have been because of defective main induction valves. I thought there must be something very seriously wrong with the whole system."

Admiral Dexter leaned forward. "Lieutenant McCrary, I must ask you once again to stick to the facts and not inject any of your opinions and conjectures. This panel will present its findings based on the evidence and nothing else. Do you understand that?"

Jack looked up at him, his ears turning red. Something told him to acquiesce, but he couldn't. "Sir, I believe that when the *Sebago* is raised, my opinions and conjectures will be substantiated by a comprehensive examination of her systems."

"Lieutenant McCrary," Admiral Dexter said, "this panel is not in existence to substantiate your opinions and conjectures. It is in existence to determine the facts in this very serious matter. I must insist that you stick to the facts. Is that clear?"

"Yes, sir."

Admiral Hill raised his hand and looked at Admiral Kane. "Sir, may we have a brief recess?"

"For what purpose?" Admiral Kane inquired.

"I believe very strongly that there's a matter that this panel must discuss privately."

"Very well, Admiral Hill." Admiral Kane looked at his watch. "This proceeding will be recessed until eleven o'clock."

The admirals rose and filed out of the room. Betsy wished she could go with them, because she knew their discussion would make a great story. It obviously had something to do with Jack's testimony.

The admirals walked down the corridor outside the hearing room and entered a conference room that had been set aside for their use. They sat around the big round table and old Admiral Kane turned to Admiral Hill. "What is it that you wanted to discuss?"

Admiral Hill had red hair and a face that looked as though it had been hacked out of rock. "Sir," he said, "I feel that I must protest Admiral Dexter's efforts to muzzle young McCrary. I believe that McCrary should be permitted to say whatever he thinks is pertinent to this proceeding."

"I disagree with that most strenuously," Admiral Dexter replied. "I think that this panel should decide what is pertinent to this proceeding and not let that decision be made by the witnesses who appear before us. A proceeding such as ours should try to elicit the facts of this matter, and not waste time with irrelevant material."

"What is irrelevant to one person may not be irrelevant to another," Admiral Hill pointed out. "I have the feeling, and perhaps I'm wrong, that Admiral Dexter might be trying to sweep under a rug testimony that might be damaging to the submarine forces."

"It is my opinion," Admiral Dexter retorted, "that Admiral Hill is trying to inject into the record every scrap of testimony, substantiated by fact or not, that tends to downgrade the submarine forces."

Admiral Kane raised his hand to indicate that he wanted them to stop arguing. "If this were a civilian court of law," he said, "opinions of the witnesses would be ruled irrelevant and immaterial. Therefore I believe that I must make that same ruling."

"But sir," Admiral Hill protested, "this isn't a civilian court of law. This is the Navy, and we have a special responsibility."

"That's true," Admiral Kane replied, "but we must be ever mindful that our primary responsibility is to civilians. We'd better proceed according to their rules if we know what's best for us. That is my final decision. I want no more quarreling in front of those reporters out there. Is that clear?"

"Yes, sir," they replied.

"Then let's return to the hearing room and resume our inquiry."

While the meeting of admirals was taking place, Helen spotted Commander Mulford in the corridor outside the conference room.

"Oh—hello!" she said, walking toward him.

He smiled as he recognized her. "Hello."

There were a few moments of awkward silence.

"Well," he said, "your brother certainly gave some interesting testimony today."

She frowned. "I suppose you could call it that."

There were a few more awkward moments.

"How have you been?" he asked.

"Very well, thank you."

Helen didn't know why she was so nervous in Mulford's presence. She fumbled in her purse for a cigarette, but couldn't find matches.

"Do you have a light?" she asked.

"I don't smoke." Mulford looked around and saw Lieutenant Nielsen standing nearby. "I say there—would you have a match for the lady."

"Of course."

Nielson stepped closer and removed a lighter from his pocket, flicking the wheel and bringing the flame to Helen's cigarette.

"Thank you," Helen said.

Mulford cleared his throat. "This is Miss Helen McCrary, and I'm Commander Mulford."

Nielsen bowed slightly. "Lieutenant Peter Nielsen, Royal Swedish Navy." He looked at Helen and admired her beauty. "You're related to Lieutenant McCrary in some way?"

"I'm his sister."

"Ah, yes—I've heard Jack speak of you."

She was surprised. "You know him?"

"I was on the *Sebago* with him."

Mulford snapped his fingers. "Of course—you were the Swedish observer on board the *Sebago!*"

"That is correct."

"You must be very happy to be back."

Nielsen nodded. "Very happy—yes."

"I imagine you're here today to give your testimony?"

"I had hoped to, but I may not be called today. I'd like to get this over with, because I'm anxious to return home."

"I'll be leaving soon also," Mulford told him.

Nielsen looked at him. "Why do you have to testify?"

"I was on the *Tioga.*"

"Ah," Nielsen said. "You are an observer in this country also?"

"Yes."

"What is your speciality?"

"Antisubmarine warfare."

Helen studied the men as they talked with each other. She thought Mulford handsome in a wholesome outdoors sort of way, while Nielsen had the aura of old world decadence about him. She wondered if he would be *different* in bed.

"I plan to be in your country," Nielsen said, "after a short visit at home. I like Britain very much."

"Oh, then you must stay a few days at my club," Mulford said. "I'd be very happy to have you as my guest."

Nielsen bowed. "That would be most kind of you."

"It's the Royal and Ancient in Saint Andrews."

"I've heard of it," Nielsen replied. "They say it's a very fine club. I certainly will look you up."

"Please do, but I shan't be there before September. If you get to Edinburgh, have a go on me; I'll write the club to expect you." Mulford turned to Helen. "If you're ever in Scotland, I hope you'll look me up, too."

Her eyes shimmered as she looked at him. "You can count on it, Commander Mulford."

The bell rang, indicating that the inquiry was about to resume. Helen put out her cigarette, and the three of them returned to the conference room.

At the end of the day Ray McCrary drove his son home through the crowded streets of Washington.

"How do you think I did today, Dad?" Jack asked,

smoking a cigarette and looking at the Smithsonian Institution as they passed by.

"I think you're being foolish, Jack," Ray McCrary replied, attired like his son in a white summer uniform. His request for retirement was being processed; he expected to be out of the Navy within sixty days.

"You mean my arguments with Admiral Dexter?"

"That's right. If you keep it up, he'll never let you command a submarine as long as you're in the Navy."

"I think you're wrong, Dad. Admiral Dexter is getting himself into trouble with old Hardtop, and if he's not careful he's the one who's liable to wind up without a command."

Ray McCrary steered around a corner. "You don't really think that Admiral Dexter will be relieved of command because of what he says to you, do you?"

"He might. Old Hardtop is getting awfully mad at him."

"But Admiral Kane has been backing up Dexter."

"Admiral Kane is getting old. He won't be around the Navy much longer, and Admiral Hill just might step into his shoes."

"Nonsense. There are numerous officers whom I could name who are senior to Hardtop Hill. You don't know what you're talking about, and if you persist in the direction you're going, you'll find yourself in trouble."

Jack looked at his father. "I'm sorry, Dad, but I have to do what I think is right. Maybe you're being too cautious."

"I'm being prudent, but not too cautious."

"I think I owe it to Ed to nail that Jew to a wall, and I'm going to do everything I can to carry through."

Ray McCrary shook his head. "Jack, you're letting your hatred for Mount get in the way of your good sense, and you'.e going to regret it—mark my words."

"I'm sorry Dad, but I feel that I've got to do it."

"Don't ever say that you weren't warned."

"I won't Dad," Jack replied, "and don't you ever say I didn't predict that things would turn out all right for me in the end."

"If they do, it'll be a miracle."

"No, it won't be a miracle," Jack said. "It'll just mean that I was right and you were wrong."

Ray McCrary braked at a red light, reflecting that Jack was headstrong and stubborn. Maybe he needed exactly what was going to happen to him. Ray McCrary was pretty sure he knew what the outcome would be. Jack's personnel file would be stamped UNFIT FOR COMMAND, and that adjudication would stand throughout his Navy career, unless something cataclysmic like a war happened.

Akiro Ito sat in the Tokyo office of Admiral Yamamoto in the Naval Ministry building. Wearing the high-necked uniform of a Lieutenant Commander in the Japanese Navy, Ito sat erect as Admiral Yamamoto read the report that Ito had brought hm.

Ito could see the Imperial Palace through the large window of Yamamoto's office in the Naval Ministry building. It was late afternoon, and the setting sun cast long shadows. On the wall to the left of the admiral was a large portrait of the Emperor, giving the office the atmosphere of a shrine.

Ito's back ached from having sat at attention for so long. He couldn't look at his watch, but he guessed he'd been sitting in that position for almost an hour. He told himself that he'd have to make his next report to Admiral Yamamoto shorter, so he wouldn't have to sit still for so long. His legs were growing numb and he couldn't wait to drink some water.

Finally Admiral Yamamoto looked up from the report. "This is very interesting," he said with a faint smile. "It's also very thorough. You've done good work, Commander Ito."

"Thank you, sir."

"I concur with your conclusion. The United States submarine forces will be severely damaged by self-inflicted wounds when this incident is over. They may suspend the production of new submarines for quite some time, perhaps years. It is possible that the role of their submarine forces will be greatly reduced for all time. All these things can only work out to the benefit of the Imperial Navy. I hope that when you return to America you will continue to deliver this quality of information and analysis to us."

"I will do my best, sir."

"That is all, Commander Ito. You may go."

FIFTY-NINE

On July 25th, after two futile efforts, the *Sebago* was raised from the mud off Block Island and towed to New London by the *Falcon*. Crowds lined the Thames River to see the famous submarine returning to port, and news photographers snapped pictures as it made its way to dock.

A special pier was roped off and declared off limits to all except the naval personnel designated to examine the submarine and removed her grisly cargo. Ambulances stood by on the pier to carry the remains of the dead crew members to the morgue in the base hospital. Admiral Mackie and Captain Robertson waited impatiently on the pier, eager to study the main induction system so that they could determine what had gone wrong.

The submarine was tied to the pier and Captain Healey of the *Falcon* declared that she was safe to be boarded. Naval personnel swarmed aboard and began their work. Admiral Mackie and Captain Robertson climbed the conning tower ladder and examined the bridge. They found that the main induction valves were wide open, just as the divers had reported.

On the afterdeck of the submarine, medical attendants opened the hatch over the aft torpedo comparment. The hatch was swung open and a young doctor lay on his stomach with a flashlight and looked down into the compartment.

He saw soggy, rotting corpses strewn over the deck and the torpedoes. One of the corpses was draped over the torpedo tubes, the arms stretched out like those of Christ on the cross.

The medical crew descended into the submarine and eased the bodies into huge rubber bags. The bags were removed from the submarine and one enterprising photographer in a low-flying airplane took a picture of them that would make the front pages of newspapers throughout the world.

Admiral Mackie opened the conning tower hatch and descended to the control room. He told Captain Robertson to stay near the main induction valves and observe them while he operated the main induction lever.

Admiral Mackie paused at the bottom of the ladder and looked around the control room. The smell was ghastly; the slop bucket had spilled over when the submarine had been raised. He looked at the chart table and realized that it was there that Lieutenant McCrary had commanded the submarine during its tragic hours beneath the sea. It must have been hell down here; Admiral Mackie could understand why McCrary had been behaving strangely ever since.

Admiral Mackie crossed the control room and looked at the lever that controlled the main induction valves. It was firmly in its closed position. He pushed it open and called up the conning tower: "Anything happen, Robertson?"

"No, sir!"

Admiral Mackie pulled the lever to its closed position, but before he could ask Captain Robertson if anything had changed, Captain Robertson shouted down: "Both valves just closed air."

Admiral Mackie pushed the lever to its open position.

"They just opened, sir!"

Admiral Mackie moved the lever to its closed position, and Captain Robertson reported that the valves had closed. Admiral Mackie opened and closed the lever again, and Captain Robertson reported that the valves were operating normally. But the next time Admiral Mackie pulled the lever to its closed position Captain Robertson reported that the valves didn't close.

They continued working the system in this manner for several more minutes; the valves usually closed when they were supposed to but sometimes stayed open.

Now the task was to determine why the valves didn't close every time.

The cortege of hearses and black limousines drove through the winding roads of the Arlington National Cemetery. Ray McCrary, Jack, Helen, and young Arabella sat in one of the limousines, looking at rows of white headstones and monuments to America's great war heroes.

Seventeen-year-old Arabella, blond like her sister and brother, was in her last year at an exclusive girls' preparatory school in New Hampshire. She was strikingly pretty, with big blue eyes and a petulant mouth. Tears rolled down her cheeks as she thought of her brother Ed, whom she'd always thought rather odd. She hadn't liked him much, not because he'd ever been mean to her but because she'd always heard the other members of her family disparage him. She'd been away to school for most of the past four years and had hardly seen him, but now the tragedy of his death was upon her and she too wished she had been kinder to him.

The cortege stopped beside thirty graves prepared in a special section of the cemetery. The families of the dead submariners got out of their limousines and gathered in an area opposite the graves while honor guards of sailors carried the flag-draped caskets.

Jack, wearing a white uniform, his hands clasped behind his back, looked around at the other mourners. He saw Gene Dunlop's wife dressed entirely in black, a veil over her face, standing between her two teen-aged sons and occasionally raising a white handkerchief to her eyes. Ensign Roy Delbert's wife, a skinny young woman with a mild acne condition, stood with her family and in-laws, and Jack could see that she was pregnant.

He saw Anthony Brouvelli's wife, a fat Italian woman who'd come down from Brockton, Massachusetts. Frank Duarti's wife and elderly parents were there from New Bedford. Jack realized that some of the *Sebago*'s dead had no one to mourn for them but their buddies. He wondered about the strange solitary men like Machinist's Mate Albert Gomez who seemed not to have been born of man and woman—who had appeared one day in a Navy recruiting station with no money, no education, and no past.

Jack looked at the group of survivors who had come to mourn. There was Jethro Keller with his arm around the waist of his wife, looking at the honor guard forming into two ranks. Nearby were Hank Burns and his wife, Al Araujo with Mark Donahue, and Vincent La Gloria, Darrell Goines, Joe Reilly—the whole gang come to pay their last respects to their mates. Lieutenant Stearns stood with *Porgie* Lieutenant McNally, who had been a friend of his at the academy.

More cars arrived, and a group of admirals got out. Admiral Dexter led the distinguished group to the podium in front of the graves. They stood and prayed with their heads bowed, and Admiral Dexter stepped to the microphone and delivered the eulogy. He spoke of the men's courage and loyalty, of their dedication to duty, and how their deaths should spur the submarine forces to greater achievements, for that would be the way their dead comrades would have wanted it.

Admiral Dexter stepped back from the podium, and a chaplain took his place. The chaplain asked God to have mercy on the departed sailors, for they had died in the line of duty. He prayed that the sailors would take their rightful places in the kingdom of heaven, and he gave thanks to God for sparing the lives of those who had survived. "From dust we have come," he said, "and to dust we shall return."

The honor guard raised their rifles and fired simultaneously into the air, the explosion echoing across the hills and up to the sky, as the caskets were lowered into the graves.

On the Lietzenstrasse in Berlin, Lieutenant Peter Nielsen descended the steps to a rathskeller frequented by naval officers employed in the War Ministry nearby. It was eight o'clock in the evening, and he'd arrived in Berlin only three hours before. He had left his luggage at the home of his Uncle Helmut, drunk a glass of wine with his cousin Karl, made a telephone call, and then come here.

He entered the huge rathskeller and heard the music of an accordion and fiddles. Through the clouds of tobacco smoke he looked to the stage and saw musicians in lederhosen dancing and singing. Buxom waitresses with ribbons in their hair carried pitchers of beer to men drinking at the long rows of tables. Empty beer mugs hung from the walls along with the stag heads and swastika flags. The atmosphere in the rathskeller was festive and joyous, and Nielsen's heart swelled with happiness. It was good to be in Berlin again.

He made his way past the tables, passing men in uniforms of all the services, and party members with swastika armbands. Nielsen could feel the excitement and sense of purpose in the air. How marvelous it was to belong to a race that was organized and on the march.

He looked around and finally spotted Lieutenant Grunberger sitting at a small table against the wall. Grunberger stood up and waved his hand. The Swedish officer waved back, and the two men met in one of the aisles.

"Peter—it's so good to see you!" said Grunberger, shaking Peter's hand.

"It's good to see you, Rudi."

They went to Rudi's table and sat down. Rudi Grunberger was blond like Nielsen, but his hair was curly, he was shorter, and his face was rounder. A pitcher of beer was on the table, and there were two steins.

Rudi poured beer into Nielsen's stein. "Let's drink a toast!"

"A toast!"

Rudi raised his stein into the air. "To you, Peter, and your miraculous escape from the bottom of the sea!"

Peter raised his stein and touched it to Rudi's, then they both drank big gulps.

"Now I'd like to propose a toast," Peter said. He raised his stein. "To the great German Reich and her great Fuehrer, Adolf Hitler!"

They touched steins and drank deeply again. A waitress walked by and smiled at Peter. On the stage the band was playing and the patrons sang:

> *With drink and fun*
> *the heart stays young . . .*

"Ah, Peter, it's wonderful to see you," Rudi said, slapping Peter on the arm. "When we heard you were on that sunken American submarine, we never thought we'd see you again."

"I never thought I'd see you again either, but here we are."

They looked at each other and smiled, for they had known each other since they were boys growing up in Berlin. They'd lived next door to each other and attended the same schools until Peter was eighteen and moved to Stockholm.

"I know that you'll make your formal report tomorrow," Rudi said, "but tell me what it was like down there in the flooded submarine."

"What was it like?" Peter asked. "It was like drowning in a toilet bowl. I think the smell bothered me more than anything else."

"Their submarines are junk, eh?"

"No, they're not junk, but they're much larger than your U-boats. They can't submerge as quickly as U-boats, and they can't move as quickly underwater. Also, they're not nearly as maneuverable."

"The Americans are a strange mongrel race," Rudi observed. "You need only compare their automobiles with German automobiles to see the difference between them and us. American automobiles fall apart if you drive them at top speed for very long, but German automobiles can be driven at top speed forever."

"Well, it's really not that simple," Peter replied. "Their submarine forces haven't had the experience that your U-boat arm has, so they haven't been able to draw the conclusions that you have. Also, they appear unable to determine whether to develop patrol submarines or fleet submarines. Many people in their navy dispute the effectiveness of submarines, but of course you have that here, too."

Rudi nodded bitterly. "Yes, all the admirals prefer big battlewagons; big, slow targets."

"The American Navy should not be taken too lightly," Peter said. "The officers and crews whom I've met were very capable and very well trained. The ones I was with on the sunken submarine really were quite heroic. I was very impressed. There was not even one instance where discipline broke down."

"That's interesting, because we don't think of Americans as being that way."

Peter smiled. "You'd better if you know what's good for you." He raised his stein to his lips and drank, then set the stein on the table and poured more beer from the pitcher. "Listen, Rudi, I'd like you to do a favor for me."

"What is it?"

Peter took a package of American cigarettes from his tunic pocket. "You're on Doenitz's staff, and I wonder if you could do something so that I could be transferred from naval intelligence to the U-boat arm. I don't like intelligence work very much, Rudi, and I really don't think I'm that effective. I'd much rather serve the Reich in the *Kriegsmarine* as a U-boat officer."

Rudi smiled and shook his head. "Oh, that's going to be very difficult, Peter."

"Why?"

"Well, you might not think you've very effective, and maybe you're not so effective right now, but in the event of war you'd be in a position to furnish the Reich with a great deal of important information."

"I was afraid that you'd think that," Peter said, discouragement in his voice.

"I wouldn't give up entirely, because one never knows what might happen in the future, but I doubt whether Doenitz would want you to leave your position in the Swedish Navy at this particular time."

Rudi looked around, then leaned toward Peter and said in a low voice, "I'm going to tell you something that I want you to promise you won't repeat to anyone, not even your mother."

"Of course I won't tell anyone. What is it?"

Rudi's eyes searched Peter's face. "We're going to war soon."

"Ah," Peter said. "Is this for certain?"

"Yes. The mobilization of troops and deployment of forces is taking place right now. I imagine you know where the first blow will be struck."

"I've been reading in the papers about the dispute the Fuehrer is having with Poland."

Rudi nodded slowly. "Yes—Poland."

"When?"

"I don't know the exact date. Probably in late August or early September."

Peter looked into his stein. "Well," he said, "we always knew that war would come, but now that it appears imminent, somehow it doesn't seem real to me."

"It will be real enough, Rudi, and it will be a kind of war that the world never has seen before."

"*Blitzkrieg*," Peter said.

"Yes, a lightning war, and we have to know what kind of threats we must expect through the Baltic Sea. That is why you will be of more value to us where you are than in a U-boat."

"I understand," Peter said. "Forget about my request for the transfer."

"I knew you'd see it that way." He raised his stein and smiled. "To victory!"

Peter touched his stein to Rudi's. There was raucous laughter nearby, and the musicians were dancing on the stage. Looking into Rudi's eyes, Peter saw the flames of war.

"*Sieg heil!*" he replied, and brought the beer to his lips.

* * *

During the final days of July and the first weeks of August the main induction system of the *Sebago* was dismantled meticulously and every component studied in a special laboratory established at the New London submarine base.

One hot summer afternoon in the *Sebago*'s control room a young engineering officer removed a gearwheel that had three teeth broken off. The gearwheel was an important part of the hydraulic system that opened and closed the main induction valves.

The gearwheel was taken to the laboratory and subjected to intense scrutiny. Ben Mount's original blueprints for the gearwheel were obtained, and a team of engineers checked the specifications. They decided that the gearwheel as designed by Mount should have been able to withstand the demands made upon it in the operation of the hydraulic system.

Metallurgical tests of the gearwheel itself showed that the alloy from which it was made did not meet the specifications set by Ben Mount. The composition of the metals was correct, but in the smelting process the alloy had hardened too quickly and at an uneven rate, causing a fault line at the base of the three teeth that had broken off.

The conclusion was that the *Sebago* had gone down because of an error in the manufacture of that gear.

SIXTY

On August 25th the special panel investigating the sinking of the *Sebago* delivered its verdict at a press conference in the room where the hearings had taken place. Admiral Cyrus Kane stood at the podium, his thick reading glasses low on his thin nose, and read the statement that had been prepared by his staff. Seated on either side of him were the other admirals who had served on the panel and behind him were several of the engineers and scientists who'd participated in the investigation, plus Ben Mount and a group of officers from the Bureau of Ships and Construction, and Jack McCrary with Lieutenant Bob Stearns.

Admiral Kane made a long introductory statement in which he discussed the impartiality of the investigation, its thoroughness, and its broad scope. News photographers flashed their bulbs in his face as he described the laboratory in New London that had tested and examined the main induction system of the boat. Betsy Kirkland was among the reporters in the gallery eagerly taking notes, and Ray McCrary, now a civilian wearing a blue business suit, was also in the audience.

Finally Admiral Kane came to the result of the investigation. He stated emphatically that the *Sebago* had gone down because of a gear that had been manufactured improperly. He held the gear in the air and nearly went blind from the flashbulbs.

"We are forced to conclude, therefore," Admiral Kane said, "that the Bureau of Ships and Construction, which designed the *Sebago* and all its systems, is completely blameless in this unfortunate and tragic matter, and that the officers and crew behaved in an exemplary manner that was in the very finest traditions of the Navy."

Admiral Kane made a few final remarks, thanking those who had participated in the investigation. Jack McCrary stared numbly at the back wall of the room. He tried to digest the awful truth that Ben Mount was not to blame for the death of his brother. He saw that he had made a terrible mistake, that his father, Betsy Kirkland, and others had been right, that he had been persecuting Ben Mount unreasonably, and that he had made a fool of himself.

Admiral Kane declared the business of the special inquiry panel over, and a crowd rushed to Ben Mount to congratulate him. They knew that his career had been on the line, and now he was cleared irrefutably. Jack McCrary watched bitterly as Betsy Kirkland shook Ben Mount's hand.

"Do you remember me?" Betsy asked Mount.

"Yes, of course—you're Miss Kirkland from the *Standard*."

"Do you think you can give me an interview now that the hearings are over?"

Ben shrugged. "I'm sorry, but I wouldn't have anything to say that I haven't said already in my testimony before the panel."

She smiled. "In other words, you don't want to give me an interview."

"No comment." He looked over her head at the

crowd in the big room. Flashbulbs were exploding, and a group of reporters were talking with Admiral Kane. Ben noticed Jack McCrary standing alone in the distance, looking in his direction.

"What a shame," Betsy said. "All you Navy people are so afraid of the press."

Ben scratched his cheek. "Well, it's not as though we didn't have reason to be."

"Isn't there anything I can say to change your mind?"

"I'm afraid not."

She threw up her hands. "Well, good luck, Commander Mount. I hope we meet again someday." She turned to walk away.

"So do I," he said.

She stopped and looked at him. "Then perhaps we shall."

"I shall look forward to it, Miss Kirkland."

Betsy walked away, thinking of Ben Mount's marvelous eyes and wondering how she could get to know him better. She considered him intelligent and exotic—a person quite different from those she usually met. She headed toward Admiral Kane, hoping to get some newsworthy remarks from him.

Ben watched her go. He would have liked to talk with her, but she was a reporter and he didn't dare. He was surprised to realize that he felt sexually aroused.

Across the room, Jack McCrary turned away from Ben and Betsy, unable to stand the sight of them anymore, and found himself staring at the face of Admiral Dexter, who scowled at him and passed him by on his way to congratulate Ben Mount.

Jack's hands were shaking as he lit a cigarette. He had risked everything on a single throw of the dice, and they had come up snake eyes. He knew he should apologize to Ben Mount, but couldn't bring himself to do it. He had set himself up as the judge of another man; he told himself he must never do that again.

"You okay, Jack?" Bob Stearns asked, walking up to him.

"I don't feel too well," Jack said hoarsely. "I think I'd like to be alone for a while, if you don't mind."

"No, I don't mind, Jack," Stearns said, looking puzzled.

Head down, Jack McCrary made his way to the door.

The next day, in the Bureau of Personnel, Jack McCrary's folder was stamped UNFIT FOR COMMAND.

Later in the day a directive was received in the Bureau of Personnel from the office of Vice Admiral Charles Hill. It ordered that Lieutenant Commander Benjamin Mount be transferred out of the Bureau of Ships and Construction and away from the continental United States. A survey of available billets was made, and the decision was reached to send Mount to England as a naval attaché.

Dell Bestsellers

- [ ] **RANDOM WINDS** by Belva Plain \$3.50 (17158-X)
- [ ] **MEN IN LOVE** by Nancy Friday \$3.50 (15404-9)
- [ ] **JAILBIRD** by Kurt Vonnegut \$3.25 (15447-2)
- [ ] **LOVE: Poems** by Danielle Steel \$2.50 (15377-8)
- [ ] **SHOGUN** by James Clavell \$3.50 (17800-2)
- [ ] **WILL** by G. Gordon Liddy \$3.50 (09666-9)
- [ ] **THE ESTABLISHMENT** by Howard Fast........\$3.25 (12296-1)
- [ ] **LIGHT OF LOVE** by Barbara Cartland \$2.50 (15402-2)
- [ ] **SERPENTINE** by Thomas Thompson \$3.50 (17611-5)
- [ ] **MY MOTHER/MY SELF** by Nancy Friday \$3.25 (15663-7)
- [ ] **EVERGREEN** by Belva Plain \$3.50 (13278-9)
- [ ] **THE WINDSOR STORY**
  by J. Bryan III & Charles J.V. Murphy \$3.75 (19346-X)
- [ ] **THE PROUD HUNTER** by Marianne Harvey ..\$3.25 (17098-2)
- [ ] **HIT ME WITH A RAINBOW**
  by James Kirkwood \$3.25 (13622-9)
- [ ] **MIDNIGHT MOVIES** by David Kaufelt \$2.75 (15728-5)
- [ ] **THE DEBRIEFING** by Robert Litell \$2.75 (01873-5)
- [ ] **SHAMAN'S DAUGHTER** by Nan Salerno
  & Rosamond Vanderburgh \$3.25 (17863-0)
- [ ] **WOMAN OF TEXAS** by R.T. Stevens \$2.95 (19555-1)
- [ ] **DEVIL'S LOVE** by Lane Harris \$2.95 (11915-4)
